SEE
YOU IN
SEPTEMBER

CHARITY
NORMAN

ALLEN&UNWIN

First published in Great Britain in 2017 by Allen & Unwin
First published in Australia in 2017 by Allen & Unwin

Allen & Unwin
c/o Atlantic Books
Ormond House
26–27 Boswell Street
London WC1N 3JZ

Phone: 020 7269 1610
Fax: 020 7430 0916

Email: UK@allenandunwin.com
Web: www.allenandunwin.com/uk

A CIP catalogue record for this book is available from the British Library.

Paperback ISBN 978 1 74331 877 5
E-Book ISBN 978 1 95253 530 7

Printed and bound by CPI Group (UK) Ltd, Croydon, CR0 4YY

10 9 8 7 6 5 4 3 2 1

For George, Sam and Cora Meredith, with all my love

And those who were seen dancing were thought to be insane by those who could not hear the music.

Attributed to Friedrich Nietzsche

Prologue

Diana
2016

It doesn't look like a scene of death. It looks like paradise. Wooden cabins dream in autumn sunshine, goats graze by the lapping waters of a lake. Even the hills seem placid, luxuriating in their pelt of native bush. She can't hear a man-made sound: only the distant chuckle of a stream, the fluting and whistling of birds. The valley is submerged in a blue haze of peace.

Paradise.

Or not. Gaudy plastic stirs among the flax bushes. Police tape: a jaunty, jarring souvenir of tragedy. There are other signs too, if you look for them. Empty buildings, marker pegs on the beach. The authorities set up camp here, she knows, and stayed for weeks. Squads of divers plunged into the lake; dog handlers combed the shadowy folds of bush. They even used a drone to take aerial footage. She imagines them tramping around in heavy-booted incongruity, coaxing and bullying statements from people who desperately want to forget.

Until a few years ago, Diana had never heard of Justin Calvin. She'd never dreamed that events in a valley on the other side of the world could decimate her family. She and Mike were pretty bog-standard people in those days. They'd been married longer than the national average, got through his army years and come out the other side. Not rolling in money, not struggling. A redbrick-and-stucco semi in South London. Most of their worry, their focus and hope were centred on their two daughters. Nobody had gone off the rails. Not unless you counted Tara's suspension for smoking behind the gym.

No sign; no sign at all of what was to come.

There's a new sound among the cabins. It's strong and clear and utterly unexpected. Someone is playing a piano: rippling, complex triplets with a haunting melody woven through them. A pair of fantails swoop and dive around Diana's head as though riding on the currents of the song. In this strange and beautiful place, after so much loss, the music seems to speak of appalling sadness. It makes her want to cry.

She has a photo of Cassy, taken as they waved her off from Heathrow. One final picture. One final smile. A butterfly in a glass case. *Have fun*, they were yelling, in the moment it was taken. *Watch out for man-eating kiwis!* Diana has used it as her desktop background ever since. She greets her elder daughter in the morning, and last thing at night, and a hundred times a day.

The girl smiling out of the screen is dear and familiar and . . . well, she's just Cassy. Voluptuous, long-legged, quick to blush. A thick plait hangs over one shoulder, an in-flight bag over the other. Her nose isn't quite straight, never has been since it was broken by a rogue hockey ball, but there's something arresting about the dark blue eyes and flicked-up lashes. She's always had that wistful expression: a downturn at the corners of her eyes, as though she knows something that others don't.

My God. Did we really make jokes about killer kiwis? If I'd seen what was around the corner, I'd have begged her not to get on that plane.

Across the lake, the volcano is a sleeping giant. The peace has a hypnotic quality. It stills your soul. It slows your breath. No wonder the media has become obsessed with this glorious wilderness. No wonder the police struggled to understand what happened here. No wonder the nation is still searching its soul, wondering who to blame.

She's often wondered the same thing herself. There have been moments over the years when she's found she has stopped. Just stopped dead. She was meant to be walking to work or feeding the cat. Instead she is far away, arms limp by her sides, gazing at the past.

It's like watching a milk bottle falling off a table. It rolls and falls in nightmarish slow motion and yet it seems unstoppable. There was a time when the family was whole, and a time when it hit the ground, milk and shattered glass spraying across the tiles. In between is the moment when she should have caught it.

One

Such a precious memory, those last minutes in Cassy's bedroom. They were driving her to the airport soon, but there were no long faces. After all, this was just a glorified holiday. She'd be back before they knew it.

Diana heard laughter and put her head around the door. There they were, her daughters: twenty-one and fifteen, both taller than their mother. Cassy had dumped everything she was taking into piles on the floor and was trying to cram it all into her backpack. Tara sprawled across the bed, hair a dark fan on the pillow, music pouring from her phone. It sounded tinny and pointless to Diana, but perhaps beauty was in the ear of the beholder.

'Mum!' cried Tara. 'For God's sake, tell Cassy she's taking *way* too many socks.'

Diana sat down at the end of the bed, glimpsing her ruddy complexion and silvery roots in the mirror. *Dowdy*, she thought, though without regret. *No other word for it*. Never mind. She could still scrub up when she had to.

Tara stirred an imaginary cauldron.

'When shall we three meet again?' she demanded in a witch's croak. 'In thunder, lightning—'

'Third of September,' said Cassy, stooping to retrieve three pairs of socks from her pack. 'We're due to touch down twenty-four hours before Imogen walks up the aisle.'

'I wish you weren't cutting it so fine,' said Diana.

'So does Imogen. She's obsessed with this wedding. Never mentions poor Jack at all. I think he's just a by-product.'

'I'm sure that's not true.'

Cassy pouted. 'She says I'm not allowed to get a tan.'

'You're *kidding* me,' gasped Tara. 'Bridezilla!'

'Yep. Apparently it'll make her look pasty if her bridesmaid is a bronzed goddess.'

'Tell her to fake it. She'll be faking it for the rest of her married life.'

Diana tried to be shocked, but her daughters mocked her. *This is 2010, Mum, not 1810!* They were a formidable team when they banded together.

'D'you want to see the bridesmaids' dresses?' asked Cassy. 'Monstrous! Hang on a sec.' She picked up her phone and flicked through the photos until she found one: a puff-sleeved nightmare in bright purple.

'Not good,' groaned Tara, shielding her eyes from the glare. 'Oh, lordy, lordy. Not good at all.'

Cassy stared at the photo in dismay. 'Becca can pull off that colour, being a skinny chick. I'll look like Barney the Dinosaur.'

'You could get your own back,' suggested Diana. 'Marry Hamish and make Imogen wear an orange jumpsuit?'

'Brilliant idea! But I wouldn't go shopping for wedding hats just yet, Mum. We're far too young.'

'True,' said Tara. 'Then again, a bird in the hand. Hamish isn't bad-looking, he's rich as Croesus and—*big* plus—Dad likes him.'

Diana listened with flapping ears. She rarely dared to pry into Cassy's private life, but Tara seemed to get away with it.

Cassy crouched by her pack, shoving in a sponge bag with both hands.

'I think I annoy him sometimes,' she said. 'We don't care about the same things.'

'You mean he isn't a raving tree-hugger like you and Granny Joyce,' scoffed Tara. 'I mean—Lord save us—he'll drink coffee that wasn't grown by a one-legged women's cooperative in Colombia. What a total bastard!' She was yawning as she spoke, stretching angular arms. 'We can't all be bleeding hearts, Cass. Oh my God, that's spooky. Your door's opening all by itself.'

The three of them looked towards the bedroom door, which creaked as it inched just wide enough to admit the family's cat.

'Pesky!' cried Cassy, picking him up and kissing him. 'Don't creep about like that.'

'He's getting tubby,' said Diana.

Cassy pretended to block her pet's ears. 'Enough with the body shaming! You want him to develop an eating disorder?'

She'd found Pesky on her way back from a party one stormy night: a mewing scrap of black-and-white, dumped in a charity bin. She got her friend Becca to lower her into the bin by her legs, bundled the half-starved kitten under her jumper and brought him home. Three years on, you'd never know the sleek king of the household had once been so close to death.

'Dad doesn't approve of this trip,' she said, once Pesky had wriggled out of her grasp. 'He was on about it again this morning. Thinks I should be doing an internship instead of gallivanting around the world.'

Tara snorted. 'What a stuffed shirt.'

Diana was inclined to agree with Tara, though she'd never say so. Mike's father had died the previous year, leaving cash to all his grandchildren. Cassy was saving most of hers but had splashed out on this adventure—her last, she said sadly, before the dreaded treadmill of work. She and Hamish planned a fortnight's volunteering at a wildlife sanctuary in Thailand, followed by a few days on a beach, before exploring New Zealand.

'I'm ready to roll.' Cassy got to her feet, bouncing up and down to test the weight of her pack.

'Passport?' asked Diana.

'Check.' Cassy nudged an inflight bag with her toe.

'Credit card? Mosquito repellent? Phone?'

'Check, check and check.'

'Condoms?' asked Tara.

Diana smothered a smile. Cassy flushed pillar-box red and said her sister was a total embarrassment.

It was around then that Diana felt a flutter of unease—shapeless, nameless and immediately suppressed. There was nothing to worry about. Nothing. Thousands of students did this kind of thing every year, with their Lonely Planet guides stuffed into their backpacks.

'Right then,' she said, standing up. 'Quick cup of tea before we go?'

•

The whole family made the trip to Heathrow, including Diana's mother Joyce, who lived in a care home nearby and liked a day out. They reached the motorway in good spirits. Mike was driving, the girls were singing along to Magic FM. Joyce had fallen asleep.

Cassy tried to plait her hair in the back of the car, but twists and twines of chestnut-brown escaped. She was wearing jeans and a grey t-shirt, a jersey tied around her waist.

It was Tara who started the trouble. She didn't mean to. She was never vindictive, just careless.

'Hey, Cass,' she said, as she sat between her sister and her napping grandmother. 'What's this about you dumping your law degree?'

'I'm not.' Cassy's denial was fast and sharp, but Tara didn't take the hint.

'Well, that's funny, because Tilly's brother reckons you are. Said you've been to see the tutors and everything.'

Mike turned off the radio. No more music. No more singing along. Diana braced herself.

'What's this about?' he asked.

'Nothing,' said Cassy. 'Honestly. Forget it. Tilly's brother is an idiot.'

'Doesn't sound like nothing.'

'Shh,' murmured Diana, squeezing his upper arm. 'C'mon, Mike. Not now. Not today.'

'Cassy?' insisted Mike. His voice was too loud.

Diana glanced around at the back seat. Cassy was biting her thumbnail, looking about six years old. Tara was pulling an agonised face and mouthing *sorry*.

'I was just wondering about my options,' said Cassy.

'Why the hell would you do that?' Mike raised both hands to head height and brought them down—*slap!*—onto the steering wheel. '*Christ* almighty! You've only got a year to go. Don't tell me you're going to throw it all away.'

'I might have made a mistake, choosing law. That's all. I maybe should have looked at something else. I'm not sure I want to be a lawyer.'

'I can't believe I'm hearing this. You're doing so well!'

'Drop it,' warned Diana. She squeezed his arm again, harder this time, but he wasn't going to be deflected.

'What modules did you say you'd chosen for September?' he asked. 'Company, intellectual property . . .'

Cassy sighed. 'Employment. Competition law.'

'Right.' Mike was eyeing his daughter in the rear-view mirror. 'By this time next year you could have a training contract in a city firm. You could be set up for life.'

'That's what worries me,' said Cassy. 'A lifetime of that.'

'What does Hamish think?'

'He thinks I'm mad.'

'He's got more sense than you. We're not millionaires, Mum and I.'

'I know.'

'We can't support you forever. We'd love to, but we can't.'

'I don't expect you to support me.'

Mike carried on ranting all the way to Heathrow, despite

Diana's attempts to shut him up. *The world's more and more unstable . . . can't live on air . . . I joined the army for a secure career with a decent pension, it wasn't for love.*

'D'you want to end up serving Big Macs and fries?' he demanded.

'No.'

'Well then! It's dog-eat-dog out there. Millions of graduates end up unemployed.'

'Leave her alone, for God's sake.' This was Tara. 'It's her life. Who cares whether she ends up working in McDonald's?'

'Stay out of this please, Tara.'

'I only asked about course changes,' said Cassy, sounding tearful. 'I only asked. But I can't do it. They said no way. I'd have to drop out and apply all over again, student loan, everything. And I'm not going to do that, so you don't need to worry.'

The exit for their terminal was coming up. Mike swung off the motorway, running his hand through his hair.

'So the upshot is you're sticking with law?'

Cassy said yes, that was the upshot, and Mike said good, because he never had her down as a quitter. Tara said some people get their knickers in a twist over nothing, and Diana—who felt it her duty—told Tara not to be rude to her father. Mercifully, Joyce chose that moment to wake up.

'Did I miss something?' she asked.

'No, Mum.'

'Hmm. Could cut the atmosphere with a butter knife.'

It was true. The cheerful day had been ruined, and Diana could have throttled Mike. Desperate to salvage things, she tried to make conversation: empty twaddle about the weather—the flight—the traffic. Nobody helped her. Mike was parking the car when a text arrived on Cassy's phone.

'Hamish,' she said. 'He's running late. Broken-down train.'

'Is it going to be a problem?' asked Diana.

'No. They're moving again already. He's checked in online. Says he'll meet us at security.'

The next half-hour or so was taken up with the maelstrom of the check-in queue, so there wasn't time for family rows. Once Cassy had dropped off her bag, Mike offered to stay back to look out for Hamish while the others headed for security. This involved steering Joyce and her walking frame through the crowds and up in a lift.

'Don't worry about Dad,' whispered Diana, once they were safely out of earshot. 'He overthinks things sometimes.'

Cassy shrugged.

'It's because he loves you,' Diana assured her. 'He wants to know you'll have a secure future.'

'I just wish he . . .' Another shrug. 'Never mind.'

They'd reached the screening point when a girl skidded to a halt beside them. She was wearing ripped jeans and a panama hat, and she grabbed Cassy around the waist.

'Becca!' cried Cassy. 'You never said you were coming.'

'Got out of work early. Bloody nearly missed you! It was hell on the Piccadilly Line.' The girl's face lit up when she spotted Diana's mother perched on the seat of her walking frame. 'Hi, Joyce! Great to see you.'

'You too, dear,' said Joyce, disappearing into her embrace.

Becca was a heartening sight after the tension in the car, and Diana was grateful to her. She was the other bridesmaid—the skinny chick who looked good in everything. Her life and Cassy's were running on more-or-less parallel tracks, except that Becca was studying psychology.

'You'd better be home in time for the Wedding of the Century,' she warned, stretching out her arm to take a selfie of herself, Cassy and Tara. 'I'm not going to be the only mug prancing about in a purple meringue.'

'I'll be there. Trust me.'

'What's Imogen even *thinking*? Imagine signing up to a life sentence at twenty-one.'

Joyce chuckled. 'I did! Fifty-one when I made my escape. You wouldn't serve thirty years for murdering somebody.'

The three girls seemed to find this hilarious. Diana didn't.

It wasn't long before Mike appeared with Hamish: a tidy young man, looking purposeful in a cycling fleece and designer stubble. Cassy scolded him for being late and pretended to cuff him around the ear. He was anxious to go airside straight away; he'd heard that security checks were taking twice as long as usual.

'Terrorist alert,' said Mike, tutting. 'Again.'

Becca appointed herself team photographer.

'Team mug shot before you go,' she ordered, holding her phone in one hand, conducting the group with the other. 'C'mon, c'mon! Huddle up. Yes, you too, Mike.'

'This photo had better not end up on social media,' said Hamish.

Becca ignored him. 'Let's see some smiles on your dials—yes, you too, Mike!'

The six of them huddled, grinned—yes, even Mike—and were immortalised.

Hamish was desperate to go through. He shook Mike's hand and muttered distracted goodbyes before hurrying behind the screen. But Cassy lingered. She'd already kissed everyone. She'd given her grandmother a gentle bear hug and a less gentle one to Mike—*Sorry, Dad*—who'd ruffled her hair and said, *Stay safe*. She had a plane to catch. And yet she turned back to her family.

At that moment Becca took one more picture. *Have fun!* the well-wishers yelled. *Watch out for man-eating kiwis!*

Cassy smiled, blew them a kiss.

'See you in September,' she said.

It was a throwaway line. Just words uttered casually by a young woman in a hurry.

And then she'd gone.

The Cult Leader's Manual: Eight Steps to Mind Control

Cameron Allsop

Step 1: Identify your potential recruit

He or she does not have to be especially young, vulnerable or gullible. On the contrary, you may want to recruit mature people with useful skills. However, their recruitment stands a better chance of success if you find them at a time of difficulty. For example: bereavement, relationship crisis, addiction, loneliness, depression and redundancy can all induce temporary vulnerability.

Look for someone who is out of their comfort zone and offer them comfort.

Two

Cassy
August 2010

Another car. Another car. Another bloody car. She turned her smile on—off—on. And all the time her life was spinning around, upside down, out of control.

They'd barely spoken in the past hour. They were hitching from outside a petrol station on the outskirts of Auckland, and it was her turn to do the work. She brandished a piece of cardboard with the word *TAUPO* scrawled across it, doing her Cheshire cat impersonation at every vehicle that passed. She'd dressed for the job in denim shorts and a clinging t-shirt—growing worryingly tighter by the day—but her legs weren't getting them any lifts.

It didn't matter whether they got to Taupo. It didn't matter how far she ran. She couldn't escape. The trouble had begun as a vague suspicion while they were still in Thailand, grew into gnawing anxiety, and now—today—had exploded into full-blown panic. She'd thrown up again this morning: jerked out of her dreams in a cold sweat, she tore out of the hostel bunk and down to the communal bathrooms. When she finally emerged from the cubicle, an Australian girl from her dormitory (Kylie? Keren?) was cleaning her teeth at the basins.

'Stomach bug,' muttered Cassy.

'Seems to get you every morning,' said Kylie or Keren, her words distorted by her toothbrush.

'Just came from Thailand. Must have been the water.'

Kylie or Keren spat into the basin.

'Yeah . . . I had one of those bugs once. Don't worry, you can have it fixed. Better get on with it though.'

Cassy felt her knees shaking and leaned against the tiled wall. She desperately needed a friend. 'Did you have yours fixed?'

'Yep.'

'Is it terrible?'

'Not too bad. A whole lot better than the alternative.'

Cassy didn't like to imagine the alternative. 'I never thought this would happen to me.'

'We never do.'

'I wasn't careless. I'm on the pill.'

The other girl zipped up her sponge bag. 'Have you told him?'

'I'm still hoping it's not . . . I mean, it still might be a bug. He won't want to know.' Cassy shut her eyes. 'Oh God, this can't be happening.'

'I think you'd better tell him,' said Kylie or Keren, as she left the bathroom. 'He's got a right to know.'

Hamish hadn't noticed anything amiss, but perhaps he had other things on his mind. He'd hated the wildlife sanctuary in Thailand so much that, in the end, Cassy had agreed to leave early and head for a beach. Now he was sitting on the grass verge, leaning against his pack, nursing a hangover. He'd spent half the night playing pool with a couple of English Gap Yah girls, swapping hyperbole about London house prices and how he was going to make his first million by the time he was thirty.

'I thought they were meant to have decent weather in this country,' he moaned, cupping his hands to light a cigarette.

'It's winter.'

The smoke made her nauseated again. Hamish unfolded the newspaper he'd picked up in a café that morning, flattening it against his knees to keep it from blowing away. The front page featured a hero with a square jaw and All Blacks jersey—as though the world was fine and dandy; as though all the human race had to worry about was a rugby player's hamstring.

Cassy knew otherwise. She was twelve when the Twin Towers came down. School classes were cancelled while everyone crowded around the nearest telly, shrieking when that second plane appeared out of nowhere. She never forgot the sight of skyscrapers collapsing like piles of Jenga. She never forgot seeing people—real people—jumping to their deaths.

'The world will never be the same again,' her housemistress had murmured, pressing her hand to her mouth. None of the girls understood what she meant at the time, but Cassy did now. From that day on, the bad news never seemed to stop. Afghanistan. Iraq. Genocide in the Sudan. A murderous Boxing Day tsunami, hurricanes, terror attacks. No sooner had 2010 begun than the earth contorted under Haiti, killing a quarter of a million people. *A quarter of a million.* The sheer scale of it was beyond comprehension. And right now, at this very moment, floods in Pakistan were drowning whole families.

'I could murder another coffee,' Hamish said, yawning. He flicked through the paper until he found the latest from the FIFA World Cup. Football was a nice, safe subject. *Life's for living* was his new motto. *Lighten up, Cass.*

A car. One male occupant. She waved her sign, trying to look happy and apple-cheeked—the sort of girl any sane man would want in his passenger seat. He shot past.

Bugger. Her hands were turning mauve from the cold.

'We must look like serial killers,' she said. 'Or maybe they think we'll be really boring and they'll be stuck with us for hours.'

'Happens,' grunted Hamish, turning a page.

'What, people being boring?'

'Hitchhikers killing drivers. Saw it on Facebook. Bloke who cooked and ate people who gave him lifts.'

'That's an urban myth. Been going around for donkey's years.' The rain began all at once, as though someone was emptying a celestial bucket of water. Hamish used his newspaper as an umbrella.

'I vote we give up,' suggested Cassy. 'Get a bus tomorrow.'

'Can't. We need to get to Taupo today.'

'It doesn't matter, does it?'

'Bloody well does. I've got my skydive in the morning.'

Pulling her rain jacket from her pack, she dragged it over her head. She didn't care about his skydive—and neither would he, once she'd told him the awful news.

She took a breath, holding it in for one last moment. *He's got a right to know.*

'Look,' she said. 'I'm really worried.'

He glanced up at her, perfectly calm. He didn't see it coming.

'Remember I got food poisoning, couldn't keep anything down for the best part of a week? It was after the exams, so . . . end of May, early June.'

'I *told* you that kebab was dodgy.'

'Okay, okay. So you do remember.' She rubbed her hands together. 'Um . . . like I say, I couldn't keep *anything* down. And now I think we might be in serious trouble.'

It took about five seconds. Then she saw it hit him—*bam!*—right between the eyes.

'Have you done a test?' he asked.

'Not yet. I've been putting it off.'

'Do a test, for God's sake! Ten to one it's a false alarm.'

'I've thrown up every morning for days. I'm so tired I can hardly stand up—all I want to do is sleep. And . . . other stuff.'

'Do a test, all right? It'll be negative, I bet you anything.' He chewed his upper lip. 'If not, you'll have to act fast. I'll help.'

'By "help", d'you mean you'll be a hands-on father?'

His reaction might have been comical if the situation hadn't been so terrifying. He looked as though she'd dropped a scorpion down his boxer shorts.

'C'mon, Cass! We're both just starting out. We've got our futures ahead of us. There's only one logical solution and you know it.' He pulled out his Blackberry. 'Let's see if I can get online . . . Fuck it, I can't. But I'm sure you can get it done here. We'll look it up when we get to an internet café.'

She knew exactly where his research would lead. She'd already done her own, on the computer at the hostel in Auckland. *Good old Google*, she thought bitterly. *Book your skydive, your pepperoni pizza and the murder of your Little Problem, all from the comfort of your armchair.*

'It'd be easy enough to fix,' said Hamish.

'It wouldn't feel easy.'

'Even if this isn't a false alarm—and I bet it is—this is still just a bundle of cells. You can probably just take a pill. It's basically contraception.'

She rubbed her face with both hands. 'I don't know what to do.'

'You don't have a choice.' He looked away from her, down the road. 'Bloody hell. Doesn't bear thinking about. Imagine Mike's reaction!'

True. Imagine Mike's reaction. There was no way—absolutely *no way*—her father could ever hear about this. He'd go right off the deep end. He'd be intensely disappointed in her. He'd think her incompetent and careless and stupid, and she couldn't bear that. She'd made the age-old mistake: she'd cocked up and now she might be banged up.

Hamish seemed to have taken her silence for consent.

'So we're agreed? Neither of us can afford to be playing happy families. I certainly don't want to play—in fact, cards on the table: I *won't* play.'

The day darkened. Headlights were on, though it was still early afternoon. A horse box. A lorry. More heartless cars, their wheels spurting drips onto her bare legs. She was shivering now, but she kept switching on the smile. Nobody was going to pick up a red-nosed, blubbing hitchhiker.

'Anyway, you seemed perky enough last night,' said Hamish. 'When you were flirting.'

'Sorry?'

'With that Swede.'

Swede? She thought back. 'You mean the Finn? The guy who made me tea while you were holding forth to Charlotte and Topsy?'

'Finn. Swede. Same difference.'

'Actually, there's quite a lot of difference. Finland is—'

'Whatever.'

'Nobody was flirting except you,' she said. 'I caught you and posh Charlotte swapping phone numbers.'

'Charlotte's father happens to be an equity partner at Bannermans.' Hamish had an air of injured dignity. 'She might be able to swing me an internship. I'd do anything to get a foot in that door. And I do mean *anything*.'

This remark took Cassy's breath away. Even by Hamish's standards—and his standards seemed to have dropped, lately—it was staggeringly shallow.

'You really are a moron, aren't you?' she said.

If he heard, he pretended not to. A pack of cyclists whirred by: giant, lycra-clad insects with sinewy thighs and goggle eyes. Cassy thought of her dad. He was always out cycling, and he looked just like one of them. *Swish, swish.* The day was taking on a nightmare quality. Perhaps they'd never get to Taupo. Perhaps they were doomed to sit on this verge for all eternity, hating each other more with every passing hour.

'Shall we go our separate ways?' she asked.

'Go our . . . ?' Hamish's mouth dropped open. 'Where's *this* come from?'

She held out her arms. '*Look* at us, Hamish. This isn't making us happy! I hate the death throes of a relationship. Might be kinder to knock it on the head.'

She hoped there was still some love. She hoped he'd put up a fight—jump to his feet crying, *no, no*, and throw his arms around her. After all, they'd been together almost two years, and they used to be head-over-heels.

But he didn't move. He didn't argue. He even looked relieved. He was trying to hide it, but she knew him too well and saw the signs: a slump of the shoulders, a poker-faced tilt of the head.

'Your call,' he said.

She muttered something about getting coffee from the petrol station, handed him *TAUPO* and walked away before he could see her cry. It was all too much. She was cold and tired and frightened. In her whole life, she'd never felt so lonely.

She was trudging across the verge—wiping away tears with the palms of her hands—when a white van pulled up at the fuel pumps. It was rusted, rattling, full of people singing at the tops of their voices. The driver's door opened and someone swung to the ground. He might have been thirty or so. Broad shoulders. Lots of fair hair, short back and sides. Pretty hot, if you were into the rugged look—which she found she was. He grinned at her.

'You okay?' He sounded as though he cared.

'Fine. *Brr*. Cold.'

He was unscrewing the petrol cap. 'Headed south?'

'Taupo.'

'We turn off at Rotorua. Puts you a lot closer.'

The van's passenger door slid open. Faces were looking out.

'These guys wanna get to Taupo,' the driver called over his shoulder. 'Have we got room for two more back there?'

There were cries of *Always!* and *Bags of room!* before a couple of girls hopped out, one carrying a small boy on her hip. Both wore navy blue dresses with blue jerseys and lace-up boots, and both had short haircuts. They were smiling at Cassy. *Schoolgirls?*, she wondered. No, a bit too old. Perhaps a choir, on their way back from some event.

'You must be freezing,' said the one with the toddler. She and the child were obviously related, with matching olive complexions and almost-black hair. 'We can't leave you out here in the rain.'

The other girl—a willowy redhead—waved a thermos. 'We've got tea!'

Cassy felt pathetically grateful. 'You have no idea how welcome that sounds,' she said. 'Hang on, I'll go and tell my wingman.'

She bounded back to Hamish, who hadn't moved.

'Good news—a lift!' she announced, grabbing her pack. 'They'll take us as far as Rotorua.'

'No way. That jalopy they're driving is bursting at the seams. Can't be legal.'

'Beggars can't be choosers.'

'I don't want to get stuck in Rotorua.'

Cassy looked back at the van. The easy-on-the-eye driver had finished refuelling; he gave her a cheerful thumbs-up as he strode away to pay. The two girls were walking towards the hitchhikers.

'Hi!' cried the one who'd offered tea. She had a Scottish accent. 'I'm Paris. This is Bali, and—' she tapped the toddler's head '—Monty. Shall we help carry your stuff?'

She was one of those dramatic redheads who suit a pixie cut, and she was blasting Hamish with both barrels of her smile. He seemed unmoved.

'Thanks, but no thanks,' he said.

'You're being a wanker,' hissed Cassy. 'We have to take any lift that's going in the right direction.'

'Not if the vehicle's a heap of junk.'

That was the moment. The pivotal moment. That was when she made the decision that would change her life forever.

'Fine,' she snapped. 'Bye then. Might see you in Taupo.'

Her arrival at the van was greeted with cheers. It sounded as though there was a party going on inside—whooping and shouts of *Hi!* and *Welcome aboard!* They treated her like a celebrity. A boy reached out to take her pack; another gave her his seat. The door slid shut with a grating thud.

'Ooh,' sighed Cassy, massaging her bare legs to get the circulation going. 'It's lovely and warm in here.'

'We'll turn the heating up to dry you out,' said Bali, who was strapping little Monty into his car seat.

The driver climbed back in and slammed his door. The engine rumbled into life.

In those final seconds, Hamish had scrambled to his feet. She saw him take a step towards the van but it was a half-hearted gesture. He could have sprinted across and dragged the door open, if he'd really wanted to.

They were pulling away from the pumps. As they passed him, Cassy met his eye. He was holding out his hands, mouthing, *What the fuck?*

Then the van was accelerating away. Twenty seconds later, Hamish and the petrol station had disappeared behind a bend.

The Cult Leader's Manual: Eight Steps to Mind Control

Cameron Allsop

Step 2: Persuade the new recruit to walk into the web

Call it something innocuous: an introductory weekend, a course, a party, a bed for the night, friendship, marriage guidance, a church meeting, even a business proposition. It doesn't matter what you call it, but get them to come along.

Three

'Shame your friend wouldn't come,' said Paris.

'His loss.' Cassy meant to sound breezy, but the shock of it took away her voice.

It was over. That was a fact. They'd still been together when they woke up that morning, and the day before, and the day before that. Two years' worth of days before that. But now it was over. *There.* She'd finally admitted it to herself. She'd thrown up five mornings in a row, and she was on her own.

The van people rallied to cheer their hitchhiker. Somebody handed her an apple; the driver turned up the heating. Her hair was dripping down her back, so they gave her a towel. Paris poured black tea from the thermos.

'It's got honey in it,' she said, watching as Cassy took her first sip.

'Lovely,' sighed Cassy. 'I was so cold.'

Her rescuers introduced themselves. Crammed into the back two rows were a Swiss couple who looked about seventy—Otto and Monika—and their two teenaged grandsons. Otto had hedgehog brows and bulldog jowls, but he smiled often. Monika was pint-sized, with sparse grey hair. She was a doctor, apparently, and still working. The grandsons' names seemed to be Washington and Riyadh, though it was difficult to hear over the rumble of the van. They spent most of the journey playing a peaceful game of I-Spy.

Amazing kids, Cassy thought. *Why aren't they squabbling? Tara and I couldn't manage a long car journey without World War III breaking out.*

Directly behind Cassy sat Bali's partner, Sydney: a quiet young man who blinked at Cassy from round-rimmed glasses. He was brought up in Cape Town, he said, but never saw a future for himself in South Africa. He travelled around New Zealand after finishing his degree.

'Then I met Bali . . . and this chap came along!' He stroked Monty's head. 'So I'm still here.'

Monty reclined in a car seat between his young parents, gazing open-mouthed at Cassy's hair. She leaned over the back of her seat, letting him play with the heavy strands.

'Don't pull,' warned Bali, but he didn't. He was a gentle child.

'What about you?' asked Cassy, turning to the boy who'd so willingly given her his seat and was now scrunched up on the floor beside a box of apples. He was in the lanky stage of adolescence, all legs and arms. He grinned, showing slightly crooked teeth. No phone, no tablet, no hoodie, no sullen silences.

'I'm Rome,' he said, holding out his hand to shake hers. 'Very pleased to meet you.'

Cassy was bemused. 'Sorry,' she said. 'This might sound rude, but . . . is it a coincidence that most of you are named after places? Sydney, Rome, Paris, Bali . . . and aren't you two Washington and Riyadh? Are they nicknames?'

There was laughter. 'Nope, real names—we're a whole planet in one van!' cried Rome.

A freckled child sat in the front passenger seat, peeking over her shoulder. Her hair was covered by a rather ugly knitted hat.

'Meet Suva,' said Bali. 'She turns eleven next week. And our chauffeur is her dad, Aden.'

Cassy was surprised. The driver didn't give off the vibes of a married man. When he met her eye in the driver's mirror, he seemed amused.

'Too many whacky names to remember?' he asked. 'We don't mind if you forget.'

The journey to Rotorua took a little under three hours, and Cassy felt more relaxed than she had in days. She counted herself lucky to have landed in the company of such thoroughly nice people. In the whole journey, she didn't hear a single word of bitchiness. There was no tension, no eye-rolling behind one another's backs. They seemed happy with life, happy with one another and genuinely interested in her. It was a new experience for Cassy: most of her friends pretended to listen for three seconds before jerking the subject smartly back to themselves. The van people asked questions and listened to her answers, laughed at her jokes, exclaimed when she mentioned that she was in the final year of a law degree.

'You must be clever,' said Suva, from the front seat.

'Nah. Law students are two-a-penny, nowadays. I kind of wish I'd done something else.'

'Such as?' That was Swiss Otto, who'd been leaning forwards to catch Cassy's every word.

'Um . . . if I had my time again I reckon I'd look at teaching. I like the way children think.'

'Well, why not?' He held out his hands. 'It's not too late! It's *never* too late.'

'True.'

'And what made you study law?'

She grimaced. 'Seemed like a good idea at the time. My dad was keen.'

'He's a lawyer?'

'No, no. He was in the army for twenty-something years. He retired as a major, and nowadays he works for a security firm. If you're doing some kind of business in—let's say—Venezuela, they'll assess the risks and provide some ex-army heavies if you need bodyguards. If there's a meltdown, they'll help you get your business out fast.'

'Wow! That's a very cool line of work.'

'Not as cool as it sounds. Mostly dull stuff. Not sure it's even ethical, helping these big corporations exploit people. But that's more than enough about me! Who are you guys?'

'Okay,' said Paris. She clapped her hands and held them together for a moment. 'Okay. Now please, Cassy, don't think we're crazy, but we all live on a farm and market garden on Lake Tarawera.'

Cassy imagined greenhouses, perhaps a vegetable stall by a road. '*All* of you? Must be a big house.'

'Not in the same house. In the same . . . village. It's a farming and gardening community.'

'Are you fruit pickers? Seasonal workers?'

'No, it's our home. We've got about five hundred hectares, not all cultivated. There's forestry and native bush. We're growing sustainably—completely sustainably—putting more back into the soil than we take out. We're off the grid for water, electricity, sewage . . . everything. But we live really well.'

Cassy sensed a change in mood. Her new friends seemed watchful, as though they were waiting for her to laugh at them.

'Yes, you have guessed it,' said Otto. His accent was strong, his delivery deadpan. 'We're just a bunch of bloody hippies.'

He winked, and Cassy smiled. They didn't strike her as being hippies. They looked neat and alert. They were glowing.

'But you use petrol,' she said. 'What about this van?'

'Runs on ethanol we've made ourselves. We had to fill up earlier because we couldn't carry enough to get us to Auckland and back.'

'So what were you doing in Auckland?'

'Just a few errands.'

'I always feel so happy to be going home,' sighed Bali. 'Gethsemane's the most beautiful place you can imagine. The lake, the hills, the bush—it's like nowhere else on earth.'

'Sounds like heaven.'

'It *is* heaven. I wish you could see it.'

When the van was forced to halt behind a school bus, Aden turned in his seat.

'Hey, Cassy—why don't you come along? Take a look at what we're doing?'

'I'd love to.' Cassy thought about the logistics, but shook her head. 'No, I'd better hop out in Rotorua. First thing tomorrow, I have to get down to Taupo. Find Hamish.'

'The guy you were hitching with?'

'Mm.'

'Boyfriend?'

'Not sure.'

Aden's smile made creases on either side of his mouth.

'We've not been getting on,' said Cassy. 'I think it might be over.'

They all looked sorry, and Cassy felt someone press her shoulder. Outside, the rain had intensified into a downpour. Drops bounced off the road; the van's windscreen wipers were struggling. A sign was barely visible through the misted window: *Rotorua 5km*.

'We're almost there, aren't we?'

'Almost,' replied Aden, and once again his smiling eyes met Cassy's in the mirror.

Once again, she caught herself smiling back. *Stop it!* She slapped her own wrist. *Get a grip*.

'If you're wondering about the smell,' said Bali, wrinkling her nose, 'it's coming from all the geothermal activity around here. Rotorua's famous for that smell!'

Cassy sniffed. There *was* a sulphurous smell, a bit like the stink bomb someone once let off in her school hall.

'People stop noticing it after a few hours,' said Rome.

Soon they were passing shops and takeaway restaurants. Suva knelt up on her seat, murmuring earnestly into her father's ear. The child was a waif, with darkness around her eyes.

'Why don't *you* ask her?' replied Aden in a stage whisper.

'Can't you?'

He poked her gently in the ribs. 'No, you.'

Suva turned right around to face Cassy.

'Please, please, please will you stay with us?' she asked. 'Dad and me. We've got a spare bedroom. It's lovely in our cabin. We'll drive you back here in the morning.'

'Aw! That's so nice of you, but I've got to say no.'

'Why?'

Where's the harm? These people obviously aren't dangerous.

'Because I can't make your dad do all that extra driving.'

'Dad doesn't mind! You don't mind, do you, Dad?'

'I certainly don't,' said Aden. 'And we refuse to drop you in this filthy weather.'

Suva was clasping her hands, pleading. Cassy didn't know many ten-year-old girls, but this one seemed unusual; nothing like Tara, for example, who'd been a bumptious pain in the backside at that age. Suva had a stillness about her, a watchfulness, as though she were guarding her happiness.

'The turnoff's up ahead,' said Aden. 'Coming?'

'There's a venison casserole on my stove,' added Bali.

The whole crew joined in. *Oh, go on, say yes . . . You're such a breath of fresh air . . . Bali's casserole is famous!*

In the years to come, Cassy would replay the next few seconds again and again. She'd wonder what it was that persuaded her to stay in that van and go to a place she'd never heard of, with people she knew nothing about.

The choice seemed easy at the time: she could get soaked to the skin, with all the hassle of finding a hostel in a strange town. She could force down her thousandth meal of packet noodles in a grubby communal kitchen. (There would be a smug Scandinavian couple wearing designer fleeces, cooking something healthy involving vegetables and a wok. There always was.) She could crawl into a creaking dormitory bunk and lie awake, waiting for the terrifying morning sickness to begin again. She could face it all on her own.

Or she could be an honoured guest in a warm house, chatting with these kind, good people over a homemade casserole. She could be cared for, pampered, wanted, liked. It was a blissful prospect.

'If you're sure,' she said, and a rowdy cheer went up.

Aden indicated left and turned off the main road.

•

The landscape had changed. The hills were steeper, the vegetation wilder. Giant tree ferns brushed against the roof of the van while rain streamed down the windows. From time to time Aden swung around a dead creature in the road, which Rome said were possums. Cassy had begun the day in Auckland, with its Sky Tower, its cafés and traffic. This felt like another planet.

As they drove on, the afternoon lightened a little. Aden had to change down two gears as the van climbed up and up, before swinging around a long bend. Suddenly the outline of a mountain came into view—a fractured giant, rearing into a whitewashed sky.

'Tarawera!' cried Bali. 'The volcano. We're almost home.'

A lake stretched into the misty distance, but it didn't look like water. It reminded Cassy of mercury: slow, gleaming, filling the scars in the earth.

'I didn't even know this lake was here,' she said.

'Imagine that,' said Paris. 'For me, it's the other way around. I hardly believe the rest of the world exists.'

The road descended rapidly before turning along the shore. At first they drove past houses—mostly holiday homes, they told her—but these petered out. As the miles passed, the road became more primitive, narrower, less well maintained. Finally it ended altogether.

The child, Suva, got out to open and shut a gate, and her father navigated down a steep bank and onto a potholed track. Soon they were bumping through gloomy native bush with no sign of human habitation. Cassy was at the mercy of total strangers.

What if they were—as her mother would say—a bunch of mad axe murderers?

At last, Aden pulled into a clearing and turned off his engine. 'End of the road,' he said in the sudden silence.

But there's nothing here.

One by one, they jumped down to the muddy forest floor and began to collect boxes from the back of the van. Mist seemed to cling to Cassy's clothes, carrying scents of bracken and moss. She heard the trickling of water in the undergrowth.

'Right,' said Aden, who'd been locking up the van. 'Gimme your pack, Cassy—we'll get it stowed.'

'Stowed where? In what?'

He nodded towards the lake. That was when she saw that everyone was making their way along a ramshackle jetty, lowering their cargo into the bow of a wooden boat.

'You're joking!' Cassy was half nervous, half delighted. 'You get to your place by *boat*?'

It looked like something out of a film: much bigger than an ordinary rowing boat, with boards for seats. Six oars. Rome, Paris, Sydney and the two Swiss grandsons hopped in and made ready to row. Bali was already sitting in the stern, Monty on her knee. He snuggled up to his mother, softly crooning a song of his own.

'She's an old whaleboat,' said Aden. 'Been used on this lake for well over a century.'

Cassy admired the curves of the hull; dark wood that had expanded and shrunk under thousands of suns. She imagined men balanced on the prow, wielding harpoons.

'You and Suva could sit next to Bali,' suggested Aden, who was untying a rope from the jetty. 'I'll be rowing. Let's shove your pack in the middle. Okay . . . in you hop.'

The next moment, six people were pulling on their oars while coots skittered out of the way with offended shrieks. Cassy looked over the side, feeling the movement of water against the hull. The lake was clear and already deep—hard to judge just how deep, but a mass of weed seemed disturbingly far below. There was no sign of a life jacket or rubber ring. Soon the weeds on the lake bed were swallowed into blackness.

'How deep is this lake?' she asked.

'Very deep, in places,' said Bali. 'But it's calm today. You'd think butter wouldn't melt in its mouth.'

Across the water, Mount Tarawera reared up with barren shoulders. It wasn't high so much as massive, broken by a series of craters. The scarred desolation reminded Cassy of the final episode of *Walking with Dinosaurs*—the late Cretaceous, when volcanic activity was suffocating the earth and a fatal meteor was about to wipe out almost all life.

'Tarawera erupted in my great-great grandmother's time,' said Bali, pointing. 'The force tore the bottom out of Lake Rotomahana, on the other side of that spur over there. This whole area was buried in millions of tonnes of ash. Lots of people died.'

It was cold on the lake; too cold to be sitting still for half an hour. Cassy was shivering by the time they rowed close to a small island. All heads turned towards it, as though it held some kind of magnetic power. A breath of smoke spiralled from the trees, and a blue rowing boat was drawn up on the beach.

'Does someone live there?' Cassy asked.

She heard murmurs from all around her; a sound even happier than laughter.

'Someone amazing lives there!' said Rome.

Cassy was intrigued by this hermitage, adrift under the shadow of a volcano. As she watched, a figure stepped out of the trees. It was a man—tall, quite rangy—strolling towards the shore. He was barefoot, wearing a pale shirt and trousers. A dog paced alongside him: a beautiful creature, like a wolf, with a heavy coat and pricked-up ears.

Rome had leaped to his feet, waving and shouting, *Justin, Justin!* All the other youngsters joined him, and the old boat rocked.

'Come on, lads,' warned Otto. 'Focus on the job. You'll have us in the water.'

They immediately sat down—though Rome couldn't resist a final wave—and picked up their oars.

The man had reached the water's edge. Cassy had an impression of spare features and fair hair lifting in the breeze. He was looking directly at her. Then he smiled and raised one hand.

Cassy couldn't look away; she kept staring back at the island, even as the boat slid into the shelter of an inlet, fringed by a grey beach.

'Who was that?' she asked Bali.

'Justin.'

'But who is Justin?'

'He's the most wonderful person you'll ever meet.'

The more she thought about it, the more Cassy was gripped by a very odd, very strong certainty. There were other people on the boat, and at least half of them had been hailing that man. Yet his greeting had been meant for her. She was sure of it.

Why me? she thought. *I'm only a hitchhiker. He didn't even know I was coming.*

And then she was struck by something else. He hadn't behaved as though she was a stranger. It was as if he already knew her.

Four

Children were pelting towards a jetty, their shouts carrying on the still air. *They're back . . . Yay!*

Cassy tried to look in all directions at once. Gauzy mist had crept across the lake, so that the whole scene seemed wreathed in magic. The forested hills here opened into a cleared and cultivated valley in which quite a large settlement had been built. She could see goats grazing and washing hung on lines beside low buildings. When they reached the jetty, Aden lobbed a rope to one of the children—a stocky, blonde girl in blue trousers—who caught it competently and turned it around a post.

'That's my friend Malindi,' said Suva.

'Are all these guys your friends?'

'Yep! All of 'em.'

'Lucky you. So you're never bored?'

'Bored?' Suva's pale eyebrows shot up. 'No, I don't think so.'

The travellers dispersed, telling Cassy they'd see her later. Cargo was passed from person to person and then to the children, who formed a procession and set off up a grassy slope. Cassy reached for her backpack but Aden was there before her, swinging it over one shoulder.

'Welcome to Gethsemane,' he said.

'I'm so happy you're here!' Suva was hugging herself.

They led her across the pasture to a wooden cabin with a long front porch. Of all the cabins, this was closest to the lake. Aden and Suva sat on the porch steps to take their shoes off, so Cassy followed suit. Then she leaned back on her elbows for a moment, taking in the sheer peace. No traffic, no shouts; just the calls of birds and the sigh of ripples on the shore. As she watched, evening sunshine lit up the torn summit of Tarawera.

Shame Hamish missed seeing this. I wonder if he's tried to call me?

'No signal, I'm afraid,' said Aden, when she squinted at her phone. 'Did you want to contact someone?'

'No problem.' Cassy resolved not to think about Hamish again that night.

'Suva will look after you,' said Aden. 'I've got a couple of chores to do before dark.'

'Come in, come in.' Suva was hopping from foot to foot, twisting her hands around each other. She'd removed her hat to reveal short, sandy hair. 'Come and see our home.'

The porch door led into a tidy kitchen-cum-living room, warmed by a pot-bellied stove. Suva stopped to stoke it while Cassy looked around her. A pine table filled much of the space; it was pulled alongside a window seat, cushioned by a squab with flowery fabric. The layout reminded Cassy of Hamish's parents' yacht.

'Right,' said Suva, smacking wood ash off her hands. 'So this is our kitchen.' She opened all the cupboards. 'Mugs in here, breakfast things in here, you can make yourself tea or anything, the kettle's beside the stove—but beware!'

'Beware?! Why?'

'Because this stuff is—*ugh*—nettle tea.' Suva screwed up her face as she brandished a jar. 'Dad says it's like drinking a cowpat. Monika gave it to him, so he pretends to like it when she comes around. We buy in tea and coffee and chocolate and

SEE YOU IN SEPTEMBER 35

things we can't make, but Monika says we have to be self-sufficient. She keeps trying her own inventions! Come and see your bedroom.'

To reach the rest of the cabin they had to go back outside, turn right, and walk along the front porch.

'Dad's room,' said Suva, opening the first door.

No frills. A double bed, a folded blanket. Two sheepskin rugs were the only covering on the bare floorboards. Canvas trousers and a dark blue knitted jersey hung over a wooden chair. There was no sign of a Mrs Aden.

The next room was little more than a cupboard.

'Mine,' said Suva.

Suva's bed, neatly made, sat under a window framed by flowered curtains. As in the rest of the cabin, the walls were tongue-and-groove boards. There was nothing hanging on them: no posters of pop stars, no photos, no mirror. Then again, the view through the window was so stupendous that there wasn't any need for decoration.

'A million-dollar view,' breathed Cassy, looking across the lake to the mountain, now rapidly fading into dusk.

'*Much* more than a million dollars!'

The room next door was bigger, with a set of bunk beds.

'Who sleeps in here normally?' asked Cassy.

'Nobody.'

'Don't you want this room? It's bigger than yours.'

'I like mine. Top or bottom bunk?'

'Um . . . top, please. I've got a sleeping bag.'

Suva said there was no need for that, and promptly disappeared. A few moments later she was back with blankets and sheets.

'Where d'you go to school?' asked Cassy, as the two of them began to make up the bed.

'Here.'

'There's a school *here*?'

'Of course.'

The child was plumping up a pillow—very adult in her actions, very busy. The pillowcase had been patched in the same flowery fabric as the curtains, and Cassy wondered about Suva's mother.

'Did you sew that on?' she asked, touching the patch.

'No.' Suva threw a sheet across the bed, and together they tucked it in. 'My . . . someone else did.'

They'd finished the task and were pushing the bunks back against the wall when Suva slapped her own forehead.

'The bathroom! Sorry, you must have been wondering if we even have a toilet. I'll forget my head next. You'll need this torch.'

She took Cassy outside and pointed to a wooden hut, raised up a few steps. 'It's a composting toilet, so throw a cupful of sawdust down after you've used it. Our shower's in there too— it's lovely in winter, because the water's heated by the stove. I'll leave you in peace.'

The little shed was perfectly civilised inside, clad in wood. The only mirror was just big enough for a man to use for shaving. A bar of handmade soap smelled of lemon balm, and there was what she assumed to be toothpaste in a small pot on the basin. No electric light, though, so she was pleased to have the solar-powered torch.

By the time she'd made her way back to the kitchen, Aden was home and lighting a hurricane lamp.

'Dinner's ready,' he said. 'Bali's parents are there. And Rome.'

Cassy's spirits nosedived. She thought of her peaceful little bedroom. She wanted to lie down under a warm blanket, close her eyes and forget her troubles for a while. She couldn't face the social effort of an evening with strangers.

Someone touched her hand; looking down, she saw that Suva had taken it.

'Hungry?' asked the child, with her wistful smile.

'Starving! Let's go.'

The smell of casserole met them as they approached Bali's cabin. It perked Cassy up. She hadn't had lunch, she'd felt too nauseated to eat breakfast, and she felt hollow. Monty was sitting patiently on the porch steps, so miniature that his feet only just reached the step below. He held out his arms to Aden.

'Hiya, buddy, you waiting for us?' Aden squatted down, his own arms encircling the tiny boy as he swung him up.

'It's like you're all family,' said Cassy.

'We *are* all family.'

'Is Monty short for Montague?'

'*Montague?*' Aden laughed. 'No! Montreal.'

'Are you kidding?'

'You commented on it, in the van. And you're right—most of us are named after places. Not all, but most. It's a bit of a tradition.'

Bali's parents turned out to be a Maori couple, Hana and Dean. Hana was the only teacher at the school. She too had short hair and wore dark blue. Like all the men, Dean was clean-shaven, and dressed in canvas trousers and a knitted jersey. He peered through the thick lenses of his glasses, smiling peaceably. They said they'd lived in Gethsemane since the community was founded. It was Hana's family who had sold the land to a European farmer, back in the 1950s. The farmer's grandson had gone on to gift it to Justin.

'So this land came back to my family, in a way,' said Hana. 'There are four generations of us here. My mother Netta—you'll meet her—and Bali, and this little fella.'

She smiled at Monty, who'd settled on the window seat with Rome and Suva on either side. They cut up his food, poured his water and let him climb all over them.

Meanwhile Dean was opening a bottle of Gethsemane peach wine. Cassy discovered that it slid down rather easily; they were soon on to a second bottle. The casserole had been on the stove since six that morning: venison, slowly simmering with carrots, yams, kumara and other vegetables Cassy didn't even recognise.

'You've no electricity here?' she asked.

They were clearly proud of their system, and spent some time explaining how it all worked. There were solar panels on almost every roof, they said, and small hydro-turbines. They used solid fuel in rocket stoves for cooking.

'We store power in massive batteries,' said Bali. 'Up at the big kitchen we've got fridges, even a freezer. My brother Seoul is catering chief. He knows everything there is to know about preserving food.'

'And venison? Where does that come from?'

'Hunting. The hills are full of deer and pigs. Beyond us it's Crown land, and we can hunt there too. Every now and again a group goes out to restock the larders.'

'So the food's all communal?'

'Everything's shared. And we have a community meal at least twice a week.'

The conversation moved on. Hana asked Cassy about the animal sanctuary in Thailand. Everyone seemed fascinated by the project, horrified by her tales of abused and injured elephants—smiling at her heavily censored description of what tourists got up to on Thai beaches. She felt as though she was in a room full of friends she'd never met before that day. There was plenty of laughter, but these people weren't vying to be the funniest or the most outrageous or the loudest. It felt like a good dream. As time passed, Monty closed his eyes, snuggling up to Rome.

'Aw, he's going to sleep,' said Cassy.

Suva kissed the toddler's head. 'Isn't he cute? He'll wake up again when the night bell rings.'

'Night bell? Is this a monastery?'

'Definitely *not* a monastery,' said Bali, who was ladling more stew onto everyone's plates. 'We're not a Christian community. Nobody's taken a vow of chastity—as you can see!' She giggled, gesturing at Monty.

'Whew. Good. *God*'s a dirty word in my family,' said Cassy. 'I was brought up by evangelical atheists.'

'What's an evangelical atheist?'

'I mean they're devout atheists, not hedge-your-bets agnostics. Mum's been one all her life. Dad was brought up Catholic, finally lost his faith when he was posted to Bosnia. So my sister and I never had the luxury of believing in fairytales.' Cassy thought about it, sipping her wine. 'Actually . . . except Santa Claus. For some reason they were prepared to fib about him.'

Aden leaned back in his chair, stretching his arms above his head.

'Mm, well, fair enough,' he said lightly. 'The world's religions have caused havoc. It's okay, you haven't landed yourself among a bunch of monks.'

'So why the bells?'

'We just choose to follow some of the rhythms of monastic life. We like to have structure to our day, our week, our year. So from time to time you'll hear the bell tolling over at the *wharenui*.'

He pronounced it *fah-re-nui*. Cassy copied him.

'Means the meeting house,' he said. 'A *whare* is a house.'

'And how often does the bell ring?'

'At least five times a day: Early Call, Morning Call, Meridian Call, Dusk Call—you might call that one teatime—and Night Call, which is last thing before bed. The times vary according to the season. But it's an invitation, not a command. We only go if we want to.'

'Which we normally do,' added Suva, 'because it's fun.'

'Are visitors allowed?'

Aden smiled. 'More than welcome.'

With darkness came torrential rain. Water bucketed down the roof, along the guttering and into water barrels. It made the lamplight seem more mellow, the stove luxurious.

'How're you going?' asked Bali, as they drank coffee. 'Tired?'

'Yes—but very happy to be here, not in some miserable hostel.'

Bali had dimples in her cheeks. 'You won't want to leave.'

A bell began to toll. It was a single, low-pitched note, repeated at a walking pace. In Cassy's state of exhaustion it seemed exotic and yet comforting, echoing steadily through the dark and rain. It called to her. Everyone immediately stood up. Even Monty rubbed his eyes.

'Cassy, stay here if you like,' suggested Aden. 'Or head back to our cabin and turn in.'

'She wants to come!' Bali lifted a woollen cloak from a hook. 'Hide under this with me and Suva. We'll all run across together.'

The night air revived Cassy. She and Bali each held an edge of the cloak while everyone scampered through the darkness, whooping when they splashed into puddles. The yellow light of Aden's lantern danced in a wild arc. The bell was still tolling as they crossed a covered verandah and crept through a door.

It was an airy, high-roofed space, filled with rows of large cushions. At one end a circular dais, perhaps a foot high, was lit by a ring of candles. There were more candles on every surface. Shadows leaped and flickered on the walls, and the air was scented with honey. It seemed a little gothic but the effect was calming. Cassy felt safe; she felt hidden.

The room was full of people, many of them children. Several smiled and waved when her group arrived. Cassy did a quick head count. There must have been over a hundred gathered in that room, but the only sounds were the tolling of the bell and rain tapping on the tin roof.

'Wanna share a cushion?' whispered Suva, plumping herself down and tugging at Cassy's hand. They were joined by Suva's friend, Malindi. The bell tolled. The rain drummed. The candles threw their shadows. The people were silent silhouettes. It was all so very peaceful.

By contrast, Cassy's thoughts began to yell at her.

Did Hamish get to Taupo? I wonder if there's a phone signal if I climb a hill? No, I'll get lost if I try that in the dark . . . I wonder what happened to Suva's mother? No woman in her right mind would walk out on Aden—kind, competent . . . sexy smile . . . I'm probably not pregnant. Hell, I hope I'm not; no no no, I won't be . . . please, God, no. Break Dad's heart. He'd despise me. Have to have a termination, I've got too much to lose. I wonder if it looks like a baby yet? Where's Hamish now? Did he get to Taupo? . . . and on and on, a ghastly merry-go-round in her mind.

The bell had stopped tolling.

From out of the silence, a tenor voice began to sing. It was a poignant melody, just four phrases long. The words were about the lake, and the mountain, and the spirit that lived in the human heart and in all things. It made the hair stand up on the back of Cassy's neck.

Then she realised that the singer was Rome. He began the song again, and this time Otto lifted a flute and played a descant. The third time through, everyone in the room joined in, along with a flowing piano accompaniment. Cassy felt a stirring of her blood as she sang along—quietly, in case she got it wrong. Next, the voices broke into harmonies and a set of drums added a new pulse. By now, Cassy knew the song and was belting it out with the best of them.

The final repetition was deafening, with cymbals and a trumpet added to the mix. It felt exhilarating. People had scrambled to their feet and were linking arms, swaying as they sang. Suva pulled Cassy up; Malindi danced with little Monty. The clamour of worry in Cassy's head was drowned out.

'That was fun!' she gasped, as they burst into the night. The rain had stopped. People milled on the verandah, chatting. It was long after midnight by Cassy's watch but there was a party atmosphere. Everyone wanted to meet her. She discovered that it was Bali who'd been playing the piano and Washington the trumpet. The drummer was a recent arrival at the community: a drooping, sallow young man they called Dublin. He said he'd been addicted to any drugs he could get hold of, including pure meth. He seemed edgy.

'I was messed up,' he confided to Cassy, and looking at his painful thinness she could well believe it. Lank hair flopped over one eye. 'Whole months I can't remember. Justin saved me.'

Otto clapped her on the shoulder. 'I heard you singing—we need singers like you. So it's decided! You have to stay!'

'Okay.' Cassy laughed, holding out her arms in defeat. 'Why not? Bugger my degree.'

Fatigue was beginning to creep up again when Aden sought her out.

'You must be shattered,' he said quietly.

'You too?'

'No, no. We're used to it. I have a few more things to do here. Suva, will you take Cassy home?'

Their kitchen was cosy, the stove gently glowing. Suva made them both hot water bottles.

'Rome's got a lovely voice,' ventured Cassy.

'I know!'

'Which of those people were his parents?'

'He lives with Hana and Dean. Soon he'll move into a cabin with Dublin and some other single men.'

'Oh. So . . . no parents?'

'I'll be right next door. Do you have everything you need?'

'I'm fine. Thanks so much.'

'Can I show you around Gethsemane tomorrow?'

I should leave in the morning, thought Cassy. *Do a pregnancy test. Find Hamish. Make decisions.*

'We'll see,' she said.

•

She lay under heavy blankets, delighting in the intensity of the darkness. It felt strange to be in a place with no streetlights, no car headlights, no electronics. Even at the wildlife place in Thailand a generator had rumbled constantly. But here the night wasn't treated like an enemy.

Suva's mother. Rome's parents. Where were all these people?

She could hear Suva moving around in her room, and then the springs as she got into bed. Later still, she heard Aden returning to the cabin. She wondered what he'd been doing.

Exhaustion was a soft cloud in her brain. She was floating in calm, warm water. It lifted her, and she drifted away.

Sometime in the night she was woken by the call of a water-bird. It sounded as though someone were playing an oboe, on just one note. It took her a minute to remember where she was. She let herself melt again, soothed by the lapping of tiny waves on the shore. She felt such peace.

It's over with Hamish, she thought. *Why don't I care more? He couldn't possibly understand what I'm experiencing here. He wouldn't get it at all.*

For the first time, she found herself imagining what might be happening inside her. Perhaps cells were dividing; perhaps life was forming. Unwanted life. Unplanned life. But life, nevertheless.

The Cult Leader's Manual: Eight Steps to Mind Control

Cameron Allsop

Step 3: Love bombing

In this fractured world, unconditional love is a priceless commodity. Shower your new member with affection, admiration and attention. Make them into a beloved king or queen for a day, or a week, or for months—for as long as it takes. Many recruits will leave. Others will blossom.

Some organisations routinely use physical or emotional attraction as an incentive to the new member to engage with the group. Never underestimate the power of sex, romance or a bond with a child.

Five

The bell was ringing.

Rolling over to peer out of her window, Cassy made out the faintest glow in the sky. A floorboard creaked in Suva's room.

Get going, Cassy scolded herself. *You're a guest. You can't loll around in bed!* Yet she felt mired in sleep. She closed her eyes for one last moment.

Then she was sitting up in panic.

No. Not now! Nausea gripped her with an iron hand. She slid from the bunk and pelted to the outdoor toilet, where she was violently sick. Exhausted, she shivered on the wooden floor. This was a disaster. She had to take control. She needed to return to civilisation. Right now.

The bell fell silent, and she heard singing. She imagined all those people gathered in the meeting house and felt oddly comforted. By the time she'd brushed her teeth and stepped out onto the wet grass, it was growing light. Her anxiety felt less sharp now, despite the terrifying sickness. The contentment of Gethsemane seemed to wash right through her. She could smell bracken, wood smoke and . . . coffee!

Aden was tending the stove when she looked in from the porch.

She'd thrown on some clothes and plaited her hair. For a moment they faced each another. It was as though they had an understanding; they knew where this was leading. *But it can't be leading anywhere. We come from different worlds, and I'm leaving today.*

'Hi!' he cried delightedly. 'Sleep well?'

'Like a log.'

'You look a bit peaky. You all right?'

Well, no. She'd just brought up most of last night's supper, and she fervently hoped he hadn't heard her. Not dignified. Not sexy.

'Fine,' she replied. 'Dandy! Bit of a stomach bug.'

He seemed to accept this, and lifted an enamel pot from the stove. 'D'you like coffee at this time of day?'

'Is the Pope a Catholic?'

He seemed confused. 'I think so. Last time I looked.'

'Sorry—maybe it's an English expression. It means yes, I'd love some coffee. Where's Suva?'

'Helping to make breakfast in the *whare kai*,' he said, handing Cassy a mug. 'The community kitchen. I thought you might like to come out to the jetty for a while. And I've got something for you. The knitting team asked me to give you this.' He laid a navy blue cable-knit jersey around her shoulders. She could smell the lanolin.

'A gift from Gethsemane,' he said.

'You can't give me this!'

'I just have. Stop fussing and put it on.'

So she stopped fussing and pulled the jersey over her head as they stepped onto the porch. A single bird called in the trees. It sounded like a football rattle, with a whistling finish. Another answered, then another, and another, serenading the morning with trills and clicks and notes as pure and fluid as those of a piccolo. Aden knew their voices: *That's a tui—hear his creaking and all the whistles? That flute is him, as well. There's a bellbird, the korimako.*

A crowd of busy little birds were pecking around the cabin.

'What are they?' asked Cassy, enchanted. 'Like tennis balls with legs.'

'Quails. They visit every day, looking for whatever we've dropped.'

The two of them wandered along the pumice sand, crunching around kayaks and a red motorboat with *Ikaroa* painted on her hull. This, Aden explained, was the fastest way to get about the lake. 'Goes like a rocket,' he said. 'Great fun.'

Cassy pointed to a long white boat lying at anchor in the bay. 'She's beautiful. I didn't notice her last night.'

'*Matariki*. Pride of our fleet. That grand lady started out as a sailing boat back in 1920. She's made of kauri.'

Matariki was elegant and old-fashioned, with a boxy cabin roof and four portholes up the sides.

'Does she use ethanol too?'

Aden nodded as they began to walk along the jetty. 'She does. She's got a shallow draft, so we can moor just about anywhere. She can carry a lot of us, at a pinch—gets a bit low in the water though! We'll take her out on Suva's birthday.'

'Will you? Where are you planning to go?'

'Suva's chosen Kereru Cove. Hot springs, even a hot beach. It's something tourists don't get to see.' An idea seemed to strike him. 'Hey, why don't you stay till then? It's on Wednesday. Less than a week away.'

Cassy narrowed her eyes, calculating, longing to say yes. 'I'd love that, but . . .'

'You have to get to Taupo?'

'I should.'

'Look, Cassy, I'll drive you to the main road any time you say the word. But you're a big hit here, and I've got an offer for you: bed and board in return for four hours' work a day. The rest of the time you can explore, take a kayak, go for walks.'

'You don't know how tempting that sounds.'

'The offer's there.'

They sat down side by side at the end of the jetty, letting their boots break the rippled satin of the water. From there the island looked like a turtle. It seemed to have a head and a body, and was swimming through gossamer skeins of mist.

'How long have you lived here?' she asked.

'Since I was fourteen. My parents came for a permaculture course. They had a smallholding and wanted to run it sustainably. They came for a week with me and Julia, my sister. We never left.'

'And their smallholding?'

'Sold it. Put the money into Gethsemane.'

'What made them decide to stay?'

Aden leaned back on his hands. 'They found what they were looking for: people who cared, a community, a way of life that was clean. Dad's a mechanic—and boy, did they need a mechanic! He keeps the machinery going. The sawmill, the tractor, the van, the boats. He likes a challenge.'

'And your mum?'

'Does the Gethsemane accounts. We're running a business here, even if we wish we weren't.'

'But you were a teenager! Weren't you pissed off?'

'Couldn't believe my good luck. It was a lot more social than our little farm in the middle of nowhere. *So* many playmates. We ran around in a gang, playing on the best rope swing I'd ever seen, swimming, fishing, putting on shows, hunting in the bush, kayaking . . . it was a perfect adolescence. There's no stranger danger here. No drugs, no bullying, no terrorism. Complete freedom.'

'Is your sister still here?'

Aden hesitated, looking down into the shadows below the jetty. A small swell washed around the posts. 'Julia didn't like it so much. She was seventeen, maybe a trickier age. She left.'

'Where is she now?'

'In Australia. She's a nurse, she's got her own family. We've lost touch.'

'What a shame.'

'We're very different people.'

At one side of the bay, the beach ended in a grassy promontory. Cassy was startled to notice a number of white crosses dotted across the headland. They looked like stickmen, marching through the tussocks, luminous in the half-dark.

'Are people buried on that headland?' she asked.

'No. The law says we can't do that. When someone dies, we have them cremated in town and scatter their ashes on the lake. The crosses are memorials.'

'So everyone comes home.'

'Everyone comes home.'

Sunrise wasn't far away. All along the eastern horizon, primrose yellow merged into whitewashed blue. Brilliance sprayed from behind the volcano.

At least it's stopped raining in time for Hamish's skydive, thought Cassy. Then it struck her that she really didn't care. She was in a fairytale valley, watching the dawn with a man who intrigued her. What more could she possibly want? It was tempting to stay—just for a day or two, just while she rested and made decisions. She couldn't imagine anywhere more healing than this place.

She was still undecided when the rim of the sun gleamed over the volcano. Seconds later, fire seemed to tear across the lake.

'*Wow*,' she whispered.

'I know,' said Aden. 'Wow.'

They sat in companionable silence, watching the day begin, listening to a cacophony of birdsong.

'Will Suva get presents?' asked Cassy.

'We don't go in for that. Possessions aren't important. The picnic's her gift from the community.'

Cassy laughed. 'I'd like to see my sister's face if someone told her she wasn't getting anything for her birthday. Heads would roll.'

'What sort of things?'

'Well, for her last birthday . . .' Cassy checked herself, embarrassed at the sheer opulence of her family's life. 'Let's just say she didn't go without. Then again, where we live is basically one giant shopping centre. Our local park is festooned with broken bottles and graffiti. There's an oily kind of drain they call the stream, but you'd want your stomach pumped out if you drank from it. So I think Suva has the better deal.'

A breeze sprang from nowhere, shattering the water into thousands of shards. Cassy heard the clanging of a gong.

'That's for us,' said Aden. He swung his legs back onto the jetty, stood up and held out his hand for hers. 'We don't always share breakfast, but this is a special occasion.'

'Why's that?'

'Because you're here.'

'I don't believe you.'

He laughed, holding on to her hand a second longer than he should. 'I never lie.'

•

The *whare kai* turned out to be a bustling kitchen and dining hall with long refectory tables. A brick bread oven was being used outside, and the comforting smell of freshly baked bread pervaded the scene. Everyone in sight was wearing navy blue or beige. At one end of the hall, a crowd of children were playing blind man's buff. Two older boys had hold of Monty's hands and were helping him to dodge.

Bali was waiting for them. A shawl was draped around her shoulders. 'Cassy!' she cried. 'You're famous! Everyone wants to meet you.'

As she spoke, a middle-aged couple bounced up to introduce themselves as Berlin and Kazan, Aden's parents. Both were sturdy and fair-haired, like their son. Berlin had what looked like engine oil under his fingernails, and Cassy remembered that he was the mechanic. Next came Seoul—Bali's older brother, the chef. He and Bali were very alike: deep brown eyes under heavy brows. He had intricate tattoos up his arms and the physique of a rugby player.

'My poor brother's in love with Paris,' whispered Bali. 'But she's refusing to be anyone's partner at the moment.'

Others followed: too many to remember, but every one of

them welcoming. An elderly woman sat peaceably at the head of a table. Her face reminded Cassy of a walnut, because of its colour and the incredible profusion of wrinkles. A walking stick rested across her knees.

'Netta,' said Bali, leaning close to the old lady, 'this is Cassy. Cassy, this is my *kuia*—my grandmother.'

'I'll be you*r* *kuia* too,' said Netta, smiling in Cassy's direction. She wore hearing aids in both ears. 'Sit down next to me, pour yourself some tea. I don't see very well nowadays.' Her gnarled fingers reached carefully for her own cup. 'But I know what *you* look like. You're a pretty lass, with a smile that melts everyone's hearts. They've been telling me how you've brought our Suva out of herself.'

Cassy looked around for Suva, and spotted her stacking plates. When Cassy caught her eye, she waved.

'See how she lit up?' said Bali. 'That's a breakthrough—a real breakthrough. It's lovely to see. She's been hurt.'

Aha, thought Cassy. *So there is a story.* She was about to demand details when a hush fell on the room. A man was standing up on a chair. He was fiftyish. Roundish. Balding. A double chin, cheerful grin and a squint—or was it a glass eye?

'Liam,' whispered Bali. 'Justin's right-hand man.'

'For this feast, we thank you!' bellowed Liam, with all the gusto of a rabble-rouser.

The company echoed enthusiastically: *We thank you!*

'For this new day, we thank you.'

We thank you!

'And for our beautiful visitor Cassy, who's already brought us joy, we thank you three times!'

This was met by shouts that raised the roof: *Thank you! Thank you! Thank you!*

And that was it. People applauded. Liam winked at Cassy before jumping off his chair. The whole thing was very good-humoured.

Bali offered Cassy some oven-warm bread. 'We didn't embarrass you, did we?'

'No! But . . .' Cassy wasn't sure how to frame her next question. 'That *was* a prayer, wasn't it? I mean . . . nobody said the word *God*, but it sounded like a prayer to me.'

'It did? Try this honey, it's still in the comb, see? Skye is our beekeeper.' Bali nodded towards a thin, laughing girl who sat at the other end of the table. 'There's nothing Skye doesn't know about bees.'

'Clever,' said Cassy, spreading a dollop on her bread. 'So are you . . . um, Christians?'

'No.'

'No?'

'Yes and no.' Bali grimaced ruefully as she touched Cassy's arm. 'Sorry, I'm not trying to talk in riddles! Depends what you call a Christian, I guess. We don't take the Bible literally. We reject the hateful things in Christianity. We *hate* intolerance. Our way of life is based on compassion and common sense. We don't judge anyone.'

'Really? Nobody?'

'No. We *never* judge. We *never* call anyone a sinner. God— or what people call God—made people who are gay and people who are straight; people who're drawn to drugs, people who go tramping in the hills, people who steal, people with mental health problems, people who've committed violent crimes. They're all welcome. No negativity here! Our way of life is based on love. Simple as that. Love. We're a family. We don't look for faults.'

'Some families look for faults.'

'Does yours?'

'Sometimes.'

'Well, we don't. We really don't.'

This didn't sound like a complete answer, but it didn't seem polite to press the point. *Never discuss politics or religion with your host*—that's what Mike had drummed into Cassy when she was fourteen and going on an exchange trip to France.

More food arrived: bacon and mushrooms, and fruit preserved in glass jars. Cassy tried some kind of curds and whey;

Bali claimed it would cure any ills. It tasted suspect—pretty much like sour milk, if she was honest—but it seemed to get on top of her nausea.

Looking around, she spotted a noticeboard with lists pinned to it.

'Our rotas for the week,' explained Bali, when she saw Cassy trying to read them. 'Otto does all that. He's our manager.'

Towards the end of the meal, Bali excused herself and went to help with the washing-up. She'd only just left when her mother took her place.

'Now,' began Hana, 'the children would love you to visit the school. They've been pestering me already.'

Why not? thought Cassy. *I can still get to Taupo later.*

'I'd be honoured,' she said.

Hana clapped. 'Yes! Thank you! After Meridian Call? That'll give us time to get out the flags and bunting.'

A stooping figure had wandered up while they talked and was standing close by, obviously waiting to be introduced. Hana beckoned him closer.

'Sorry, Kyoto—I mustn't monopolise Cassy. Take my seat. Cassy, this is Kyoto, our chief carpenter. He built most of this place. He's one of the Companions.'

'One of the what?'

'Companions. Elders. *Kaumatua.*'

The carpenter had a head of grey wire, like a pot scrub. Cassy was fascinated to see a pencil stub stuck into it, presumably for safekeeping. His fingers were yellowed, his teeth in pretty bad shape. He set his teacup onto the table with a clatter.

'So where are you from?' he asked.

'My parents live in London.'

'London!' He slapped his knee. 'I was born there. Came over here as a kid with my parents. I've buried them now, and both my sisters. But I'll tell you what . . .' He leaned closer. 'These people saved my life.'

'Really?'

'Spent half of it in prison. Nobody would give me the time of day, and fair enough because I've done things that should've disqualified me from the human race. Fifteen years ago, Justin came and got me from Mount Eden jail.'

'And brought you here?'

Kyoto nodded. His eyes had reddened.

'Sorry . . . it still gets to me. *I promise you, Chris,* he said—that was my name then—*I promise your life is going to be worthwhile from now on.* He trusted me when nobody else did. I'd done a joinery apprenticeship, so he set up the carpentry workshop just for me. And look at me now, I've turned my life around. I've got myself a beautiful lady—Athens, you'll meet her, she runs the woollen mill.' Kyoto tapped the table, fixing Cassy with a bird-bright gaze. 'If it wasn't for Justin, I'd be dead by now. No ifs or buts. *Dead.* Plenty of us here could tell the same story.'

'I haven't met Justin.'

'You will.' He picked up his teacup, took a noisy sip. 'And once you've met him, you'll never worry about anything ever again.'

•

'Our phone's down at the moment,' said Aden, as he unlocked the office. 'Sorry about that. We've got satellite internet. I think it's a miracle, but visitors complain that it's slow and it cuts out a lot.'

The office was a standalone cabin. There were filing cabinets and a desktop computer, coffee rings and piles of paper clips. Cassy half expected a bouncy secretary to pop out and start doing her nails.

'So who works in here?' she asked, as they waited for the computer to start up. 'Your mum, I guess, doing the accounts?'

'A few people. We trade produce and buy in stock. I use the internet to find breeding rams. People do distance learning: Paris is studying midwifery, Rome's doing computing. We run residential courses, like the permaculture one my parents came for. There's a bunkhouse up at the back.'

'Any other courses?'

'Sustainable living—things like beekeeping and weaving. And retreats for recovering addicts. Rome runs our website. He's very good.'

Cassy's curiosity had got the better of her. 'Doesn't Rome have any parents?'

'The whole community brought him up. His mother died after he was born.'

'Sad. And where's his father?'

Aden shrugged. 'It's not a secret. His father's Justin.'

'The man we saw on the island? People keep talking about him. Who is he?'

'Ah! Looks like we've managed to get online.'

Aden said he'd give her some space, then left the room.

Cassy had only just opened her email account when Suva's head appeared around the door, offering a guided tour.

'Hana's let me out of school especially,' she said.

'Five more minutes?'

'Okay.' The child loitered, swinging against the doorpost.

'Scram,' said Cassy. 'Five minutes!'

She could have taken hours to find the right words for Hamish. She could have typed, edited, cried and typed again—it wasn't much fun to be pronouncing their relationship officially dead.

Hi Hamish,

I hope you got to Taupo ok and you're skydiving right now. I haven't been able to text because there's no phone coverage here. Dodgy internet too.

I think we should call it a day. We can call it mutual agreement, can't we? I don't regret the time we've had, it's been wonderful. But your reaction to you-know-what proved what we both already knew, that we don't have a future together. I'm pretty sure you've come to the same conclusion.

Good luck with the million pounds before you're thirty! I promise I won't come asking for any of it ;)

And thanks for all the fun we had.

I'm at a sort of farm called Gethsemane. They've offered me bed and board in return for work. I haven't decided yet, but I might stay for a few days. Save me a fortune.

If we don't meet up before, I'll see you in Christchurch when we fly out.

Hope the skydiving was fun.

Take care.

Love,

Cassy xxx

She reread the message three times.

Her hand gripped the mouse.

Send.

Job done, decision made.

•

The rest of the day passed in a blur. She was shown greenhouses and beehives, worm farms and composting systems. The gardens were vast and apparently chaotic: a baffling riot of winter vegetables grew among herbs, soft fruit and a hundred other plants she didn't recognise, all under a canopy of nut and fruit trees, alive with birds and insects. It looked more like a jungle than anything else. Cassy thought of her father's military rows of carrots, and smiled.

She met brown hens, dust-bathing in their mobile run; she patted goats, and ewes with teddy-bear lambs. She had a whistle-stop tour of the workshops. And all day long she saw contented people.

Gaza, the permaculture expert, took time out from pruning fruit trees to talk. 'It's all about the soil,' she said, while Cassy nodded and tried to think of intelligent questions. The gardener was perhaps forty or fifty—it was difficult to tell—and dauntingly vigorous. She reminded Cassy of a white falcon she'd once seen in a wildlife park, tearing at a bloodied chunk of meat. Beautiful, for sure, but her eyes were an unsettling ice blue, her nose slightly hooked, white-blonde hair cropped and spiky. Cassy had the feeling she was wondering which bit of her to eat first.

'Gaza is Malindi's mother,' said Suva later. 'She's a Companion.'

Cassy was surprised. 'Malindi, your lovely friend? Well . . . they both have that Nordic colouring.'

'Yeah, but Malindi's much jollier and fatter!' chuckled Suva, before whispering, 'Gaza is very, *very* pure, that's why they made her a Companion, but she can be a bit scary. She came to Gethsemane when Malindi was a tiny little girl.'

'Is Malindi's dad here too?'

'No! He was a horrible man. He used to bash Gaza. Some Gethsemane people were running a stall and they saw her with a broken jaw and blood everywhere. So they brought her and Malindi here. Malindi says that was the best day of their lives.'

Next stop was a sewing workshop, where people were stuffing sheep's wool into pillows. Cassy was hailed by a plump, comfortably smiling couple. They introduced themselves as Breda and Chernobyl.

'I hear you met our sons in the van,' said Breda, patting a chair so that Cassy would sit down.

'Your sons! So you must be . . . ?'

'Otto and Monika are my parents. Washington and Riyadh are our sons. They came home raving about this fascinating hitchhiker.'

'Look out,' warned Chernobyl. 'Riyadh wants to marry you!'

Finally Cassy visited Hana's school, which housed about thirty pupils between the ages of four and seventeen. As she arrived they broke into a welcome song, waving banners. *It's like being a film star*, she thought, as excited children lined up to present her with pictures they'd drawn for her. The building consisted of two classrooms, a well-stocked library and a small kitchen that was also used for science lessons. A couple of parents were acting as teacher's aides.

After Cassy's royal tour of the school, she and Hana shared a pot of tea on the porch. The children made dens in the trees, or charged around with a rugby ball, or took turns on a rope swing that hung from a branch. Some were playing a version of hide-and-seek that Cassy recognised as Kick the Can but which Hana called Kick the Shoe.

'Does this take you back to your childhood?' asked Hana.

'Not really. I went to boarding school, and it wasn't at all like this.'

Hana looked aghast. 'How old were you?'

'Nine.'

'No!'

'It's okay.' Cassy shrugged. 'We moved all the time because my dad was in the army, so there would have been no continuity in my education. Boarding school's really common for military families. The government even helps to pay for it.'

'Weren't you homesick?' Hana was leaning forwards, kindly brown eyes focused on Cassy's face. It was such a mellow afternoon, and the teacher was so very sympathetic. Cassy found herself telling the truth.

'I hated that place from the first day to the last. At the end of every holidays I used to chew around my nails until the skin was sore.'

'Poor wee girl!'

'But I came home for sixth form. Dad had retired and they'd bought our house, so it was all change. In a way we *all* left the army and finally had a home of our own—a home in one place! I went to a local school. That was a lot more fun.'

'What about your sister? Did she hate it too?'

'She didn't go.' Cassy saw Hana's surprise and hastily explained, 'Tara's six years younger than me—Dad was retiring at about the time she'd have gone away to school. He was forty-five, he'd earned the full pension and still had time for another career. So there was no point in her boarding. She had a very different kind of childhood to mine.'

'A happier childhood?'

'Well . . . different. More relaxed, maybe? Dad was in civvy street for most of it.'

Hana poured more tea. She seemed thoughtful.

'You're a magnet to children,' she said, changing the subject. 'You have a natural gift.'

'I don't have a gift. I just like children.'

'And they like you.' Hana seemed to be weighing her next words. 'Cassy, we desperately need another teacher. I'd train you. I think you would be the most amazing asset. We lost our last one three years ago, and I've been struggling.'

'Sorry!' cried Cassy, flushing with both embarrassment and pleasure. 'I love your school, but I'm definitely no teacher.'

'Ah, well.' The older woman's smile didn't falter.

'What happened to the one you lost?'

'Kerala.' Hana laid down her teacup. 'A tragedy. She seemed a deeply spiritual person.'

Cassy braced herself for a sad story. It sounded as though this Kerala woman had died.

'As it turned out,' said Hana, 'she wasn't spiritual at all. She met a man when she was out recruiting, and—'

'Recruiting?'

Hana blinked, but continued smoothly: 'For our courses. We run stands at agricultural shows, things like that. She met this fellow. She sneaked away in the night with her two boys, never said goodbye to anyone. Can you imagine? Poor Suva was broken-hearted.'

'Hang on.' Cassy's jaw had dropped. 'Don't tell me this is Suva's mother you're talking about? Aden's wife?'

'That's right. Kerala.'

'Suva has *brothers*?'

'Two of 'em. Perth and Medan. Never seen again. We hear they've got into drugs.'

Cassy was appalled. 'What kind of a woman could *do* that to her family?'

Before Hana could answer, the building began to creak. The

legs of Cassy's chair turned into wobbling jelly. Her cup rattled on its saucer, the tea rippling in concentric circles. At first she assumed a lorry must be passing by. Her student flat always shook when a juggernaut went up the road.

But there is no road. There are no lorries.

And then it was over. Hana smiled at Cassy's bewilderment.

'You've never felt an earthquake before?'

'Well . . . no. They aren't terribly common in Croydon.'

'The earth's crust is thin here. We often feel the forces underneath. The planet has tantrums—like a teenager.'

'So you know my sister!'

Hana laughed, leaning down to pick up a ball that had just bounced onto the porch and lob it back to the children.

The world was still again, but Cassy was left disturbed by the experience. It had been eerie to feel the stirring of the earth. She looked across the lake and wondered whether its surface had rippled in giant concentric rings, like the tea in her cup.

Six

Oh God, no. Not again.

The nausea must have come upon her as she slept. Cassy slid off the bunk, grabbed her new jersey—no time to put it on—and raced outside. Retched, retched, retched again under a stand of cabbage trees. It went on too long. She felt too weak.

Who was she kidding? This was no false alarm. She was the proud owner of an unwanted gift, like the novelty ties and fitness videos that ended up on eBay after Christmas. *Unopened, still in original packaging.* Her hands crept across her still-flat stomach, cradling the tiny mistake. For a few moments she allowed herself to wonder who this person might be.

As the sky paled, the bell began to toll. She'd been crying, her nose was running and the smell of vomit in her hair appalled her. Her mouth felt revolting. She didn't want anyone to see her in this state. Pulling the jersey over her knickers and t-shirt, she hurried towards the beach. She needed to wash. She needed to think. She needed solitude.

Lake and sky were mirrored immaculately, as though the two were identical twins. The water's embrace was brutally, numbingly cold. She stood thigh-deep, teeth chattering, splashing icy purity over her face and hair. It felt penitential.

What am I going to do?

The way she saw it, she had two options.

Option one: Go home. Have the baby. Be a single parent living on benefits in a grotty flat. Be despised by her dad, patronised by her mum, pitied by everyone else.

Option two: Find a clinic, hand over a credit card and try not to think or feel or care. Get a job, buy a house, start a pension fund. Be a successful citizen of this ridiculous world. Make her father proud.

'Oh God, oh God, oh God,' she moaned aloud, as her tears dripped into the water. 'Help me.'

A voice in the stillness. 'Hello, Cassy.'

She swung around, peering towards the shore. Whoever had spoken was male, his accent New Zealand—but that didn't narrow the field very much. She was pretty sure it wasn't Aden or Liam. Kyoto the carpenter, maybe? How did he get so close without her hearing him?

'Hi!' she said, with a self-conscious little laugh. 'The water looked inviting.'

'I often do the same thing. Bet it's cold.'

She could just make him out now: a tall figure on the beach, a wraith in the morning twilight. Flustered and embarrassed, she began to wade towards him on her numbed feet. In her haste, she stubbed her toe against an underwater rock—now *that* she certainly *did* feel—and hopped in agony, swearing under her breath.

'All right?' he asked.

She was in danger of falling over, arms windmilling. The next moment he'd walked into the water, his trousers soaked to the knees, and reached out a steadying hand to take hers.

That was when she recognised the man she'd seen on the island. He seemed somehow aristocratic: a long nose and broad forehead, framed by thinning, sandy hair. Pale green eyes with a fan of smile lines. A cable-knit jersey very like her own. Bare feet.

Once they were on the beach, he stooped to look at the gash on her big toe. Blood was trickling onto the sand.

'Ouch!' he said, wincing. 'Quite a war wound.'

'Can't feel a thing.' She tugged her jersey as far down her bare thighs as it would go. 'I'll stick a plaster on it when I get back to my cabin. Thank you so much. You've got wet! I'm sorry.'

'Sit down,' he insisted, pointing towards a natural ledge, formed where the grassland fell away to the beach.

She sat, because it would seem rude to refuse.

'I think I saw you on the island,' she said.

'You did.'

'Are you Justin?'

'For my sins.' He'd taken a handkerchief from his pocket and was dipping it into the lake. His dog came trotting along the beach, with waving tail and massive paws. 'Peter, meet Cassy. Keep her company.'

The grey wolf lay down with his chin on Cassy's lap, letting her warm her hands in his coat. Justin knelt at her feet and began to clean the laceration on her toe. She protested—'It's okay, honestly, I'm fine'—but he ignored her.

'Would your parents like it here?' he asked.

'Um . . . my father would last five minutes. Mum might manage ten.'

'Why would that be?'

'The idea of sharing everything, of not owning things. They'd hate it. They like to stay in their own box. They don't believe people can be unselfish.'

As she talked, she noticed a long, white scar on the palm of his right hand. She wondered about it, but didn't ask. He tore a strip from the handkerchief and wrapped it around the toe. His strategy worked. The bleeding stopped, the pain calmed to a dull ache.

'Good as new,' said Cassy. She stood up, testing her weight. 'Thanks. You've ruined your hanky!'

'Plenty more where that came from.'

He wandered back to the water and stood with his hands in

his pockets, gazing towards the mountain. Perhaps she should find this man creepy and stalkerish. After all, he'd appeared out of nowhere, he knew her name, and she wasn't wearing very much. Yet she didn't. He seemed fatherly rather than predatory. Peter had followed him and was splashing around in the shallows. She hobbled across the sand to join them.

'I can hear your thoughts,' said Justin.

'My thoughts?'

'Mm. Blaring at you like a radio. Constant noise. Constant worry. It must be exhausting.' He stooped to pick up a flat stone and weighed it in his hand. 'You can turn off that blaring radio. It takes practice, but you can. And when the white noise stops thundering away in your head . . . *then* you'll hear the music.'

With a flick of his wrist, he sent the stone spinning. It kissed the water, bounced, bounced and bounced again.

'Well done,' said Cassy. 'I counted five.'

'I'm not a good skimmer. Suva puts me to shame.'

Cassy's father had once tried to show her how to play ducks and drakes. He'd made a science of it. *The secret's in choosing the right stone, Cass . . . turn yourself to this angle . . . no, not like that! Tip your stone up twenty degrees . . . and spin!*

She remembered trying to do exactly as he said, mirroring every movement; she remembered the inevitable, disappointed click of his tongue when her slate plopped into the pond.

'Your turn.' Justin handed her a stone. 'Life isn't always tidy, is it? Things can get messy. And that can disappoint the people we most want to please. Sometimes the person they *want* you to be isn't the person you really *are*.'

Tears again. Why had she turned into such a crybaby all of a sudden? What was wrong with her? She lobbed the stone. Hopeless. *Plop.*

'My dad thinks I shouldn't be in New Zealand at all,' she said. 'He wanted me to do an internship to jack up my CV. He says it's a dog-eat-dog world out there, and I've got to be the one doing the eating.'

'Dog-eat-dog!' Justin looked comically startled.

'Maybe I do need to be a bit more . . . carnivorous.'

'I don't think you're a carnivore, Cassy.'

'I owe it to them. Mum and Dad invested all they had in our education. It came before holidays, before everything. They have a mantra: *There is no more valuable investment than education*.'

'So that you would grow up to be a thoughtful, empathetic person?'

'So that I'd have a good career. I'd be able to afford my own children's education, give the next generation a leg-up onto the same treadmill. Gotta scramble onto that treadmill, even if it means standing on heads to get there. Then round and round you scamper, little rat! And on, and on, and on it goes.' Cassy bent to stroke Peter's ears. 'I'm being a bitch.'

'You're being honest.'

'They want me to be a success. In their worldview that means being stinking rich. They can't imagine any other model for a successful life.'

'Yes, I see.' He nodded calmly. 'What would they say if they knew you were pregnant?'

She stood blinking at him.

Did he just say what I think he said? How the bloody hell does he know? Even I don't know for sure!

'I've got no idea what you mean,' she retorted, trying to sound haughty. She knew she was blushing.

He smiled, laying a hand on her shoulder. Then he searched along the beach, found another good skimming stone and gave it to her.

'This time, leave your wrist behind.' He demonstrated with his own hand. 'Throw *out* and *down*.'

The stone bounced once. Just once. Justin punched the air.

'Yes!' he cried, and found her another. 'Turn a bit more sideways, and *flick*.'

It was like a holiday from worry. For half an hour or more they didn't talk about her troubles; in fact, they didn't talk much at all. They simply combed the sand and pumice for the best stones and concentrated on making them dance across the ripples. Cassy managed two bounces, then three, and once—incredibly—eight. She felt her heavy heart being lifted up.

'Stay here a little longer,' said Justin, as they were walking back to the settlement together. 'You make us so happy.'

She didn't answer at first. She felt herself to be on the brink of something terrifying and wonderful. The person her parents thought they knew had been made of wax. She was melting. She was changing shape. A new Cassy was emerging.

'Maybe just another couple of days,' she said.

Seven

Diana
2010

They had no idea. No idea at all. Not until it was too late.

It was Tara who first sounded the alarm. Tara, stomping into the kitchen with a mug in her hand and disgust on her face.

'My tart of a sister,' she said. 'I've poked her, I've messaged her, I've texted her. Not a single word.'

Mike didn't look up from his paper. 'She's got a *real* life. Doesn't need to waste hours glued to a screen.'

Tara curled her lip at him before turning to Diana. 'You heard from her, Mum?'

'Not since Auckland. She does seem to have gone off the air.'

'She was meant to send photos of Hamish skydiving.' Tara tipped the remains of her morning cuppa down the sink. She didn't really like tea, though Diana doggedly delivered a mug to her room each morning, out of a need to be nurturing. 'Selfish bitch.'

'Language,' warned Mike.

Sometimes, thought Diana, it was hard to believe her two daughters came from the same stable. Cassy was the easy one, even as a baby, always trying to please. Tara came into the world screaming with colic and didn't much care whose toes she trampled on. Her features were sharper than her sister's. So was her tongue.

'Okay, Dad,' she said coolly. 'I'll rephrase. Selfish. Self-centred. Witch.'

'If you worked half as hard as Cassy did at school, you'd have a future as bright as hers.'

'Here we go. Change the tape, for God's—'

'Now, now,' Diana interrupted hastily.

Tara had a summer holiday job as a waitress in a local café. The dress code was black but beyond that, it seemed, there were no rules. Her skirt stopped several inches above her knees, and her makeup was frankly . . . what was the word? *Tawdry*. She'd come home the previous week with more ear piercings—three in each, now. Mike was pretending he hadn't noticed.

'You've got a point though,' he said, folding his paper. 'Cassy hasn't reported in for a while.'

He sounded irritated. He wasn't used to things not happening in an ordered way. You'd think being father to two children would have taught him something about chaos, but he was a slow learner when it came to human frailty.

Diana picked up the phone. 'Okay, well, let's give her a bell. It's . . . um, nine in the evening over there.'

She had the call on speakerphone. They all heard Cassy's message.

Hi. This is Cassy. Either my phone's switched off, or I'm out of credit. Leave a message. Bye.

'See what I mean?' said Tara.

'She's probably out of signal range,' said Diana.

Mike looked at his watch and mumbled, 'Bloody hell, is that the time?' Two minutes later, husband and daughter had slammed their way through the front door, hurrying to work and railway station, leaving a hum of silence. *This is what it will be like when Tara leaves home too*, thought Diana as she stacked plates into the dishwasher. *The empty nest. And what about me? What will I have achieved?*

She had a degree in history and was training to be a museum curator when she met Mike. Her career had been subsumed by his, because of the frequent relocations of army life. Perhaps she had no right to resent it—she'd known the score when she married him—but sometimes she felt a little bitter all the same. More than a little. She didn't want that for Cassy or Tara.

Better keep my life full of futile activity, she told herself, *or I'll start to question the point of my existence.*

Summer was always a good time for futile activity. As soon as they were settled in South London she'd found part-time work at the local arts centre. Today she had a meeting lined up with the man running the photo booth for the fundraising ball. Apparently, photo booths were mandatory nowadays. People couldn't just dress up and dance like flapping chickens any more. No, they had to record it for posterity.

Before leaving the house, she sent Cassy another email. *Keep it light*, she decided. *Keep it jolly.*

> *Darling Cassy! I'm just off to work, all's well here. Hope you're having fun. What's the news?? Get in touch when you've a moment. Mum xx*

•

At lunchtime, she visited her mother. Joyce lived in a tiny studio in a retirement village. She'd nicknamed it the One-Stop Shop, because people came in able-bodied and bought flats, then descended through the serviced studios, the nursing home, the hospital wing and, finally, the Chapel of Rest.

'No bugger gets out of here alive,' she said cheerfully.

Joyce's studio smelled of rose-scented talcum powder and tea. Residents weren't allowed their own toasters because people kept burning the toast and setting off the fire alarms, and that meant everyone had to be evacuated; but they could have a kettle, and she always put hers on as soon as a visitor arrived.

'I've got chamomile and ginger, Earl Grey or builder's,' she said, opening a tea caddy with arthritic hands.

'Builder's, please. You know that, Mum. I've never had anything different in about forty years.'

'Always a first time.' Joyce nodded at the biscuit tin. 'Have a rich tea. A drink's too wet without one.'

The biscuit was soft. Diana made a mental note to take her mother shopping.

'Now,' said Joyce, 'what news of my Cassy?'

'No news.'

'Must be having fun, then.'

Diana perched on the edge of the bed. Joyce wouldn't sit in the lounge. Too many old people, she said, and the telly would make you deaf if you weren't already.

'She's not going to stick with Hamish, is she?' asked Joyce, settling in the armchair. 'Hope not.'

'You don't like Hamish?'

'He lacks soul.'

'You've only met him twice.'

'Twice was enough.'

'Mike likes him.'

'I'm sure he does,' said Joyce, with just a pinch of nastiness.

Diana silently counted to ten.

She'd been at university when her mother buggered off to save the world, spending the next five years at Greenham Common, camping in a sea of mud from which all men were banned. To Diana and her bewildered father, self-sacrifice had never looked more selfish. Joyce had thrown herself into the nuclear disarmament cause with indecent enthusiasm. She was arrested four times, once in full view of TV cameras. Young Diana—along with half the nation—watched her on the news: wild-haired, passionate, dressed in homespun rags and screaming, *I want a safe world for our children!* as she was dragged away by two burly policemen.

The world hadn't felt any safer for it. Diana hadn't felt proud of her warrior mother. She'd felt abandoned. Sometimes—in her darker moments—she wondered whether she'd married a military man in order to get her own back.

Joyce didn't look like a warrior any more. Back then she'd

been small but upright—defiantly, angrily upright—but over the past decade osteoporosis had left her shrunken and bent. Her hair was white and fluffy, her hands veined. She looked the epitome of a little old lady, and people talked to her as though she were a child. Diana heard a care home manager do that, once. She took the woman aside and showed her a YouTube clip of the arrest at Greenham Common.

'*That's* Joyce?' The manager seemed incredulous.

'That's Joyce. Don't patronise her.'

'Cassy needs someone with a bit of spark,' declared Joyce now. 'A bit of a rebel. Otherwise she'll wake up at my age and wonder where her life went.'

'No, Mum. She doesn't need to rebel. The world's her oyster.'

Joyce snorted. 'The world of law and commerce, you mean.'

'What d'you want her to do, join hands around an airbase? Make a public exhibition of herself?'

'Oh dear.' Joyce took a tissue out of her sleeve, carefully touching it to her mouth. 'You're not *still* harping on about that? It wasn't easy, you know, it wasn't a picnic. Some winters we almost died of cold. Do you have any idea how close the human race was to blasting the crust right off the earth, destroying all life forever?' Joyce held up a thumb and forefinger. '*This* close. The planet's clock was set at three minutes to midnight.'

Diana huffed and looked away. They'd had this argument too many times.

'D'you want to go shopping tomorrow?' she asked, breaking the silence. 'Anything you need?'

'A visit to the library would be nice.'

'Right.' Diana forced down the last of her tea—it was still hot and brought tears to her eyes. 'Fine. Four-thirty?'

'Thank you, dear.'

Diana was rinsing her mug when Joyce called out to her.

'Let me know,' she said, 'if you hear anything from Cassy.'

•

Tara stood in the kitchen and held out her phone, so that her
parents could see a string of unanswered texts. Then she showed
them Cassy's Facebook page. The most recent update was from
Auckland, almost a week earlier. Imogen had tagged Cassy in
no less than seven posts about her wedding. The result had been
resounding silence.

Tara's was the last post on the page.

*WHAT HAPPENED TART, DID YOU GET LOST
IN MORDOR??? YOUR FAMILY ARE OBVIOUSLY
SOOOOO EEFFFFFING BORING NOW L*

CASSY? CASSY? CASSSEEEEEEEE!!!!!

Eight

Cassy

They were all friends, working and chatting: Paris, Bali, Aden and some others, preparing beds for spring planting, bringing compost in wheelbarrows and adding it to the soil. The morning's frost had burned away, leaving the air glittering. Cassy had gained new blisters on her fingers over the past few days, but it was no hardship. She liked the rhythm of their spades, the rich compost scattering as Aden shook a handful of weeds. There was something pouring into her lungs; something that tasted of hope.

Aden looked over Cassy's shoulder. 'Ah! Here's Monika.'

The tiny doctor was heading their way, wearing her usual blue cotton trousers. Her gait was slightly duck-footed, and she had a sweet smile.

'Aden,' she called, 'can I please borrow your guest?'

'Only if you promise to bring her back! She's too popular. Hana wants her to teach, Otto wants her to sing, Kyoto wants her to be a carpenter—I've said no, Cassy, don't panic. If you're looking for an assistant, Monika, you'd better join the queue.'

'I'm not in the business of stealing people,' said Monika, taking Cassy's arm. 'Lemonade? Or I've got elderflower.'

It wasn't really a request. More of an order. Cassy had a suspicion there was a warhorse inside Monika's wiry little frame.

'So you're the GP here?' she asked, as they walked across the grass.

'I am. Luckily Gethsemane folk aren't ill very often.'

Cassy asked about Otto's background and was surprised to learn that he'd once been CEO of a medical research company. She tried to picture him as an executive, hiring and firing, striding up and down a boardroom.

'He seems so benign,' she said. 'So laid-back.'

'He is now! He wasn't in those days. It was stressful.'

They sat on the front porch of the surgery, drinking Monika's lemonade. Cassy was entranced by the sight of two newborn goat kids, snuggled close to their mother at the foot of the porch steps.

'That's Marigold,' said Monika. 'She's the tamest of our flock, doesn't mind being tethered. But—oh dear—she does like to eat the washing! We kept a goat at home, when I was a child.'

'How long have you been in New Zealand?'

'Many years. We used to go to Justin's Gethsemane centre in Wellington.'

'Gethsemane began in Wellington? I didn't know that.'

'Oh yes! Otto and I were a part of it. So were Liam, Hana and Dean, Netta and a few others. When Justin set up this community at Tarawera, he said he needed a doctor and a good manager, and please would we come too? We were both hating our work at the time. So we said yes, please! Our daughter Breda joined us later.'

'So you're founder members.'

'We are.' Monika nodded. 'You can tell, because we have our original names. The giving of new names didn't begin until later.'

'Why are people named after places?'

'Ah, well. We care about this beautiful, beleaguered planet. We're thinking about every corner of the earth. So we name ourselves after those corners.'

'I like that idea,' said Cassy. She was fighting a yawn when the older woman—without changing her tone—said something that made her eyes snap wide open.

'Now, my friend,' she remarked, 'I think you may have need

of me, as the doctor who's delivered every child in Gethsemane.'

Cassy had just taken a mouthful of lemonade and almost spat it out. Monika, by contrast, looked serene—as though they were swapping recipes for carrot cake.

'How are you feeling?' she asked. 'Tired? Nauseated? Often the case in the first trimester.'

'I'm not even sure I'm—'

'Oh, I think you're pretty sure. Let's call it a miracle.' Monika was beaming now. 'Because it *is* a miracle.'

Cassy forced herself to breathe. *In . . . out.*

'Look, I can't have a baby. I just can't.'

'Because?'

'Because I'm alone.'

'That's one thing you are *not*. You're in Gethsemane. You'll always have family here.'

'I'm twenty-one years old. I haven't finished my degree, haven't even got a boyfriend any more. If there *is* a baby—and I'm still hoping there isn't—it doesn't fit in with my plans.'

'Your plans?'

'For my future. For my life.' Cassy knew how it sounded. She was a spoiled child. *My* plans. *My* life. 'In ten years' time I might be a good mother.'

'The baby doesn't come in ten years. The baby comes now.'

'It's not the right time.'

'You know what I think? I think this is exactly the right time. How about we do a test? Then we'll know for sure.'

'What if I don't want to know?'

Monika got to her feet and opened the door.

'Coming in?'

•

It was real, then. It was happening.

She sat in a wooden armchair, arms wrapped around her waist. *Banged up. In the club. Stupid, stupid girl.*

Monika pulled up a stool.

'You're safe here,' she said, giving Cassy's hands a little shake of affirmation. 'You're *not* alone.'

'What am I going to do? My parents . . .'

'Will forgive. Or perhaps they will not. But this isn't their child.'

'How far gone, do you think?'

'I can't do a scan here, but based on the dates you gave me, we have ten, eleven weeks from conception. He or she will be . . .' Monika held up her finger and thumb, close together, and said in a singsong voice, '*this* big.'

'So little.'

'Yes, *so* little, but the heart is beating.'

'Eleven weeks?'

'More or less.'

'That's not too late for a termination, is it?'

'Not too late,' said Monika, shaking her head mournfully. 'But I know you won't make that decision.'

Cassy pressed her face into her hands. Tears ran through her fingers. 'How can I be a mother? Look at me! I can't provide a decent childhood.'

'You are *already* a mother.'

'I don't want this. I don't want this. I don't want this.'

The doctor's accent was heavy and melodic. She seemed to make the words blend together. 'The baby hears all your words, you know. Yes! He does. Your heartbeat is his constant music, his comfort, his world. To this child you are the only being in the universe.'

'But I can't—'

'*Shh.*' Monika used the back of her thumb to wipe away Cassy's tears. 'Yes, you can. Because to him, you are God.'

Nine

Diana

Becca phoned. She sounded hesitant.

'Um . . . just wondering if you've heard from Cassy at all?'

When Diana admitted that they hadn't heard a word, Becca clicked her tongue.

'Bother. I wanted to ask her about this coffee machine we're giving Imogen and Jack. There's one that's a bit more expensive, but with its own grinder. I'm not sure which to . . . Never mind, it can wait.'

'Just go ahead, Becca,' said Diana. 'Get whichever you think. I'll pay Cassy's half.'

They talked about this and that. The wedding. Becca's holiday job in Starbucks.

'Anyway,' said Becca, when she was about to ring off, 'tell her to answer my messages!'

After the call was over, Diana took a bottle of wine out of the fridge. Mike was watching her.

'Are we worried yet?' he asked.

'No. She's not in a war zone. But I wish she'd get in touch.'

'Hang on!' Mike held up a finger. 'I think I might have Hamish's number.'

'Won't it seem a bit clingy if we call Hamish?'

'Who cares?' He snatched his mobile from the dresser and began scrolling. 'Yes! We're in luck. What time is it there? Eight in the morning—high time they were awake. It's ringing.' Mike walked around in a little circle, staring down at his feet. Walking in circles was what he did when a call agitated him: when he was phoning to complain about his electricity bill or the bin men not collecting on the right day.

Someone answered; the rumble of a male voice.

'Hamish,' said Mike, his tone expansive. 'I didn't wake you, did I?'

No, no, lied the voice from the other side of the world.

'Just trying to track Cassy down. She with you now?'

A short silence; then the rumble again.

'Not since you left Auckland?' asked Mike. Diana felt a moment of panic until he looked at her and mouthed, *It's okay*.

'She's doing what? *Roofing?*'

Laughter down the line; more words.

'How're you spelling that? Oh, I see. *Wwoofing*. Well, that makes sense. She told us it's expensive down there. The high New Zealand dollar . . . yes, yes . . . oh, I see.'

He listened again.

'No phone coverage. Ah, that explains it! We thought there would be a simple reason. Right . . . right. Where?' Mike scribbled a couple of words on the back of an envelope. 'Oh good. Well, I'm sorry the two of you . . . obviously it's better to break up now than later.'

There was small talk: mention of skiing and the weather. Diana was pouring two glasses of wine when Mike ended the call. He replaced the phone—carefully, as though it contained something delicate—and stood for a moment, looking down at his shoes, his cheeks puffed out.

'They've split up?' Diana asked, putting a glass into his hand.

He sat down, fingering the stem. 'He's in the South Island now—a long, long way from where he last saw her. He reckons Cassy was in a "funny mood". Any idea what that means?'

'Probably means she was heartily sick of him.'

'The pair of them were hitchhiking. Cassy took a lift and Hamish didn't. A van full of hippies, he said. The next day she sent him a Dear John email, told him she'd been offered bed and board in return for work. You know what wwoofing is, don't you? It's an acronym: Willing Workers on Organic Farms. Hamish says it's all the rage over there.'

'Where is this place?'

'He last saw her heading for . . .' Mike checked his scribble. 'Rotorua. Apparently the farm's called Gethsemane.' Mike spoke the word with a slight sneer, as though he thought it a silly name for a farm.

Diana raised her glass. 'Well done! This explains everything. And as for Hamish? Well. Perfectly nice boy, but . . .'

'Smug?'

'Image conscious.'

'No,' said Mike. 'Focused.'

'Mum reckons he lacks soul.'

Tara had just breezed into the kitchen, an iPod in her top pocket, half jiving to whatever music was being piped into her ears.

''Sup?' she asked, looking from one face to another.

When they told her what was up, she stopped dancing. She even took out one of the earbuds.

'Whoa, back up!' she cried. 'Can we just get this straight? Cassy left Hamish standing by the side of a road?' She whistled. 'Go girl! What a badass she's turned out to be.'

'That's one word for it,' said Mike.

'She hasn't changed her Facebook status to single.' Tara sounded disapproving. Her sister had committed a regrettable faux pas in neglecting to make the public announcement. *I post, therefore I am.* 'Anyway, this means I get to hook up with Hamish myself! He's rich, and he's hot, and he'll be on the rebound right now.'

Mike pretended to be shocked and called her a minx.

'Marrying for money is back in fashion,' she told him, resuming her jiving. 'I thought you'd approve, Dad! I'm planning for my future. Like you always say, it's a dog-eat-dog world out there.'

Diana imagined Cassy wandering around some idyllic farm, sitting by a campfire, maybe singing wholesome songs while someone strummed a guitar. Perhaps she was having a passionate— if slightly sordid—fling with one of those commies, leaving her poor mother to handle the fallout back home.

She nipped up to the bedroom and tried Cassy's number again. No good. She left a foolish, chirpy message; but even as she spoke, she had the feeling that her voice would never be heard. Something felt echoingly empty, as though she were shouting into an abandoned well.

Half an hour later, she tried again.

And again.

And again.

The Cult Leader's Manual: Eight Steps to Mind Control

Cameron Allsop

Step 4: Sell, sell, sell!

Show how happy you all are, how terrific the product you're selling. There must be no dissenting voice. You are a living advertisement, and this product has made you happy. So smile!

Get the recruit to agree in principle that they want what you're offering. Don't they want to be happier, slimmer, purer, richer, more popular, more likely to go to heaven? Of course they do. And you can show them how.

Ten

Cassy

Suva's birthday. Sickness wrenched Cassy out of bed again, but it didn't bring the same terror. She no longer carried the secret alone. People knew, and they didn't despise her. When the bell tolled for Early Call, she and Aden crunched across the frosty grass towards the *wharenui*.

'Where does that trail go?' Cassy asked, pointing out a path marked by two large rocks that began behind the school.

'To the top paddocks. I've already been up this morning. We've got three more lambs.'

Cassy looked back at the trail. It turned sharply uphill before disappearing into the dense shadows of the bush.

'It's not even light yet, and you've already hiked up to the top of a massive hill and . . . done whatever you did?'

'Yep. There's a vehicle track too, if I need to take the tractor. This one's the shortcut.'

Cassy felt acutely aware of the man who loped along beside her, his hand sometimes brushing the back of hers. She wasn't sure what it was he made her feel. Lust, for sure, but that wasn't all. She caught herself wondering how it might be if they walked side by side every day; if they were together every night.

What if this was my life?

The song that morning was sung especially for Suva, though the words didn't make a lot of sense to Cassy.

We celebrate your precious daughter
Born beside these sacred waters
May she dance in love and light
And keep the watches of the night!

A sense of expectation followed the song: a ripple of pleasure, like a breath of wind on the lake. Cassy felt it herself, though she didn't know why.

Then Justin was among them. He seemed to bring his own gravitational pull. Everything was drawn to him; even the air folded around him. He moved unhurriedly, touching people on the shoulder, speaking to one or two before moving on. When he came to Suva, he knelt down and they talked. Cassy saw Suva giggle and throw her arms around his neck.

Then he got to his feet, turning to Cassy with a clownish grimace.

'Ooph,' he groaned. 'Poor old knees.'

His face was as she remembered it: thin, ascetic, with the narrow mouth and pale green eyes. For some reason, she desperately wanted him to like her.

'How's the foot?' he asked.

'Fine! Thank you.'

'I've been hearing great things about you, Cassy. You're a miracle.'

'There's nothing miraculous about me.'

'Really?' He raised an eyebrow. 'Then why are Suva and Aden happy again? No ordinary woman could have done that. Have you thought about my suggestion? Will you stay with us a bit longer?'

'Ooh, that would be . . .'

'Good! Hurray! So you'll stay?'

'I can't. I have to get back to the real world.'

His eyes crinkled, and he touched his palm to her cheek.

'This *is* the real world.'

•

Twenty picnickers set out in the old launch, *Matariki*. Aden explained that it was possible to walk to Kereru Cove, but with Netta and other elderly people in the group it was easier to take everyone along the lake.

Justin didn't come. They saw him in the red speedboat, travelling very fast in the other direction. Cassy felt a bewildering sense of loss.

'He often heads off for a few days,' said Bali.

'Where does he go?'

'He collects people in trouble. He meets members of Gethsemane who can't live with us.'

'Who looks after Peter when he's not here?'

Bali looked amused. 'Gaza. He'll be running riot in the garden right now. She *dotes* on that dog!'

Aden was teaching Rome to drive *Matariki*. The teenager held both hands on the wheel, craning his neck to see past the cabin roof. There was a definite look of Justin about him: he'd inherited his father's sandy hair and green eyes, and some of his effortless authority. Malindi was hanging around the cockpit, looking nonchalant. She had round cheeks, a wide smile and long eyelashes, which she tended to flutter at Rome. He treated her like a little sister.

'What happened to Rome's mother?' asked Cassy.

'Tripoli? She drowned.'

'No!'

'Long time ago.' Bali was holding a finger to her lips, so Cassy dropped the subject.

They were approaching a narrow inlet with its own beach. Tendrils of steam rose from the shallows, and Cassy spotted a cabin peeking out through ponga and vines. It looked ludicrously picturesque.

'Kereru *whare*,' said Bali. 'One of Gethsemane's bush huts. For people on spiritual retreat.'

'How romantic!'

Bali chuckled. 'Well, it's meant to be for meditation and regeneration. But yes, it can be romantic too.'

The boat had come to rest by a natural wharf, and Aden leaped ashore to tie up.

'Nice job,' he called to Rome, as he wound ropes around trees.

The expedition force moved out, heading along a path into the bush. Someone had brought a wheelchair for Netta. Four men picked it up and carried her aloft while she smiled impishly from her litter.

As Cassy began to follow, Suva galloped up and grabbed her hand.

'Close your eyes!' she ordered.

'Why?'

'Because this is a surprise.'

It takes courage to be led with your eyes shut, especially along an uneven path by an overexcited child. They climbed steeply uphill, and Cassy could hear the rushing of a stream very close by. She moved slowly, shuffling over tree roots, puzzled by a feeling of heat through the soles of her sandals and whiffs of the sulphurous smell she'd noticed in Rotorua.

'Have faith,' said Suva. 'I won't lead you anywhere dangerous. Another minute . . . okay, now you can look.'

Cassy opened her eyes.

It was a dream world. Forest gloom. Giant ferns and moss and glittering jewels of sunlight. A stream cascaded over rocks, forming a series of pools—some wide and deep enough to swim, some the size of a bath. The water was green glass, shot through by clouds of tiny bubbles, half hidden by billowing clouds of steam.

'Am I awake?' asked Cassy.

'Yes!' Suva was stumbling over her own words, desperate to point everything out. 'That little pool's the hottest, too hot for me. See the rock slide? Malindi's already sliding down it! And look—' pointing into the lush undergrowth '—a mud monster!'

Cassy stared at the patch of grey mud. It swelled and dimpled as though some weird creature was writhing beneath the surface. Then—*gloop!*—a miniature eruption. The effect was unearthly.

'Come on,' said Suva, tearing off her clothes to reveal a swimming costume. 'It's the best feeling ever. Even Netta's going in.'

By early afternoon, the lavish picnic was over. Adults were luxuriating in the pools or taking naps on sun-warmed rocks; children played Kick the Shoe among the trees. Aden and Rome had walked into the bush to check possum bait stations.

Cassy, Paris and Bali stood under a waterfall so clear and smooth that it could have been an ice sculpture. Hot water cascaded onto their necks, spraying off their shoulders. Cassy was fascinated by her friends' casual attitude to all this geothermal activity. She'd never before seen the earth so fiery and dynamic, a pressure cooker ready to blow. She tipped back her head, looking through the canopy to the delicate blue of the sky.

'When did the volcano last erupt?' she asked.

'In 1886,' said Bali, promptly. 'When Netta wakes up, ask her to tell you the story.'

The grandmother had been dozing in her wheelchair, with a blanket around her shoulders. Her eyes snapped open.

'You girls gossiping about me?'

'You've got big ears!' Bali laughed. 'We're talking about the eruption, Nana.'

'Oh! That.'

Cassy kept out of the conversation. She suspected there were all sorts of cultural minefields around her feet, and she didn't want to step on one.

'Tell Cassy about the phantom canoe,' urged Bali.

'Some of that plum wine would be nice.'

Bali rolled her eyes. 'Nothing comes for free, does it?' She hauled herself out of the pool—steaming in the cold air—scurried across to a basket and scurried back.

'Here we are,' she said, placing a clay cup in her grandmother's hands. 'Got it?'

'Yes.'

'Don't drop it.'

'I'm not senile, thank you.'

Cassy moved closer, the better to hear Netta's voice above the gushing of the falls. For a long time the old woman sat with the cup on her lap, lips moving silently as though gathering history around her.

'You have to understand how it all began,' she said. 'The Te Arawa tribes have lived under the mountain for centuries. They used the boiling springs for cooking, and their *whares* were warmed by the hot ground. The peak was a burial ground. They left the bones of their ancestors up there, but they knew the rules. The mountain is *tapu*—sacred. It has to be treated with respect. Then Europeans came, and things changed.'

'I bet they did,' muttered Cassy.

'Missionaries and explorers at first, but word spread, and in came the tourists. They travelled from all over the world to visit the pink and white terraces at Lake Rotomahana.'

Cassy looked enquiringly at Bali. 'Terraces?'

'Like giant flights of stairs,' said Bali. 'Made of silica. You haven't heard of the pink and white terraces? They were called the eighth wonder of the world! Even royalty came to see them.'

'Another hole in my education.' Cassy felt ashamed of her ignorance.

'We've got pictures in the school library. Old-fashioned English ladies with lace parasols. The local Maori became guides and boatmen, you see. They made a lot of money.'

'Who is telling this story?' demanded a peevish voice from the wheelchair.

'You are, Nana.'

'So shush. Now, where was I?'

Bali smiled. 'The tourists.'

'Yes. The tourists. Well, one of the most famous guides was

a very clever woman called Sophia. Once day she was guiding a party across Lake Tarawera—they were in a whaleboat, just like ours—when they saw something that froze the blood in their veins.'

Netta paused, long enough for her audience to grow impatient.

'A war canoe,' she said at last. 'It appeared out of the morning mist and began to race silently alongside Sophia's boat. There were two rows of men in this *waka*—one row sitting and one standing. Imagine it! Those standing were wearing flax robes and their heads were plumed as if for burial. Sophia hailed it . . . and hailed it . . . but there was no reply. It was as though they were the souls of the dead being ferried to the sacred mountain. And then—' Netta reached out a hand, grasping at a ghost '—the *waka* disappeared.'

'Did they all see this?' asked Cassy. 'Everyone on Sophia's boat?'

'They all saw it. Sophia, the crew, the tourists. Everyone.'

'Maybe some people were using a war canoe that day, for some reason?'

'Yes, yes, yes.' Netta closed her eyes, tutting. 'But you see . . . no such canoe existed on Tarawera. No such canoe has *ever* existed on Tarawera. No. That *waka* was a phantom. They asked the old *tohunga* what it meant, and he said, *It is an omen, a warning that all this region will be overwhelmed.* And eleven days later, his prophecy came true.'

The cup tilted in Netta's hand; drops crept down the blanket.

'My grandmother's family lived in a village right under the mountain, but that winter she went to stay with cousins at Lake Rotoiti. On the night of the tenth of June they were woken by an earthquake. Everyone rushed outside and—oh! Such a terrible sight. The sky above Tarawera was on fire, with a giant column of black smoke, and lightning flashing, and explosions. Then half the earth was hurled into the sky. My grandmother knew that was the end of her family.'

'How old was she?'

'Little. About seven or eight. The stars went out, and ash began to fall. They huddled in the *whare* and stayed there all night, listening to ash pattering on the roof like rain, watching the roof bending under its weight. My nana was sure she'd be buried alive. The family said prayers while they waited for their end.'

Cassy was transfixed by the story. She saw frightened eyes in the darkness, a thatched roof bulging, a whole family expecting to die.

'When they looked out in the morning . . .' Netta shook her head. 'There *was* no morning. The sun had gone out. And the landscape around Tarawera was gone. Villages were buried under fifty feet of mud and ash. They're still under there.'

'How many people died?'

'Nobody knows. The Europeans estimated around a hundred and twenty, but my grandmother said it was far more, perhaps even thousands. And the pink and white terraces were lost forever.'

'What happened to her?'

'Nana? She lived to be ninety-two. She had eight children.'

Cassy splashed hot water over her shoulders, doing calculations in her head. Netta's grandmother must have been born about 1879. She'd lived through the complete obliteration of her family, and both world wars, and reached the age of ninety-two. Quite an innings.

'She never forgot,' said Netta. 'Even when she could no longer remember the names of her own daughters. She never forgot the night the sacred mountain tore itself apart. She never forgot the day the sun went out. Everyone thought it was the end of the world. And for many of them, it *was* the end of the world.'

•

A sunset cruise in the winter evening. Slanting light. Mist lay upon the water in an opalescent veil, but no ghostly *waka* appeared.

Rome and Aden were boatmen again. Cassy and Paris sat on the white roof of the cabin. They could hear talk and laughter from below, where people were making hot drinks on a propane stove. Monty was curled up beside Sydney. Other children were playing a hand-clapping game, merry silhouettes in all that beauty.

They're not worried, thought Cassy. *They're not stressed. They've got the answers.*

'What d'you reckon about that phantom canoe?' she asked Paris.

'Well . . .' Paris narrowed her eyes, considering the question. 'They saw something, all right. The four tourists described it in their letters home, and others saw it at around the same time. Someone even sketched it.'

'I wonder what it was, really.'

'Perhaps it was exactly what the *tohunga* said: a warning. This is a very spiritual place.' Paris lay down flat, copper hair gleaming. 'It feels a very, very long way from Edinburgh.'

'D'you ever go back to visit?'

'God, no!' Paris looked sickened. 'I've nothing in common with anyone there.'

The story emerged, as *Matariki* slid across the glassy water. Paris's father and mother had been fighting ever since she could remember. They'd both remarried, both begun new families, and neither had much time for the daughter they'd created together.

'My name was Rachel,' said Paris. 'I felt like an outsider in both households. I finally left because . . . okay, I'll tell you. I killed my best friend.'

Cassy did a double take.

'Isla,' said Paris. 'Isla Wallace. We'd been to a party to celebrate our exam results, and I was driving us home. We were so happy, we were singing. I stopped to text my boyfriend, then pulled back onto the road—and this lorry slammed into us. To this day I don't know where it came from, I just remember the headlights. We rolled down a bank, landed upside down. Pitch black.' Paris shut her eyes. 'Isla was killed outright.'

'Oh no,' breathed Cassy. 'That must have been . . .'

'She was eighteen.'

Otto's voice boomed from the cabin below, followed by hoots of laughter from his appreciative audience.

'There was gossip,' said Paris. 'That I was drunk, that I was texting. I got away with a fine, not that I cared. I wouldn't have cared if they'd strung me up. It felt like I was carrying this lead weight, every minute of every day. I tried to escape, working my way around the world. I worked in bars, I cleaned rooms in hotels. I drank, I smoked God-knows-what, I slept with more guys than I can remember. But it didn't matter how far I ran, how wasted I got, I couldn't put down the weight I was carrying. I was working in a café on the ski fields at Ruapehu when I met Sydney.'

'Monty's dad?'

'Mm. There wasn't anything going on between us, but when the ski season ended we hitched together. One day we got picked up by the Gethsemane van. And . . . long story short, I met Justin. He saw I was in trouble. He always knows. He invited me to his island, and he just listened. I talked all day. All night. All the next day. He listened like nobody had ever listened to me before.' Paris's eyes were overflowing; she wiped them with her sleeve, and took a moment to steady her voice. 'He heard everything I said. He heard the things I didn't say. And all of a sudden . . . it was amazing . . . I felt as though he'd picked up that weight in his own arms. I felt as though maybe—just maybe—it was okay for me to be alive. For the first time, I slept without hearing Isla screaming.'

Cassy felt flattered that Paris had confided in her. 'Is that why you've stayed here?'

'Yes! I'll never leave Justin. I owe him my life. He set me free.'

'So you've somehow got a residence visa?'

'Otto sorted that out for me. I had to pretend I was in a permanent relationship with Seoul!'

The engine note changed. *Matariki* was turning in a wide arc, heading back towards Gethsemane. Cassy caught Aden's eye, and they both smiled.

'Hey! Want to drive?' he called.

'Go on,' said Paris. 'It's fun.'

Cassy made her way down to the cockpit. Rome cheerfully relinquished the wheel and went to hang out with the other youngsters.

'Good day?' asked Aden, once he'd shown her what to do, and she was steering in a more or less straight line.

'One of the best in my whole life,' she said. 'You're so lucky to live like this.'

'You could always stay.'

'No. No, I really can't. I have to go back and finish my degree, and pretend that easements and covenants and the registration of titles are of existential importance to me.'

'Why?'

She tried to keep her voice light. 'Because then I can get a posh job, and a smart car, and a foot on the bottom rung of the property ladder.'

Aden merely grinned. He didn't need to say anything.

The past days had been magical, intriguing, unsettling; like falling in love. Little by little, moment by moment, Gethsemane and its people were becoming her own.

Eleven

Diana

They were just ordinary days, and yet they didn't feel quite ordinary. Something was out of place. A dark thing had begun to grow and spread, though they tried to blow it away with brittle breeziness.

It wasn't fear. No, no. That would be ridiculous. Cassy was nobody's fool, and she was in one of the most stable countries in the world.

Not fear. Diana liked to think of herself as a chilled-out mother, not a neurotic worry-wart. So they couldn't get hold of Cassy . . . Well, so what? If some tragedy had happened, they'd have heard by now.

Not fear.

It was four-thirty in the morning when she found Mike in his cramped workspace under the stairs. He was hunched in front of the desktop, looking vulnerable and tousled in his tartan dressing-gown and slippers. Light from the screen painted blue rivers on his face.

'I've found them.' Relief in his voice. 'They *do* exist.'

She stood with her hands on his shoulders. His hair was definitely thinning on top. Greying a bit too. But fifty was barely middle-aged nowadays, and Mike was in better shape than most men half his age. Only that morning he'd cycled twenty miles. She wasn't entirely sure why he bothered.

'This their website?' she asked, peering at the colourful images on the screen.

'Mm-hm. They look pretty harmless.'

They did indeed. It was a slick website. The main photograph was taken from the end of a jetty, looking inland. It showed buildings scattered against a backdrop of wooded hills, with a gang of adorable lambs in the foreground. The main heading read *Gethsemane,* and beneath, in a smaller font: *Whether you stay for a day or for a lifetime, the doors of Gethsemane are open to you.*

There were thumbnail pictures of happy-looking people holding up vegetables; there were goats, beehives, and a wooden cabin with a group of very beautiful youngsters on its front porch. Links were arranged along the top: *About Us; The History of Tarawera; Our Courses; Wwoofing; Contact; Testimonials; Gallery; Book Now.*

'What are the courses?' asked Diana.

'Permaculture, whatever that is. There's one for recovering addicts.'

'Sounds very laudable.'

'There's all sorts of hyperbole about the beauty of the scenery, the expertise of the tutors, the . . . you know, the purity of the environment. It reads like a tourist brochure. Have a look at *About Us.*'

A picture of a lake swathed in mist appeared, with text super-imposed over the top.

The Gethsemane community was established in Wellington in 1985. It moved to its present home on the shores of Lake Tarawera in 1990, after the land was generously gifted by the Svenson family. Gethsemane has stewardship of over five hundred hectares of New Zealand's native bush, inter-spersed with permaculture gardens, forestry plantation and pastureland.

The landscape of New Zealand, like so much of our planet, has been ravaged over the past century: intensive agricultural methods, urbanisation, imported pests and the thirst for fossil fuels have led to wholesale destruction. The human race has travelled far from its spiritual roots. Here we live sustainably and work with the environment, not against it. We nurture our soil. Our buildings and systems are designed to have minimal impact. We are carbon neutral. Our way of life is built upon love in its most simple and yet profound sense, remembering always that we are stewards—not landlords—of the earth.

Gethsemane offers refuge to everybody, without question. Nobody has ever been turned away. Many of our number have lived successful lives as professional people, but were drawn to Gethsemane because they felt something vital was missing. Others come for healing, or to learn more about themselves while treading lightly on our fragile earth. If you are recovering from trauma, from addictions or from the stresses of life, there is a home for you here.

Visitors are always welcome. There is no obligation to take part in the spiritual life of the community. Those wishing a deep experience of the peace of Gethsemane can join in one of our courses, or simply rest among us for as long as is needed. The doors of Gethsemane are open to you.

We welcome you.

'Sounds ghastly,' said Diana. 'I'm surprised Cassy can stand all that holier-than-thou smugness.'

'She's pretty tolerant.'

Diana pointed at the screen. 'What's their "spiritual life"? Are they some kind of Christian outfit? Buddhists? New Age?'

'They don't say anywhere on this bloody website. My money's on New Age. But look—*Contact Us*.'

Mike clicked on the link. No phone number, and just a post office box, but there was an email address: watchmenofgethsemane@gmail.com.

'Might come in handy,' said Diana.

Mike stretched, blinking at the kitchen window. 'Good Lord, it's getting light. I thought children were supposed to stop keeping their parents awake all night?'

'I don't think that ever happens.'

'Coming back to bed?'

'In a minute. I might just send Cassy another email.'

From: Mike and Diana Howells
To: CassyHowlerMonkey@gmail.com
Subject: How are you?

Hi Cassy,
Hamish told us you've split up. Never mind! Just checking you're okay. Drop us a line, would you? We're not worried. Just wanted to make sure you're still alive, not kidnapped and sold into the white slave trade!!! Haha ☺
   Mum xxx
   PS Tara says hi. So does Pesky.

The Cult Leader's Manual: Eight Steps to Mind Control

Cameron Allsop

Step 5: Reduce autonomy, induce dependency

Begin to introduce rules and routines into the life of your new recruit. They can be quite random: dress, food, sleep patterns, behaviour. Remove familiar possessions. Keep your recruit isolated and out of touch with their usual networks. You need them to depend on the group for all information and support.

Many organisations use a special vocabulary. This gives a mystical quality to the group's activities, and the recruit begins to feel that they 'belong' as they learn the words.

The stupefying properties of sleep deprivation cannot be overstated. A person who is sleep-deprived becomes disorientated and malleable, a fact well known to military interrogators. Sustained sleep deprivation will lead to a loss of grip on reality.

At the same time, the group should offer rewards for obeying the rules: love, support, comfort, rest. The carrot and the stick.

Twelve

Cassy

She'd been in Gethsemane ten days now. Even if she left tomorrow she wouldn't have enough time to explore the country before flying home. She didn't care. She'd learned more about herself in ten days than she would in ten years of travelling. She still hadn't made a decision about the pregnancy. She knew she was running out of time—if she didn't hurry up it would be too late, and the decision would have been made by default. Yet even this didn't feel quite so urgent any more.

They'd had supper and cleared away, and now she was lying on the window seat. Every cabin in Gethsemane was kept immaculate, but everyone worked together. The genders were absolutely equal. It was one of the many things Cassy admired about her new friends.

Suva had a piano lesson with Bali. Aden was sharpening a chainsaw on the kitchen table, whistling under his breath. He'd been cutting firewood all day and come home smelling of wood resin. He and Cassy were content in each other's company—more than content, though they still hadn't acknowledged it. Sometimes she'd wake in the night and wonder what would happen if she tiptoed along the porch and slid into the warmth of his bed. She imagined tracing the muscles of his back, running her fingers down his stomach. She was pretty sure he wouldn't kick her out.

'Aden?' she said.

'Mm?'

'You must miss your sons.'

For a moment there was silence, and she wondered if she'd overstepped the mark. Then he carried on with his task.

'Every day,' he said.

'How old are they?'

'Perth will be fifteen by now. Medan's thirteen.'

'Have you ever heard from them?'

'No. They know I love them. I'm still hoping they'll come back.'

He moved the chain along, sharpened the next link. The gentle whistling began again.

A peaceful sensation fizzed in the back of her head. At Monika's request, she'd handed over her watch to be put in the safe, along with her wallet, phone and passport. There were no clocks in Gethsemane, so she didn't know the exact time. All she knew was that Night Call was late, and everyone was up again before sunrise. Her intellect seemed to have melted. She'd never thought of lack of sleep as a state of being before.

She remembered talking to her glamorous cousin, Yvette, at a family funeral. Yvette was a big shot in a shipping company, constantly held up as a role model by Mike (*You'll have to pull your finger out for these exams, if you want to be as successful as Yvette*). She earned gazillions and worked eighty hours a week until her first child arrived.

The woman sprawled in an armchair hadn't looked like a big shot. Her eyes were puffy, her skirt crumpled, and she had a baby jammed up her blouse. Three mugs of tea were lined up on the coffee table.

'He keeping you awake?' asked Cassy.

'You can say that again.' Yvette drank the first of the mugs straight down with the air of an alcoholic knocking back a shot.

'Teething?'

'Oh my God. The bloody child's nocturnal.'

'You must be knackered.'

A heavy smile crossed her cousin's face. Her voice drawled, her eyes drooped. 'Don't tell anyone I said this, but . . . you know what?'

'What?'

'It's actually quite a pleasant sensation, as long as you don't have to use your intellect. It isn't motherhood per se that mushes people's brains, it's sleep deprivation. It's like a weirdly chilled trance. I tried to fight it, but now I've given in. Five o'clock this morning, I'm pretty sure I was starting to hallucinate.'

'I never want to go through that,' declared Cassy. 'Uh-uh. Never.'

Yvette's laugh ended in a yawn. 'This little cherub has turned two intelligent beings into worshipping ninnies.'

Aden's whistling sounded far away.

I'd better have another go at contacting Mum and Dad, Cassy thought. *I bet there's a pile of emails from them by now. Maybe they know about Hamish and me? They'll make a drama of it.*

The whistling fell into the folds of her consciousness. Thoughts flickered in and out like flames in the stove: some inconsequential, some bright, some distorted. The chainsaw bumped against the table—a harsh sound, grating through the fog—but then it was her father, dropping his briefcase onto the bedroom floor.

She was very small; her head came to his waist.

'Are you pregnant?' He looked disgusted, as though he could smell something revolting.

'We're very disappointed in you,' said her mother. 'We're going to send you away.'

They pulled her trunk out of the cupboard. The very sight of it made her feel homesick. It was like a coffin, and her name was on the lid: *Cassandra Howells*. She started to cry. Her nose was running.

'It'll be fun,' said her mother, cheerfully lobbing things into the trunk. 'You'll have lots of new friends.'

And then the bell began to toll. It was the most blissful,

welcome sound. She wasn't in disgrace. She wasn't being sent away. She was loved.

Aden was damping down the stove. 'Hello there, sleeping beauty! Coming? You don't have to.'

But she wanted to go. She wanted to be a part of that happy, hopeful crowd. Her friends would dilute the loneliness of her dream.

'The bell's reassuring,' she said, as they walked in the icy dark. 'I love the fact that someone rings it at the same times every day. The planet might be in chaos, my life might be a mess, but as long as that bell keeps tolling, all is well.'

'Did you know that here at Gethsemane we keep Vigil?' asked Aden.

'Vigil?'

'Mm. All night, every night.'

'What does that involve?'

'At any one time—day or night—there will be people awake, normally in the *wharenui*. There's never a time when everyone is asleep.'

'Who stays awake?'

'We take it in turns. But someone is always keeping watch.'

'Keeping watch for what?'

'Just keeping watch. A member of Gethsemane is called a Watchman.' They were approaching the *wharenui*, drawn by the buttery light from its windows. 'Suva's going to take her turn too, now that she's eleven.'

Cassy liked the idea. Even while she slept, she was never completely alone. People were watching over her, and over the world.

'There's so much I don't know,' she said.

'You will. You'll know everything.'

'If I stay?'

'If you stay.' He paused, one foot on the steps. 'I'd very much like you to stay.'

•

The *wharenui* felt as it always did at night: warm and safe. Beeswax in the candles added an intoxicating sweetness to the air. The Watchmen weren't shadows in the dark any more; they were friends.

Otto led the community in sharing news: a seventieth birthday, a child who'd broken her arm. Kyoto's partner Athens—a gypsy queen with dark eyes and silver-streaked hair—announced that the mill had won a national award for a range of knitwear. Apparently, Gethsemane shawls could be bought in smart shops all over New Zealand. Then came the song: mellow this evening, and reflective. They were still singing when Justin joined them.

'Hello, everyone,' he said, as he stepped onto the dais. 'I couldn't stay away.'

There was laughter and a murmur of greeting. The music continued, but very quietly.

'Now,' said Justin, 'who has a confession to make?'

A handful of people came forwards to stand in front of the dais, facing the crowd. Dublin the drummer; a woman called Valencia, whom Cassy had seen sewing blue dresses; Malindi; and two older men whose names Cassy didn't yet know.

'Negativity breeds in dark corners,' said Justin. 'Bring your negative thoughts out into the sunlight! Humble yourself, and be nothing.'

Cassy didn't like the sound of this. She was afraid it was going to be some ghastly public humiliation, but the ritual seemed pretty benign. The people confessing didn't have much to be guilty about: seeing a water-skier on the lake and feeling jealous . . . snapping at someone in anger . . . eating apples on a fasting day.

Justin spoke privately to each of them and touched his or her forehead. 'This is the touch of forgiveness,' he said. 'Love yourself again.'

It was all over in a matter of minutes. The five went back to their places looking happy.

Cassy thought Call must end soon, and they'd all be getting some sleep, but the music floated on.

'Now,' began Justin, sitting on the step of the dais, 'shall we talk about God?'

Cassy groaned inwardly. *Please, no!*

He was looking at her. It was as though he'd heard.

'I know what you're thinking, Cassy. But will you listen for a while? Let the words flow into your mind. Just let them flow in . . . flow in . . . that's all I ask. You can leave at any time, and we'll understand. Will you listen?'

She nodded, blushed, and mouthed, *Okay.*

It was easy stuff at first. Justin spoke calmly and fluently. He said the Old Testament was no more than a jumbled collection of pagan fables, twisted to mean things that were never intended.

'They somehow managed to dream up this place called hell—hell!—the ultimate naughty step.' He shook his head in bemusement. 'Mankind, eh?'

People chuckled. Cassy smiled too. So far, so good. Even her parents could buy into this.

Justin talked about Maori gods of earth and sky, forest and sea, earthquakes and volcanos. Their names sounded exotic and compelling, rising above the haunting music.

'Those ancient stories of gods are images of the Infinite Power,' he said. 'Images from the minds of men. Do you see? Christian missionaries tried to disinfect, to kill off what they saw as the dangerous bacteria of deep spirituality. They called those ancient beliefs "superstition". What do I call them? I call them wisdom. I call them seeing the universe with eyes and minds that are open to the Infinite Power.'

His voice was mesmeric, a lullaby in her profound exhaustion, dulling the analytical part of her brain. He talked for a long, long time—she estimated an hour. She tried to think critically, to deconstruct ideas such as 'spirituality' and 'Infinite', but they streamed like water: impossible to catch between her hands before he'd moved to another. People swayed as the voice flowed on and on. Sometimes phrases would be repeated many times, waves stroking the beach—gentle, hypnotic, insistent.

'What is God?' he asked, stepping down from the dais and wandering among his listeners. '*Who* is God? God is the Infinite Power that rolls through the universe. Human beings can't imagine infinity. They try to imagine, and they make up stories, and throughout the centuries those stories grow into religions over which wars are fought and atrocities are committed and millions die. And *where* is God?' He turned in a full circle. 'Not in the trenches, not in the bloody battlefields, not among the fallen boys.'

He'd arrived in front of Cassy.

'But if we free our minds, we can glimpse the glory of the Infinite Power.' He looked into her eyes, speaking quietly. 'Cassy, we'd like you to come with us on a journey. It's quite safe. You don't have to leave this room.'

She nodded. She wanted to follow where he led. She wanted to see beyond the ordinary.

'Well done.' Justin laid both hands on her head before returning to the dais. 'Close your eyes, then. Follow me. Follow me.'

The music stopped, leaving a charged silence. Cassy closed her eyes and let her consciousness drift. As time passed she lost awareness of the room, of Aden beside her, even of herself. The chatter in her head was gone. Her mind had been freed from her body, and she was floating in the dark.

'You feel the night air,' Justin was saying. 'Do you feel it rushing through your spirit? You're flying over the ruffled water . . . soaring up the flanks of Tarawera. Higher and higher, until you reach the summit. All the world is spread before you . . . all the world . . . all the stars in their billions. Feel the wonder. *Feel* the wonder. Do you hear the song of the universe?'

She *could* hear it—she was drenched in it. The night sky was pulsating with music. She was on top of a bare mountain, buffeted by winds, her hair tangling around her face. She could see forever. She could see the chaotic stain of humanity, spread across the earth.

'Look into the stars,' said Justin. 'And now look far, far beyond them. You're seeing everything that is, and everything that was. You're seeing everything that will be. You're looking into infinity.'

Cassy was dimly aware of shouts and laughter, followed by thuds. Justin raised his voice, shouting above the clamour.

'And now you're communing with another mind. Yes, yes, the mind of the Infinite! You feel an unimaginable presence. You feel love, lifting you up in a tide . . . do you feel it?'

Yes! She felt it—like a wave, so powerful that it knocked her right down. She felt something far greater than she'd ever imagined, with senses she had never known existed: an overwhelming awareness of a vast and loving consciousness. It reached into her and filled her heart with love, then lifted her and carried her. She was laughing with joy—what did anything matter? Why be afraid, ever again?

She was lying at Justin's feet. She had no idea how she'd got there. All around her, people were laughing and weeping. Some seemed to be having fits, their bodies convulsing. She saw people fall, thudding onto the wooden floor. Justin moved among them, laying his hands on each one.

Cassy felt tears coursing down her cheeks, but she wasn't embarrassed. She'd travelled far beyond vanity.

Justin crouched beside her.

'What did you feel?' he asked.

'I was in the presence of someone . . . something. I can't describe it. But I don't think I'll ever be the same again.'

'Oh, Cassy, you are amazing.' He pulled her head to his shoulder. He seemed intensely moved. 'You've looked into the face of God.'

Thirteen

Diana

Mike shut his paper. He folded it in half, then into quarters, smoothing the creases.

'This is ridiculous. Why the heck hasn't she been in touch?'

Diana was checking her emails yet again. Spam, spam, spam . . . school reunion . . . electricity bill . . .

'Eureka!' She was crowing with relief. 'Here she is!'

From: CassyHowlerMonkey@gmail.com
To: Mike and Diana Howells
Re: How are you?

Hi Mum and Dad,
Thanks for all your messages. Sorry, I don't get much time and the internet's hopeless here. Soooo . . . you know about Hamish and me. It was a mutual thing.

I've got to tell you about this place. I wish I could trans-port you here, like on Star Trek. *It's a farm beside a lake, and I get bed and board in return for work. At the moment I've got gardens to dig and I'm helping to produce a musical at the school! You'd be proud of me, Dad—I get up early in the mornings now. Can't see myself being one of those students again, pouring a whole load of bottles into a bucket and drinking it and then throwing up. I've discovered a new me.*

Imagine being among the happiest, kindest people you've ever met. Imagine finding they like you straight away, no questions asked! Imagine a micro-nation in a beautiful micro-world, where there's no stress and no rat-race. Old people are cared for and respected, not shoved into homes. There's a very simple rule, here: no negativity, only love.

Imagine a place where the children don't hunch over smart phones or computers or Xboxes. No sharing of photos of one another having sex, or drama queen posts about how miserable they are. There is NONE of that! Children play in total freedom. There's no paedophile to groom them, no car to run them over, no school bully to make them cry. Nobody's ever left out.

Imagine people who never bitch, who don't have credit cards, who aren't scrabbling to drive bigger cars than their neighbours. They own nothing. They share everything. And they're happy! I haven't heard anyone say 'pension' or 'mortgage' or 'dog-eat-dog' since I've been here.

Imagine people who have such a capacity for love that they collect addicts and criminals and drop-outs, and give them a home and a purpose.

Now. Imagine being welcomed by these wonderful people. They value me. They want me to stay. It's only an idea, but do you think I could put my degree on hold for a year?

I hope you're all OK. How did Tara's exams go? Can't get online much so don't worry if no contact for a while.

Love U.

Cassy xxx

Mike took off his reading glasses. 'What d'you make of it?'

'All very wholesome,' said Diana, who had found the message terrifying. 'On the face of it.'

'Mm, yes.'

'I'm sure she doesn't mean it about staying on.'

'God, I hope not.' Mike's forehead was furrowed with misgiving. 'D'you think she seems a bit high?'

'No, not high. Enthusiastic.'

'Well! Good. As long as she's happy. And safe.'

When Tara appeared, her parents were still trying to reassure each other.

'Ah, the prodigal sister!' she cried. 'I'm not talking to that girl. If she can get online she could have answered my twenty million messages.'

All the same, Tara took a look at the email. As she read, she whistled.

'What do you think?' asked Diana.

'I think it sounds like she's on something. That lazy tart, getting out of bed early? Bollocks.' While she talked, Tara was riffling through a drawer. 'I need batteries for my calculator. How come we never have any the right size? Oh, we do.'

The next half-hour was filled with the business of a weekday morning: Mike gulping down another cup of coffee while polishing his shoes; Tara learning German verbs while having a text-argument with a friend; Diana opening a bank statement while wondering what Cassy was doing at that moment. They all left the house together.

A heatwave was gathering strength. Midday temperatures were forecast to reach about thirty degrees.

'Are you going to reply to Cassy, or shall I?' asked Mike, as Diana locked up the house.

'I'll do it.'

'There are so many other places to see. That would be my angle.'

'I'll say that.'

'Maybe she should come home now, if she's not going to make the most of being over there.'

'I'll say that too.'

He stood running his hand down his tie again and again,

smoothing it against his shirtfront. It was something he did at times of stress, as though by controlling his appearance he could manage everything in life.

'Don't worry,' said Diana, pecking his cheek. Such empty words. She might as well have said, 'Don't breathe.'

She arrived at work to find a flashing answer machine and a pile of funding applications in her in-tray. She ignored them all, and began to compose a message to Cassy.

Fiona appeared, bravely decked out in one of her floral tents. Diana's colleague was a widow who had her own worries in life. Her daughter Stacey had left her no-good husband and moved back home with three children. Fiona tackled it all with determined jollity and an awful lot of doughnuts.

'Cuppa?' she asked, miming a tipping mug with one hand.

'Please.' Diana didn't want tea; she wanted Cassy to come home and be safe. But she said, *Please*, because that was What One Did.

'Isn't it hot?' gasped Fiona, returning with mugs. 'Whew. We need air-conditioning in here. How did you get on with the funding applications?'

'Nowhere,' said Diana, massaging her temples.

Fiona stood stolidly in her gold sandals. 'Something up?'

'Cassy's up. We had this email. It's rattled us a bit, to be honest. Have a look.'

Fiona rolled her desk chair across and sat down, squinting at the message. 'Sounds as though she's found heaven on earth,' she said, once she'd read it.

'There's no such thing.'

'I wish Stacey and the kids could have a life like that. Cassy's learning things that might have more use than law, when the chips are down.' Fiona had taken off her glasses and was rubbing her eyes with the back of her hand. 'Jarred's gone and got himself suspended again.'

'Oh dear! What for?' Diana wanted to care about an off-the-rails grandson. Really, she did.

'Caught watching porn at school. They've got access to every-thing on the internet.'

'Too true.'

'Stacey had to go and talk to the teachers,' said Fiona, 'so I took the little ones to the play park. And guess what we found?' She replaced her glasses. 'Needles! Not the knitting kind. Just there, for any child to pick up. I worry about their futures, Diana. I do. I worry. What kind of a world are we passing on to them?'

'They'll be okay. They've got you.'

'If my lot had the chance to follow Cassy out to this bit of paradise, I'd jump at it.'

They drank their tea together, talking about an upcoming exhibition. Then, at last, Fiona moved back to her own desk and Diana returned to her email. She read it through once more. Cheerful but firm. A reality check.

She clicked her mouse and listened for the sound—like a miniature firework—as her words took flight and shot around the world.

•

Cassy

From: Mike and Diana Howells
To: CassyHowlerMonkey@gmail.com
Re: How are you?

Darling,
That all sounds lovely. We look forward to seeing the photos when you get home. BUT don't forget all the things you wanted to do in New Zealand!! Remember you have the rest of the money Grandpa left you still sitting in your savings account. We know you earmarked that for other things but it does give you flexibility.

   Dad and I think you should leave that place now and carry

*on with your trip, or else come home early. There's no point in
wasting time and money by sitting in one place.*

   *Don't mess up your life, Cassy. Please stay in touch and
tell us you're moving on now.*

   Lots of love,
   Mum xx

Cassy banged her head onto the desk. 'My *bloody* parents!'

Paris and Bali were in the office with her—they had a couple
of admin jobs to do, they said—and were by her side within
seconds. They looked, then groaned in sympathy.

'No respect, is there?' said Bali. 'It sounds as though they
don't know you at all.'

'*That all sounds lovely.*' Cassy was mimicking her mother's
voice. 'For Pete's sake, it's how you'd talk to a toddler!'

Paris perched on the edge of the desk. 'It can be hard for
parents to let go.'

'You mean it's hard for them to stop being bloody controlling.'

'I think you should write back straight away. Be honest with
them. Be upfront! Love is *always* honest.'

'Might be best if I did it tomorrow,' said Cassy, chewing her
lip. She was rereading Diana's message and feeling more indignant by the second.

'Why tomorrow?'

'Because right now—*right now*—I feel like telling them to
fuck off.'

Bali began to plait Cassy's hair.

'Why not do it now?' she suggested. 'Don't let it fester. You've
got time before Call.'

Cassy sat very still, soothed by the gentleness of her friend's
fingers on her scalp.

'It's time to be honest about how you feel and who you are,'
said Paris. 'Honesty and love go hand in hand.'

'Okay.' Cassy bent over the keys, typing furiously.

*I've only got a few mins—but v v quickly, aren't you inter-
ested in what I was trying to say? Couldn't you tell that this
matters to me? Or didn't you care?*

*I'm going to be honest. There hasn't been enough honesty
in our family.*

*You like to think I'm going to become a partner in some
massive firm, so I can work ninety hours a week and you can
show off to your friends. Read my lips: I AM NOT THAT
PERSON!! I'm sick of living out your fantasy of the perfect
daughter. You have to accept me for who I am, not who you
expect me to be. TBH right now I'm not sure I want to finish
my degree. I don't think I fit into that life any more. I never did.*

*I haven't decided if I'll be catching that flight home. I may
delay.*

Love,

Cassy

'Perfect,' said Paris, when she'd finished.

'You think?'

'Mm. It's totally honest.'

'Maybe a bit too angry-woman?'

'It's time they knew who you really are.' Bali was still plaiting
Cassy's hair. 'You're a truly extraordinary person,' she said. 'Sad
that they don't seem to see it. Better press *send*, though, before the
internet crashes. Hey, after Call, 'd'you want to take a bottle of
wine down to the rocks and light a bonfire? Aden will come, I bet.'

'That sounds fun.'

'The lake's like a mirror this evening.' Bali peered at the
screen. 'Haven't you sent that message yet? Come on, chop chop!'

Cassy clicked, and the message disappeared from her outbox.

'Well done,' said Paris.

'Proud of you,' said Bali.

They were both hugging her. Cassy felt enveloped in their
sisterly warmth.

'Thanks, guys,' she said.

Fourteen

Diana

> *From: Mike and Diana Howells*
> *To: CassyHowlerMonkey@gmail.com*
> *Re: How are you?*
>
> *Darling,*
> *Were you in a bad mood when you wrote that? I'm sure those people seem very exciting, but we think you've been there long enough. Of course you will go back to Durham, and you will finish your degree. We aren't going to let you throw everything away. Please get to a proper phone and call us STRAIGHT AWAY.*
> *   Mum and Dad xx*
>
> *From: Mike and Diana Howells*
> *To: CassyHowlerMonkey@gmail.com*
> *Re: How are you?*
>
> *Cassy, we're worried. Just phone, PLEASE, so we can talk to you.*

Facebook message from Tara Howells

Mum and Dad r going nuts. For fucks sake fone them just to get them off my back!!! You r coming home aren't you??

From: Mike and Diana Howells
To: CassyHowlerMonkey@gmail.com
Re: How are you?

Cassy,
Are you sleeping with someone out there—is that what this is about? If so, please see it for what it is. They may call it free love, but I call it cheap love! Your future is worth more. I hope you know that.
   Love,
   Mum

Facebook message from Tara Howells

CASSSSSSEEEEEEEEE!!!!! WHAT THE FUCK???

From: Mike and Diana Howells
To: CassyHowlerMonkey@gmail.com
Re: How are you?

Cassy, this isn't funny. If we don't hear from you straight away we'll have to take some kind of action. PLEASE PHONE ASAP. We expect to be meeting you at Heathrow next Friday. We will be there!!

•

On the Saturday before Cassy was due home, Becca and Imogen turned up unannounced. Diana was cheered to find them standing on her front step, wearing sundresses and smiles. It made Cassy seem closer.

'Come in,' she cried. 'Ready for the big day, Imogen? Wow, you look all radiant and bridal!'

Imogen and Becca had known each other forever, and met Cassy when she started sixth form at their school. It was a friendship that had carried the three of them through the stresses of A levels and early adult life—and, in Imogen's case, her on-again, off-again obsession with Jack.

Imogen's froth of hair seemed unusually blonde that day; Diana suspected some serious money had been spent in one of the posher salons. They talked about wedding flowers while she led them out to the garden table. It was a breathless, yellow-haze evening. Train tracks were buckling in the heat. Imogen said she'd been stranded at Clapham Junction, and getting home from work had been a bloody nightmare, and she hated bloody Southern Railway.

'Any news on our lass?' asked Becca, as Diana opened a bottle of prosecco. 'We've not heard a dicky-bird.'

'Oh dear, I was hoping you could shed some light,' said Diana, filling their glasses. 'I don't understand what's going on. She says she might not be back on Friday.'

'She *has* to be back!' Imogen looked appalled. 'She's my bridesmaid.'

'I know, I know. I was going to call you. Hang on, you can see what she wrote.'

Diana fetched her laptop, brought up Cassy's most recent message and watched their shocked expressions as they read.

'Ouch,' said Becca, wincing. 'Steady on, Cass.'

'She's sick of living out our fantasy of the perfect daughter, apparently,' said Diana, who'd been cut to the quick by Cassy's message. 'I didn't know I had such a fantasy. I really, really didn't.'

'I always thought she liked being perfect,' said Imogen. As soon as she'd spoken, she smacked herself in the mouth. 'I mean . . . sorry, that came out bitchy.'

'I don't recognise this voice,' said Becca, wrinkling her nose. 'It doesn't sound like Cassy.'

Imogen leaned back in her seat. 'We've heard something about

Hamish. I don't know whether it's true, but . . .' She held up her hand. 'Don't shoot the messenger, but according to Facebook he's very matey with someone else already. She's called Charlotte Someone-double-barrelled. There are photos of them skiing together.'

'Well!' Diana took a moment to digest this news. 'That *is* a bit of gossip.'

'I didn't really know him, but I always thought that man was insincere,' said Imogen. 'Too smooth by half.'

Soon after that, the girls downed their drinks and said they'd better be off.

'We're not telling anyone about Cassy,' said Diana, as she saw them out. 'We're still hoping she'll be home on Friday. If you could just keep this under your hats?'

'Sure,' said Imogen. 'But if she doesn't front up at my wedding, people are going to wonder why.'

Becca stopped to kiss Diana's cheek. 'Don't worry. She'll be on that plane.'

'I'm sure she will.'

●

It was one thing to be half rational while sitting in a sunlit garden; not so easy after dark, when the air felt like a smothering blanket. A migraine was gathering. Green-and-red psychedelic balloons floated and flashed in the dark periphery of Diana's vision.

She lay on her side of the bed and listened to Mike worrying. He turned over. He sat up, threw himself down again. She understood. It was the witching hour, when horrors seemed to crawl out from under the rocks. She imagined sickening things: Cassy kidnapped, chained in a dungeon (did they have dungeons in New Zealand?); Cassy lost in a wilderness, or dead in a ditch.

Don't be silly. Don't be so bloody silly. You know exactly where she is.

Yet the images kept coming.

Mike didn't bother to whisper. He knew she was awake.

'Why is she doing this to us?'

Diana sighed. 'I don't know.'

'Christ.' He hit the pillow. 'I feel so bloody useless.'

She didn't want his agitation; she had enough of her own. She could hear his breathing, heavy and irregular, as though he'd just run a race.

'She could be in real trouble,' he said.

'Hardly likely.'

'But we don't *know*, do we? We don't know who wrote those messages. All we know is that she accepted a lift from strangers and we haven't heard her voice since. Not her actual voice. That's the truth, Diana. Those are the bare facts.'

She rolled onto her back, blinking at the psychedelic blind spots. 'Maybe we could write to those people?' she suggested. 'To the email address on their website.'

Two minutes later, they were both heading downstairs. Better to be doing something than sweating in impotent terror.

'Polite and concerned?' asked Mike. 'Or angry and demanding?'

'Polite and concerned. First time, anyway.'

Pesky flopped in through the cat door as soon as the downstairs lights went on. Diana bent to pick him up while Mike searched for the Gethsemane website.

'Where is she, Pesky?' she murmured into a twitching ear. 'Where's your mistress?'

Dear Sir or Madam,

We are enquiring about our daughter, Cassandra Howells, who we believe has been working for you. There are some matters of family business that we need to discuss with her urgently. We've had difficulty communicating with her, and understand this may be because there is no mobile phone coverage in your area.

We'd be grateful if you would please ask her to telephone us. Could she perhaps use your landline, if you have one? We really do need to speak to her as soon as possible.

Thanking you in advance,
Michael and Diana Howells

For the rest of the day—Sunday—they were on tenterhooks, watching their emails like cats outside a mouse hole.

'I can't stand that noise,' said Mike, when church bells began to ring. 'I'll take my bike out. I'm meant to be training for the cycle challenge.'

This wasn't news to Diana. He was always training for one race or another. She watched out of the sitting-room window as he set off—pedalling crazily, as though he had a pack of wolves after him.

•

On Monday, heat melted tarmac in the roads and filled the parks with sunbathers. Diana jumped every time there was a new notification on her phone.

'Nothing?' asked Fiona. She was suffering—florid and shiny-faced—and had bought a fan for the office.

'Nothing.'

'She's due home any day, isn't she?'

'Friday.'

Fiona parked herself in front of the fan. It rippled the skirt of her flowery dress. 'Don't worry. If she chooses to stay a bit longer, it's because she's happy.'

•

By Tuesday morning the household was ready to explode. Mike shouted at Tara for refusing to do the washing-up. Tara hurled a pot into the sink—tsunami over the floor—and stormed off to school, tripping over the cat on her way out.

Mike and Diana were left looking at each other.

'It'll be okay,' said Diana. 'Her plane takes off in forty-eight hours. She'll be on it.'

'Christ, I hope so.'

They both heard it: the *ping* of a message arriving on Mike's computer.

Mum and Dad,
I hear you wrote to Gethsemane. Please DO NOT do this again. This is between you and me. It's nothing to do with these good, kind people.
I've made a decision. I've cancelled my flight.
I'll be in touch.
Cassy

The Cult Leader's Manual: Eight Steps to Mind Control

Cameron Allsop

Step 6: Denounce and renounce

Can you persuade your recruit to denounce their close friends, or even their family? If so, you're well on your way.

Fifteen

Cassy

She never forgot the day she began to hate her parents.

Winter was meant to be over, but a polar blast had splashed a bright line of snow along the upper slopes of Mount Tarawera. It was a fasting day in Gethsemane. Justin called for these about once a week, and everyone took part; even children went hungry with very little fuss. Justin did the same himself. In fact, he often fasted for several days at a time.

'You don't have to join in, Cassy,' Aden had told her. 'You're not a Watchman, and you're eating for two.'

But she insisted. She couldn't eat if others weren't, and fasting days always ended in a lovely midnight feast in the *whare kai*. All the same, by late afternoon she'd begun to feel distinctly odd. She, Bali and Paris had been cleaning all three of their cabins together, but the others had both left for other duties. It wasn't until she was alone that she took a break from cobwebbing and looked out of the window. High, high up—just a glinting speck—an aircraft inched among the clouds.

Hamish was on his way home. Today. Right now.

She could be sitting beside him, watching films, eating peanuts out of little packets. The family would have met her at Heathrow, and on Saturday she'd have been Imogen's bridesmaid.

What am I doing here?

She heard running steps on the porch before Rome appeared in the doorway. The teenager was out of breath.

'Cassy,' he said, 'I'm sorry . . . but the Companions want to see you in the office, straight away.'

'Why?'

'I don't know.' He seemed nervous. Tension made his voice fluctuate from bass to falsetto and back again.

Cassy was already pulling on her boots, feeling breathless with anxiety. 'All of them?'

'Liam, Gaza, Otto and Monika.' His eyes flickered towards the office. 'They didn't look very happy.'

Rome and Cassy trotted up the slope without speaking. He opened the office door for Cassy and followed close behind her. It was reassuring to have her young friend at her back. After all, he was Justin's son.

The four Companions were shadows, sitting on the far side of a table. The room felt very cold.

'Thank you, Rome,' said Liam. 'You don't need to stay.'

'I don't mind.'

Liam made a jerking motion with his head. 'Off you go, son.'

Cassy felt Rome press her arm, and then heard the door closing behind him. She was alone, and shivering. She was the accused. They didn't invite her to sit down.

'Your father's sent another email,' said Gaza. 'Shall I read it to you?'

The letter sounded absurd when read out in Gaza's clipped tones, especially as she laid a contemptuous inflection over some of the words. Cassy felt her face grow hot.

'*Dear Sir or Madam, I am writing with considerable concern about Cassandra Howells. In my opinion she has been abducted by you. I warn you that I work for a major international security firm with contacts in police, intelligence agencies and governments all over the world. I demand your assurance that Cassandra will return home immediately. If I do not receive that assurance within the next forty-eight hours, you will leave me no option but to use my influence with the authorities in New Zealand. This will not end well for your outfit. Yours faithfully, Michael Howells.*'

'Oh God,' groaned Cassy, trying to cool her cheek with the back of her hand. It seemed profane—her father's pomposity in this sacred and simple place. 'That's the stupidest thing I ever heard.'

'We agree,' said Gaza. 'But we don't like being threatened. We don't have friends in high places, unlike your father.'

'Don't listen to him! He's just rattling his cage.'

'Are you sure?' asked Monika. 'Are you quite sure?'

'He does work in security, but it's nothing to do with police or . . . you know, spies and things. It's just for businesses who want extra protection in places like Baghdad. My father's never even *been* to New Zealand. I'm telling you, it's all bluff.'

They were staring blankly, slightly over her head, as though she were nothing but a nuisance. Any minute now they'd drag out her trunk and start packing it for her.

'Do you want me to leave Gethsemane?' she asked, panic thumping in her chest.

No answer.

She desperately didn't want to leave. She knew that now.

'You don't want me to go, do you?' She was begging, her breath coming in gasps. 'Please don't throw me out.'

'That depends,' said Gaza. 'You've been a gateway through which negativity has arrived. We have to be sure that this gateway will never be opened again. *Never* again. Otherwise—yes, I'm sorry, but you'll have to go.'

'Does Justin want me to leave?'

'He's asked to see you after Night Call.'

The floor tilted. Cassy reached for a chair but missed it and staggered. She felt a firm hand on her elbow, guiding her.

'Steady.' It was Monika's voice. 'Sit down for a moment. Take your time, that's it, head down . . . right down . . . better?'

Suddenly—wonderfully—they loved her again. Otto fetched a cup of water. Liam put his arms around her shoulders as though she were his own daughter. Their kindness brought tears.

'Don't cry,' said Gaza, though she too was smiling. 'It's not The Way.'

'The Way?'

'The Gethsemane Way. You need to learn it, and follow it.'

Cassy brushed her sleeve across her face, tried to say *sorry* and sobbed instead.

'Ooh—I'd like to give your father a piece of my mind!' railed Monika. 'You're sheet-white. I want you to go and eat something, right now.'

'I can't! It's a fasting day. I don't want to break any more rules.'

'Doctor's orders. Go and ask Seoul for some soup.'

Afraid they'd see her crying again, Cassy promised to head straight for the kitchen. Then she fled from the office and right into the arms—literally, into the arms—of Aden, who happened to be walking past. For a moment she wondered what he was doing there; he was meant to be up in the top paddocks.

'Whoa,' he said, leading her around the corner, out of sight. He looked into her face. 'Hey. What happened?'

'My parents. My ignorant, patronising, interfering, *fucking* parents.'

She felt his strength absorb her hurt. She felt his calm. He was her friend. He respected her, which was more than could be said for her own family.

Since Mum assumes this is about sex, she thought furiously, *I'll just go ahead and make it about sex.*

Grabbing the neck of his shirt in both fists, she kissed him on the mouth. It was as though she'd opened a floodgate. For perhaps ten seconds the rest of the world seemed to disappear.

Then he disentangled himself.

'Not yet,' he whispered.

She was baffled. Mortified. 'Why not yet?'

He laughed—caught his breath—and rested his forehead against hers. She fought the urge to kiss him again.

'You're forgetting Justin,' he said. 'Nothing happens without his blessing.'

'Nothing? Not even—'

'Nothing.'

•

Night Call had come and gone. They knelt on the floor of the meditation room, a small chamber off the *wharenui*. Justin had asked Paris, Bali, Aden and Monika to join him and Cassy. Outside, the air crackled and glittered with frost; inside, it crackled with expectancy.

'Cassy,' said Justin, 'share your feelings. Bring them into the light.'

Candlelit shadows. She'd been awake for twenty hours, had eaten almost nothing, and felt as though she were submerged in a dream. Perhaps the others felt the same; perhaps they were all dreaming the same dream.

'I think my parents don't know me,' she said. 'I tried to tell them about Gethsemane, but they weren't interested. To them I'm a doll: dress me up, put me on the shelf. My mother assumes I'm sleeping with someone here. Why did she have to assume that? She obviously thinks I'm shallow.'

'They've hurt you,' said Justin. 'Families can be toxic. They control and demean.'

Something was engulfing Cassy, a foaming blackness that made her want to hit out.

'That's it exactly! You know those walking reins people put on their toddlers? Control, control, control. I feel as though I've had those on me all my life. I feel them jerking me back from the other side of the world.'

'How do you feel, when they tug on those reins?'

'I feel . . .' She shivered. 'Abused.'

'Abused,' repeated Justin, and Cassy sensed the word fluttering among them. 'I wonder why you use that particular word. I wonder what's locked away in your memories.'

He was on his feet, though she hadn't seen him move. He strolled around the circle, stopping to touch each of them on the forehead, his voice rhythmic and soothing.

'You are here,' he said quietly, as he touched. 'You are *here*, Monika; you are *here*, Bali. Right here. You don't need to move a muscle to find yourself. You don't need to take a boat to find yourself. You don't need to take a bus, or hitch a lift. You don't need to look in a mirror. You are *here*.'

His voice was inside her head. Her brain seemed to tingle.

'You are *here*, Monika . . . you are *here*, Aden . . . you are *here*, Paris. Bali. Cassy. You are *here*.'

As his fingers pressed her forehead, Cassy felt her mind opening its doors.

He sat down again, folding his long legs, letting the silence breathe into the corners of the room.

'You don't need to talk. You don't need to think. You don't need to do anything. Just be here. Just be. Just . . .'

He spoke for a long time, and his woven words were the piece of silk that a magician throws over his hat. She couldn't quite make sense of them, and yet they floated and billowed, transforming her into a white dove. Yes, she saw it all clearly now! Her family was irrelevant—why did she care what they thought? They were small, selfish people with small and selfish lives. The only reality was right here, in this room.

'They sent you to boarding school?' said Justin. 'Just you? Not your sister?'

'It was because of my father's work.'

'Was it really?' The green eyes were gazing at her, as though he could see right into her soul. 'Cassy, you're harbouring a monster. You locked it away in a dark place, didn't you? Yes. So let's bring it into the light. It's frightening, this monster, but we're with you. Okay?'

She nodded.

'Close your eyes. Walk right up to the door of your childhood. Are you there, at the door?'

'Yes.'

'Open it.'

Her mouth was dry as she grasped the handle. Something was in there, lurking in the darkness, just out of sight.

'I'm afraid to look inside,' she said.

'We're here with you. Step through the door. Be that little girl again,' urged Justin. 'Can you do that? Yes?'

'Yes.'

'Well done . . . well done. You're very small. I think you're very unhappy.'

The trunk was there. The coffin-trunk. Cassy touched the painted lettering on its lid. *Cassandra Howells*. It was packed and ready to go.

'Don't they love me?' she asked.

'We're here with you. We'll never abandon you. You're very frightened. Did you make your father angry—can you hear him shouting?'

Justin's voice was caressing her mind. Justin was her friend, guarding her as she explored the dark maze. One by one, images burst open like bubbles of poison: chewed thumbnails when a school report arrived in the post. Terror when she scratched the car with her rollerskates. Seeing a tabby kitten on the other side of the road and running to rescue it, the honking of a car horn, and Mum screaming, *Casseeee!* before Dad pelted across the road to smack her three, four, five times.

And that wasn't all. There was something worse, something monstrous. She felt the grip of fear in her stomach.

'What's he doing?' asked Justin. 'You're very scared.'

'He's just put the phone down. My teacher called, she said I stole somebody's pencil case. But I only borrowed it. His face is ugly.'

'He's going to hurt you.'

'Yes.' She was shrinking away. 'He's walking around the

kitchen. I feel really . . . really . . . I want to hide. He's gone and got—'

She stopped, her mouth open. *No.* She hadn't known this. Not this. She'd forgotten this ever happened.

'What, Cassy? What's in his hand?'

She remembered it all, with a clarity that made her scream. She saw the wooden spoon in his hand, and heard the *swish, swish,* and felt it thud and smack against her leg. Again and again he hit her, on her bare thigh with the skirt pulled up and out of the way, while she howled and struggled and her mother did nothing to stop him. It was happening right now—the humiliation of it, the shock and the horrible pain. Her heart was breaking, because they didn't love her at all—they hated her. They *must* hate her, to hurt her so much. Then her father walked away, and her mother pushed her up the stairs and told her to go to bed, didn't even give her a hug. They left her alone in her room, while bruises blossomed like flowers on her leg.

'Cassy,' said Justin's voice. 'Can you hear me? You're out of their reach now. Let them go. Let them go.'

She was retching. Her thigh was on fire. She thought it might be going to explode. But she wasn't alone any more. Hands were protecting and supporting, voices were a kindly chorus in her ear. *Poor little girl. We love you!*

Justin's was the first face she saw. He crouched in front of her, holding out a mug. She recognised the taste: St John's wort and chamomile. Warmth, honey and a ghost of steam in the gentle light.

'Are you with us again?' he asked.

'I think so.' Her tongue felt heavy. She wasn't sure where she was, or how she'd got there. She was lying against someone—it turned out to be Aden—and she felt as though she'd been running for her life.

As the candles burned lower, the throbbing in her leg subsided. Her heart stopped pounding. The nightmares were fading.

'You've cast them out,' said Justin. 'Those demons of your past.'

'I hope so.'

'You're free. Believe me. You are free.'

She took her time, prodding her mind for tender corners. Then she exhaled in a rush. '*Whew*. Yes. I can breathe.'

Justin nodded. 'Cassy, we love you. No reins! Do you believe me?'

'Of course.'

'Then here's my suggestion. Stay with us. Have your baby here. Let Gethsemane be your family. Where else would you want to bring up a child? He or she will have a perfect father in Aden, and Suva will have a mother again.'

It took a long time for his words to sink in.

'You mean forever?'

'I mean forever. Become a Watchman. You and Aden will be united as Partners in the Watch. You'll never be unhappy again—that's my promise to you.'

Something shifted in her brain; it was flooded by a shining, purring sensation. She looked around at Aden.

'Have you agreed to this? You've only known me a few weeks.'

He shrugged, smiling. 'A few weeks. A few minutes. Doesn't matter. Our future was fixed the moment you stood beside that road and held up your soggy cardboard sign. I was meant to give you a lift. You were meant to come to Gethsemane.'

Her choice looked blindingly clear. This wasn't about lust, or infatuation, or a rebound from Hamish. It wasn't even love in the Disney-romantic sense. It was much greater than those things. She and Aden were two threads woven together as part of a magnificent tapestry. The tapestry was Gethsemane itself, and the weaver was Justin. This was her future.

'So it's yes?' asked Justin.

'It's yes,' she said. 'Thank you.'

Justin threw up his arms in celebration. 'This is wonderful news! From now on you're our daughter, sister and friend. And oh, how we love you.' He drew her to her feet. 'I'm going to ask you to do one last thing—right now, tonight—as a symbol and proof of your freedom.'

'I'll do it. Whatever it is, I'll do it.'

'Call your parents and tell them. Cut their reins.' He put his hands on each side of her face, kissing her head. 'You can do it, Cassy. You *can*. Gaza and Monika will go with you. They'll be right beside you.'

'We'll protect you from their manipulation,' promised Gaza.

'But . . . what do I say?'

'Tell them you'll be making Gethsemane your home,' said Justin. 'But don't mention your unborn child. They don't need to know about that, do they? No. Then send a message to your ex, assuring him there's no pregnancy. That would be a kindness to him, wouldn't it? Let him off the hook?'

'Yes—yes, then he can stop worrying. But couldn't I just email my parents? They're going to go nuts.'

'Ah, well.' Justin shook his head sadly. 'That'll be their choice, won't it?'

Sixteen

Diana

'Darling? Diana!' Mike was shouting up the stairs, his voice high and excited.

She was in Cassy's bedroom. In theory she was looking for a physics textbook for Tara, but really she was sitting on the bed. Just sitting. Cassy could have nipped out five minutes ago. The smell of her cocoa butter; a long hair on the pillow; a trashy novel on the bedside table. Books about the laws of contract and tort. Babar the Elephant, soft and threadbare, who'd been Cassy's friend since she was one day old.

Diana had heard the phone ring, and shut her eyes.

Please be Cassy. Please, please be Cassy.

'Diana!' Mike yelled again. 'It's Cassy on the phone!'

She was already pelting down the landing with Babar in one hand, snatching up the bedroom phone.

'Cassy! Oh, this is great! Hello?'

Silence. Then Cassy's voice, but blast-frozen.

'Hello, Diana. Hello, Mike.'

There was no love or life. She'd never called them Diana and Mike; they'd always been Mum and Dad.

'Where are you?' asked Mike.

Later, when they analysed the conversation, they felt sure she was reading from a script.

'I'm here at Gethsemane, Mike. You know that.'

Diana had the receiver pressed to her ear, eager to catch every word. '*How* are you, darling? We've been beside ourselves.'

'You emailed Gethsemane again. I specifically asked you not to. You made threats. You're—'

Mike was already losing his temper. 'For Christ's sake, Cassy! What the bloody hell did you expect? Do you think we're going to—'

'No negativity please, Mike.'

'—watch you throw away your life? You think we'll meekly stand by and let them kidnap you?'

'No negativity please, Mike.'

'What have those people done to you? Evil, manipulative—'

Cassy spoke over him. 'I don't want to hear your anger. We don't have negativity here. Only love.'

Diana couldn't bear Mike's ranting, or Cassy's unnatural calm.

'Cassy,' she begged. 'Please, darling, listen to us.'

'No, Diana. You listen to me. I've reached a decision. But if either of you shout again, I'll end this call. Do you understand?'

'Yes,' said Diana quickly. 'Yes, we do. Shh, Mike! Please.'

Maybe Cassy was taking a long breath; maybe checking her script. When she spoke again, Diana thought she detected a catch in her voice.

'Okay,' she said. 'I'm going to stay here permanently.'

Mike exploded—*Oh, for the love of God!*—but Diana intervened. 'Not forever, surely? You talked about deferring your degree for a year.'

'I told you: I'm not that person any more. I feel as though I've only been half alive until now. This is a different world, a different way of living. I've experienced pure love.'

'Cassy—'

'I've had an encounter with God.'

She might as well have lobbed a grenade down the line. To her atheist parents, an encounter with God was final proof that their daughter's mind had been hijacked.

'Which God?' asked Diana. '*Whose* God?'

'I don't believe I'm hearing this,' thundered Mike. 'What drugs have they been giving you?'

Cassy was inexorable. 'You're so hidebound and buttoned-up and full of hate and fear and negativity . . . your eyes are shut, you're holding your hands over your ears, so you'll never glimpse the glory. All we have here is love and sharing. No greed, no possessions. All that *they* have is mine. All that *I* have is theirs. I'm going to give them the rest of the money I inherited from Grandpa.'

'You have to be joking!'

'Mike, I *will* end this call. Final warning.'

The conversation dissolved in a maelstrom of words. Mike and Diana argued, they pleaded, they threatened. It was like talking to a pre-programmed robot.

'Can't you see you're being manipulated?' barked Mike, when Cassy had said *no negativity, only love* for the third time in a row. 'Love, love, bloody love—it's a scam—this isn't about love! Cassy, for God's sake, stop spouting that mantra and use your brain.'

'I am using my brain.'

'They want your money, that's all they're after. Anyone in their right mind can see that! Once they've got your money, they'll throw you out.'

This was met by another silence—a long one this time, perhaps twenty seconds. Diana thought she heard the murmur of voices in the background.

'I'll be staying here,' said Cassy. 'Gethsemane is my family.'

'*We're* your family,' whispered Diana.

'A toxic family. I've remembered things about my childhood. Things you hoped I'd forget.'

Diana held Babar to her cheek. 'What d'you mean?'

'You know.'

'But darling . . .' Diana searched her memory bank and came up with nothing. 'I honestly don't.'

'It's sad that you can't even admit it. I'll stay in contact if possible, but it has to be on our terms. There are rules. No, no—' she was speaking over Mike, who was blustering '—Mike, don't interrupt me again. You've said enough. If you breach any one of the rules, we'll have no choice. We'll cut you off. Permanently.'

'It's *us*, Cassy!' cried Diana. 'It's Mum and Dad. We love you. Don't you love us?'

'Emotional blackmail won't work.'

'What about Granny—what do I tell her? What do I tell Tara?'

'Here are the conditions.' Again, Diana had the sense that Cassy was reading from a script. 'First, don't say anything negative about Gethsemane. Not to me, not to others, not to the media or on the internet. Remember the code we live by: no negativity, only love. Second, do *not* ask me to leave. No manipulation. No games.'

It's a nightmare, thought Diana, sliding off the bed until she was crouching on the floor, smothering sobs with her free hand. *Please, please make it a nightmare. Please let me wake up.*

Cassy might have been reading out a shopping list, ticking things off.

'Above all, you're *not* to try coming out here. If you set foot anywhere near Gethsemane, you'll never see me again. Do you understand?'

All hell broke loose. Mike was bellowing that she'd been brainwashed and to stop buggering about and come home *right now* or he'd be calling the police on the bastards. Diana piled in too. *You're not well, Cassy. You need help.*

Cassy didn't even say goodbye. There was a click, and she was gone. That was that. End of story; end of Cassy.

Again and again, in the weeks and years to come, Diana and Mike replayed the conversation in their minds. Replayed it, relived it, longed to turn back time and somehow change the outcome. They would lie awake on their own sides of the bed, not touching, wondering where they'd gone wrong. Sometimes, as she was falling asleep, Diana would hear that click; and then silence.

The email arrived an hour later. It must have been sent at about five in the morning, New Zealand time.

'Maybe they're giving her amphetamine,' said Mike. 'Speed. To keep her awake.'

'She wouldn't take drugs.'

'How d'you know? We can't pretend to know anything about her any more.'

Diana read the message fearfully—hopefully—longing for a miracle: *Just kidding!!! I'll be home tomorrow.*

But it wasn't a miracle.

You're intractably negative, and we can't allow negativity to come into our world. Your cynicism is poisonous.

I will neither send nor receive further messages. Genuinely urgent news can be sent via Gethsemane's email address. If you love me at all, you'll be happy for me.

Please don't think about coming to find me. If you do, you'll be trespassing. I won't see you, and your lack of respect for my wishes will only make me despise you.

I feel sorry for you. You're living under the mud at the bottom of the lake, and you can't see anything but mud. I would save you if I could, especially Tara, but I know now that's impossible.

I wish you well. I pray that one day you'll rise to the surface and feel the warmth of the sun.

Cassy

•

Friday morning. Cassy was meant to be coming home today. It said so on the bedside calendar.

CASSY HOME! ☺ 11.10 AM

They woke in despair, and dressed in silence. Mike sat on the edge of the bed, knotting his tie.

'I feel so impotent,' he said.

He didn't have government contacts in New Zealand; that had been a bluff. He and Diana had appealed for help from the New Zealand police as well as the British High Commission in Wellington. Both had been polite but bemused. *So your daughter's alive and well, not asking for help? And she's an adult? And you know exactly where she is?* They clearly thought these were clingy parents who needed a reality check.

'I didn't see this coming,' said Diana, resting her head on Mike's shoulder. 'Of all the bogeymen I've feared over the years, this wasn't one of them.'

She couldn't resist looking into Cassy's room. It still smelled of her; it still looked as though she'd be back today. *She wouldn't let me down*, Imogen had insisted tearfully, when they'd talked the night before. *She just wouldn't.*

A grey pall hung over the house. Neither of them wanted breakfast, though Mike made a pot of coffee.

'Tara going to work in the café?' he asked.

'Not today. I think she'll need a bit of TLC.'

'Poor kid.'

They both started at the sound of a door crashing against a wall, followed by footsteps hurtling down the stairs. Tara burst in, tears smudging last night's mascara.

'She's shut down her Facebook page,' she wailed.

'Facebook!' said Mike, thumping his chest with his hand. 'I thought you'd found a dead body in your cupboard.'

'Don't you know what this means?'

'It's social media. It doesn't mean anything.'

'No, Dad! Fuck's sake. First, it means she's been on that page, she's seen all my posts and messages and . . . fucking *pleading* with her to get in touch. She didn't reply with even one word.'

'That's hurtful,' said Diana.

'That page meant she still existed. I could still see photos of her, I could say things to her. I keep it open, whatever else I'm doing. It was there last night. Now it's gone. It's like she's dead.'

Diana could have cried. It was heartbreaking to think of poor Tara, who pretended to be so tough and sassy, leaving offerings on the shrine of her sister's Facebook page.

'C'mon, lovely,' said Mike, holding out his arms, his own eyes red-rimmed. 'Give me a hug.'

Tara allowed herself to be comforted for a few seconds before pulling away again. 'We have to go to Heathrow. We have to meet that flight.' She shrugged her shoulders up and down—a miserable, childish gesture. 'If we pretend everything's normal, maybe everything will *be* normal. She'll just walk into the arrivals hall with Hamish.'

Her parents looked at each other helplessly. They had nothing in their toolkit for dealing with this.

'Please?' begged Tara.

'She's not on that plane,' said Diana. 'We have to face it. She's not coming home.'

·

Hamish phoned that evening. He sounded shaken. He'd expected Cassy to be at Christchurch Airport, he said; couldn't believe it when she didn't turn up. Someone else had been sitting in her seat. It wasn't until he arrived home that he found a brief email from her, explaining that she was staying in New Zealand.

'It's my fault,' he kept saying. 'It's my fault.'

Diana didn't mention Charlotte Someone-double-barrelled. The poor boy sounded quite guilt-ridden enough.

'You're not her keeper,' she said.

'I got a lift five minutes later. Five minutes! Nice couple, plenty of room in their car. If only . . .'

He seemed haunted by the van: the battered white van, full of people who sang and offered tea.

'I wish I'd got in the bloody thing with her,' he groaned.

'Thank goodness you didn't. It wasn't a lift; it was a trap.'

'I'm sorry,' he said. 'Tell Mike, will you? I'm just so sorry.'

Seventeen

Cassy

She and Justin spent most of the next day and night in the meditation room, digging up forgotten memories. Poisonous images: her father's gritted teeth, her mother's cold shoulder; a fist here, a shout there; abandonment, rejection and fear.

Sometime during the early hours of Saturday morning, Justin asked Monika to let Cassy into the office so that she could transfer everything in her bank accounts to Gethsemane. Cassy was tired beyond thought and sickened by her newly unearthed memories. Her happy childhood was a lie. Gethsemane was true.

'None of us own anything here,' Monika said, as she cut up Cassy's bank cards with a pair of scissors. 'Otto and I sold our house, our investments, signed over our pensions. And *pow!*— our stress was gone.'

The computer was on. Everything was ready. At the last moment, Cassy hesitated. 'What if things don't work out for me here?'

'Are you thinking about divorce before you're even married? You have to earn our trust if you're going to become a Watchman.' Monika peered into Cassy's face, frowning. 'Are you sure you *want* to be a Watchman?'

'I'm sure.'

'Well then, do this one last thing. Then it'll be chamomile tea, and snuggle down, and off to sleep. Tomorrow's going to be very special. The children are putting on *Joseph*. We'll have a barbecue.'

Monika's voice was calm and reassuring. Cassy's hands seemed to move by themselves, typing in her bank's address and navigating the security system. Once she'd begun, it felt easy to log into her accounts and transfer everything in them to Gethsemane. *Click, click, click.* Thirty-two thousand pounds. *There.* Now she was free.

●

Joseph and the Amazing Technicolour Dreamcoat was a big success. Rome brought the house down as a laid-back pharaoh; Monty and a gang of other tiny tots played an adorably chaotic flock of sheep. Suva, Malindi and an older girl called Beersheba had created Joseph's rainbow coat by sewing together hundreds of rags. Spirits were high and the audience easy to please.

Cassy stayed behind to help sort out costumes and props. Then she and Aden wrapped their arms around each other as they wandered towards the beach, where barbecue smoke twined over a backdrop of glittering water. One day soon—they didn't yet know when—they'd become Partners. For now, they were in a blissful hinterland. Aden was humming 'Any Dream Will Do'.

'Gets in your head, doesn't it?' he said.

'Tell me about it.'

Spring had melted the snow on Tarawera, and the valley seemed to be smiling; but Cassy had something on her mind.

'Aden?'

'Mm?' He was watching Justin and some children who were paddling in the shallows, hampered by Peter, who cavorted around them.

'How do you feel about Kerala now? I mean . . .' Cassy felt mortified to be raising the subject of his first wife, but she persisted. 'She was a Gethsemane girl. You had three children.

Now you're starting out again with a townie who knows nothing about farming or sustainable living. I'm just wondering whether I should be jealous.'

He sounded bewildered. 'Jealous?'

'I don't want to be battling with the ghost of a perfect woman.'

He stopped walking and turned to take both her hands. For once there was no trace of a smile. 'Kerala and I were only seventeen. Gethsemane was smaller in those early days; there really wasn't anyone else for either of us. We weren't perfect together, but we made the most of it. You, Cassy, are my destiny. It's not comparable in any way.'

'Really?'

'Stop asking, or I'll set Gaza on you.'

They were standing close together, smiling goofily at each other, when Liam appeared.

'Sorry to break up the party,' he said with a chuckle. 'But we need your muscle, Aden. That stage is bloomin' heavy, and it's got to be moved before Dusk Call.'

'Shall I come?' asked Cassy.

'No!' Aden rubbed her back. 'You can't be lifting.'

Cassy watched him go before walking on to where Rome was organising a game of rounders.

'First post, second post, third, fourth!' he yelled, jogging the perimeter of an imaginary circle and dropping jerseys to mark the bases. 'Who's got the gear?'

Malindi came scampering from the direction of the school, clutching a bat and a yellow plastic ball, holding them out to Rome with a grin of pure adoration.

'You're a star, Malindi. Okay—who's bowler for this team? You, Jaipur?' He tossed the ball to Athens' son: the dark-eyed, athletic pin-up of a teenager who'd played Joseph in the musical. 'I'll be backstop, then, if nobody else wants the job. Ah, Cassy! Please will you keep the score for us?'

The batting team sat on the grass to wait their turns, and Cassy lazed with them. Suva and Malindi were giggling about

Jaipur, who they both thought was 'lovely'—though Malindi thought Rome was '*really* lovely'.

The lovely Jaipur began the game by bowling to a four-year-old called Zanzibar. She could barely lift the bat and swung about three seconds too late.

'Aw,' said Malindi, sounding motherly. 'Zanzi's such a cute little button.'

Jaipur came and stood within arm's length of the tiny batter.

'Look at the ball, Zanzi,' he said quietly. 'Don't take your eyes off it. That's right. Ready?'

She planted her feet wide apart, eyeing the ball as though it were made of gold. Jaipur aimed it right at her bat, so that she couldn't miss. There was a *tock* of plastic on wood before the ball plopped onto the grass a couple of feet away, and both teams cheered. Zanzibar stood with a dazed smile, drinking in the applause.

'Now you have to run,' explained Jaipur.

Everyone yelled, *Run! Run, Zanzi!*, but she didn't move.

'C'mon, little sis,' said Rome. Abandoning his duties as backstop, he took the child's hand and trotted alongside her. He was more than twice her height and had to stoop as they ran. Meanwhile the fielding team gamely pretended to lose the ball among some cabbage trees until Zanzibar was safely home.

'Who's Zanzibar's mum?' asked Cassy.

'Skye,' said Malindi.

Cassy had seen Skye out at the colourful beehives, wielding a smoke box while she collected honey. She was always singing under her breath; bright eyes in a thin face.

'Beekeeper Skye? She's just a child herself.'

'I think she's about twenty,' said Suva, adding casually, 'Justin rescued her from being a prostitute. This man was making her do horrible things.'

'Poor girl,' said Cassy. It didn't seem the sort of discussion she should be having with two eleven-year-olds, so she dropped the subject.

One by one, the batters took their turns while Cassy kept score in her head. She lay on her back and looked up at the sun, idly wondering what time it was. Then—abruptly—she sat up.

It's Imogen's wedding day.

That same sun would soon be shining through her friend's bedroom window. She, Becca and Cassy had planned to share a bottle of bubbly while they got ready. They'd dance around to music as they did one another's hair. It would have been fun. What kind of a bridesmaid doesn't even get in touch on the wedding day?

'Feeling okay?' asked Suva, peering at her anxiously.

'I have to go to the office.'

'Why?'

'To contact my friend. She's getting married today! How could I have forgotten?'

'Um . . .' Suva was blinking rapidly. 'Have the Companions said you can do that?'

'Surely I don't need permission?'

'They have the office key,' said Suva, leaping up and brushing grass off her knees. 'I'll go and ask.'

'Shall I come?'

'No. Stay here.'

And she was gone—whirling down the hill as though her life depended upon it. Cassy watched the stick-thin figure disappear among a crowd of people on the beach. Until now it had felt liberating not to be bothered with communication and technology, but today she longed for a smart phone and a few bars of signal. Then Zanzibar plonked herself down, stuck out her feet and asked Cassy if she thought she had funny toes.

The batting team was all out when Justin came strolling up. Rome threw him the bat. 'You're in, old man!'

'Okay,' growled Justin, crouching like an ace at Wimbledon. 'Do your worst, Jaipur.'

Cassy had never seen Justin so playful. He smashed the ball up the hill, prancing around the circle of jerseys while the fielding team scrabbled to shake it from the clutches of a kowhai tree. He took clownish steps, pretending to be riding a bicycle—turned and jogged backwards on his long legs—then tiptoed with his arms up, like a tall, thin ballerina. Peter bounded beside him, and even the dog seemed to be laughing. Justin finally put on a turn of speed when he saw that Rome had the ball and was about to hurl it at fourth post.

That last-moment sprint was a second too late. The ball hit the jersey—Rome and Jaipur both screamed, *Gotcha!*—and the fielding team did a victory dance.

'Betrayed!' cried Justin, as he trotted back to Cassy. 'By my own son!'

'You did it on purpose.'

'Who, me?' He took her arm. 'Come for a walk?'

It was an honour to have him to herself. Everyone in Gethsemane wanted a piece of this man, and he'd given her so much already. They skirted the beach and made their way onto the headland, climbing among the wooden crosses.

'They don't have names on them,' said Cassy.

'No. They're here to mark the life of a Watchman as part of the whole, not as an individual. But I know each one. This,' said Justin, gently laying his hand on a cross, 'was for a lady called Barbara Svenson. She and her husband gave this land to Gethsemane, and died here.'

The little hill wasn't high, but it was steep. Peter galloped to the top and back three times before Cassy and Justin had reached halfway.

'I hear you're worried about your friend's wedding,' said Justin.

Cassy was embarrassed, but grateful to Suva for telling him, not one of the Companions. Justin was a safe haven.

'I am. Imogen.' She paused for breath, her hands pressing into her sides. 'I was meant to be a bridesmaid. I feel awful about it! She'll be really upset. I thought if I could phone, wish her luck, say sorry . . .'

Justin sighed. 'But, Cassy, you've made your decision. You've chosen Gethsemane. In a week's time you're going to become a Watchman.'

'I am.'

'And when you made that choice, you knew what it meant, didn't you? All of us have given up our Outside lives. Narcissism and negativity creep in from the world. We work hard to keep them out.'

Cassy felt crushed. 'I know. Sorry.'

He'd begun to smile. 'Still. This is important to you. So give me Imogen's address, and your message, and we'll have flowers—chocolates, maybe?—delivered today.'

'Justin, that's brilliant! Thank you! If I could get into the safe and grab my credit card . . .'

'No, no.' He waved his hand, dismissing her offer. 'You haven't got one any more, remember? Gethsemane will foot the bill. It's our gift to you.'

She tried to thank him again, but he wouldn't hear of it.

'No more thanks,' he said. 'But from now on, you have to let go of your past.'

They'd reached the highest point of the headland. A single weathered cross commanded a view of all Gethsemane. Below them, clear water washed against a rocky outcrop. They gazed at the ridges and creases of hills, cloaked in bush and pine forest. The volcano crouched like a sphinx, guarding the lake. Cassy could hear the children playing rounders, the chatter of the picnic. *This is my home*, she thought.

'Will I have a new name?' she asked. 'When I become a Watchman?'

'Of course.'

'Who will I be?'

Eighteen

The rose-bright dawn. A chorus of birdsong. Mount Tarawera seemed to blush as the rising sun caressed its shoulders.

Her friends had come to wake her during the night, and help her to get ready. It had been fun, like the pre-wedding morning she might have shared with Becca and Imogen. During this time, she'd given up the last of her possessions: her clothes, her backpack, her medicine kit, toiletries and jewellery; even a pendant Hamish had given her. Everything was taken away. She had nothing except the clothes she stood up in and her walking boots. In the early hours of the morning, Bali cut her hair. Cassy relaxed into something close to sleep as she listened to the hungry sound of the scissors and watched her hair fall in dark swathes across the wooden boards. She felt light and unencumbered. That was her vanity being sloughed away; that was the shallow ambitions of her parents. Her Outside family was toxic; her Gethsemane family was pure and good.

All of Gethsemane sang in harmony as they walked with her in a procession towards the lake, led by Otto's flute. Monika had explained what to expect of this ceremony: what questions Cassy would be asked and what answers she should give. Cassy didn't understand every word, but it seemed far less off-the-wall than the complex rituals of her paternal grandparents' Catholicism. *Smells and bells*, her father called it. She and Mike had stifled giggles at Yvette's baby's christening, when the priest started thundering away about Satan, prince of darkness—rolling his rrr's while sweeping about in an embroidered robe.

Justin stood alone on the shore. No embroidered robe. Just himself, waiting for her. He took her hands and led her out until they were waist-deep in water. She gasped as the icy cold punched the air from her lungs, but he seemed oblivious. Many of her friends waded in too, while others gathered on the beach and jetty.

Aden and Suva stood on either side of Cassy: her Partner-to-be, her daughter-to-be. Bali, Paris and Rome were nearby. Three black swans drifted out of the morning mist, pale light glinting on their feathers.

Justin bent his head. 'Ready?' he asked quietly.

'Ready.'

'No stubbed toe?'

'I've got better at negotiating the rocks.'

He laughed. He seemed excited today, and youthful. He straightened up, raising his voice. 'Cassy! For the last time, I call you "Cassy". Do you ask to join us, and make Gethsemane your family?'

'Yes! I ask to join you.'

'Will you make yourself nothing? Will you follow the Way?'

'I will make myself nothing and follow the Way.'

'Will you keep the Vigil, and look towards the Last Day?'

'I will keep the Vigil, and look towards the Last Day.'

'Then we welcome you.' He laid his hands on her shoulders. She felt their weight. 'At sunrise, your life will begin.'

The world held its breath. Gusts skipped across the surface of the lake, ruffling Justin's hair. Then—quite suddenly—a point of light was gleaming above the volcano. It swelled and flamed, tipping gold into the valley.

Justin smiled. 'Goodbye, Cassy!'

She'd been taught what to do next. Stretching her arms wide, she fell straight back into the water. She felt hands pushing her under.

The cold. The incredible cold. It gripped her brain; it stunned her body. She made herself breathe out, releasing silvery bubbles of air as the hands held her far beneath the surface. She lay with her eyes open, a visitor to this alien world, the freezing gloom and dancing streaks of light. The water was purifying. It was giving her new life. Above her, the surface looked like shattered glass with brilliance beyond. As the seconds passed, her lungs began to scream for oxygen. She felt the first stirring of panic, and willed herself not to struggle. Perhaps this was the end for her? Perhaps she'd failed in some way, and the hands would hold her under the water until she died.

Then they lifted, and she was up and out, through the shattered glass and into the world of air and light. She was laughing, gasping and shivering; light-headed with cold and the taste of death, exhilarated by the nearness of God.

Justin's triumphant shout skimmed across the water, all the way to the mountain and back.

'Welcome, Cairo!' he cried.

Aden and Suva were embracing her; so was Rome, so were Paris and Bali, swiftly followed by Liam and Otto and Malindi and . . . too many for her to take in. As she splashed back to the beach, Monika came hurrying to meet her, carrying towels. They felt luxurious, warm as hot water bottles.

'I kept them in the bread oven. Now—quickly—come with us,' the doctor chivvied. 'We've got a bath for you!'

Some of the women ran with her up the hill and into the small meditation room. The stove was lit. A tub stood beside it, filled and steaming.

'Take off your clothes, give them to me,' said Monika, holding out her hand.

'But everyone got wet, not just me.'

'Chop chop! In you get.'

Cairo obeyed, lowering herself into the delicious heat. 'I haven't got any dry things to put on.'

'D'you imagine we hadn't thought of that? Look beside the stove! There are your new clothes. See? Everything you need, waiting for you.'

And so it was that the newest recruit arrived in the *whare kai*, to be greeted by all of the community. She was wearing a navy blue dress and a knitted jersey, and her hair had been cut very short. She felt as though she was shining. This was the most important day of her life.

She'd come home.

Nineteen

Diana

'I've had a letter from Cassy,' said Joyce, taking a piece of paper out of her novel. 'Came in the post.'

Diana sank onto the edge of the bed, feeling for the crocheted blanket with the palm of her hand. She'd lied like a flatfish every time her mother asked for news. She lied to almost everyone, including herself.

Turning up at Imogen's wedding had felt like acting in a strange, deceitful play. Tara had cried off; said she wasn't going to pretend everything was okay when everything was fucking awful. But Diana and Mike flew the flag, chortled through embarrassing speeches, toasted the happy couple. They even took photos of the cake-cutting—Imogen glowing, Jack imitating a rabbit in the headlights—'to send to Cassy'.

Imogen and Jack had just begun their first dance when Diana felt a hand on her knee. Mike had left his chair and was squatting beside hers. There was sweat on his forehead.

'Please can we go?' he asked.

She nodded fervently, grabbing her handbag. They slid away like thieves—through a back door, without saying goodbye to anyone—and drove home in silence.

Joyce was spreading out the letter. One of the carers had

parked her wheeled table so that it stretched over her lap. She kept her battle equipment on its formica surface: glasses, a book of crosswords, a biro and a large-print crime novel with a blood-spattered gun on the cover.

'When were you going to tell me?' she asked accusingly.

'I hoped I'd never have to.' Diana's gaze was riveted on Cassy's scruffy, familiar handwriting. 'Can I read it? What does she say?'

'She says she's getting married.'

Diana felt her stomach drop away.

'A lovely man.' Joyce put on her glasses. 'Bit older. In his thirties. A farmer. He was the driver of the van that picked her up.'

'Oh my God. So old! She must have been forced into it.'

'Rubbish. Your father had a good ten years on me.'

'But Dad was . . .' Diana couldn't take it in. 'They won't be actually, legally married, will they?'

'Maybe it's just to get a visa.' Joyce held out the letter. 'Marriages can be ended, Diana. This isn't the worst thing that could have happened to her, not by a long chalk.'

Diana scanned through Cassy's ramblings. If she'd hoped to learn something new, she was disappointed. Apart from the bombshell about her impending marriage, Cassy was churning out the same old script.

> . . . *no negativity, only love. Nobody's ever lonely . . . live sustainably and simply. At first I missed the mod cons but I've got used to it now, and I'm so much happier for not being crouched over a screen . . . the hours I wasted! We have a shared goal, which is to take care of this planet and of one another . . . encounter with God . . . love . . . love . . . love . . .*

Blah, blah, blah, thought Diana. *The salesman's spiel. I've heard it all before.*

One line stood out: *We're led by an amazing man called Justin Calvin—he has more love in his little finger than most people ever feel in their whole lives.*

The letter was signed *Lots of love, C,* with three kisses.

'Justin Calvin,' said Diana. 'Justin Calvin. Who the heck is Justin Calvin?'

'A very loving man, apparently. Perhaps you should take that at face value.'

'He's bewitched her! Him and his weird acolytes.'

'She's made a decision,' said Joyce, reaching out her hand to take the letter back. 'You may disagree with that decision, but she's made it. She's found people who care about the same things she does. She's happy. I've written to congratulate her. They use a post office box.'

Diana passed the letter back and watched as Joyce stashed it away. Her mind was in freefall.

'No,' she said suddenly. She got up off the bed, stooping to straighten the blanket. 'No. No! This is not going to happen to our family. You hear me? It's *not* going to happen.'

'Don't do anything silly.'

'That's the pot calling the kettle black. You and Cassy have the monopoly on doing silly things.'

She was heading for the door, planning to slam it behind her. She wanted to make the whole place shake. Cassy and Joyce were in league together—they held the moral high ground because they *cared*. She was the shallow conformist who didn't care enough to abandon her family.

'Are you flouncing off?' asked Joyce.

Diana had one hand on the handle. 'D'you need anything?' she asked, with a coldness that demanded the answer 'no'.

'Some more socks would be nice. I keep putting holes in them.'

'That's because of your toenails. I wish you'd let me . . . oh, never mind. Socks. God. Okay, I'll get some.'

'Help me move this bloody thing,' Joyce said, pushing at her table. 'I want to get up.'

Diana almost pretended she hadn't heard. Maybe, just this once, *she* could be the one to walk away. Sighing, she turned back, moved the table aside and lifted her frail mother to her feet.

'There you go. D'you need to use the bathroom?'

Joyce was balancing with one hand on the arm of her chair. 'Yes. But first, I want to give you a hug.'

•

Poor Mike. The blood drained from his face and left him white—ghost-white, as though she'd shaken a tub of flour over his head.

'My girl?' he whispered. 'Getting married?'

'I think it's time we went to find her.'

'Is this human trafficking? Is she a sex slave?'

'I don't know, but we have to do something. I've been racking my brains to think of someone who could hold the fort at the arts centre. Fiona's taken her grandkids to Tenerife.'

'I'll go alone.' Mike brought up the work diary on his phone. 'I can leave the day after tomorrow, if I call in some favours.'

'I've got to come.'

He shook his head. 'You can't get away soon enough, and every day could be crucial! Also, it'll be rough on Tara if we both go. This place obviously has some magnetic power, like a black hole. People get sucked in.'

Diana realised she'd begun to gnaw at her nails, and clasped her hands in her lap. 'Could we wait, maybe? Next month . . .'

'We've already dithered too long. We need to stop this farcical marriage.'

They talked for half an hour, batting the subject around and around. Diana made some phone calls, trying to find cover at work, but failed. In the end she agreed to let him go alone.

'Right then,' he muttered, pulling a credit card out of his wallet. 'Finally, I get to *do* something.'

'I hope this isn't a mistake.' She was biting her nails again. 'They've been one step ahead of us all along.'

'What have we got to lose?'

•

Heathrow again. Diana stopped at the drop-off zone and got out of the car while Mike took his bag from the boot.

'I wish I was coming with you,' she said.

'*I* wish you were.' He was standing with both feet together and his back very straight: a soldier on parade, ready to move out. She sensed his nervous energy.

'Good luck.' She kissed him, and they held each other for a last moment.

'I'll bring her home,' he said. 'I promise.'

Twenty

Cairo

She was barefoot, wearing a crimson dress with shoestring straps, its bodice embroidered with brilliant native birds. Justin was performing another ceremony on the lakeshore. This time, it was to join Aden and Cairo as Partners in the Watch.

She'd been overwhelmed when Bali and Suva brought the dress to show her.

'I embroidered this one, it took me hours and hours,' said Suva, proudly touching a tui among rata blossoms. 'Bali did this guy—' pointing to a bellbird '—Monika did this lovely kereru . . . and d'you see the pukekos?'

'They're gorgeous.'

'I know! Malindi and Rome sewed them. Um . . . oh yes, these tiny green riflemen were Kazan and Hana. Oh! See the little ruru? The morepork?' She laid a reverential hand on New Zealand's native owl. 'Justin did that!'

'*Justin?*'

'Yes!' Suva was bubbling over. 'It took him two whole days. He did nothing else all that time. He really loves you.'

The needlework was exquisite. Cairo imagined the sumptuous garment in some smart boutique, with a price tag of a thousand pounds.

'We had help,' said Bali. 'Beersheba and Valencia made the dress, and fixed up our mistakes.'

On the morning of the ceremony, Cairo secretly wished there were a proper mirror in Gethsemane—or, better still, a camera. She wanted to see how she looked on her wedding day. The pregnancy wasn't obvious yet, and the nausea had stopped, but she was sure her body had changed.

'Bustier than ever,' she muttered, squinting down at herself. 'Reckon I'm a double D.'

'You look like a princess,' said Suva, who was pinning flowers into her hair.

'So beautiful,' whispered Aden, when he took her hand to walk with her down the slope to where Justin stood waiting.

The whole community celebrated. The organisation was immaculate, as it always was in Gethsemane. Otto was on the case: Otto, the almost-invisible manager. He'd been zipping around for days, carrying lists and rosters and schedules. Cairo had developed her own theory about the Companions: Liam was the affable frontman; Gaza the muscle; Kyoto the loyal jack-of-all-trades; and Monika the shrewd adviser. Otto made everything run smoothly.

Seoul and his kitchen team produced a Pacific Island feast. As a wedding present, the community gave Aden and Cairo a luxurious blanket, soft and dark brown, knitted with enormous stitches. The band played jazz, and Gethsemane jived the hours away to syncopated rhythms—everyone, including the very old and very young. Justin was the life and soul of the party. He must have danced with every woman or girl—and some of the men—in the place. Cairo was beginning to flag when she saw that he'd leaped up onto a table and was holding out his arms for quiet.

'It's time for you two to set sail,' he said, smiling at Cairo. 'I'm told that your vessel is ready and waiting.'

There was no sneaking out. The raucous crowd escorted the newlyweds down the hill, carrying lanterns. A rowing boat was moored at the jetty, loaded with provisions for two days at Kereru Cove.

'In you hop,' ordered Justin, holding up a lantern. Cairo hitched up the lace skirt of her dress and scrambled down, followed by Aden. The boat rocked alarmingly, making her laugh.

It wasn't the wedding, nor the send-off, nor the bridegroom, nor the honeymoon she'd dreamed of when she was a little girl. It certainly wasn't what her parents would have imagined. *Poor Mum. No mother-of-the-bride outfit, no sobbing in the front row.* There would be a formality later, in a registry office—to help Cairo's application for permanent residence—but this was the real marriage. Cairo had just promised her life to a man she barely knew, and her going-away vehicle was a rocking rowing boat.

'One each?' suggested Aden, picking up an oar.

'Yep! I bet we end up rowing round and round in circles.'

Justin untied the painter and threw it down to them.

'May the Infinite Power watch over you,' he called, 'this night and always.'

Their first few strokes were chaotic, provoking catcalls from the crowd on the shore. But they tried again, and found a rhythm. The boat was moving out of Justin's lantern light when Cairo heard something that made the hairs stand up on the backs of her arms.

'Aden!' she whispered. 'Listen.'

It sounded like an enchantment. They shipped their oars as the flute's liquid voice cried to them across the water: 'The Skye Boat Song'.

A hundred voices belted out the chorus: *Speed, bonnie boat, like a bird on the wing, Onward! The sailors cry.* A fair amount of Gethsemane wine had been consumed that night, which was probably why the singing was more enthusiastic than tuneful. Cairo felt tears on her cheeks.

'Time to go?' asked Aden.

She nodded, picking up her oar. She sensed the movement of his body, close beside hers, and smiled. Soon the lantern lights were swallowed by the night.

•

She woke in darkness, roused by the sorrowful cry of a ruru. It called again, and then again, as though searching for something lost.

The rowers had been guided into Kereru Cove by the glowing embers of a fire on the pumice sand.

'Who's done all this for us?' asked Cairo, as they waded in the warm water, hauling the boat onto the beach.

'Good fairies.'

The fire was a heap of embers, but firewood had been stacked close by. Aden blew the flames into life while Cairo fetched some blankets from the hut, exclaiming at all the trouble someone had gone to. The *whare* had been cleaned, the bed made up and flowers arranged in jars. There were even chocolates on the pillows.

When she came back, Aden was opening a bottle.

'They've left us the best wine,' he said, filling two clay cups. 'Blackberry! Here you are.'

They knelt facing each other. Firelight danced on the embroidered birds, bringing them to life. Cairo felt exultant.

'Look at that,' she said, gazing at the raging fire of the Milky Way. 'There never was such a sky.'

'A firework display, in honour of you.'

'Well yes, of course.' She chuckled. 'The universe is all about me.'

He held his cup to hers, with that rueful smile that made her want to tear his clothes off.

'To my hitchhiker.'

'To my getaway driver.'

She downed the wine, delighting in the tang of it. Then she let the cup roll away across the sand. 'So the waiting's over?'

'Oh yes. Definitely.'

She ran her fingers beneath the shoestring straps of her dress. First on one side, then on the other, she slid them off her shoulders. The embroidered bodice fell to her waist.

'Well,' she murmured as they tumbled together onto the blankets. 'The best things come to those who wait.'

•

The ruru cried again. She imagined the owl, sharp-eyed and hunting in the bush. The air was glass-clear and profoundly still, so that even the giant ferns seemed frozen. Tomorrow they'd stroll along the forest path to bathe in the pools, and this time they'd have the place to themselves.

Aden's arms were around her. She pressed her mouth to his neck, feeling the rhythm of his pulse under her lips, inhaling the faint musk of his skin. Then—unable to resist—she brushed her lips against his. He stirred, and she felt his arms tighten. For a long time she lay still, luxuriating in the memory of the past few hours.

The Milky Way had surely never been so immense, so dazzlingly bright. It was pulsing, exploding, singing with a billion voices. Orion seemed to salute her as he strode through the sky.

'Thank you,' she whispered to the Infinite.

One of the stars broke free and glided across the vault. Cairo turned her head, watching the meteor arcing down, and down, towards the dark bulk of Tarawera, until it disappeared into nothing.

Twenty-one

Diana

Mike sounded surprisingly alert for someone who'd just travelled around the world.

'No jet lag?' asked Diana. She'd suffered through a sleepless night and was still in her dressing-gown.

'I think I'm running on adrenaline. It's been hard to track these people down.'

'Under the radar.'

'Mm . . . and can you believe this? They're not accessible by road!'

'How then? On foot?'

'I've found a bloke with a boat. He says he knows where they are. He's taking me first thing tomorrow. Just think, Diana . . . in a few hours' time I'll have seen Cassy. Hopefully I'll be bringing her out.'

Diana switched the phone to her other ear. 'That would be wonderful. But if you could even check she's all right . . .'

'I'm not leaving without her.'

Mike was keyed up. She could hear it in the heaviness of his breathing, the jagged excitement of his speech patterns. She imagined him pacing his motel room, mussing up his hair. He couldn't stand inaction. These past weeks had been torture for him.

He'd thought about nothing but rescuing Cassy, and now he was so close. *So* close.

'This time tomorrow,' he said, 'she'll be out.'

Diana shut her eyes and imagined Cassy standing at the front door. It had become a vivid, hallowed image, as close to prayer as she'd ever come. Opening her eyes again, she saw that Tara had wandered into the kitchen with bed hair and fluffy slippers.

Dad? she mouthed, and Diana nodded.

Mike was still giving himself a pep talk, like a coach before a big match. He'd *insist* on seeing Cassy. He *wouldn't* take no for an answer from those bastards.

'And as soon as I've got her out, I'll head for Auckland.'

'Give her a kiss from me.'

'I will.'

'Tell her I love her.'

'Me too,' called Tara, pressing her palms together. 'Tell my sister to get back here. Pronto.'

●

When the post arrived, two letters for Cassy lay among the charitable appeals and adverts for takeaway pizza. Bank statements, by the look of them. Diana carried them into the kitchen.

'Think I can open these?' she asked, holding up the letters. 'They're confidential.'

'Duh!' Tara made a *you-are-an-imbecile* face. 'Seriously, Mum? Gimme, gimme.'

She held out her hand. Seconds later, final statements were fluttering onto the kitchen table.

'*Shit*,' said Tara, staring. 'Tell me this doesn't mean what I think it means.'

All the inheritance—*whoosh*. Gone. All the accounts were closed, even the credit card. It was as though Cassy was trying to erase herself from history.

'She's crazy,' said Tara. 'She's . . . oh my God. How's she living, with no money?'

They passed the hours in a state of nervy excitement, constantly checking the time in New Zealand. They even allowed themselves to hope. After all, Mike was over there. He'd see Cassy. He'd fix everything.

'He'll be with her now, won't he?' Tara kept saying. 'They should be on their way home. Shall we call him?'

So they tried Mike's number, but he didn't answer. Perhaps he too had disappeared into the black hole.

They jumped every time the phone rang. First it was Joyce, eager for news; then Mike's brother Robert, who wanted to moan about his divorce; then one of Cassy's flatmates from Durham. She'd heard a rumour that Cassy wasn't coming back; was it true, and if so, why? Should they find someone else to cover the rent?

'I've never felt so tempted to go into a church in my life,' said Diana, as she and Tara tried to eat last night's chicken tikka. 'Light a candle. Maybe even . . .'

'Pray?'

'Well. You know.'

'Been there, done that. Don't bother. It doesn't work.'

Tara dumped her plate in the dishwasher, reached into her schoolbag and pulled out her laptop. 'We need more info. I bet I can dig up some dirt on Gethsemane.'

It was better than doing nothing. Tara began to wade through the thousands of hits that came up when she searched *Gethsemane New Zealand,* complaining about the fact that there was a country music band and several gardens with the same name. Meanwhile Diana researched destructive cults, and new religions, and old religions, and pyramid selling, and self-help groups that went too far. It wasn't reassuring.

I lost my son to the Moonies.

Scientology took thirty years of my life.

We had to kidnap my brother from the Family of Heaven.

'I can't believe this is going on,' she said. 'There's a whole industry built around the manipulation of minds.'

'Isn't that called school?'

'Listen . . .' Diana read out a harrowing account by a mother who'd lost her son to an organisation that claimed to be a church. *They used the internet as their fishing grounds. They spread their nets and Danny was caught. He used to spend hours shut away in his room, on his computer. From being a warm, loving boy he became this stranger who wouldn't speak to us. In the end he left home. He works for them now, collecting money on the streets.*

Pesky had wandered in. Finding his food bowl empty, he began to strut up and down Diana's keyboard.

'Oh, all right,' she said, getting to her feet and opening the fridge. 'You won't starve, Mr Bossy. It's *your* mistress we're trying to rescue.'

'What's that leader bloke's name again?' asked Tara.

'Calvin. Justin Calvin.'

Tara said the name under her breath as she typed.

'Genius! Look at this, Mum.'

It was a blog from 2009, written by someone who called himself Ian the Sparky—an electrician from Brisbane who'd gone travelling. It consisted mainly of selfies of a bald man standing beside landmarks around Australia and New Zealand.

Then this:

Hi all, sorry for the long time with no posts. I've just spent 3 weeks wwoofing for the Gethsemane community at Lake Tarawera. I was upgrading their solar power system.

They're awesome people, it's a fantastic location and I learned a lot about permaculture, which was why I went in the first place. Their leader's called Justin Calvin. What an amazing man. He was in prison himself once, and he's passionate about giving everyone a second, third or fourth chance. So he goes and collects people who're in trouble, and brings them back to turn their lives around. I can honestly say I've never met anyone like him.

They wanted me to stay, but in the end it wasn't for me. One or two things grated. One example of this was that everyone gets given a new name by Justin. He calls them after geographical locations, so people have names like Athens, Berlin, Gaza etc. etc. This just felt too weird. Also, the longer I stayed, the more I got the feeling there's a religious thing going on. Everyone wears the same clothes and the women all have short hair, and every time a bell rings they all troop off to a kind of church.

It's been a mind-blowing experience and I'll never forget it, but 3 weeks was long enough so here I am in Wellington. Happy to be back in the real world. Next stop Rarotonga— got my grass skirt on!!!

'Does that mean Cassy has a new name?' asked Tara.

'Gosh, I hope not.'

Tara squinted thoughtfully at Ian's photo. 'He could leave whenever he wanted. And this Justin sounds like a good person.'

'Yes, that's reassuring,' said Diana, with more conviction than she felt. 'I expect we'll hear from Dad soon.'

•

Midnight found mother and daughter in a state of nervous exhaustion, watching rubbish on television and working their way through a packet of chocolate biscuits. Tara was lying with her head on Diana's lap, something she hadn't done for years.

'He'd phone if he'd got her out, right?' she asked.

'He would. He will.'

'Try and call him again?' Tara fetched the phone and handed it to Diana. 'Can't do any harm.'

This time, Mike did answer. He sounded agitated.

'I'm in the police station,' he said.

'Did you see Cassy?'

'Never got anywhere near her. I bet I'm not the first angry father to turn up there. I hadn't even got off the jetty when a reception committee arrived. Smiling Gestapo. Two guys, and a blonde witch with the coldest eyes I've ever seen—Christ, I wouldn't want to meet her on a dark night. They had a couple of heavies standing guard.'

'But you asked for Cassy?'

'They said she's not here. I said fine, I'll wait. The White Witch said she doesn't want to see you, and you're trespassing. They frogmarched me back to the boat. I think they'd have thrown me off if I hadn't gone quietly.'

'Oh, Mike. That must have—'

'So I've walked into the police station and said I want to report a kidnapping. I think I've finally managed to stir things up. They'll go and see her.'

She told him about the bank statements and heard him swear under his breath. 'It's *all* gone?'

'Every penny. She can't even buy a bus ticket.'

Tara was listening to Diana's end of the conversation with reddening eyes. Diana reached along the sofa to touch her ear.

'It's okay,' she whispered. 'Dad's sending in the heavies.'

Twenty-two

Cairo

'Policemen?' cried Cairo. '*Here?*'

They'd been so happy as they rowed home. Their short honeymoon had been a time of glorious intensity, as though they'd jammed two years' courtship into two days. Aden had only to touch Cairo, or even look at her, and she felt energised. She seemed to have the same effect upon him.

Their homecoming was meant to be triumphant: the day their family life began. They'd hoped to find Suva waiting for them, but they hadn't expected her to be hysterical, tears on her freckled cheeks. She threw herself against Aden's chest as soon as he stepped onto the jetty.

'They came in that boat,' she gasped, pointing at a launch.

'Shh.' Aden dipped his head to look into her face. 'It's okay. Where are they now?'

'Monika invited them into the *whare kai*. She's giving them tea. They say they won't leave till they've seen Cairo, because her dad's made a complaint.'

'You've done really well,' said Aden. 'Just run back and tell them she's on her way.'

The child pelted up the slope towards the kitchen block, arms held out for balance. Cairo watched with sick anxiety. This news was a gunshot, tearing through the perfection of the day. Their homecoming—their *home*—had been violated.

'The Companions will be furious,' she said. 'I've brought the police right into Gethsemane!'

'Shh.' He put his arms around her, and they rocked together. 'Justin will already know they're here. He always knows. He won't let anything go wrong.'

For the first time, she felt as though pregnancy was slowing her down. Her lungs felt compressed. As they were climbing the steps onto the porch of the *whare kai*, she stopped to catch her breath.

'I feel so ashamed,' she whispered.

'This isn't your fault. And Gethsemane has nothing to hide.'

The two men were sitting at a refectory table but got to their feet when Cairo appeared. They didn't belong here, with their stab-proof vests and radios. They were aliens from another world.

'Cassandra Howells?' That was the older of the two: a balding giant with a quiet voice.

'I prefer to be known as Cairo. My parents sent you, didn't they?'

'Well, you can understand why they're concerned.'

'Not really.'

They introduced themselves as Senior Constables Rua O'Connell and Tony Smith. Then they noticed Aden.

'Mind if you wait outside, sir?'

'*I* mind,' said Cairo. 'This is Aden. My husband. We're just back from our honeymoon.'

'Congratulations,' said the older one, O'Connell. 'All the same, if you would, Aden? Just so there's no suggestion of coercion.'

Aden looked at Cairo. 'I'll be on the porch. Call if you need me.'

Meanwhile Monika was bustling around, making herself pleasant, plying the unwelcome visitors with tea. She seemed tiny and wholesome and slightly doddery, which might have been why nobody asked her to leave.

The officers pulled notebooks from their pockets. *Sorry to bother you*, they said. *Just a few things we need to clear up.* They asked innocuous questions at first. When had Cairo arrived, and in what capacity? Then O'Connell came out with it.

'Can I just ask . . . are you here of your own free will?'

'Of course I am.'

He coughed gently. 'If I could put it another way: do you feel safe?'

'Yes, I feel safe. I *am* safe.'

'Your dad disagrees.'

'He can't accept that I'm an adult. Does he think I've been kidnapped or something?' Cairo read their expressions and saw that she'd hit the nail on the head. 'Ridiculous. He's wasting your time.'

O'Connell stole a glance at his notebook. 'He says you've handed over a fortune.'

'It was my money.'

'So it's true?'

'Yes, yes, yes.' She was rolling her eyes. 'God, this obsession with money! I didn't need it, so I gave it away to a good cause— you'd think they'd be proud of me.'

'He reckons you've been brainwashed.'

'I know he does.'

'Why would he think that?'

'Because he's a control freak. He thinks anyone who doesn't agree with him must have been brainwashed. Look, I'm not a fool. I'm an educated, adult woman. I've found a new life here, I love my husband and I've chosen to stay. I have a right to do that.'

'Okay,' said O'Connell, and he shut his notebook. 'So just to confirm: you're definitely not asking us for any help?'

'Definitely not! I'm sorry. You've been sent on a wild-goose chase.'

'Not to worry.' He glanced curiously around the kitchen. 'Makes a change. Never been on this property before.'

The other officer didn't seem happy to leave it there.

'There's something you might not have taken into account,' he began, laying hairy forearms on the table. 'Are you aware that your father was here yesterday?'

Cairo stared. 'Here? You mean . . .'

'He only got as far as the jetty.'

Dad in Gethsemane? No, no. He can't have been. The walls had dropped away. Her father had looked into her world, and she had nowhere left to hide.

'They didn't tell you?' asked Smith, glancing meaningfully over his shoulder at Monika. 'Came all the way from Britain to find you. I wonder why nobody's thought to mention it?'

'Cairo returned from her honeymoon twenty minutes ago,' said Monika, who was standing behind the men, drying cups. 'She was at a cabin accessible only by boat. She couldn't be contacted.' As she spoke, Monika met Cairo's eye. Neither of them mentioned the fact that Kereru Cove was only forty minutes' walk along a bush path.

Dad was here. Dad was in my home. He's found me.

Smith pressed his point. 'There was quite an altercation, apparently.'

'Indeed there was!' snapped Monika, wielding her tea towel with offended little jabs. 'That man should be ashamed of his performance! He could be heard for miles around, shouting and swearing. He even offered violence to my husband, who is over seventy years old.'

'He threatened Otto?' asked Cairo.

'And Gaza. It was nasty.'

'Okay, okay.' O'Connell held up his hands. 'Look, whatever the rights and wrongs, this man's travelled the whole way around the world to see you. He's in Rotorua at this very moment. We can take you back with us right now. Don't you at least owe him ten minutes?'

'Um . . .' Cairo glanced at Monika, who gave a small shake of her head. 'No. I can't do that.'

'Can I ask why not?'

'He can be very controlling. Very manipulative. He could do a lot of damage in ten minutes.'

O'Connell sighed. 'I just feel sorry for the poor bloke.'

'Poor bloke?' echoed Monika, fixing the officer with an indignant glare. 'Poor *bloke*? Don't you have any training in dealing with the victims of family violence? Do you understand what you're doing? You're asking this woman—this *pregnant* woman, by the way—to face the abuser she fled. He's pursued her all around the world. It's sinister. It's threatening. And you call him a *poor bloke*?'

Cairo felt as though her head was being pressed in a vice. She wanted to run outside, grab Aden and flee to the sanctuary of Kereru Cove.

Monika slid quietly onto the bench beside her.

'Hey there,' she said, patting Cairo's hand. 'Don't you think it might help if the authorities knew what he's like?'

'I just wish he'd leave me alone.'

'I know. So tell them.'

Cairo touched the table with her forefinger, tracing a swirl in the grain of the wood. She tried to recall Justin's reassuring presence, as he'd led her through the catacomb of buried memories. He'd helped her to open the locked doors and look into the darkness. She listened for his voice. He would know what she should do.

'Justin wants this,' whispered Monika.

It was a direct order.

Cairo raised her eyes and looked squarely at the visitors.

'There are some things I'd like to put on record,' she said. 'Just so you know. Just in case he ever comes back.'

Twenty-three

Diana

She met him at Heathrow. Among the bustling stream of travellers, he stood out as utterly defeated, limping home from the battlefield.

'I'm sorry,' he said. 'I've failed.'

She wrapped her arms around him. Then she whispered, *Come on*, took his bag and steered him towards the car park.

At first he seemed too weary to talk, slumping in the passenger seat as the car crept down to ground level. She'd heard little from him since he left Rotorua: only a brief call to say the local police had visited Cassy, and that he was giving up and coming home.

The barrier lifted. Mike roused himself.

'The cops didn't want to know,' he said. 'Not once they'd talked to her. They strongly suggested I leave town.'

'Could they make you leave?'

'No point in staying. I don't know what the hell she told them.'

'But you'd got so close!'

'There was nothing I could do.' He looked ten years older, cheeks sagging with failure. 'There's no sneaking in. It's bloody miles up this godforsaken lake.'

He was trying valiantly to stay awake, but his speech became more and more slurred. Finally he gave in to exhaustion. Diana drove smoothly, not wanting to disturb the shattered man. She felt light-headed with rage. She wished Cassy could see what she'd done to her father.

When Diana parked in the driveway, he opened his eyes. 'Tara?'

'At school.'

'It's good to be home.' He squeezed her hand before stumbling out of the car. Soon he was flat on their bed, eyes closed, breathing heavily. He'd removed only his shoes.

'It doesn't get worse than this,' he said, when she brought him a mug of tea.

But he was wrong.

•

It started with the doorbell. Dark figures behind the glass. A man and a woman, neither of them in police uniform. They introduced themselves and showed their warrant cards, but Diana wasn't listening.

'Can we come in for a few minutes? It's about Cassandra Howells.'

This is it, she thought. *It's all over. Cassy's dead.*

As she was showing them into the sitting room, she saw Mike at the top of the stairs. Her eyes met his, and she knew they were thinking the same thing. They'd lost a child. The unbearable thing—the nightmare that happens to other people—had come into their lives.

The visitors suggested that Mike and Diana sit down, so they did: side by side on the sofa, gripping each other's hands.

'Tell us,' said Diana. 'What's happened to Cassy?'

The woman reached into a case, taking out a typed document.

'Cassandra has made some allegations to our counterparts in New Zealand.'

'Allegations?'

'Allegations of physical abuse.'

Mike punched the sofa. 'I knew it! Those bastards! Is she safe now? Have they got her out?'

Diana squeezed his hand tighter. She saw what was coming. She was sitting on a track with Mike, watching a train bearing down on them, knowing it was about to smash them both to pieces.

'The alleged abuse didn't happen in New Zealand,' said the woman.

'No?' Mike sounded bewildered. 'Then where?'

And so it began. Cassy was accusing *them*. She said she'd been hurt in her own home, as a little girl, by the people who were meant to love and protect her. She described a controlling brute of a father and a weak, colluding mother. She made them sound like monsters.

'But *none* of this is true,' protested Diana. 'She's twisted every incident, every loss of temper, every mistake. All parents make mistakes.'

'Some of her allegations go beyond reasonable chastisement,' said the man.

'Is this an official interview?'

'Not at this stage. Just a chat.'

'So we can ask you to leave?'

'You could. But wouldn't you like to get this cleared up?' He scratched his nose—delicately, with his forefinger—a misleadingly casual gesture. 'Do you remember an incident involving a wooden spoon? We'd be talking maybe fifteen years ago.'

Mike's features crinkled in mystification. He turned to Diana. 'Any bells?'

The woman began to read an extract from Cassy's statement. Diana felt physically sick to hear it: a vile story about Mike pulverising five-year-old Cassy. It was described in detail: a frenzied attack on a tiny girl, who was left bruised and screaming, locked in her room all night. *My father carried out the assault, but my mother stood by and did nothing, and afterwards she put me in my room. Not long after that, they sent me to boarding school.*

Mike's head was in his hands. Diana wanted to run to the bathroom and throw up.

'This is pure fantasy,' she whispered. 'And she didn't go to boarding school until she was nine. Ten, even. I can't remember. She went because of army life, not because of any sinister child abuse thing. Most army children go—not just officers' children.'

She'd talked herself to a standstill. The visitors were looking at Mike, who seemed too broken to defend himself.

'I know what you're thinking,' protested Diana. 'You're thinking no smoke without fire. But you're wrong. I'm not going to pretend we've never smacked our children. I'm not going to pretend we've never shouted, either. But this man she describes— this maniac, spitting aggression and violence—that is not—I repeat *not*—Mike. He's just not that kind of man. He was an army officer for twenty-three years, for heaven's sake, with an exemplary record. And he adores his girls.'

'So you're saying this incident never happened?'

'It *didn't* happen.' And it didn't; Diana was sure of that. She'd been racking her brains and never—not even after Bosnia, when Mike was a mess—had there been such a horrible event.

The woman raised her eyebrows. 'Mike, can I ask you: any idea why Cassandra might make these claims, if they're not true?'

At last, Mike lifted his head. It seemed very heavy. 'I think she's been brainwashed.'

'Brainwashed?'

'By these people. They've got a hold over her.'

The nightmare went on, backwards and forwards. Mike and Diana only wanted to talk about Gethsemane; the police only wanted to talk about family violence. Diana felt tears coming, and rummaged in her pocket for a tissue.

'You call her Cassy,' said the woman, 'but she doesn't use that name.' Diana and Mike both looked blank, so she held up the statement. '*I was born Cassandra Alexandra Howells, but I am known as Cairo.*'

'My God,' whispered Mike. 'Is there anything of her left?'

Diana leaped to her feet at the sound of a key in the front door. 'Tara,' she muttered, and hurried to meet her daughter. Tara

was dumping her bag on the stairs, breathing fast as though she'd
run back from school.

'Hi, Mum. Dad home?'

'In here,' said Diana. 'But we've got a problem. The police—'

Tara stopped dead at the scene in the sitting room.

'Hang on a minute,' she said. 'Whoa. Would someone mind
telling me what this is about?'

'It's about Cassy,' said Diana, adding quickly, 'It's okay, she's
fine.'

'She can't be fine! The police don't come knocking on people's
doors just for the fun of it. She's not dead, is she?'

Diana explained why the police had come knocking on their
door. As Tara listened, her mouth fell open.

'You have got to be *joking*! Oh my God, that lying cow.' She
confronted the visitors square on: chin up, knuckles on her hips.
Her eyes were sparking. 'Let's get this sorted out right now.'

They tried to stop her. Diana heard the man mutter something
about child protection issues.

'I'm not a child.'

He was shaking his head. 'These alleged events took place
at around the time you were born, so you can't help us. It isn't
appropriate to—'

'*Appropriate?* What does that even mean? I'm going to set the
record straight, because this stops right now. That's what I call
"appropriate". You listening?'

Oh yes. They were listening. Diana would have laughed if the
situation hadn't been so ghastly. Tara was a force to be reckoned
with when she was riled.

'My sister's gone off her head in New Zealand. Literally. My
dad is a great big teddy bear. He doesn't even swipe the cat away
when he licks the butter. No—he cuddles him instead. That's
how dangerous he is! This man—' she gripped Mike's arm with
both her hands, kissing his cheek '—never hurt anyone in his life,
except maybe when he was in some war, but that's different. I'll
admit he's a pain in the bum sometimes, he's OCD, he drives me

nuts and most days I want to give *him* a slap, but there's no way he ever abused Cassy and I'll swear to that in court. Okay?' She glared at them. 'Just leave him alone, will you?'

They thanked her, said they'd be in touch and made a rapid exit.

The family was left shell-shocked.

'Welcome home, Dad,' said Tara.

'They won't take it any further,' said Diana. 'Cassy's made all this up and they know it. Anyway, she isn't here to give evidence.'

Mike ran his hands underneath his glasses, pressing his fingers into his eyes. 'I didn't do it, did I?' he whispered. 'I didn't do that awful thing and block it out?'

'Of course not.'

'Why does she hate me so much?'

'She doesn't hate you.'

'She must do. She really must. I must have been an awful father.'

He didn't want anything to eat; didn't want a cup of tea. He dragged himself back to bed, and this time he didn't even bother to remove his shoes. Diana did it for him. As she was closing the bedroom curtains, she spotted Tara out in the garden. She was lying face down, draped across the swing seat, using her feet to turn around and around until the chains were twisted and bunched. Finally she let go and spun—joltingly, wildly—dark hair flying.

It was Cassy who'd taught her that game—years ago, when they were living in officers' housing, and Tara was a tiny pre-schooler who worshipped her big sister. They used to make themselves dizzy. Diana would hear the pair of them giggling as they staggered about on the lawn.

Another hour passed before Tara came stomping in through the kitchen door. Her face looked shuttered, like a house closed up for winter.

'I'll never forgive her,' she said. 'Never.'

'They've put things into her head.'

'Stop making excuses.' Tara kicked a wooden chair, sending it clattering across the tiles. 'She's broken Dad's heart with her fucking lies! He loves her, that's why he went to look for her—and in return she's trying to get him locked up. How could she say those things about him?'

'I don't know.'

'She's a selfish, lying, vindictive bitch. And I hate her.'

Diana didn't argue. At that moment, she hated Cassy too.

The Cult Leader's Manual: Eight Steps to Mind Control

Cameron Allsop

Step 7: Patience

Do not rush into the introduction of core beliefs. Some new religions require their members to study for months or years before they learn the entirety of their creed. Before telling them what you're really about, you need to be sure that your recruit has invested heavily in the organisation, has become reliant upon it, and is immersed in its magical thinking. They will then be prepared to accept a belief system that might seem laughably absurd to the uninitiated.

Twenty-four

Cairo
January 2011

The cool of the morning. The hollow slap of water against a wooden hull. No sight of the shore or the sky.

Aden had woken her an hour ago by nuzzling her ear. Cairo felt as though she'd only been asleep five minutes. She had her own class of the smallest children at school now, as well as the duties on Otto's rotating roster: Vigil, gardening, kitchen, firewood, laundry, crèche and workshops. She'd fallen into bed after Night Call and slept right through the unborn baby's kicking, and the mosquitos, and the heat.

She sat up, disorientated, heaving her clumsy body around. It was still dark.

'What's happening? Can't be time for Call already?'

'Shh . . . no. Justin's going to take you fishing. Here, I brought you tea.'

She rubbed her eyes. The baby was nowhere near due but she wondered how much bigger it could possibly grow. She felt as though all her organs were being squashed to make room, and she'd developed the pregnant woman's waddle.

'Fishing? In the middle of the night?'

'It's not for us to question.'

'How d'you know? Is he here?'

Aden handed her some clothes. 'I just know.'

Minutes later, they were on the jetty. Cairo had become attuned to the natural world and sensed that dawn wasn't far off. She inhaled the morning freshness as she took Aden's arm. Their partnership had been an arranged one, she knew that, but it made her very happy.

'Can't you come too?' she asked.

'Don't question Justin.' Aden's voice had a sharp edge, which wasn't like him. 'He never asks for anything we can't give, or anything he wouldn't give himself.'

'But . . . what are we being asked to give?'

He didn't answer. She heard oars on water before Justin's boat appeared out of the gloom, with Peter tail-wagging on the bow.

'Morning, you two!' cried Justin, throwing the painter. 'Coming fishing, Cairo?'

They left Aden standing on the jetty. He waved as Justin pulled away, and she waved back. Seconds later he'd melted into darkness.

Justin was a strong rower, but it took some time to get out to the deep part of the lake where he wanted to fish. They talked about the pregnancy, and Cairo watched the evening star as it sank towards the horizon. At last Justin stored the oars, humming to himself as he pottered about. Peter sat on a piece of sacking and watched his master's every move.

Cairo tried not to think of the lightless depths that lay beneath the flimsy wood. There were no life jackets on board and she felt hopelessly heavy. She wouldn't survive long if she fell in there. She'd drown, and the baby would die with her.

'Don't worry,' said Justin. 'I've never sunk one yet.'

'I wasn't worrying.'

'Fibber.'

They both smiled.

'Coffee?' he asked, producing a thermos and pouring some into a tin cup. 'It's a beautiful brew. I made it myself.'

'Thank you.'

She watched as he broke a muffin in half to share. She hadn't expected luxuries like this. She knew that Justin's lifestyle was spartan, even more so than that of the Watchmen. Yet here he was, taking her on a fishing trip with all the creature comforts. Like a father.

Like a father. A memory flitted through her mind; it ran in and out, playing hide-and-seek with her consciousness. Her dad on a weekend, gleefully bringing out the sandwiches. *This is the life, eh Cass?* The reservoir wasn't big. They could have walked around it in ten minutes. He showed her how to tie on the fly, and how to cast. *Have a go. Let the line just . . . ooh, watch the trees.*

A world away, and half a lifetime.

'Worrying about something?' asked Justin.

'My father,' she said. 'We used to go fishing.'

'Sounds like a good memory.' He was opening a tackle box. 'Of course you have good memories. Your family aren't evil.'

'No.'

'But they can never understand Gethsemane. Okay, we're ready. Would you like a go?'

'I'd rather watch you.'

She heard the swish of the rod, the whirring of the reel, followed by a small splash as the line hit the water.

'It was *my* father who taught me to cast,' said Justin.

'Your father?'

'Mm. Well, the man who called me his son. He used to take me to a canal, somewhere in Essex. I was about four. We caught nothing but supermarket trolleys.'

'Where is he now?'

'He died. Motorbike.'

'I'm sorry.'

Justin said not to worry, it was a long time ago. Then he asked about the children in Cairo's class, every one of whom he knew and loved. He understood their individual foibles, and who was best friends with whom, and who needed extra care. He wondered whether there were any resources Cairo needed, and she mentioned more early reader books.

'Talk to Rome,' he said. 'He'll order them.'

Without fanfare, the sun hauled itself over the horizon and into a layer of cloud. Justin cast again and again, the line snaking onto the milky opacity of the water.

'Do you ever hear voices, Cairo?' he asked.

She was startled. 'No! Should I?'

'I think you will one day. I foresee that for you . . . hang on, have I caught something?' He peered, shook his head, and unhurriedly cast again.

Cairo was leaning closer, watching and listening. Six months ago she'd have been looking for some way to escape (*Help! Trapped on a tiny boat with a raving nut job!*) but she was a different woman today. She knew that human existence was a speck in the universe. She'd communed with the Infinite.

'I've heard voices ever since I was a little boy,' said Justin. 'Not mad, hallucination voices. Real voices, of real beings. I'm perfectly sane, I promise you . . . *Aha!*'

The rod was bent almost double. This was the part she didn't like about fishing. She'd never really wanted to catch anything, though her father always put the trout back. That was the rule, in the little lake.

'Isn't it stressful for the poor thing?' she'd asked once, looking at the gasping mouth and pulsating gills.

'Not if you're very careful,' Mike had said. 'Not as stressful as being banged on the head.' He'd lowered the fish into the water with both hands and held it there, and they watched it come to life and flick away.

Justin let his line out, wound it in, let it out. 'He's a big fella,' he said. 'Look . . . there! See him?'

She did—a silvery flash of tail, churning the water. Little by little Justin brought it closer, finally dropping a magnificent trout into a net. It lay flapping, rainbow scales shining, while Justin lifted a vicious-looking knife out of the tackle box.

'Glorious creature,' he said, taking hold of the fish. Cairo winced and looked away, despising herself for being feeble. When she turned back a second later, Justin had cut its head clean off. 'Seems a bit barbaric,' he said, 'but it's a lot kinder than clubbing it or leaving it to suffocate.'

He dropped both head and body into a bucket. Then he sat down and grabbed the oars.

'Back to my place for breakfast?'

They pulled the boat up the beach together. Once she was on dry land, Cairo stood entranced. Justin's island was a miniature paradise, covering perhaps a quarter of an acre. Rocky coves and pumice sand surrounded a bush-clad interior. She heard the melodic sweetness of a tui and caught a flash of his white pom-pom among the crimson flowers of a pohutukawa. She'd thought the Gethsemane settlement was peaceful, but this was another world again.

'Welcome!' declared Justin. 'Here's my cabin, up in the trees . . . come along in, we'll make some more coffee. I have a propane stove. Bit of a luxury.'

It was a simple cabin, smaller than her own and very bare: just a few books, writing paper and a pen lay on the table. The floor was swept, the stove unlit. The porch looked straight across the lake to the mountain.

'What a magical place,' said Cairo.

'Yes. Yes, it is.' Justin was gutting the fish, then lacing fillets along a couple of sticks.

'Not lonely?'

'I need to be alone. But I have Peter for company. And the birds—so many birds! Rome visits me often. Sometimes I have guests to stay.'

'Guests?'

'Watchmen, when they need special care. Maybe they're fighting their demons, maybe depressed. Maybe just overwhelmed by life.'

'Like Paris. She told me that you were the only one who listened. And Dublin. And Kyoto.'

'Or it's just a friend, like you, who's good enough to while away an hour or two with me. Right, I think we're ready. Let's sit outside.' He led the way out to the beach and nodded to a ring of pumice. 'If you'd just add a couple of bits of wood to the fire and blow on it?'

Within minutes, the fish was gently cooking. It smelled exquisite. Justin and Cairo settled on smooth wooden stools under the cicada-hissing trees, their feet in the sand, watching wisps of smoke in the wavering air.

'You said you heard voices,' ventured Cairo.

'One in particular,' said Justin. 'He's been visiting me—on and off—since I was five years old. He calls himself Messenger. I was a sad kid. My mother and I were refugees, in a way, and things weren't good. Messenger promised that one day I'd rule over the people who were hurting me. *Wait, Justin*, he used to say. *Your time will come.*'

Cairo began to have a very odd, very intense sensation. A mist was clearing from her mind. Something extraordinary was being unveiled.

'I grew up with a lot of violence,' said Justin, 'and I gave a lot back. By the time I was Rome's age I hated the world and everyone in it.'

'I can't imagine that.'

'Ask Liam! He knew me back then. People were afraid to look me in the eye. They saw the rage. I was a one-boy crime wave—petty theft at first, then drugs kicked in and I got nastier. The shrinks said I had conduct disorder, the police thought I was a psycho who was going to kill somebody. And one day, I almost did. An innocent stranger.'

Cairo saw only a serene, middle-aged man with sea-green eyes, a man whose love chased away shadows. He looked like a university professor, perhaps, or a distinguished actor.

'Was it a car accident?' she asked, thinking of Paris.

'It was a knife. I drove a knife into a young man's stomach.' He saw her shock and nodded. 'Yes. *Yes.* I know about sin. I know about hate and anger and shame. I know about forgiveness.'

'Has everyone in Gethsemane heard this story?'

'Only those I trust.'

It was his gift to her. She hugged his words. *Those I trust.*

'What happened to him?' she asked.

'He survived. We were both lucky.'

'And you?'

'I descended into hell. I crawled into a hole and tried to die. And it was at that moment—the darkest of my life—that Messenger returned. He brought reinforcements, thousands of them—an army! They came to tell me who I am.'

His gaze held hers, affectionate but a little severe. She sat absolutely still. She couldn't look away.

'Cairo,' he said, and smiled. 'Cairo. Don't you know who I am?'

The answer was dazzling. It was in the air, in the lake, in the sky. It was in the drifting smoke, the rattle of cicadas, the music of the birds. It was in every atom of the universe. She was on her knees in the sand. How had she been so blind?

Old Cassy—the one who'd never been to Gethsemane—would be scoffing right now. *What a load of old bollocks*, she'd be saying. *Get yourself out of there, girl.* But Cairo's mind was open, her eyes were open, and she could see clearly. She knew she was in the presence of the light of the world, of Jesus Christ himself.

'Of course!' she cried. 'Of *course* I know you! I've known you all my life.'

Bliss rippled through her body and her mind. Even her unborn child seemed to somersault.

'The baby's dancing,' she said, laughing. Then she burst into tears. 'He knows exactly who you are!'

For an hour or more she knelt at his feet. She never wanted to be anywhere else. He broke the white flesh of the fish to share with her. While they ate, she asked about his previous mortal life. He described his mother, who always believed in him. He reminisced about his cousin John, brutally murdered. He remembered siblings and friends who resented him.

'The same patterns this time,' he said. 'And the same old guard, vested interests—modern-day scribes and Pharisees. Though I've kept a lower profile. The idea this time around isn't to get myself executed.'

'Is the Infinite your father?' she asked. 'Are you the Son of God?'

The question made him chuckle. He held out a scrap of fish for Peter.

'We've watched humans tying themselves in knots with their clumsy theology. Century after century, war after war; Judaism and Christianity and Islam and Hinduism and all the others, splitting into a thousand different sects. They've all got it hopelessly, catastrophically wrong! You'd think Christianity would have done better, since I do actually exist. But no. I mean, the Trinity? *Seriously?* Where on earth did that come from?' He held up his hands in exasperation. 'And the Creationist narrative! Beggars belief. The sheer ignorance and arrogance of it makes me weep. Transubstantiation would be hilarious, except that people have been tortured to death for questioning it, which isn't funny at all.'

'Tell me the real story. I want to understand.'

'You can't. It's on a scale that even you, wise Cairo, can't come close to comprehending. But you can make a start by accepting that the natural universe has dimensions and physical laws that are beyond all possibility of human knowledge.'

'*More things in heaven and earth?*'

'Exactly. The Infinite is far beyond understanding. There are realms beyond realms; heavens beyond heaven, peopled by divine beings. Ironically, science is much closer to understanding God than any religion. But even the most brilliant scientist can't comprehend infinity.'

The lake licked the shore; the volcano merged into the hot sky. Justin talked, and Cairo floated in the mystery of his words. He was describing the indescribable. She was dazed by the time he emptied his flask of coffee into their cups.

'Do you remember your baptism, Cairo?'

'That was the best day of my life.'

'It was a wonderful moment, wasn't it? I asked whether you would keep the Vigil and look towards the Last Day. And you said yes. You didn't know what it all meant, but you said yes. You trusted me.'

'I did. I do.'

'I once asked my followers to keep Vigil while I prayed. They fell asleep. You've heard the story, I'm sure.'

'The Passion. In the Garden of Gethsemane. I was brought up by atheists but even I know that story.'

He shuddered. 'None of the Gospels do justice to the horror of those hours. They got quite a lot of facts wrong . . . but the core is true. It was the most terrible night of my human life, and my friends couldn't even stay awake. Well, now I'm back, and this time a lot more is at stake! We can't afford to fall asleep on the job. That's why we keep Vigil. A Watchman is always awake, always watching for the Last Day.' He threw the dregs of his coffee into the fire, and it sizzled. 'You know it's coming, Cairo. You were already afraid when you came here. You were afraid for a world that's going to hell in a handcart. The Devil is doing her work—oh! So merrily.'

She couldn't read his expression; she didn't know whether he was serious or not. 'The Devil?'

'You don't believe in her?'

'I thought it was an allegorical concept,' said Cairo. 'Not a sentient being.'

'You see her work. Buchenwald. Bosnia. The Killing Fields of Cambodia. Rwanda, the Congo . . . the casual cruelties in homes and schools and offices and factories and farms . . . on and on, day after day. Our planet is sick. The temperature is rising, the ice is melting, while humans squabble and deny. They've got their fingers in their ears, their eyes shut—they're singing *la-la-la*, refusing to hear or see. I warned them! Earthquakes, I said. Tsunamis. Famine, war, plague. It's all there, in the Gospels. The Last Day is coming for mankind.'

'When will it come?'

'Soon. In my present lifetime.'

'But all those innocent people. What about the children?'

'Let me worry about them. Here at Gethsemane we've made an oasis in the chaos. I promise you—I *promise* you—I won't leave you or Aden or this beautiful new child of yours. You'll be with me in the Kingdom of Peace.'

He began to describe a fiery cloud of glory, a legion of angels—more than the stars in the sky—and how he'd regain his divine form. There was too much to take in, especially as Old Cassy still whispered: *This stuff is just weird! Get out while you can.*

Justin gave her hands a shake. 'Wondering if I'm a basket case? I wouldn't blame you. History is littered with people who think they're Jesus Christ. There are plenty of false messiahs in the world today.'

'There are?'

He gave a startling shout of laughter. Peter swept his tail across the sand.

'Enough to make up a football team! They've all got loyal followers, and they're mostly very rich men. Hardly any women. I hate to say I told you so, but . . . I told you so. One of the last things I did was to predict the false messiahs, and the false prophets.'

His laughter was gone. The shadows were back.

'Do you love me, Cairo?'

'You know I do.'

'I have a job to do. It might take courage. Will you help me see it through?'

'You only ever have to ask.'

He reached down, laying his hand on Peter's head.

'No matter what?'

'No matter what.'

Twenty-five

Diana

As the months passed, she survived on autopilot. Tara seemed perpetually angry. Mike lost interest in life; he even gave up cycling. He stopped talking about Cassy, and then he stopped talking about anything at all. He and Diana began to turn down invitations. Their social circle shrank.

'At least Cassy's not dead,' friends would say, trying to be reassuring. 'Gotta look on the bright side!'

Then those same chirpy Pollyannas would pass around photos of their own daughter's graduation—or wedding—or adorable children.

One foot after another. One day after another. Autumn, winter.

In December, the police rang to say that they'd be taking no further action regarding Cassy's complaint. Diana waited for some kind of an apology, or at least some explanation as to why they'd let the family dangle for so long before making a decision. But no. She and Mike weren't innocent, it seemed, just not demonstrably guilty.

They went through the motions of that first Christmas, inviting Joyce for lunch. Pesky was pleased about the tinsel. Everyone did their best, but Cassy's absence made a mockery of the day. Even Joyce's optimism was faltering.

'Seems odd,' she fretted. 'She only wrote to me that once. Well, as long as she's happy.'

On New Year's Eve, Tara headed off to a party dressed as a slutty Tinkerbell and arrived home too drunk to stand up, with crumpled wings and her head down the loo. *I want my big sister back. Where's my sister?* Diana spent the rest of the night sitting by her bed in case she choked. She couldn't afford to lose another daughter.

In January, Joyce slipped in the shower and broke her hip. After a month in hospital she had to give up her studio and move into the nursing wing. She spent her days in a high-backed armchair in the lounge, between a woman whose strokes had left her unable to speak and a man who cried all the time.

'I hope I slip away in my sleep,' she said calmly, while Diana was brushing her hair one wet February evening.

'Mum!'

'Don't "Mum" me. I'm not asking for sympathy. I just pray to die in my sleep while I still have my faculties. Everybody here prays to die in their sleep. It's our ambition. We've seen the alternative.'

You want to abandon me again, thought Diana, and she brushed more vigorously, which made Joyce wince.

'Ouch! Okay, my hair is perfect. Now, I've been thinking about Cassy and I cut this out of the paper.' Joyce fished into her latest crime novel and produced a press cutting. 'Here.'

It was an interview with a man called Dr Cameron Allsop who, according to the write-up, was an anthropologist based at the University of Sussex, and director of something called the Destructive Cults Information Trust.

'Take it home,' said Joyce. 'Let me know what you think.'

•

Mike had been held up at work again. He'd been coming home later and later, and often not at all. He had to go overseas, or he had to work all night because of time zones. Any excuse, Diana thought, to avoid the sadness in this house.

Tara was out. Probably drinking. Diana sat on the sofa with her legs tucked under her, and unfolded Joyce's article.

PEOPLE ARE CHAMELEONS, SAYS CULT EXPERT.

Dr Allsop's story was intriguing. He and his wife had joined an organisation that claimed to be about life coaching, but which began to demand that they take part in group sex. He was shocked and left, but his wife didn't. A year later, she was accusing him of the sexual abuse of their five-year-old. Fortunately, her accusations didn't hold water.

The group destroyed my marriage, and could have put me in prison. I was left wondering what had hit us. What was the nature of this beast who'd stolen my wife's mind? Years of research followed, during which I wrote my PhD thesis on destructive cults and new religions. People are like chameleons. They change in order to fit in.

The article was wide-ranging. Allsop described the chain of events that led to the deaths of almost a thousand people in Jonestown in 1978; he discussed the tragedies of Waco and Heaven's Gate, and the ghastly murders carried out at the behests of Charles Manson and Aum Shinrikyo. But it was the passages about his wife that most fascinated Diana. They could have been written about Cassy.

Her mind was hacked, her memories corrupted. The techniques are popular with hypnotists and the wilder evangelists, with dodgy psychiatrists, even with controlling partners. The organisation isolated her in a controlled environment before using the power of suggestion, again and again, to plant these obscene thoughts into her mind.

Diana read the article twice. Then she opened her laptop and searched for *Destructive Cults Information Trust*.

Bingo. There was Dr Allsop. He looked like a caricature, with a nose and eyebrows that dwarfed the rest of his face. There were links to his publications and videos of lectures he'd given all over the world. If anyone could help, he could.

She clicked on his email address and began to type.

Twenty-six

Cairo

Her son was born on the morning of 22 February 2011: a glowing, dreamy day, when the blue waters of the lake seemed to merge into the blue heavens, and the mountain shimmered in late-summer heat.

Cairo had learned a great deal during the long hours of the night.

First, she learned that when women say things like *childbirth doesn't really hurt*, they're lying through their teeth. She cursed every one of those double-dealing women. She screamed for pain-killing drugs. She was sure she was going to die.

Next, she learned that pain on such a scale transports you into a secret war bunker. She discovered another part of herself; a part that rolled up its sleeves and took over, ignoring Monika's quiet movements and Paris rubbing her back. There was nothing but the pain and the job in hand.

Finally she heard that first cry, and saw the miraculous new life, and felt the wonder of it. She couldn't have imagined such love. *Now* she understood why all mothers lie.

He was born in his parents' bedroom, just a few steps from the lakeshore. Monika showed Cairo how to feed him while Paris was spreading clean sheets onto the bed. It wasn't the custom at Gethsemane for fathers to be involved in the births of their children, but Aden and Suva came bursting in as soon as Monika tapped on the window.

Nobody watching the scene would have guessed that this wasn't Aden's biological son. He held the little one with easy confidence; this was his fourth child, after all. The baby looked comically miniature in his father's arms. His eyelids were translucent, like butterfly's wings. His mouth had fallen open, squashed against the blue fabric of Aden's rolled-up shirtsleeve. Suva tiptoed closer, her lips rounded in a silent *ooh*.

'Your new brother,' said Cairo. 'Isn't he soft? Look at his tiny fingernails.'

'We heard you scream.'

'I didn't scream, did I?'

'No, no.' Aden's smile took over his whole face and corrugated his forehead. 'Well . . . yes, actually. Quite a lot.'

'And quite a lot of swear words!' said Suva, giggling.

Cairo dozed while Suva brushed her hair. The baby slept, woke, fed, and slept again. Outside, the calm rhythms of Gethsemane continued: the bells, the steady tramp of feet, the talk and laughter. Cairo felt as though she'd lived here all her life. In seven months she had left the valley three times, and then only to travel as far as Rotorua. At first it had felt odd to be so profoundly cut off, but gradually it had become normal, even desirable. All media was monitored by the Companions. They brought the news to Call: sickening stories of murders, famines, wars, floods and landslides. Gethsemane was a haven.

Kazan and Berlin came as soon as they could. Berlin held their new grandchild in his mechanic's oily hands, and they both gushed over him.

'You and Aden mustn't do any cooking,' Kazan told Cairo. 'The community provides meals for at least two weeks after a birth. We're here for you. Any time you'd like a cup of tea and a bit of a moan—you know where I am!'

After they'd gone, Aden carried the baby to the window.

'That's the lake,' he said. 'You'll swim in there on a hot day like today. See the children jumping off the jetty? And there's Tarawera, the sleeping dragon. It breathes fire.'

'I'm in heaven,' said Cairo.

'Halfway to heaven,' Suva corrected her. 'Heaven is like this but a thousand times happier. Heaven will begin when the world ends, on the Last Day.'

Eventually Aden went back to work and Suva to school. They'd not been gone long when Bali dropped by. Monty—three years old now—was in the crèche. Monika poured celebratory elderflower cordial for everyone, while Paris waltzed around with the new arrival.

'I wonder what your name is?' she murmured, kissing his downy head as she twirled. 'Who are you, darling?'

'I thought Alex, short for Alexandria,' said Cairo.

The effect was instant. The temperature dropped. Paris stopped dancing.

'You don't choose,' she said. 'It's not the Way.'

Cairo lifted her chin. 'Alexandria is a city in Egypt. Appropriate, since I'm Cairo. Alexandra was my second name.'

'Justin will name him.'

'But surely he'll ask me? I've carried this baby for nine months! It's me who's been in bloody agony half the night. He's *my* baby.'

Bali was looking scandalised. 'You're talking about a human being, not a possession! We don't own anything here. We certainly don't own one another. Aden will not support you in this.'

'Where I come from, it's the parents who choose a child's name.'

At some unspoken signal, Monika, Paris and Bali had formed a hostile battleline. Cairo tried to stand up, to face the three women. She felt light-headed.

'This is a free country,' she insisted, but with less certainty.

'Free!' scoffed Paris. 'Is *that* what you call it? Last week a three-year-old girl—in *this* country—was kicked to death by her mother's boyfriend. Kicked. To. Death. He delighted in torturing her, had been doing it ever since she was born. Who is free?'

The baby didn't seem to like such loud voices. He cried—a quavering, tragic sound—but when Cairo tried to take him back, Paris stepped out of her reach. The message was clear.

'He needs me,' said Cairo. 'He's hungry.'

'We have bottles.'

She couldn't believe this was happening. Her friends stood like sentinels, as though she'd turned into a raving lunatic who must be contained. After seven months of isolation, Cairo had become reliant on these people. She had nobody else. She was hopelessly vulnerable, a snail with no shell. As the baby's quavering grew into wails, she felt milk soaking her shirt.

'Please,' she begged, trying desperately to get to him and finding her way blocked by Bali. '*Please.*'

'You're not yourself,' said Monika. She sounded kind but detached. She might have been explaining why a child needs to be whisked off to the intensive care unit. 'I think we need to take him away, until your faith is stronger.'

'Monika, please!'

'For his safety. Until you're well again.'

'Aden won't let you do this.'

'Oh yes he will,' said Monika. 'I assure you he will. Aden knows the Way. This baby isn't yours, and he isn't Aden's. He's a child of Gethsemane.'

'I was already carrying him when I came here.'

'And we opened our homes and our hearts to you! Didn't we?'

Cairo wilted in the face of Monika's coldness. She was always so kind; she was the friendly doctor who cared.

'You did,' she said. 'You were lovely.'

'The Companions thought you were very special, very spiritual,' continued Monika, shaking her head. 'Justin put immense trust in you. Is your faith so much weaker than we thought? Are you so vain that you can't accept the gift of a name?'

'We'd be very sad to lose you,' said Bali.

The words opened up a bottomless abyss. *We'd be very sad*

to lose you. They would take the baby, and Cairo would be sent away. She'd have nothing to live for.

'I'm sorry,' she whispered, dropping back onto the bed. 'I don't know what I was thinking.'

The springs creaked as Monika sat beside her. Cairo was in tears. Her rebellion was over—completely and permanently. She felt only fear, and a desperate longing to be loved again.

'I'm sorry,' she sobbed. 'I'm so sorry.'

Now, at last, there were arms around her; murmurs of love and reassurance. Bali crouched to take her hands. Cairo leaned forwards and pressed her forehead into her friend's shoulder. She felt a painful kind of joy, the type that hurt—it couldn't be swallowed; it swelled and blocked your throat. She'd glimpsed the void. She must never risk rejection. Never, ever again.

'You love Justin,' said Monika. 'Yes? Yes. He loves you, and he loves this brand-new Watchman even more than you do. Lucky, lucky child! Your son will be honoured with a name chosen by our Messiah. Isn't that wonderful?'

They were a tableau: the three around the bed, and Paris at the window, cradling the baby against her shoulder. He'd calmed down and was dozing off. Their backdrop was utterly still: water, sky and a mountain with torn flanks.

Then the earth began to quiver. It slid from side to side quite gently, as though they were standing on a railway carriage while it was being uncoupled. Cordial rippled in its jug. Paris took hold of the window frame with her free hand.

The shaking wasn't strong, but in those few seconds the birds stopped singing, the goats bleating. Invisible hands rocked the cabin on its wooden piles. Cairo had noticed, in her months at Gethsemane, how people always fell silent during a quake. They focused on it, feeling it, gauging whether this one was going to turn into a monster or not.

Not this time. The world was still again. The baby had slept right through it.

It wasn't until the next day that a group came back from a shopping trip with tragic news: the quake had been a monster after all. The city of Christchurch had suffered wholesale destruction, and one hundred and eighty-five people had died. The cathedral tower had come crashing down, a symbol of lost hope. That elegant, prosperous city would never be the same again. The country was in mourning.

'Another sign,' said Justin, as he walked among them in the *wharenui* that night. 'We pray for the victims of the earthquake. We ache for this turbulent world.'

Cairo sagged against Aden in the heat. She hadn't told him about her rebellion. She felt nothing but shame and fear when she remembered that scene. Her friends seemed to have forgiven her immediately, behaving as though it hadn't happened. She hoped it could be quietly forgotten.

Their son was making his first outing into society: a communal child with over a hundred adoring aunts and uncles and cousins. It wasn't long before he became restless, screwing up his face and nudging at her dress. Cairo wasn't sure what to do. She didn't think she could feed him in here, and she had never heard a baby cry in the *wharenui*. *Shush*, she whispered anxiously, jiggling him against her shoulder. *Shush, shush. Don't make a fuss. Please don't make a fuss.*

When she looked up, Justin was standing in front of her.

'May I?' he asked, and gathered the baby into his own arms. 'Our newest friend . . . *hello, mate* . . . has been born in the last days of our world,' he said. 'But that isn't a sad thing; it's a wonderful thing.'

Justin seemed to have a magic touch with all children, perhaps because they sensed his calm. The baby relaxed, contenting himself with squinting up at the ceiling. Cairo felt her heart swell. Then everything fell apart.

'But Cairo,' said Justin, without looking at her, 'I hear you've been questioning the Way. Is this true? D'you want to say something to us?'

She felt the blush. It started on her neck and spread right up to the roots of her hair. *Who told him?* Aden's hand was squeezing hers. She let go of him, and walked to stand on the step of the dais. Her friends were looking at her. Aden was looking at her. They were waiting for her confession.

'I wanted to name him myself,' she said. 'I was vain.' She felt tears begin to spill, and let them fall. *Humble yourself, and be nothing.* 'I said terrible things. I said I knew better than Justin, because it's my child. *My* child. I'm sorry, Justin.'

Justin turned his back on her and walked away, showing the baby to Dublin, to Beersheba, to everyone. Cairo was left alone.

'Isn't he beautiful, Hana?' exulted Justin. 'Berlin and Kazan, you must be happy grandparents! Look at those perfect little hands.'

At last, he returned to Cairo.

'The Way exists to protect you and to protect Gethsemane,' he said.

'I know.'

'Temptation is a living thing: a creeping, cunning creature. If you open the door for it—even a little crack—it will slink in.'

'I know. I'm sorry.'

'Will you fight temptation from now on?'

'Yes.' She wiped tears with her sleeve. 'I'll never question you again.'

The shadow was lifted. He laid his cool fingers on her forehead.

'This is the touch of forgiveness,' he said. 'Love yourself. Be free. And this young man's name? Welcome, Damascus. You will be a wise counsellor.'

The future counsellor didn't seem especially impressed by this prophecy. He began to fuss again.

'I think it's his supper time,' said Justin, handing him back to Cairo. 'You'd better go and feed him. Suva, you could keep them company.'

It was a warm, still night. Cairo and Suva sank onto the porch steps. From inside the *wharenui*, they heard the music begin.

'Do you feel better for confessing?' asked Suva, as Cairo struggled to get the baby to latch on.

'Much.'

'It's awful, confession. Makes you feel like a nasty little worm.'

'We have to be prepared to stand before our friends and say, "I was wrong," and know that we'll be forgiven. That's what Justin's love is all about. *Ouch.*'

'Teeth?'

'Powerful gums.'

Suva giggled. Then she said, 'My mum had to confess lots of times.'

'Really?'

'Mm. She caused trouble about things like us children having to fast. One day she started crying. I asked her what was wrong, and she said it was complicated and I wouldn't understand. And now I *do* understand. Demons had got to her. They tempted her with lies and promises, and she let them in. So . . . one day we were recruiting, and I heard her talking to a man. She was planning on taking us all to the farmers' market on the Saturday. This man was going to wait with a car, and she was going to tell us some lie, and we were going to get in, and then he was going to drive away! I saw them kissing—my mum, kissing another man!'

'You poor love.'

'How *could* she?' Suva spoke as though she'd heard her mother plotting to drive them all off a cliff. 'People who leave Gethsemane go mad, or die . . . and they die twice, because they've lost the chance for eternal life.'

'What did you do?'

'I told Gaza. As soon as we got home, the Companions called Mum into the *wharenui.*'

'Oh dear.' Cairo felt a grudging sympathy for the woman. 'How awful.'

'They were there all night. I think Justin cast out demons. I was in bed, but I thought I heard the screaming as he cast them out.' Suva leaned back on her arms. 'In the morning I saw her getting into Justin's boat.'

'Going to the island?'

'Mm. It seemed like ages before she came home to us.'

'Was she better?'

'Well.' Suva thought for a moment. 'Yes, but she was like a cushion that's been sat on too long and gone flat. She said she was glad I'd told on her, and asked if I could forgive her. And I said yes yes *yes*, of course.'

'Was it hard to forgive her?'

'No! Justin says forgiveness is one of the things that sets us free. But we didn't forget. Justin said I had to watch what she did, in case she needed more help.'

Justin asked this child to spy on her own mother. The thought was unwelcome: a fly buzzing in a peaceful room.

'I didn't watch carefully enough,' said Suva. 'In the end, Mum and the boys snuck away like rats. She left a note under my pillow. She wanted me to join her Outside. She said she loved me . . . but she must have loved herself more, mustn't she? So I never saw any of them again. Oh, I did once—Medan ran up to me in Rotorua and gave me a letter. I told him I didn't want it and I threw it straight in the bin.' There was contempt in the child's voice; a determined boredom. 'She's dead. Maybe not in her body, but in her life. She made her choice, and now she's lost. So . . . yeah.'

Suva had rushed to tell the story. Now she slumped onto the grass, her pale face turned up to the sky. Damascus had fallen asleep in mid-slurp. Cairo kissed his nose, revelling in the intoxicating newborn smell. These two were her children. She loved them both.

'You'll never leave us, will you?' asked Suva.

'Never.'

'Promise?'

'I totally and absolutely promise.'

•

Damascus was less than three weeks old when the Infinite sent a far greater and more terrifying sign even than Christchurch. A massive earthquake, measuring 9.0 on the Richter scale, struck off the coast of Japan. It triggered a tsunami that swept onto the land, swallowing towns—casually, as though people were ants. Their cities and roads, their technology and cleverness meant nothing. The ocean had no pity.

Justin arrived in the community within minutes of the news, though how he always knew what had happened was a mystery. The Companions arranged for footage to be projected onto the whitewashed inside wall of the *wharenui*, and the Watchmen gaped in horror as the wave roamed on and on in its murderous spree. They saw fellow human beings vainly trying to escape in their cars; or running, holding the hands of their children. It looked like a disaster movie.

Hours later a reactor at the Fukushima Daiichi Nuclear Power Plant melted and exploded. Justin called the whole community to a Vigil that lasted two days. The Watchmen took turns to rest but Justin didn't sleep or eat at all. He became more and more withdrawn. All day, all night, he led Vigil in the *wharenui*, or stood on the lakeshore, staring out across the water.

On the second morning Cairo joined Rome, who was watching his father. 'What's he doing when he stands on the beach?' she asked.

'Waiting for Messenger.'

'Doesn't he ever sleep?'

'He's not a man.' There was pride in Rome's voice. 'Not an ordinary one, anyway.'

'I'll go and see if he needs anything.'

As she approached, Peter looked around to see who was coming. There was tension in the dog's stance. He was ready to defend his master. Justin didn't seem aware of anything at all. There was an unsettling emptiness in his gaze, almost as though he were having some kind of fit. Cairo stood by his side, just like faithful Peter, and waited.

At last, Justin stirred.

'Cairo.'

'Are you all right?'

'This is a foreshadowing of what's to come. The next wave will be one of terror.' He looked dazed, the green eyes bloodshot.

'We're not scared. We have you.'

'This isn't a children's story. I'm not Aslan. Not Gandalf. I'm not Dr Who, the Time Lord who saves the human race once a week. I'm not even the genocidal maniac of the Old Testament—smiting and drowning and burning. Humans are so small. They have no chance against the savagery that's stalking them.'

'But you're going to save us.'

Justin seemed to be struggling with some unspeakable sadness. Perhaps seeking comfort, he reached down to bury his hand in Peter's warm coat.

'There's a price to pay for being saved.'

Twenty-seven

Diana

Dr Cameron Allsop's office at the university wasn't tidy, and neither was he; but he had a precise way of speaking, teamed with a gentle manner. It was he who'd suggested they pay him a visit. There was no fee, he said, though a donation to the Destructive Cults Information Trust would be very welcome.

'I don't have a solution,' he'd warned them. 'All I can offer is moral support. But come and see me.'

Every news channel that day was dominated by the apocalyptic events in Japan. For a while the three of them talked about the tsunami and the Fukushima nuclear disaster. It seemed wrong not to, somehow.

'Right,' said Allsop, once they were settled around a low table with mugs of coffee. 'Cassy.'

He sat with clasped hands while they gave him their full story, filling in the details. When Diana mentioned that Cassy's new husband was the driver of the white van, Allsop tutted. 'Textbook stuff, I'm afraid.'

'Really?'

'They found her at a vulnerable moment. Lucky break for them. Sounds like she'd had a row with the boyfriend and she was far from home. Some of these groups do it with military precision. They're experienced, and they're disciplined. They offered community, made her feel wanted, used the man as bait. Classic techniques.'

Mike was gripping the arms of his chair, fingers drumming. 'But she's not an airhead.'

'I'm sure she's not,' said Allsop. He peered at Mike for a moment, as though checking he hadn't caused offence. 'These destructive cults—or "new religions" is the PC term—tend to target people with something to offer. There's a perception that it's all about oddballs and no-hopers with low self-esteem, but that's way off the mark. Your daughter fits the profile: a youngish adult, educated—and maybe at the idealistic end of the spectrum?'

'I don't think she's idealistic.'

'Oh, Mike, of course she is,' said Diana, exasperated. 'You *know* she is.'

'We brought her up to think critically. She's well educated, she's smart.'

'That's certainly true,' Diana conceded, 'but she worries about every stray dog or cat or human being she sees. She worries about melting ice caps, and child soldiers in Uganda, and . . . remember when she phoned home from school after they'd been learning about climate change? Floods of tears. *The world's ending, Mum. The world's ending.*'

'Okay, so she's got a social conscience. It doesn't make her reprogrammable. You make her sound like a total drip, Diana.'

Allsop had been listening to this exchange, cradling his cup in one hand. 'As I said in that newspaper interview, people are chameleons. They'll change their colours to blend into any society, if they're manipulated effectively. Hostages often align with their captors—it's well documented, you'll have heard of Stockholm syndrome. Children learn the slang and join the gang. A perfectly normal teenager from Manchester becomes a suicide bomber. A battered wife covers her bruises and tries to be *exactly* what the man wants.'

'But Cassy wouldn't care about blending in,' said Mike.

'She already has.' Diana tapped his arm. 'C'mon, we've got to be realistic. They've somehow uninstalled critical thinking from her brain—*ping!*—and downloaded this Stepford wife.' She turned back to Allsop. 'They've even taken her name away. She calls herself "Cairo" now.'

'As in Egypt?'

'As in Egypt.'

'Mm. I imagine you know about Heaven's Gate? All those pleasant, smiling people died in the certain belief that a space-ship was going to take them to the Next Level, and that their leader was the Second Coming of Jesus Christ. They had the most eccentric names you've ever heard. Names are powerful, aren't they? Every school bully knows that—Smelly, Freak, Four-eyes. A change of name helps to disconnect the recruit from their old identity. It disorientates them. I interviewed a woman brought up among the Children of God. She had eleven different names before she was fifteen. She had no idea who she was any more. When this man Calvin persuades people to accept an outlandish name, he's putting a collar and lead on them.'

It was a horrible image. For a moment Diana didn't trust herself to speak. She shook her head and sipped her coffee, waiting for her dismay to subside.

'You talk about hypnotism in your article,' said Mike. 'Do you mean literally—' he mimed a fairground hypnotist, holding up a pendulum '—hypnotism, like in the films? *Tick-tock, tick-tock, you are going to sleeeeep.*'

Allsop nodded enthusiastically. 'Sometimes, yes! I do mean that. A clever manipulator can implant all sorts of ideas in a person's head. It can be a crowd phenomenon. Ever seen a video of the Nuremberg Rallies? Or . . . have you been to one of those fundamentalist awakening churches?'

'Heck, no. Never.'

'Look on YouTube. Stirring music—like a rock concert—big stage, clever lighting, charismatic speaker promising the earth, often in a singsong voice, lots of repetition, a crowd sky-high on collective emotion. Before you know it people are falling down and babbling and giving themselves to the Lord. And, incidentally, a lot of cash to the church.'

'Amazing,' said Mike. 'We've got one of those places at the end of our street. So, are you saying there's no line between a religion and a cult?'

'Big question. I have a tutorial group arriving in ten minutes to discuss exactly that.' Allsop put down his cup and leaned forwards in his chair. 'Look, here's the bottom line: the destructive cult is exactly what it says on the tin. *Destructive*. If a group encourages people to cut off their families, if it uses mind-control techniques, psychological coercion, if it takes their money, if it controls their daily lives and isolates them . . . if it uses deception to recruit and fundraise . . . well, then the alarm bells start to ring. And there's almost always a self-appointed, charismatic, messianic leader.'

As Mike told Allsop about his disastrous visit to New Zealand, and about Cassy's allegations, Diana listened with half an ear. She was wondering about the white van. *They were singing*, Hamish had said. *They were friendly*.

'I wonder what they were thinking,' she said suddenly.

Allsop and Mike both looked at her. 'Who?'

'Sorry. I mean those people in the van. What were they actually *thinking*, when they lured her in? They can't all be evil bastards.'

'They're not,' said Allsop. 'I think someone who's been inculcated is more than just an actor. They truly believe the role they're playing. I dare say they believed they were saving her by taking her into their loving community.'

'So she's one of them now? She's the bait?'

'Quite possibly.'

'Which means we can't hate them for it.'

'I don't think you can. If the leader's done his job well, he has complete control. In extreme cases—Heaven's Gate, Jonestown, the Solar Temple—they will die for him. They'll accept any amount of abuse from him. They seem to forget what normality is.'

'And what about him?' asked Mike. 'Calvin. What makes him tick? He doesn't believe his own bullshit, does he?'

'I don't know about Calvin in particular, but as a general rule I'd suggest most leaders have narcissistic, sociopathic tendencies. Generally it's about money, power or sex. Or all three. They may pretend to be altruistic—they may even *believe* themselves to be altruistic—but altruism is probably not their moral imperative. Even if they start out with ideals, it all gets out of hand.'

'Power corrupts,' said Diana.

'When it goes unchecked, yes.'

It sounded as though students were congregating outside Allsop's door: footsteps and chatter and—from the sounds of it—a tennis ball being thrown repeatedly against a wall. Allsop glanced at his watch. It was a subtle movement, but his visitors took the hint and got to their feet, thanking him for his time.

'One last thing,' said Mike. 'I've heard of families having people kidnapped to get them back.'

'Probably land yourselves in the criminal courts and get you kicked out of New Zealand for good.' Allsop drew the flat of his hand across his neck. 'Nope! You really can't go around kidnapping people.'

'I thought you'd say that.' Mike looked gloomy. 'It'd be a long shot, anyway. This place is pretty inaccessible.'

'Sorry.'

'Any other advice?'

'I'm afraid it's a waiting game. One day she may phone and say, "Come and get me." In the meantime, write to her. Some of your letters might get through. Let her know you love her. And don't rubbish those people!'

'Too late,' said Mike gloomily. 'We've already made that mistake.'

'Hang on a minute.' Allsop riffled through a cardboard box on his desk before handing them each a leaflet. 'I dole these out at events. It's very simplistic. Just a potted guide. Might help when you're trying to explain it to friends and family.'

The leaflet was a sheet of A4 folded in three, with the
Destructive Cults Information Trust logo at the top. The printer
had used the sort of font Diana associated with old-fashioned
typewriters. It was titled *The Cult Leader's Manual: Eight Steps
to Mind Control.*

Twenty-eight

Cairo
July 2011

'D'you ever think about your parents?' Aden asked, as they lay in each other's arms. A storm was sweeping down the valley. Gusts of gale-force wind threatened to tear away the cabin's roof, and rain had turned the pasture into a quagmire.

Cairo hesitated. The wrong kinds of thoughts were always trying to creep in.

'Sometimes I daydream that they'll join me here and be as happy as I am. Because I'm rich,' she declared, snuggling closer to him. 'I'm a billionaire.'

It was true, though over the past year there had been moments when she hadn't felt rich at all. Some days she'd felt tired and hungry and stifled, and had been sorely tempted to scream at somebody. Those thoughts always left her ashamed, and she had to confess them at Call. So she'd learned to smother them, plunging into the next task with a brilliant smile. *No negativity, only love.*

Perhaps the most testing moment had come when she asked Monika about contraception.

'You're breastfeeding,' the doctor had pointed out. 'That should stop you conceiving for a few months.'

'I was hoping for something a bit more reliable.'

'Why?'

'Because one child's enough for now.'

Monika's eyebrows shot up. 'You think so?'

'I'm still only twenty-two.'

'Get on and have Aden's child. It's only fair.'

'I'd like to pace myself.'

'You don't have time to *pace yourself*. Have you forgotten the Last Day? Create a Gethsemane family as fast as possible.'

Cairo felt a surge of anger. This was too much. She needed to take a stand. 'It's *my* body,' she said. 'I'd like to control what happens to it.'

Flick of a switch. The love went out.

'You can follow the Way, or you can follow your own inclinations.' Monika shrugged and looked out of the window. 'It's your choice.'

The alternative was unspoken. *Follow the Way, or be selfish. Be a bad person. Be unloved. Follow the Way, or leave Gethsemane.*

'I'll just let nature take its course, then,' whispered Cairo, and immediately—without missing a beat—the doctor was all smiles and grandmotherly clucking over Damascus.

Another gust raked the cabin.

'It'll feel pretty exposed out on the island,' said Cairo.

'Justin's used to it.'

'Yes, but Bali isn't. She's over there tonight.'

'*Bali's* on the island? How d'you know that?'

'I talked to her this afternoon,' said Cairo. 'She was on the jetty with Monty and Sydney. Justin's invited her to stay for a while. She's having a break from family life.'

'How did she seem?'

'Fine. She's not ill or anything, it's just that she needs a rest. Justin came and got her in his rowing boat. Sydney and Monty stood on the jetty and waved them off.'

Aden seemed to be thinking about this news. She laid her ear against his chest, listening to the slow, regular thud of his heartbeat.

'I didn't know that,' he said at last. 'I'll go and see Sydney tomorrow. He'll need a friend.'

'Why? D'you think she's in trouble of some kind?'

'No. But whatever it is, Justin will take care of her. He takes care of anyone who needs his love. The old, the young, the sick, the weak and the beautiful—like Bali.'

'That sounds wonderful.' Cairo sighed, running her fingers into his hair. She loved the way it curled around his neck. 'And I'm stuck here in this cabin, with you.'

'You should count your blessings. You found the perfect man, hopped into his van and got rid of that wimpy Pom you had in tow.'

Rain arrived suddenly, thundering on the tin roof. She laughed, and kissed Aden, and forgot all about Bali and the island.

•

Three weeks after the storm, Gethsemane celebrated the first anniversary of Cairo's arrival with a lunch party. Justin came, and he'd brought Bali home. Monty saw his mother before anyone else did. He hurled himself across the room and spent the rest of the meal clinging to her.

Someone must have gone to fetch Sydney, because he came tearing in to fold Bali into his arms. His eyes were closed, and Cairo glimpsed tears behind the round-rimmed glasses.

'Thank you for coming back,' he kept saying. 'Bali, Bali. Thank you, thank you.'

Justin made a fuss of Damascus. The baby was nearly six months old, with a fluff of shining brown hair and a wide-mouthed, two-toothed smile. He was dressed to kill in an all-in-one suit knitted for him by his Nana Kazan.

'Does this child ever stop grinning at the world?' asked Justin. 'Seems to be his default setting.'

He presented Damascus with a gift: a set of alphabet blocks in a flax basket. Cairo turned each of them over, marvelling at the craftsmanship.

'Thank you,' she whispered. 'Justin, I don't know what to say.'

'No need to say anything.'

'Did you make these?'

'Rome and I.' Justin looked around until he spotted his son, who was trying to tango with Malindi. 'He spent hours sanding the edges until they were baby safe.'

Rome had shot up over the past year and now—at seventeen—he was nigh on six foot. His shoulders were broadening, both literally and figuratively. He'd adopted Cairo and Aden as his own family. She thought of him as the younger brother she never had, and said so to Justin.

'Good!' cried Justin, throwing Damascus up and catching him, making the baby gurgle with laughter. 'Thank you for being the big sister *he* never had! I wish his mother could see him now.'

'What was she like?'

'Tripoli.' Justin's smile faded. 'She was innocent.'

It seemed an odd way to describe his son's mother, a woman who'd died so tragically. Cairo had expected him to describe Tripoli as *spiritual*, or *wonderful*, or even *the love of my life*. But she'd been in Gethsemane long enough to know not to pry.

Liam and Otto were hurrying up, anxious to bend Justin's ear about something. She heard Dublin's name as the three men walked away.

After lunch, the community went back to its normal routines.

'Not you, Cairo,' said Justin. 'And not Suva either. Buzz off! Go and enjoy the sunshine, it's precious at this time of year.'

So they wandered down to the beach and sat on the coarse sand. The winter sky was a white canvas, washed with streaks of mauve. Damascus sat propped up, legs stuck out in a V-shape, dribbling over his new wooden blocks.

'I'm glad you got into our van.' Suva shuffled closer to Cairo, leaning against her. 'I spotted you first, you know. I said to Dad, "Look at that girl!" and he said, "Oh yes. Look at that girl, let's stop and get some fuel."'

Cairo blinked in astonishment. 'You mean he didn't really need petrol?'

''Course not! We had a jerry can. No, Dad knew you were the girl for him as soon as he saw you. Love at first sight.'

Cairo had never heard this version of events before.

'That's . . . well, I'm flattered.'

'Paris and Sydney were hitchhikers too,' said Suva. 'We picked them up in the rain, just like you. They said exactly the same thing you did, when you got in.'

'Which was what?'

Suva imitated a frozen hitchhiker, rubbing her hands together. 'Oooh, it's warm in here!'

Cairo laughed. 'I didn't know that either. There's so much I still don't know.'

They pressed close together, faces turned towards the weak sun. Suva asked what it was like to travel on a plane, then she asked what happened at university, and Cairo did her best to describe student life.

'I'll never go.' Suva sounded very sure.

'No?'

'I couldn't live Outside! And anyway, the Last Day will have come before then. I don't really know why we bother with school.'

'Does that ever scare you?' asked Cairo. 'Knowing the Last Day is coming?'

'Scare me?' Suva laughed. 'That's like asking if I'm scared of my birthday! I've been waiting for it all my life. It's what we're here for, isn't it? Justin's going to be transformed into his true divine self, and there will be an army of angels, and we'll be taken up in a fiery cloud of glory. Then the Kingdom of Peace will begin.'

Damascus wanted to be a part of the conversation. He'd somehow shuffled closer to Suva and was bashing her knees with a wooden block.

'Hello, baby bro.' Suva bounced him up and down while he flapped his arms, crowing in delight. 'Are you dancing?' she cried, her voice high to match his yells. 'Let's waltz. DAH-da-da, DAH-da-da!'

Someone roared like a lion—*Rarrr!*—hurling himself off the grassy cliff and onto the sand, making both Suva and Cairo shriek. It was Rome: half adult, half child, bent double with laughter. Five seconds later, Malindi followed him. His shadow. She was twelve now, and so cheeky and fun-loving that Cairo wondered how she could be icy Gaza's daughter.

'Like sitting ducks,' said Rome, throwing himself down next to Damascus. 'Hello, wise counsellor! We didn't scare *you*, did we? No, because you're clever. You saw us creeping up.'

'I always wanted a little brother,' said Cairo. 'And now I know how annoying they are!'

The three youngsters began to play with Damascus and his blocks. Cairo pulled her cloak around herself, lying on her back, watching the evening star begin to glow. She sat up at the sound of a dog barking on the water.

'There goes my father,' said Rome. He sounded wistful.

Sure enough, the blue boat was heading away from the jetty.

'Is that Dublin with him?' asked Malindi.

'It is,' said Suva. 'He's having thoughts of going back to drugs. He's really unhappy. Justin will heal him.'

They watched the boat as it made its leisurely journey. The inlet was a sheet of mirrored glass, reflecting the pastel sky. As the boat neared the island, Peter leaped into the water and paddled ashore.

'Dublin and Beersheba are meant to be Partners one day,' said Malindi. 'She told me. She's really happy. But Dublin has to be healed first.'

Beersheba was a slightly clumsy, very bubbly eighteen-year-old with a high-pitched laugh, like Betty Rubble from *The Flintstones*. It was she who'd masterminded the embroidery on Cairo's wedding dress. Hard to imagine her with the slouching drummer.

'How will Justin help Dublin?' asked Cairo.

'Compassion and listening,' said Rome. 'People who go to the island get the full blast of Justin's love. It even happened to Otto once. D'you remember, Suva? No, I guess you were too little.'

'*Otto* needed help?' Cairo was astonished.

'Mm. His brother turned up from Switzerland and tried to persuade him to leave. He kept hanging around. He even hired a helicopter and came in that way. It was exciting.'

'I bet it was.'

'The brother gave up in the end, but poor Otto went to pieces. Justin took him across to the island. He lived there for ages. I used to visit. I remember, once, they'd been fishing, they were cooking trout over a fire. The pair of them just sat talking, old friends, so happy. I lay listening to their voices while I got eaten by sandflies.'

'That sounds lovely.'

'It *was* lovely! It was beautiful. Otto never wobbled again.'

Suva was hugging her knees. 'Think of growing up Outside, scared all the time, never feeling safe. Like my brothers are now.'

The teenagers shivered, imagining the horrors of life Outside. It occurred to Cairo that Malindi was the only one of the three not born in Gethsemane, and her only memories of the world involved a violent father.

It had grown darker while they talked, and a freezing mist was gathering on the lake. Their thoughts turned to a warm stove and hot drinks. Cairo invited Malindi and Rome for supper.

'Can we play cards after Call?' asked Suva as they stood up, brushing sand off their clothes.

'Good plan,' said Cairo. 'Let's all snuggle up and play whist. It will be a perfect end to a perfect year.'

Malindi was smiling, her round cheeks dimpled, eyes dancing. Suddenly she stretched up and kissed Cairo's cheek.

'What was that for?' cried Cairo, kissing her back in a rush of affection.

'For being you,' said Malindi. 'For being our friend.'

Twenty-nine

Palmer and Young Investigation Services
Wellington

15 September 2011

Dear Mr and Mrs Howells,

Thank you for engaging our services to investigate the Gethsemane community. Please find enclosed the hard copy of our report together with supporting documentation. As we discussed on the telephone there are other avenues that could be pursued, including a visit to Gethsemane. However, you felt that this might be counterproductive.

We enclose our final invoice and would appreciate payment within 14 days.

Please do not hesitate to contact us if we can be of any further assistance.

Yours faithfully,
Duncan P. Palmer

Report regarding Gethsemane community, Tarawera, Rotorua District, New Zealand, with reference to Cassandra Howells

Justin Calvin
Records show that a Justin Calvin was born in Essex, England,
in 1964. His parents are recorded as Marion Black and Gary
Ian Calvin. It seems that Justin and his mother emigrated to
New Zealand after she married a New Zealand merchant
seaman, Bruce Heeringa.

I have spoken to Mrs Carol Foster, who was a neighbour of
Calvin's family when they lived in Wellington. Her son Liam
was a founder member of the Gethsemane community and is
estranged from his mother. According to Mrs Foster, Heeringa
was a very violent man who beat both Marion and Justin.
Mrs Foster describes the young Justin Calvin as 'an evil little
boy' who led her son into delinquent behaviour. She recalls
that he was removed from home by the authorities at the age
of ten, and from then on lived in children's homes and foster
care. He continued to influence Liam, who would frequently
travel across town to see him. Calvin's mother Marion has
since died.

I have not been able to verify Mrs Foster's claims. The
accessing of criminal records is against the law in New
Zealand, but it is fair to say that during the 1970s children
regarded as delinquent were frequently removed from their
parents. This is something of a national scandal.

What can be confirmed is that a few seconds after midnight
on New Year's Day, 1981, Calvin was involved in an alterca-
tion outside a Wellington bar. He was on bail for drug offences
at the time. According to newspaper reports, he stabbed a
male student in the abdomen, apparently unprovoked. His
victim suffered life-threatening injuries. Calvin pleaded guilty
to wounding with intent to cause grievous bodily harm and
was sentenced to four years' detention in a youth facility. I
enclose copies of press reports.

Three factors seem relevant. First, there were concerns
about Calvin's mental health. He reported auditory and
visual hallucinations of a religious nature. He talked about

the devil and angels. Press coverage of his sentencing refers to a psychiatric report in which it was suggested that his psychosis might have been triggered by the use of hallucinogenic drugs.

Second, Calvin impressed those professionals who met him during the sentencing process. The reports were very positive. He expressed intense remorse and concern for his victim.

Third, Calvin's counsel placed much stress upon the bleakness of his childhood. He was said to have been devastated when his mother emigrated, because he lost contact with his birth father, who was subsequently killed in a motorcycle accident. Life with his stepfather was described as a reign of terror. Despite this he was extremely distressed when removed from his mother at the age of ten, and tried to run home to her on several occasions. He reported serious physical and emotional abuse while in state care. Again, this is possible: the scale of abuse of children in state care during this period is only now coming to light.

Through contacts in the Department of Corrections I learned that Calvin has remained in touch with his borstal chaplain. The Rev. David (Dave) Watkins retired some years ago and now lives in a rest home in Wellington. Calvin still visits him, which seems extraordinary given that their relationship was inmate/chaplain.

I visited Mr Watkins, who is not in good health. He was happy to talk to me and allowed me to record the conversation. He told me that Calvin took advantage of opportunities to educate himself while serving his sentence. He was a committed Christian who began a popular Bible study group. Staff soon began to rely on his leadership abilities, calling on him whenever there was trouble. On one occasion he talked an inmate down from a roof. He was also said to have quelled a riot.

At this time Mr Watkins' own faith had been weakened by the loss of his wife, but he claims that it was resurrected by *his contact with Calvin. He said: 'To know him is to love him.' Calvin was seventeen years old when he was sentenced. It seems remarkable that at such a young age he was able to bolster the faith of an experienced youth facility chaplain.*

When I mentioned Calvin's mental health, Mr Watkins became guarded. He reminded me that history is full of mystics and saints who claim to have heard voices. He quoted Joan of Arc. He said: 'Nowadays when people believe God speaks to them, they're locked up and given antipsychotic drugs. What does that say about modern life?'

Mr Watkins told me that upon his release, Calvin was welcomed by a charismatic church in Wellington. However, during the mid-1980s there seems to have been a falling-out and he left, taking many of the congregation with him. At this stage Calvin set up his own church in a warehouse, calling it Gethsemane. In 1990 he established the community at Tarawera.

While I was with Mr Watkins, his daughter Jennifer visited. She is a retired teacher who has met Justin Calvin and describes him as 'compassion personified'. Later, she privately volunteered the information that Calvin is paying the care home fees for her father. She said that Mr Watkins would dearly like to live at Gethsemane but is unable to do so as he needs specialist medical care. He wishes to have his ashes scattered there.

The land at Tarawera
In 1990, 520 hectares of land was gifted to Calvin by Thomas and Barbara Svenson, founder members of the Gethsemane church. The Svenson family had bought it from Maori Iwi in the 1950s. This elderly couple was childless and gifted the land in return for the right to live on it and be cared for until their deaths, which took place in 1993 and 2001 respectively.

While searching the land records I discovered that the gift was contested (unsuccessfully) by the donors' nephew, Mr Rick

Svenson. Mr Svenson lives in Australia but I was able to speak to him by telephone. He remains very angry about what he calls a 'theft'. He believes that Calvin 'brainwashed' his relatives, who talked as though he was 'Jesus riding on a fucking donkey'. He pointed out that the gifted land is far more valuable now than it was in 1990, and that Calvin is a multimillionaire as a result.

Gethsemane

I visited the area and spoke to business owners. The community has little impact, and locals seem barely aware of its existence. Members use dentists, supermarkets and other services in Rotorua. They're seen as polite people, known for excellent produce and craft products.

The community runs its own school, registered as a private school with the Ministry of Education. The government's Education Review Office (ERO) reported on the Gethsemane school in 2007. The report is available online. No significant alarm bells were rung.

I spoke to an ex-colleague in the Rotorua police who confirmed that the community is generally 'no trouble'. His chief contact with them has been in issuing and renewing firearms licences to members who hunt in the surrounding hills. He noted that on several occasions over the years, relatives have appealed for help in 'rescuing' members of the community, but that on each occasion the member in question has refused to leave. He was unaware of Mr Howells' visit, but recalled an incident in 2007 when a former member walked into the station, asking for a police escort so that she could go and collect her daughter. However, the following day she rang to withdraw her request. This was Kerala Louise Tillich, now living in Auckland.

Kerala Tillich

I telephoned Ms Tillich. She seemed extremely anxious and

was unwilling to speak to me. When I explained that I was acting for parents of a new member of Gethsemane, she agreed to give me a few minutes.

Kerala Tillich's parents were founder members of Gethsemane. She married (or entered into a marriage-like arrangement with) another member at the age of seventeen and went on to have three children. She told me that marriages are arranged by Justin Calvin, and that he is 'really good at it' because he 'sees into people's hearts'. She added a few moments later, 'But, then, so does the Devil.'

Ms Tillich left Gethsemane in 2007. She was able to persuade her sons to come with her but was forced to leave her seven-year-old daughter, whom she has never seen again. She suffers from anxiety, and her sons have been expelled from school. I had the impression that she regrets her decision to leave. She told me: 'Hell is a world without God, and that's where I am, that's where my boys are.'

I pressed her for details of life in Gethsemane but she became agitated and ended the conversation. My impression was that Ms Tillich is on the verge of a breakdown of some sort.

Conclusion
Gethsemane appears to be a peaceful community. No criminal activity has been reported since its establishment in 1990.

Justin Calvin is something of an enigma. He enjoys the respect and even love of many, such as Mr Watkins and Jennifer, and the Svensons. Even Kerala Tillich refused to speak ill of him, except with that one phrase: 'But, then, so does the Devil.'

On the other hand, it seems that Calvin has a remarkable degree of control. The community owns its own land, grows its own food and pays no wages. If all capital and income including pensions are paid to him, then he may be a very rich man indeed.

On the positive side, my investigation has brought up nothing to indicate that Cassandra is in physical danger at Gethsemane.

Please let me know if I can be of any further assistance.

Duncan P. Palmer
Palmer and Young Investigation Services

The Cult Leader's Manual: Eight Steps to Mind Control

Cameron Allsop

Step 8: Zero tolerance of criticism

Shame any who question, shun any who leave. Your message should be constantly reinforced: your ideology is the only truth, and you as leader are above criticism. Only those who remain in the group are saved, enlightened or valued. Those outside the group are not saved, not enlightened, not valued. Anyone who is critical of the group must be rejected, as must anyone who chooses to leave.

Thirty

Cairo
October 2011

It was like watching the gathering of storm clouds. Throughout that winter and into spring, the news brought by the Companions to Call was unremitting dark. The Watchmen feared as the Arab Spring descended into murderous chaos. They prayed for the dead and bereaved when an earthquake rocked Turkey. They wept over extremes of climate: drought and starvation in East Africa, lethal flooding in South America and Asia. They watched footage of riots in British cities, with looting and arson. Cairo could scarcely believe her eyes. She *knew* those places. Otto showed her a press photo of a building she recognised, not far from her old home, up in flames. The world she'd known was in deep trouble.

'Yet still humankind dreams on,' said Justin. 'Oblivious.'

But in Gethsemane the skies were clear. Spring filled the valley. The most vicious frosts had passed, the larders were full, and blossom frothed in the food forest.

Dublin came home from Justin's island a changed man. He no longer slouched. He smiled all the time; looked people in the eye. He picked spring flowers and delivered them to Beersheba in the sewing workshop. Within a week, Justin had joined the pair as Partners in the Watch. Beersheba laughed when Dublin first kissed her, startling a flock of mallards who had been snoozing on the beach.

Now that the mornings were milder, Cairo and Aden took to drinking their early-morning coffee on the steps of their porch. They huddled under a cloak and threw crumbs to the quails.

'This is my favourite time of day,' said Aden. 'Cold but promising. Like you.'

She pretended to slap him. Then she told him the news she'd been hugging to herself for a fortnight.

'Pregnant!' he cried, pulling her to her feet and waltzing her up and down the porch.

'Shh, you idiot,' she hissed, giggling. 'You'll wake the children.'

So he waltzed her gently, as though she were made of the finest crystal.

'I love you,' he said. 'You've brought me to life.'

•

Justin appeared at Night Call with Peter at his heels. He seemed incandescent, as if coals were glowing inside him.

'Do you feel it?' he asked. 'Do you feel the Last Day coming closer?' He was walking down the hall as he talked. The Watchmen seemed to rustle in his wake, like fallen leaves.

'Today is the thirty-first of October 2011. Why do I mention the date? Because today the population of this planet reached seven billion. Seven billion! D'you know what the head count was when I was here in the first century? I'll tell you: three hundred million. Three. Hundred. Million.' He shook his head in wonder. 'And frankly, that was more than enough. *Seven billion*. The earth groans under the weight of that seven billion. They exploit, they defile, they will ultimately destroy. That's why I'm here now.'

He stopped to take Netta's hand as she sat in her wheelchair.

'The Messiah has returned quietly, in a backwater,' he said. 'Why not descend from heaven in a superhero cape, waving my cross like a wand and generally kicking arse as I save humankind?

Because my cross was never a magic wand. Last time I offered to save them all. My offer was rejected. This time I can only save a few.'

Malindi's hand was in the air.

'Malindi!' cried Justin cheerfully, heading in her direction. 'What can I do for you?'

'Justin, there are people in the Outside who give us money, aren't there? And people who pray for us? Will they be saved?'

'Good question,' said Justin. 'Yes, they'll be saved too. All of us here will be taken up in the fiery cloud of glory—or 'flames of devouring fire', as it says in the book of Isaiah. But I'll send for those friends of Gethsemane who aren't with us on the Last Day, and they'll join us. Okay?'

Malindi was nodding vigorously. 'Okay.'

'I think we should sing about the long-awaited Last Day. Dublin, how about you bring us in with a bloodcurdling drum tattoo?'

Dublin grinned and brought his drumsticks crashing down, to be joined by Washington on the trumpet. Beersheba whooped and began to dance.

Justin's euphoria was infectious. Cairo, Aden and Suva were still bubbling as they hurried home to their cabin; even Damascus was chattering away in his father's arms. They'd reached the porch when Liam came trotting out of the darkness.

'Got a minute, Cairo?'

The Companion waited until the others had gone inside, then rubbed his hands together.

'Good news!' he announced. 'Your first recruiting trip.'

'When?'

'Tomorrow. A festival in Hamilton. Kyoto's flogging his new sustainable building course.'

'Hamilton?' stammered Cairo, who felt ambushed by her own anxiety. 'Isn't that a long way?'

'Be there and back in a day. It's a Christian music festival. We've had success there in the past. Lots of Christians are starting to wonder whether the promise of the Second Coming might be wearing a bit thin. Have we got news for them!'

'Who's going with me?'

'Kyoto, Sydney. Rome's driving. He needs the practice, he's got his test coming up. Oh—Paris. She brings 'em in. She's pretty.'

'So what's my job?'

'You know the score. Look out for anyone who needs us. Waifs and strays with nowhere to stay, anyone who could do with a rest. If they've got useful skills, all the better. Show them how lovely we are—but don't scare them off with too much information.'

This wasn't news to Cairo. Over the past year she'd seen a number of potential recruits arrive. Out of about fifteen visitors, three had stayed. Two more had come on a course and also stayed. The deepest beliefs of Gethsemane weren't revealed at first; it was a gradual process, like landing a fish. The truth was trickled to them little by little as they became more detached from the outside world, more spiritual, more ready to believe. It wasn't dishonesty, it was necessity. Cairo was certain there were still things *she* didn't know.

'Just one other thing,' said Liam. 'Keep an eye on Sydney, would you? Bali won't be coming.'

'An eye out for what?'

'Negativity. You'll know it if you see it—and I'd like to hear about it if you do. Okay?'

Cairo was surprised, but she knew better than to question a Companion. If Liam wanted her to keep an eye on Sydney, she'd do it. In fact—if she was honest—she felt just a little bit chuffed at being taken into his confidence. She was trusted.

'Sure thing,' she said.

He gave her a thumbs-up, and hurried off into the night.

•

The recruiting party gathered on the jetty before dawn, rugged up in cloaks and gloves and hats. They'd been joined by Lima and Colombo, an earnest couple who'd once lived in a tepee in a

New Age community, but had become disheartened by infighting and moved on. They had an adorable two-year-old called Xian, who'd been left in the crèche for the day.

Rome and Kyoto were already on board *Ikaroa*, messing about with the motor. A bitter wind made whitecaps race across the lake. Cairo stamped around on the jetty, feeling the first twinges of morning sickness and wishing she could have stayed in her warm bed with Aden until Early Call.

'Anyone seen Sydney?' asked Paris.

'I'll go and get him,' said Cairo, and headed down the jetty. She had to knock twice on the cabin door before Sydney answered.

'Ready to go?' she asked brightly.

'No.'

'Nearly ready?'

'We're not coming. Monty's got a dose of the runs.'

'Poor little man! But can't Bali—'

'No, she can't. She's gone back to the island. Apparently it's an honour.'

Cairo wasn't sure how to react to this. As she hesitated, Sydney stepped out onto the porch.

'Don't you ever get sick of this bullshit?' he asked. She could smell alcohol on his breath. 'Don't you ever wish you could burn this place down?'

'Sydney!' Horrified, she glanced over her shoulder.

'There are things you don't know. Things they never want you to know. Try asking them what happened to Rome's mother. Go on. Ask them *where* she is. And while you're about it, ask how Justin gets about when he goes on his mysterious jaunts. He doesn't use the van. Where does he go? And where does all the money go?'

No negativity. She covered her ears, screaming the mantra in her mind, desperate to drown out his voice. *No negativity, only love, be nothing.*

He grabbed at her hands. His voice was high and loud in the pre-dawn silence.

'Cairo, open your ears! We give everything. *Everything.* We give our whole lives. We eat when we're told, we sleep when we're told. For fuck's sake, we even screw when we're told! But it's never enough for him, is it? Never enough. He always wants more.'

Monty's voice came quavering from inside the cabin. 'Daddy? Dad?'

'Coming, my friend,' croaked Sydney. He bent double for a few seconds, as though winded, then took off his glasses and wiped his eyes with the palms of his hands. 'Cairo . . . oh God, this is . . . look, I want you to know that I'm sorry. I helped get you into the van that day. I thought we were saving you.'

'You were. You did.'

'No.'

'See you tonight,' she said. 'Okay?'

He shook his head, and disappeared inside.

•

The Hamilton party was all aboard when she ran up the jetty.

'No Sydney?' asked Paris, as Rome motored into the wind.

'He can't come. Monty's under the weather.'

'Couldn't Bali look after him?'

'She's gone back to Justin's island.'

'*Has* she?' Paris turned her head to look across at the island. She sounded intrigued, even envious. '*That's* an honour.'

'That's what Sydney said. But he . . . anyway. That's what he said.'

She saw Paris's eyebrows go up. Then Rome opened *Ikaroa*'s throttle, and they shot across the water.

•

Here she was, doing nothing more dangerous than sitting in the back of a rattling van, but she was shaking as though on her way to the gallows. Every turn of the wheels took her further from safety.

Paris slipped an arm around her shoulder. 'You okay, lovely girl?'

'Not really.'

'We all feel panicky when we travel anywhere. You've not been out much, have you? Don't worry. You're safe, as long as you stick with us.'

'Okay.'

'Just remember to smile.' Paris demonstrated a friendly grin. 'See? Show how happy you are.'

For the rest of the day, Cairo concentrated on smiling and showing how happy she was. It helped to control the heart-thudding, palm-sweating sense that she was prey to some unseen predator.

Once they'd arrived at the festival, Paris and Lima went off to look for waifs and strays, leaving the rest of the Gethsemane posse to man the stall. Cairo had expected the turnout at a Christian music festival to be conservative and a bit happy-clappy, but the reality was a bewildering, diverse procession of humanity. Kyoto was evangelical about his new course, 'Build your own Ark!'. Cairo, Rome and Colombo smiled, chatted and handed out leaflets. Nobody said a single word about Justin, the Infinite Power, or the Last Day.

During a quiet moment, Kyoto collared Cairo.

'So,' he said. 'What's the story with Sydney?'

The Gethsemane mind begged her to tell him everything—*honesty is love*—but she couldn't bring herself to denounce her friend.

'Monty's not well.'

'And that's all?'

She tried to sound casual. 'I think so.'

The carpenter looked at her shrewdly, scratching his grey curls. 'I hope it is, because we don't have secrets at Gethsemane.'

To her relief, a couple wandered up at that moment and asked him about 'Build your own Ark!'. By the time they'd gone, Cairo was talking to a boy whose tent had flooded in a downpour.

'Come and stay at Gethsemane,' she urged, pressing a leaflet into his hands.

'Where?'

'Our farm. Warm beds, hot showers and there's a stew already cooking. We'll give you a lift, no strings attached.'

He handed back the leaflet. 'Too fucking good to be true,' he muttered, before disappearing into the crowd.

By the time Rome began to dismantle the stand, Cairo's smile was slipping. Paris had had more luck, though, and arrived at the van with a couple of young women in tow, carrying backpacks and a guitar. They were horticulture students from Christchurch: friendly, interested and knowledgeable. Their tent had also flooded, so the offer of warm beds and stew had proved irresistible.

'Sounds special,' said one of them. 'What you're doing. In this cynical world, you people really seem to care.'

'We do care,' said Cairo. 'And I can tell you do too.'

Their names were Melanie and Raewyn. 'We're a couple,' announced Melanie stoutly, and they put their arms around each other. 'If that's a problem, you'd better say so now.'

'Definitely *not* a problem,' Paris assured her. 'We don't judge love at Gethsemane. We celebrate it.'

Cairo opened the passenger door.

'Hop in! We'll turn the heating up high. That'll soon dry you out. We've got a thermos of tea with honey.'

And she smiled, and smiled, and smiled. Then she slid the door shut behind them.

•

The visitors spent a happy evening in the cabin Paris shared with two other single women, being plied with smoked fish and plum wine. They were celebrities at Night Call—Melanie played her guitar—and decided to stay for a few days.

Cairo was dead on her feet by the time Call was over. Aden began Vigil duty while Suva went to Paris's cabin to talk to the new girls. Cairo headed home alone, with Damascus asleep in his cloth on her back. She was yawning when two figures loomed out of the dark: one sharp and upright, one rolling and round. Gaza and Liam.

'Good trip?' asked Gaza.

'I think so. We brought back those girls.'

The pair fell into step, flanking her. Escorting her.

'Melanie and Raewyn,' said Liam. 'Fantastic. Know much about them?'

'They're horticulture students—really impressed by your methods, Gaza. They used to go to an evangelical church but people tried to tell them they were sinners.'

'Always helps,' said Liam. 'Nothing like a bit of bigotry to drive them away.'

Suddenly Gaza halted, grabbing Cairo's wrist. 'Now. What about Sydney?'

'Monty was ill, and—'

'Be careful, Cairo.' Gaza's grip was like a vice. It was beginning to hurt. 'Be very careful. I don't like being lied to.'

They know. Cairo felt like a rat in a maze: wanting to run, but with no idea which way was out.

'We're asking for honesty here.' Liam's tone was genial enough, but he was standing much too close for comfort. 'Negativity's best out in the open. Otherwise it spreads. Rotten apples and barrels. Justin's worried about Sydney. He can actually see his negativity, hanging over their cabin in a dark cloud. That's why Bali went back to the island.'

'We need honesty and love,' said Gaza. 'Not lies and hatred. If you hide negativity, you're colluding in it.'

There was no escape. They knew everything. They knew she'd listened to Sydney's bitter ranting and failed to report back. She was in terrible trouble.

'Cairo, we think you're very special,' said Liam. 'We even see you and Aden as Companions in the future.'

'Really?'

'Yes. Yes, we do. As long as you don't disappoint us.'

They were offering her a gift: the chance not only to redeem herself, but even to climb another rung on the Gethsemane ladder.

'You wouldn't want to hold Aden back, would you?' asked Gaza, who was still grasping her wrist.

Somewhere in the depths of her mind, Old Cassy was banging on the walls of a padded cell. *Keep your trap shut! Who cares what these tin-pot tyrants think?* But Old Cassy had no say in the matter. She was fading into history. Soon she'd disappear altogether.

The night was moonless and intensely cold. The hills were frozen shadows. Somehow it seemed easier to betray Sydney to people whose faces she couldn't see.

'He's in a hell of a mess,' she said. 'I think he needs help.'

'Tell us all about it,' said Gaza.

•

Aden arrived home from Vigil with half an hour to spare before Early Call. She heard him stomping across the porch and knew from his footsteps that he wasn't happy.

'Trouble last night,' he said, pouring coffee before falling into the window seat. 'Poor old Sydney.'

Her heart missed several beats.

'What's happened?' she asked.

'Seems he'd let negativity take over. The Companions finally called him in, and it was worse than any of us realised. He's been secretly using the internet at the library in Rotorua! He's been in touch with his family. They've flooded his mind with doubts. Families *always* do that if they get the chance. We spent all night trying to get him back.'

'Could you help him?'

'I think he's lost his faith. Quoting statistics at us—did we realise the world has never been safer, less disease, longer life spans? He even mocked Justin's divinity! *He's no more Jesus Christ than I am.*'

'No!' Cairo was shocked by the blasphemy. 'Was Justin furious?'

'He wasn't there. Sydney asked to talk to him, but Gaza said he wasn't coming because Sydney no longer believed. Then he panicked and started trying to apologise, but it was too late. In

the end he was curled up on the floor, crying, asking to see Bali
and Monty. It was pretty rough. Poor guy.'

'Where is he now?'

Aden dipped his head to his mug, not meeting her eyes.

'Gone.'

'Gone where?'

'You didn't hear *Ikaroa* leaving? They'll take him as far as
the bus station. He'll be given a hundred dollars. His family's in
South Africa, I'm sure they'll help.'

'I don't believe it.' Cairo was staring out at the jetty. 'They
can't just chuck him out—they can't *do* that. We're his family!
What about Bali?'

'She's said goodbye.'

'And Monty?'

Aden grimaced. 'It's sad for him.'

'Sydney will go to court, he'll try to get custody of Monty. He
won't just leave quietly.'

'He will.'

'But he loves that little boy.'

Aden seemed completely spent. He lay down, stretching his
length along the window seat. 'He does love Monty. He really
does. But he won't make any trouble. Gethsemane has been
through this before, Cairo. Kerala gave up Suva. People who
leave Gethsemane are fighting demons already—they don't have
the strength or the money to fight us too. And they know—in
their hearts, they know—that if they take their children away
they're condemning them to death at the Last Day. Sydney
knows Monty is only safe if he's here. He'll give him up. They
all do.'

She imagined Sydney sitting alone on a bus, leaving his wife
and child and everything he loved behind. *He must be terrified*,
she thought. *He must be heartbroken*.

'I shopped him to Gaza and Liam,' she said miserably.

'Look, this wasn't your fault. They already knew. The truth
is, he never really belonged here. He stayed because he loved Bali

and Monty, not because he loved Justin. He was never really a Watchman.'

Cairo held the coffee pot between her hands, wondering how to frame her next question.

'The last time I spoke to him, he said something about Rome's mother. Tripoli.'

'Mm?'

'He said I should ask *where* she is now. But she's dead, isn't she?'

'Yes, she's dead.'

Aden held out his arms, inviting her, so she slid behind the table to lie beside him. There was barely room on the narrow seat, but they managed. She heard goats bleating, and the murmur of human voices as the milking team arrived.

'Tell me,' she said, her face close to his.

'There's nothing to tell.'

'Tell me what happened.'

He closed his eyes. She felt his chest rise and fall.

'Tripoli went swimming. At night, alone, in winter. The lake had ice in it.'

'Why on earth would she do that?'

'Nobody knows why. Rome was a few weeks old. She left him with Monika, walked out of the cabin and never came back. Justin was beside himself. He had us searching . . . the whole community was out in the hills, in the bush, on the lake. Took us two days to find her.' He drew a long breath, before adding, 'Actually, *I* found her.'

'Where?'

'Further down the shoreline. She'd drifted.'

'That must have been . . .'

'Yes,' he said. 'It was.'

A female voice yelled, *Stand still, Marigold! You'll kick it over!* The milking team was having a bad day. The bell began to toll. Suva had got up and was moving around in her bedroom. Drawers opening and shutting.

'It's forgotten now,' said Aden. 'We don't talk about it. And I've been awake all night—' he broke off, yawning '—and I've got to patch up the roof on the tractor shed before the next storm comes through.'

Minutes later, the family left for the *wharenui*. Damascus snuggled into his cloth on Cairo's back with just his smiling face showing. Suva was in a good mood, holding on to her father's arm and bouncing every few steps. When they were halfway up the hill, Melanie and Raewyn came dashing over, already under Gethsemane's spell.

'Why would you ever leave?' exulted Melanie. 'This place is paradise!'

Cairo put an arm around each of the girls as though they were her best friends. The three of them walked in step, savouring the exquisite purity of the air. The bell sounded mysterious in the half-light. Watchmen were gathering, smiling, embracing; making ready to begin another day.

But on the porch of the *wharenui*, Cairo turned to look out at the gunmetal expanse of the lake. She wondered what a new mother must have felt in her last moments, as the ice took her breath away.

Thirty-one

Diana
December 2011

It was Cassy's twenty-third birthday. Diana had sent her some earrings, but with little hope that they'd reach her. Mike had signed the card and written a note. Tara refused to be involved.

'She wants to talk to me,' she said, 'she can lift up the phone.'

Tara had gone out for the evening; said she wasn't going to sit at home and be depressed.

'Twenty-three years ago,' said Diana, as she and Mike ate at the little kitchen table. 'Do you remember? My waters broke, and you ran that red light.'

'I'd rather not talk about it.'

'We can't pretend she never existed.'

'She seems keen to pretend *we* never existed.'

They cleared away the meal in silence, watched the news in silence, made their way to bed. And still, there was silence.

Diana used to think they had a pretty good marriage. Good enough, anyway. They'd managed the separations and upheavals of army life, including ten moves in eighteen years. Their greatest test—or so they thought—had come after Mike's second tour in Bosnia. He seemed to lose himself for a time: jittery, drinking, flying off the handle. He was never violent, but she was pregnant with Tara and it was a grim year. Diana and Cassy—a little girl, then—learned to tiptoe around him. Yet they'd weathered the storm. It was ancient history, never mentioned, almost forgotten. Tara knew nothing about it.

This, though. This thing with Cassy. It was in another league. It left them bruised in every part of their souls. It made everything seem pointless. Diana wondered whether their shared investment in their daughters had been a kind of glue. When it began to dissolve, there seemed to be nothing holding them together.

The private detective had been their last hope. They had researched carefully before choosing him and spent more than they could afford. Palmer was a New Zealander, an ex-policeman who'd been in the business for years. He had experience, a wide network and a knack for getting people to talk. But he admitted to being baffled. He'd never heard people speak about anyone the way they did about Justin Calvin.

'It's not just admiration,' he said, when Mike and Diana phoned to discuss his report. 'More like *adoration*. That prison chaplain's attitude blew me away. Calvin talked a suicide down from a roof, stopped a riot, persuaded an elderly couple to hand over their land. He started his own church, and he was still only about twenty-one. People flock to him. Then again, Kerala Tillich was a helluva mess.'

'So what are we dealing with?' asked Mike.

'I don't know.' Palmer sounded frustrated. 'I'm sorry. You want answers. Heck, you paid me for answers! But I honestly can't decide whether this guy is Jesus or Hitler.'

They thanked him, paid him and filed away his report. After that dead end, Mike lost hope. He had no interest in anything or anyone. Night after night, month after month, Cassy filled their silence. Diana couldn't stand it any longer.

'Speak to me,' she said to his turned back on Cassy's birthday.

'I don't know what to say.'

'Well, for a start we should talk about Tara. She's drinking. She's doing no schoolwork at all.'

'At least we know where she is.'

Diana wanted to shake him. She understood his despair—of course she did—but what gave him the monopoly on grief? Easier to be alone, surely, than lonely in your marriage.

'D'you think you might have depression?' she asked.

'No.'

'Sure about that?'

Nothing.

'Mike?'

Still nothing. It was infuriating.

'Okay,' she said. 'Well, I think you're depressed, and I wish you'd get help because you're impossible to live with. For God's sake, it's not just you who's suffering! I want to stop crying for her too. I want to have one single day when I'm not wondering whether she's still alive.'

Still no response.

'Enough,' she snapped, reaching out to flick on her bedside lamp. 'Enough, Mike. You're bloody well going to tell me what's going on in your head.'

He was hunched up, hiding under the covers like a small boy. She laid her hand on his hair just as a sound escaped him—a long, falsetto whine that appalled her.

'Go away.' He was sobbing—helplessly sobbing, his chest heaving, tears streaming down his nose and onto the sheet. 'I don't want you to see me. It's my fault. It's me who drove her away. It's me she hates.'

There could be something in that, she thought.

'Of course it's not your fault,' she said.

He grabbed a pillow and wrapped it around his face. The movement was distressingly childlike. She'd never, in all their years together, seen Mike break down like this. Anger, yes, but never tears.

'Please go,' he begged again. 'Please.'

She grabbed her dressing-gown and fled. There was only one room in the house that brought her any comfort, and she headed there now.

Tara had come to hate Cassy's room. She wouldn't go into it. *Like a frickin' shrine*, she said. But it wasn't a shrine. It was just a beloved girl's bedroom, waiting for its occupant to come home. Seventeen months had passed since they watched Cassy pack, but it could have been yesterday. The corkboard was festooned with photos and to-do-before-I-go lists; the Greenpeace calendar still showed the page for July 2010. A row of Russian nesting dolls—a tenth birthday present from Mike's mother—kept sentinel on the windowsill: big, medium, small, very small, tiny, their painted faces locked in the permanent rictus of a smile, eyelashes like sunbeams. The dreamcatcher with its nets and feathers had hung forlornly all this time, with no dreams to catch.

Diana cleaned the room each week, dusting the law books and photos, the bottles of moisturiser and nail varnish, the tangled collection of jewellery in the mother-of-pearl box. Cassy's room must be ready for the day she came home.

Pesky was curled up on the bed. When he saw Diana he stretched, purring sleepily.

'You miss her too, huh?' whispered Diana. 'Budge up, fatso.'

She burrowed under a duvet that still—with a little imagination—smelled of Cassy's cocoa butter. The sheets felt profoundly cold.

'Cassy,' she said aloud, 'please come back. We're falling apart.'

Her voice sounded lonely. Futile.

The curtains were open. She could see drizzle on the glass and the orange mist of a light-polluted sky. Cassy wasn't even under that same sky. She was far away, in bright daylight, beside a beautiful, poisonous lake.

'Happy birthday,' said Diana. 'Wherever you are.'

Thirty-two

Cairo

If Monty cried for his father, he did it behind closed doors. He seemed thoughtful sometimes, and tired, and he took to sucking his thumb. Sydney hadn't been gone long when Bali announced that she too was pregnant.

'They'll be like twins,' she told Cairo, as they celebrated. 'Your baby and mine.'

'Will you get a message to Sydney?'

Bali blinked. 'He's gone back to South Africa. This is a child of Gethsemane.'

Melanie and Raewyn were baptised as Watchmen and became Kiev and Tunis. They laid out a new herb garden, inspired by a medieval abbey. Soon, even more aromatic plants were finding their way into Seoul's stews and Monika's medicinal teas and salves.

Cairo's twenty-third birthday fell on a weekend in December. There was a community breakfast to celebrate, and her school class sang a song they'd been practising for her.

It had rained all week, but that morning the sun came out. Cairo and Bali were rostered to help in the crèche, and decided to take their tiny charges for a walk along the bush path to Kereru Cove. It was a couple of miles, the path zigzagging over several steep spurs, but the children were used to walking everywhere. They scampered along like puppies and burst onto the beach, tearing off their clothes.

'Tidy piles, please!' ordered Bali. She was puffing. Impending motherhood made her radiant, opulent and a bit ungainly. 'Prague, don't chase the poor ducks. How would you feel if a giant duck chased you?'

The preschoolers made obedient piles out of their clothes before tumbling into knee-deep water. Two-year-old Xian—daughter of the tepee couple, Lima and Colombo—couldn't quite manage, and was stuck with her dress halfway off her head.

'There you go, darling,' said Cairo, disentangling the little girl and ruffling her hair. Gethsemane children of both genders had their first haircut on their third birthday. Xian still had a frizzing mass of ringlets, a halo in the sunlight. Suddenly—unbidden—Cairo was reminded of Imogen.

I wonder how she's getting on. Do she and Becca ever think about me? I wonder what Becca's doing now. I'd love to talk to them both.

'You look sad,' said Bali.

It was an accusation. Nostalgic thoughts about the Outside amounted to negativity.

'No! Not sad. I was thinking that Xian's a kitten,' said Cairo, blushing as she folded the child's tiny blue dress. 'I wish she could keep all those lovely ringlets.' She noticed her friend's sharp intake of breath. 'Not that I'm questioning the Way.'

Bali's eyes were shining. 'Careful, Cairo,' she warned. 'One day you're wishing Xian could keep her ringlets, the next you'll be wishing your own hair was long again. That's how negativity creeps in.'

'I know.'

'I've already lost Sydney. Please, please don't make me lose you too.'

Old Cassy very nearly exploded. *You can piss off*, she wanted to snarl. *What gives you the right to be Mrs Purer-than-Thou?*

What gives you the right to tell me what to think? You're so sodding bossy.

But that was dangerous thinking. Appallingly, suicidally dangerous. Bali was close to the Companions, likely to join them one day. She was a powerful figure—and a good friend too. So Cairo forced a smile and apologised, chanting in her head: *No negativity, only love, be nothing.*

Xian provided a merciful distraction by falling face down into the water. Both women dashed to pick her up.

'Whoops!' said Bali. 'You okay, sweetie? Got sand in your eyes? Don't rub it, you have to blink. No, don't cry! No crying! Be brave. Blink-blinkety-blink.'

The child stuck out her lower lip, screwing up her face as she opened and closed her eyes.

'Better?' asked Bali.

'Yuss.'

'I need to see a smile.'

Xian forced a comical grin before galloping back to her friends. A few minutes later Bali took off her own blue cotton trousers and waded into the water to give Monty a swimming lesson. Cairo stood alone on the warm sand, feeling ashamed of her anger. She'd allowed negativity to creep up. Even though she'd suppressed it, she had still felt it. She'd have to confess the whole thing at Call, and she dreaded that.

This little bay was the scene of some of the happiest hours of her life. It was an oasis of calm, undiscovered even by the trampers who sometimes barged in from the Outside, carrying their packs and their tents. Splashes and children's laughter sprayed like diamonds.

It was heaven on earth. She needed to remember that.

•

That night, as she lay beside Aden, she heard him thinking. She could hear it in the beat of his heart, the shallowness of his breathing.

'I saw Justin today,' he said. 'He came and found me in the top paddock. Took off his shirt and helped me swing a gate.'

'That sounds like him.'

The moon was rising over the lake. Its pale gleam dazzled her even when she shut her eyes.

'We were talking about a Partner for Rome,' said Aden. 'Justin intended that to be Malindi when she's older. But now he thinks there may not be time before the Last Day.'

'Malindi? Not Suva?'

'It can't be Suva.'

'She and Rome are really good mates.'

'Not Suva.'

'I don't see why not.'

Aden pushed himself away and sat on the edge of the bed, his back turned to her. She knelt up behind him, running her arms around his chest.

'I'm not trying to question Justin's choice,' she said, pressing her mouth against his shoulder. 'I just wondered. Suva and Rome are like brother and sister.'

Aden grunted. It wasn't quite a laugh. 'That's because they *are* brother and sister.'

There was a missed beat as she wondered whether he was teasing her.

'Suva and Rome?'

'Suva and Rome.'

'That's not possible.'

Again, the sound that wasn't quite a laugh. 'It *is* possible, and they're living proof of it.'

'You've never told me this before.'

'It wasn't time for you to know. I wasn't allowed to tell you. But now the Companions trust you to understand.'

'Understand what? How can they possibly be brother and sister?'

She felt his hand seeking hers as it lay on his chest. 'I'm not Suva's father.'

'Of *course* you are.'

'Not biologically. I was charged with the responsibility of fostering her. I'm her dad, but not her father.'

'Then who is?'

Another missed beat. Then he said, 'Justin.'

Cairo was stunned. Her mind was scurrying around, trying one possible explanation after another, but she couldn't find any way in which this piece could be fitted into the jigsaw.

'Justin's the father of lots of Gethsemane children,' said Aden.

'Like who?'

'Like Jaipur.'

Jaipur's mother was Athens. Cairo had assumed Kyoto to be his father—though now she thought about it, there was no physical resemblance at all.

'And Xian,' added Aden.

'Little tiny Xian with the curly hair? You're kidding me! That means Justin and Lima must have . . .'

'And Zanzibar.'

'No . . . Zanzi? Skye was a prostitute, wasn't she, and Justin rescued her? She can only have been about sixteen at the time. I assumed she was pregnant when she arrived.'

'She's the mother of a princess. Justin's building a new people, and these are the children of God. They carry the light of divinity within them. They'll be royalty in the Kingdom of Peace.' Aden seemed diminished. His strength and certainty weren't enough tonight. Not for this.

Cairo rested her cheek against his cool skin. 'But I don't see how . . . I mean, Kerala was *your* Partner.'

'We don't own anything in Gethsemane. She went joyfully to his island and stayed there until she was pregnant. She was the lover of the Messiah, mother to his child. She wasn't the first. She certainly wasn't the last.'

'You didn't mind? *She* didn't mind?'

'We were happy,' he said, though she felt the stiffening of muscles in his neck. 'It was an honour.'

'And a sacrifice.'

He shrugged. 'Sacrifice is a part of the tapestry. Justin sacrificed his life, dying in agony. This wasn't much to ask. Everything's
shared here.'

'Even our bodies?'

'*Everything.*'

She closed her eyes, letting the bewildering jumble of new
information settle into order. After eighteen months of immer-
sion in the life of Gethsemane, she'd left behind the hang-ups
she'd brought with her from Outside. There was a time, she knew,
when she would have been outraged. Kerala, expected to sleep
with the boss and bear his child? Aden, obliged to feel honoured
by it? Lima, Skye, Athens, Kerala. How many women had made
that visit to the island? How many men were bringing up Justin's
children?

But that was Old Cassy, conventional child of conventional
parents. She despised that person. She refused to be shocked.
After all, Aden wasn't Damascus's biological father either.

'Does Suva know?'

'She knows, but it's never talked about. She's grown up in
the quiet knowledge of her divine half. Rome is different. He is
Justin's first son, his special one, and he has no mother. Justin has
always acknowledged him as his son.'

Who else? Cairo searched her memory, and then it hit her.
'Oh. Oh, I get it. Bali.'

'That's right.'

'And Sydney couldn't handle it! I was there. I saw him standing
on the jetty, waving goodbye while Justin rowed her away. That's
why he went off the rails.'

'It was a test. Sydney would have been foster father to a divine
child. He failed the test.'

'Will Justin ever choose me?'

'No.'

'Why not?'

'He promised. He said I've made the sacrifice once, and he'll
never ask me to do it again.'

She imagined how it would feel to be one of those women: to be Justin's lover, confidante and constant companion, living with him on the island for weeks at a time. It was an oddly stirring idea. Justin was king of Gethsemane and saviour of the world. There would be glamour to it, like sleeping with a rock star. Her lover would be divine; her next child would be royalty.

Then again . . . She imagined the physical reality and recoiled.

'I love Justin as a father,' she said. 'Not as a man. Not like that—no! It would seem a bit like incest.'

'Lucky you've got me, then. Not remotely divine.'

She hugged him tighter. 'You are to me.'

'I don't know whether that's blasphemy or flattery.'

She made him lie down again and laid her head on his chest, wanting to comfort him and smother her own unease. She felt the new baby kicking and guided Aden's hand so that he could feel it too.

'Meet your son or daughter,' she said.

Everything was good in their world, and the world to come, whenever that might be. Except that she was haunted by an image of her man, standing alone on the jetty, watching as a boat was rowed away.

•

In April, Bali gave birth to a baby girl. Paris, Cairo and Monika were with her. It was very early in the morning, but by some divine instinct Justin knew. He rowed across straight away.

'Little one,' he whispered, cradling the child, 'born into a world that's clinging to the edge of the abyss. I'll call you Helike.'

Cairo was in the late stages of her own pregnancy. She snatched a few hours' sleep before Call, but it didn't seem like enough. It was during the song that she was startled by the first twinges of pain. She leaned against Aden, breathing in . . . and out . . . until they faded away. *Whew.* This couldn't be the real thing. She wasn't due for another fortnight.

'All right?' Aden whispered, putting his arm around her.

'I think I just need coffee.'

By mid-morning Cairo and her pupils were standing at the classroom windows, watching the mountain disappear behind a wall of mist and rain. She was about to suggest they paint the storm when another spasm gripped her. And another. And another. She hurried to set up easels and paints, then fetched Suva from Hana's class and asked her to find Rome.

'Tell him I need him to look after my class today,' she said.

'Why, though?' Suva seemed confused. 'What will you be doing?'

The next one took Cairo by surprise. It knocked the breath from her body, the words from her mouth. She bent in agony, resting both hands on a desk.

Suva whirled around and headed for the door. A moment later, she was sprinting through the rain towards Monika's surgery.

•

Tarawera often saw four seasons in a day. The evening sky was a brilliant turquoise when Monika handed Cairo her baby boy. Later, Justin named him Quito.

'Two new Watchmen,' said the doctor, standing with her hands on her hips. 'Two in one day. What a blessing, and what great friends they'll be. But oh dear, I'm worn out. Please—nobody else go into labour!'

Cairo's son was simply breathtaking. His head was covered in a fluff of silky hair, his features smooth and round and delicate. He accepted the fact of his birth with complete placidity, chewing his lower lip and making faces. She felt overwhelmed by love. An idea forced itself into her mind before she could bar the way.

Mum and Dad don't even know.

'Perhaps I could write to my parents?' she asked.

'Why?' Monika looked astonished. 'That would simply invite harassment.'

'I thought . . . just a few words, to tell them they have two grandsons.'

'It will start everything again. You want another visit from the police?'

'No.'

'No. And neither do we.' Monika peered out of the window. 'I see your handsome Partner standing outside, as he has been all day! Shall we call him in to meet his son?'

The Cult Leader's Manual: Eight Steps to Mind Control

Cameron Allsop

Congratulations! Your recruit is now a part of your organisation, has invested heavily in it and has bought into your belief system. They are highly motivated to work with the group to perpetuate its existence.

Remember that continuing control relies upon every member having an irrational fear of leaving the group or of questioning your authority. Ensure that there are constant reminders of the evils of the world beyond. The only news they hear should be bad news.

Thirty-three

Diana

20th February 2014

Darling Cassy,
I have no idea whether my letters have been reaching you,
but I keep writing them in the hope that some of them will.
In the years since you left there's never been an hour when
I haven't thought about you. You're as important and real
and loved as ever.

The main reason for this letter is to tell you that Granny
has died. She slipped quietly out the back door of life when
nobody was looking. This is exactly what she prayed for, so I
must be happy for her. But I would have liked to say goodbye.
She had her marbles right to the end but I'm afraid her body
let her down. I do wonder whether those years at Greenham
Common are partly to blame.

She asked about you every time I saw her, and she always
sent her love. By the end it was difficult for her to write. That's
why her letters to you got shorter and shorter.

Becca came to the funeral. She also sends love. She's an
industrial psychologist now, as you'll know if you've been
getting her letters. She's just landed a marvellous promotion,

and will be moving to New York! I wouldn't have expected her to be the one who ended up high-flying.

She tells me Imogen and Jack are divorced. Imogen had an affair and it's all been terribly acrimonious. So that's sad. Thank goodness there are no children involved.

Dad's still living in the horrid flat he's renting. He comes for dinner at least once a week. I know that seems strange, since we're separated, but I have to make sure he gets one hot meal!

Tara's been rather a worry. We don't see much of her now that she's left home. So many times I've wished you were here to talk to her.

I'm enclosing the service sheet from Granny's funeral. She always said she wanted it held at St Luke's, and I have to admit there was a kind of comfort in all those old, familiar words. The vicar was really good. Also, I learned things about her. There were people who knew her when she was a real firebrand, getting herself arrested. To me it was betrayal but to them it was heroic. An icon! My mother! I'll put in a photo of her, and some of me, Tara and Pesky (who now struggles to fit through the cat flap—the vet's put him on a diet).

I'm sorry to be writing with sad news, but I thought you would want to know about Granny.

If you do read this, darling darling Cassy, please know that I love you. You're in my thoughts when I wake, and when I go to sleep. And always. And forever.

Mum xxx

PS Please, PLEASE get in touch. I promise I will not say one word against your friends there. Just a phone call would make me very happy!

PPS I hope you've been getting my letters.

Cairo

January and February were breathlessly hot that year. The grass dried and withered. Barbecues were banned. Sheep and goats huddled in patches of shade, serenaded by the thunderous hiss of cicadas. Cairo, Aden, Suva and the two little boys swam whenever they had a free moment. In the mosquito-buzzing nights, when it was too hot to sleep, they all crept down to the water and lay in the luxurious cold.

Autumn brought crisp, bright mornings. Fruit and nuts swelled in the food forest, and the Watchmen harvested enough to feed an army. On the day of the first frost, a recruiting team brought home a Japanese language student: a self-possessed, elegant girl. She was baptised Palmyra, and became Partner to Washington.

Paradise in the valley. Chaos Outside. The storm clouds were growing darker. Week after week the Companions brought news of atrocity or disaster: one horror after another, on and on. The Watchmen began to write them up on a wooden blackboard in the *wharenui*. Soon the board was full and they had to start another. And another. And another.

Civil war had been raging in Syria for years now, creating a hell on earth. Nigeria mourned as Boko Haram slaughtered towns and kidnapped hundreds of schoolgirls. A ferry full of children capsized in South Korea. Africa was caught in the grip of the Ebola virus. Earthquakes struck in Chile, the Solomon Islands, Alaska, Mexico and Fiji. A passenger plane disappeared into thin air; another was shot down. Russia invaded Crimea and there was talk of nuclear war. Tragedy unfolded in Gaza. Most terrifying of all, a new group had reared its head with a ferocity and success that defied belief: the Islamic State or ISIS, they called themselves, and they seemed to glory in hatred and cruelty and death on an unimaginable scale. As the year wore on even Justin seemed to tire, as though the weight of the world's evil was dragging him down.

Cairo's third child was born on 1 November 2014. A girl, this time: a strong-willed burst of life whom Justin named Havana.

Damascus and Quito were barely more than toddlers themselves, and they weren't quite sure what to make of this strange creature called a sister. The two small boys would stand hand in hand beside the wooden crib and prod her to check she was still breathing.

'You and Aden do make gorgeous children,' Monika said when the new baby was six weeks old. 'But three is enough, especially with the Last Day so close.'

She took a diaphragm out of a cupboard at the back of the surgery and explained how to use it. Cairo was happy to comply, because three children were indeed enough. In any case, it didn't occur to her to question the decision. She'd long since given up struggling to preserve those trappings of autonomy. The perfection of life in Gethsemane came at a very small price.

Monika was in a mood to chat. She settled herself in her armchair, dotting adoring little kisses over Havana's scrunched-up face.

'So you think the Last Day will be soon?' asked Cairo.

'Look at the signs. How much longer can this go on? Everyone on the Outside must be terrified! I was afraid it wouldn't happen in my lifetime, but now I'm sure it will.'

'How will we know?'

'We'll know. That's why we keep watch. We'll be ready, and Justin will lead us into the Kingdom of Peace. And *you*, darling—' the doctor snuggled Havana against her bosom '—will be coming too. Imagine that, little one. You'll be taken up in a fiery cloud of glory! Your lullaby will be sung by throngs of angels!'

Cairo looked out of the window to where Damascus and Quito—one dark head, one fair—were practising their somersaults with nonstop chatter. Two-year-old Quito's idea of a somersault appeared to involve rolling sideways down the slope. They were a picture of security and happiness.

But fear was on the march. She kept glimpsing it out of the corner of her eye. The Last Day was coming. The end of the world. The end of her parents, of Tara, of Granny Joyce; of Becca and Imogen and Hamish, and billions of others.

'I wish Justin could save them all,' she said.

•

In the dead hours of the night, Gethsemane was woken by the bell. It tolled faster than usual, reverberating through the unremitting dark, making the Watchmen stream from their cabins to the *wharenui*.

'Is it the Last Day?' asked Suva, pulling a jersey over her head as they hurried up the hill. She sounded excited. 'This could be it! It's really happening! Who was on Vigil? Maybe Justin's been transformed.'

Justin was waiting for them, but he hadn't turned into a glorious being. Nobody had ever seen him unshaven before, and the grizzled stubble made him seem old. There was wildness in his eyes, in the thin set of his mouth. He gave them the news himself: seven gunmen had attacked a school in Peshawar, Pakistan, systematically murdering as many children as they could. It had taken them hours to do their work.

People wept openly, sobs echoing in the open space. Tears were allowed when they were shed for the world.

'Hatred with no bounds,' said Justin. 'Evil unleashed. What will She think of next? No more. *No more.* I beg the Infinite Power to bring an end to the world's suffering. Let it end. Let the Kingdom of Peace begin.'

•

Two nights later Cairo was sitting on her porch feeding Havana, who seemed to have an insatiable appetite. It was one of those quiet hours after Night Call, when most Watchmen were deeply asleep. The moon was full, the lake as smooth and bright as a cymbal. Mother and daughter were both beginning to doze when a shout echoed across the valley.

Cairo's first instinct was to block her ears and go quietly

indoors, because in Gethsemane it was wise not to be curious. Then she heard it again—a long, ululating yell, coming from the direction of the island—and recognised Justin's voice. Holding Havana against her shoulder, she sprinted down to the water.

A lean figure was clearly visible on the island beach, under the spotlight of the moon. He'd fallen to his knees with his arms held wide.

'Why?' he was screaming, his head flung back. 'Why? *Why?*'

Cairo stood on the shore, clutching her baby, wondering whether she should get help. *Not mad, hallucination voices. Real voices, of real beings. I'm perfectly sane.*

'Messenger,' said a voice behind her, and she turned to see Liam scrambling down to the sand.

'But isn't Messenger his friend?'

'His friend, yes.' Liam came to stand beside her. 'But a friend with a sharp tongue. Or it might be the Devil. She plagues him. She whispers in his ear.'

Cairo felt a shiver run down her spine. In this moonlit wilderness, listening to Justin's unearthly cries, it was all too easy to imagine the whispering of the Devil.

'Can't we help him?'

'Not now. No human being can help him at a time like this. People don't know how lonely it is for him, to be divine and marooned on earth. Later on, I'll row across. He'll be shattered.' Liam stared across the water, tugging anxiously on his earlobe. There was no trace of his usual bluff jocularity. 'I hate seeing him suffer like this. I've loved him ever since we were little kids, terrorising Wellington.'

'What was he like as a child?'

'Ran rings around me. I was the weirdo with a squint who nobody likes, and he was the clever kid everybody's scared of. But he made me his friend. I followed him everywhere, into every kind of trouble. And I've never stopped.' Liam shook his head. 'Never stopped. Never will stop. I worshipped him then, and I worship him now.'

Justin had begun storming up and down the island, arguing with some invisible adversary.

'I'd do anything for him,' said Liam.

'I know you would.'

'No. I mean *anything*. I'd die for him today if he asked me. I wouldn't want to live a single second without Justin Calvin.'

Cairo had known Liam for more than four years, but it struck her that she'd never understood him at all. She'd cast him as an affable sergeant-major figure who enjoyed his power. But he wasn't motivated by power; he was motivated by loyalty and by love. She had no doubt that he meant what he said. He'd die for Justin, right now, today.

Another scream tore through the silence. This time it was loud enough to startle Havana.

'*You promised! You bloody promised! Why does it always have to be me?*'

'You'd better be getting back to your cabin,' said Liam.

Thirty-four

Justin
1981

'Happy New Year,' he said.

The blade went in more easily than he'd expected. He stood there counting—*one, two, three*—and then the guy started screaming blue murder.

By one minute past midnight, he and his mates were darting down the alleyways, left, right, right. Until now they'd have followed him anywhere. They fed off his energy. But he heard the high-pitched terror in their giggles and knew he'd gone too far this time. One by one they slunk away. Lame excuses. When the going got tough, the tough went home to their mums.

Only Liam was loyal. The pair of them ended up hiding behind a shed near where the commercial fishing boats tied up. Liam kept moaning, *Fuck, it's freezing*, even after Justin gave him his beanie. It was midsummer, but Wellington didn't care about the seasons.

'D'you think you killed that guy?' Liam whispered. His squinting eye was all over the place. It did that when he was upset.

'He didn't look dead to me,' said Justin.

'Why'd you do it?'

He'd done it out of rage. He'd done it because all the world was celebrating the birth of another year, and he was sixteen years old and couldn't see the point of his own existence.

'He had a Hawaiian shirt,' he said.

He'd sliced his hand on razor wire while they were climbing the perimeter fence. The wound gaped open like a mouth. The blood looked dark and slippery in the yellow wharf lights, as though he was leaking black engine oil.

Liam was shivering noisily. 'Do anything for a cup of tea.'

'Fuck off home,' said Justin. 'Go on.'

'What about you?'

'For Christ's sake.' Justin gave him a push. 'Just sod off.'

So Liam sodded off, still wearing the beanie. Justin heard him crashing over the fence, then his clumsy footsteps, then nothing.

That left diesel and rotting fish. It left the mean wind, the blackness that rang in his ears. The fireworks were over. The party was over. For days he'd been high on rage and hooch and vodka, but even they'd deserted him now. He had nothing. He was nothing.

Curling on the cold ground, cradling his throbbing hand, he tried his very best to die.

•

Someone was shouting in his ear: *Justin! Justin Calvin!*

He knew that voice. His old friend.

'Messenger?' he cried, crawling from behind the shed. 'Where are you?'

The night was thinning. Seagulls scolded and scrapped around a rubbish bin, dragging out fish-and-chip papers. He staggered to the wharf and stood right on the edge, balancing above the oily water and massive ropes of fishing boats. The sea began to glint in the light of a new day.

Something was going to happen. He knew it. He *knew* it. He could feel his power growing and swelling. His mind filled with a deepening roar, as though a vast crowd was applauding.

'Messenger!' he screamed. 'Here! I'm here!'

And then it happened. Dazzling fire hurtled across the water like an arrow from a bow, straight into his eyes. It was a pointer, marking him out. Messenger was coming, yelling a triumphant greeting, but this time he'd brought an army. They flew in ranks, shining squadrons singing with a million voices. Justin had never felt like this before. Their love was a swollen river, lifting him up and carrying him in a tide of shining gold.

He stood with his arms stretched towards the Host. They were made of white light, blindingly bright, pieces of the sun. His head felt ready to explode with the power and glory of their singing. He laughed, and shouted, and sang with them.

He didn't notice the two policemen walking up the quay. Only when they reached him did he hear the crackle of a radio, and a voice saying they'd found a teenager who fitted the attacker's description and he was in la-la land.

They didn't know. They could never know. *Poor fuckers*, he thought, *they can't see what I can see*. He wasn't afraid of being locked up. What did any of that matter? He was in the presence of beings from another realm altogether, and their message changed everything, forever. It changed everything for him, and for the men who stood beside him, and for the entire human race.

At last, he knew what he was doing on this earth. He knew what he had to do next. He knew everything.

He remembered who he was.

Thirty-five

Diana

15th July 2015

Darling Cassy,
I've been thinking about you today, because this is the fifth anniversary of the day you left us. Five years!

I wonder what you're doing. Perhaps by now you have children? I hope you're happy. I often imagine you in that place. It does sound truly lovely.

I've had an email from Hamish, much to my surprise. He's based in Dubai now. He's going to be in London at the end of August and wants to drop in. So I've asked him for lunch. That will be nice. I haven't clapped eyes on him since you left.

Good news on the Tara front. She seems to have turned a corner at last. She's got herself into an apprenticeship program in IT and loves it. Fingers crossed.

Dad's still living in that wretched flat. They've had financial problems at work and I think he's quite stressed. I'm still at the arts centre three days a week. Same old, same old. Fiona's found a man who loves her. He does wood turning. It's nice to see her happy.

Pesky's sitting on my lap and keeps nudging my pen with his nose. He's making it rather difficult to write. He's getting a few grey hairs. Aren't we all?

Darling lovely girl, as always this comes with all my love. If you ever need anything, please let me know. I am here for you. I will always be here for you.

SO much love,
Mum xxx

Cairo

Almost five years in Gethsemane. Five years of watching the seasons chase one another across the lake and the volcano playing hide-and-seek in the mists.

Paris and Seoul were to become Partners at last, and the community was getting ready for a party. Cairo's job was to harvest the last of the winter vegetables: broccoli, parsnip, leeks and spinach. Havana was swaddled against her back, snoring like a small steam train. Rome, Malindi and Suva had come to help her. Malindi was sixteen now, and Suva soon would be. The two girls were closer than most sisters, and fun to have around: lively, clever and utterly unaware of how beautiful they were.

'Seoul's been in love with Paris for years,' said Suva. 'It's a bit romantic.'

'She's lucky!' said Malindi, her blue eyes widening. She appreciated good food. 'Imagine having him cooking for you every day.'

There was frost in the air and a high, ice-tinted vault of sky. Malindi's blue skirt swirled as she danced among the bushes. She lifted a booted foot when Rome was reaching for his basket and kicked him on the bottom. If she was hoping for a reaction, she was disappointed. He merely twitched a moody half-smile before carrying on with his work. The young man had turned twenty-one and looked more like Justin every day, but he seemed to be living under a shadow recently. He smiled less, frowned more. He didn't tease the girls as cheerfully as he used to.

The conversation turned to Washington and Palmyra, whose first child was due at any moment.

'Otto and Monika will be great-grandparents,' said Malindi. There was a streak of mud on the curve of her cheek. 'Whew. That sounds *really* old.'

She and Suva began to speculate about whether the baby would be a boy or a girl, and what name Justin would choose. Cairo half listened, crushing a ragged sprig of rosemary in her hand. She'd first met Washington on the day she got into the van. He was just a child then, enjoying a game of I-Spy with Riyadh and Rome. Incredible to think he was about to become a father.

When she tried to recall life before the van, she found she couldn't. The memory seemed antique, dusty, tinged with sepia. *Was that really me?* She'd been like a fish in the depths of the lake, unable even to imagine the brilliance of the world beyond. Then she accepted a lift and began her journey into light.

The boards in the *wharenui* covered a whole wall now. The planet was in flames. Millions of refugees were pouring into Europe, though many drowned on the way. Nepal mourned the deaths of thousands, killed by earthquakes. The so-called Islamic State was terrorising the world. Bombs turned crowded markets and bus stations into charnel houses. Cairo felt grateful—guiltily grateful—that she and her children were safe.

Old Netta had died in the autumn, aged ninety-two. Her ashes were consigned to the lake, and a new cross joined the others on the headland. Yesterday they'd added another: that of a man called David Watkins. Cairo had never heard his name before, but Justin wept as he scattered his ashes off the promontory. He seemed grief-stricken, and rowed back to the island without speaking to anyone.

Cairo was wondering who David Watkins might have been when she spotted Gaza marching through the food forest.

The gardener worked harder than anyone in Gethsemane, which explained why the larders were so well stocked. Physical work and fasting had hollowed her face, and the sinews stood out in her arms. Cairo quailed at the very sight of her.

What does she want? What did I do wrong?

Malindi stood to attention. Suva swiftly wiped the mud off her friend's face.

'Hi, Mum,' said Malindi. 'We've nearly finished.'

Gaza's eyes swept over their baskets. 'Right,' she said. 'Cairo and Rome, you're to take *Ikaroa* down to Kereru to set up the cabin for Paris and Seoul.'

'Now?' asked Cairo.

'Now.'

Cairo didn't want this job. The short winter's day was going to turn bitterly cold within an hour. She had a baby on her back and a family meal to cook. But Gaza's ice-blue gaze was upon her.

'Sure,' she said. 'Be happy to. Suva, could you take Havana?'

Mist had begun to seep across the lake when they left the bay. Rome was usually cock-a-hoop when speeding along in *Ikaroa*, but this evening he seemed to have something on his mind. He slowed to a crawl before Kereru Cove, scanning the shoreline.

'Can I tell you something, Cairo?' he asked.

'That depends.'

'Just between you and me. Nobody else, not even Aden.'

Cairo grimaced. Secrets were always uncovered. Somebody always confessed.

'I have to tell someone,' said Rome. 'And I trust you. If the Companions knew, I think I'd be expelled.'

'They'll never expel you! You're Justin's son.'

'Sons get sacrificed.' Rome turned the motor off, letting *Ikaroa* drift. He was gripping the sides of the boat. 'I'm in touch with Perth.'

'Perth? Suva's brother?'

'I bumped into him in Rotorua. In the bank. He gave me

his phone number, so I took a few dollars out of the cash I was banking and bought a phone. I've even found a spot where I can get a signal. Behind the laundry—it's only two bars, but it works. I've been calling him.'

'Rome, please don't tell me any more.'

'I've met up with him. We've done a lot of talking. A *lot* of talking.'

Cairo wished he hadn't confided in her. She would have to pass on the information to the Companions or be complicit in it.

'He needed me,' insisted Rome. 'He's on bail for selling drugs. And he's alone. Doesn't Justin teach us to care for people in trouble? Isn't that what Gethsemane is all about?'

That was true. Justin would never turn his back on someone in need.

'Does Perth want to come back?' she asked, as a hopeful thought struck her. 'Aden would collect him tomorrow—he'd collect him tonight!'

'No.'

'No chance at all?'

'Perth doesn't want Aden to know. He says Gethsemane is a hellhole.' Poor Rome looked beleaguered. 'He's told me stuff. It's got me thinking.'

'You're mad to listen!'

'Have you ever wondered how Justin always knows what's going on? He *always* knows. Perth told me—'

'Stop.' Cairo had leaped to her feet, making *Ikaroa* rock. 'Stop, stop! I don't want to hear any more.'

'But—'

'Not another word. I'll jump off this boat if you say another word. I mean it.'

They drove on to Kereru *whare* in silence. Vines and undergrowth were begining to engulf the cabin, so they cut them back. They made the bed, put out chocolates, swept the floor, laid the fire, organised food and a bottle of wine. Then they motored home through the first spits of rain.

'Please don't tell Aden,' whispered Rome, as they tied up at the jetty.

She'd been thinking about this, and had come to a reluctant decision.

'I won't,' she said. 'I hate not telling him, but I won't. But you mustn't open the door to Perth's negativity. Don't listen to him. Hey, little brother? Do you promise?'

Rome didn't promise. In fact, he didn't reply at all.

•

The following day saw two happy events occur at Gethsemane.

First, Paris and Seoul were joined as Partners. Neither of them stopped smiling from dawn until dusk. The celebrations were in full swing when Washington came running in, jumped up on a table and announced that he was a father. Palmyra had just given birth to a boy, weighing in at an eye-watering four kilograms. Justin named him Fez.

'I was midwife to my own great-grandchild,' said Monika the next day, when she dropped by for tea with Cairo. She'd mellowed as she approached the age of seventy-six.

Cairo laughed. 'Wow! I bet there aren't many who could say that.'

Monika nodded, fingering her cup. She seemed uneasy. For the first time in five years, Cairo sensed a hairline crack in her friend's serenity.

'I hope my dear little Fez has a bit of time to grow up,' she said. 'A bit of a childhood before the Last Day.'

Thirty-six

Cairo
August 2015

There was an urgency about Justin nowadays, like that of a commander before battle. He ordered that shopping and recruiting trips be kept to a minimum.

'Stay close,' he said. 'Be ready—2015 is going to be the Last Year.'

He walked past a row of blackboards, trailing his hand across the catalogue of disaster—a constantly updated timeline, leading to the Last Day.

'The signs are unrelenting.' He stopped to tap one of the boards. 'Remember this . . . and this? Right across the world. Another Nigerian town massacred. Children crucified by Daesh. A passenger plane deliberately flown into a mountainside. And Syria's agony goes on and on and on, and has drawn in the world's powers. I predicted all of this when I was here last. *All* of it. Wars, and rumours of wars. Nations rising against nation. Famines, pestilences, earthquakes.'

A toddler was grizzling. It was Xian's little sister, Cuba. Her parents looked mortified.

'Sorry, Justin,' said Lima.

'Cuba! Can I have a cuddle?' asked Justin, holding out his

arms. He balanced the tiny girl expertly on one hip and, with a conjuror's flourish, produced a biscuit from his pocket. 'I brought this especially for you.'

Cuba accepted his gift with a complacent smile. Another child had her hand up. It was Zanzibar, Skye's daughter, who'd been so useless at playing rounders all those years ago. She was an outgoing nine-year-old now. Justin sat down on her cushion, still holding Cuba.

'Fire away, Zanzi.'

'What will actually happen?' asked Zanzibar. 'On the Last Day. How will the world end?'

'Terrific question! I'll tell you. Humankind has been so distracted by Syria, and all the refugees, that they haven't noticed the real danger. Nuclear weapons have already fallen into the hands of the wrong madman. He's just a madman, plain and simple, as so many powerful people are. Soon those forces will be unleashed—shock waves and radiation, thousands of times more terrible even than Hiroshima or Nagasaki. The earth will shake, volcanos will blow themselves apart. Oceans will rage and cover great stretches of land. The sun will go out. There will be total darkness.'

Zanzibar sat very straight, listening to every word. Justin dropped a kiss on her shorn head.

'But don't be scared, because you'll be safe, Zanzi. And your mum. And all of us. You know why? Because you trust me. Messenger and his army will come, and I'll be transformed into my real self. You'll need your sunglasses, because my *real* self is brighter than a thousand suns!'

'You'll be a god again.'

'Yes, and you'll be one of my special friends. I'll make the earth stop shaking, I'll tell the oceans to go back into their proper places. And *then* my reign of peace will begin.'

Zanzibar was nodding happily.

'All right?' Justin tickled her behind the ear, making her giggle. 'Well done.'

Monty led the song that day, singing unaccompanied just as Rome had at Cairo's very first Call. He was seven now, with a pure treble voice that brought tears to Cairo's eyes. Today's song was very different to Dublin's triumphant drum tattoos, or the euphoric harmonies that made everyone want to dance. It was simple and melancholy: a requiem to the world.

Cairo happened to be watching Justin. He was on his feet again, still holding Cuba, swaying as he sang to her. Then—out of nowhere—something seemed to hit him, making him stagger and clutch at his head. Lima ran to take Cuba back. The next moment Liam was by Justin's side, helping him out by a side door.

The Watchmen saw, but they were too disciplined to comment. They kept singing. They kept smiling. They kept smiling.

•

When Cairo left the *wharenui*, Rome fell into step with her.

'I've seen Justin do that before,' he whispered.

'When?'

'Couple of days ago, on the island. He said I wasn't to tell anyone.'

'Has he talked to Monika?'

'He won't. He says his body's disintegrating so that his divinity can emerge.' Rome turned in a full circle, checking there was nobody in earshot. 'Perth's being sentenced this afternoon.'

'You're not going!'

They argued in furious whispers. Otto had given him permission to go to Rotorua to buy a new computer, because the antediluvian one in the office had finally died. Perth was to be sentenced at two, and Rome planned to be with him.

'Let me tell Aden,' begged Cairo. 'He'll want to be there.'

'No! I promised Perth. He's terrified of anything to do with Gethsemane.' Rome grabbed her arm. 'Cairo, if you tell Aden . . .'

He didn't have to finish the sentence. They both knew where it was going. *Aden might tell the Companions.*

'You're playing with the Devil,' warned Cairo.

'No. I'm standing by a friend. If Justin was in his right mind he'd see that. In fact—' He broke off to grin—widely and unconvincingly—over Cairo's shoulder. 'Hi, Suva!'

'What would Justin see?' asked Suva, who seemed to have materialised from nowhere.

'That Malindi and I should be Partners,' said Rome, without a moment's hesitation. 'Now. Before the Last Day.'

'Ooh!' Suva rubbed her hands. 'Well, I don't think she'd say no.'

Cairo was shocked by the smoothness of his lie, but she had to go along with it. An hour later, she looked out of her classroom window to see *Ikaroa* disappearing behind the headland.

•

School was over for the day. Cairo was carrying a basket of washing to the laundry when *Ikaroa* returned. She changed course and met Rome on the beach.

'Find what you wanted?'

'A laptop for Gethsemane.' He dropped his voice. 'Perth got twenty-one months.'

'How was he?'

'Realistic.' Rome rubbed his face with his hand. He looked twitchy, his gaze darting around the settlement. 'Kerala was there.'

'Oh no. You didn't talk to her, did you?'

'I did. And she told me something terrible. I don't know what to do.'

All of a sudden, he was crying. She needed to get him off the beach. Eyes could be watching from any one of the cabins.

'Come to our place,' she muttered. 'The boys have gone to Kazan and Berlin's for tea.'

As soon as they reached the cabin, Cairo checked every room to make sure Suva wasn't around, then swung Havana from her back and settled her with some toys. Rome was pacing, talking fast.

'She told me this thing.' Cairo was shocked to see how his hands were shaking. 'This awful, awful thing.'

'It'll be all right.'

He pressed his fingers against his eyes, as though trying to block his tears. 'It's *not* all right. She told me what really happened to my mum.'

Cairo knew she should shut this down, but Rome was suffering. And besides, she'd always been intrigued by Tripoli's story.

'She was a child when she got pregnant with me,' said Rome. 'She was only sixteen. Sixteen! Like Malindi and Suva. They're still just kids.'

'Young people do become Partners here. Aden and Kerala were seventeen.'

'But she wasn't *from* here, and he didn't make her his Partner. He picked her up in Wellington. She'd run away from home and was begging on the streets. He found her going through the bins for food. Kerala says she was far too thin, but very pretty and very, *very* young. He took her to his island. He told her she was Mary Magdalene—you know, reincarnated. He said all the speculation was true about him and Mary Magdalene. She was his wife.'

'*Really?*'

'That's what he said. He called Tripoli—my mum—the Bride of God. She worshipped him. We all do, don't we? But according to Kerala this was even more . . . she was just crazy about him, followed him around like Peter does now. They lived together on the island until I came along. I was born in Monika's surgery. Apparently I came out the wrong way round, and Kerala heard my poor mother screaming for hours. After I was born she cried all the time, didn't even want to look after me. All she wanted was to get back to the island. A couple of times she managed to paddle out there in a kayak, but Justin kept sending her back.'

'Why?'

'There was always some reason. He went away on one of his trips and came back with Athens. He said she had to stay with him, because she was a recovering alcoholic.'

Jaipur's mother, thought Cairo, with a horrible rush of understanding.

'Athens *was* an alcoholic,' she said. 'She's told me so. Justin found her passed out on a park bench. She doesn't touch our wine.'

'Yes, but that wasn't the only reason she stayed on the island! And Jaipur was the result.'

Havana had crawled off to the cupboard and was pulling out all the pots. Cairo ignored her. There was a time for worrying about the mess, and that wasn't now.

'Go on about Tripoli,' she said.

'When I was two weeks old, Justin took her out fishing. He told her she could never live on the island again. He said he loved her, but Messenger had reminded him that he is *everyone's* Messiah, so he can't love one person more than another. He dropped her off at the jetty. Kerala and Aden were good friends of hers. They tried to look after her, but she was broken. That same day, the Companions had every boat removed from the beach and the jetty. They were all hidden. Late at night people saw my mum looking for them. She was crying. She told Kerala that if she could only get to Justin, she'd make him love her again.'

'Oh no.' Cairo could see where this was going. 'No.'

'My poor mum was trying to swim to the island. But it was too cold, and too dark, and too far, and she was only a little girl really.'

Pity overwhelmed Rome. Tears streamed down his face. He tried wiping them with his hand, then with his sleeve, but there were too many. Cairo fetched a handkerchief and sat him on the window seat. She sat too, and hugged him.

'You know what else Kerala told me?' he said, when he could speak again. 'Justin and the Companions didn't want any investigation into her death. Nobody Outside knew she'd been here. He picked her up off the street, remember? They put Breda down as my mother when they registered my birth. Tripoli became one of Gethsemane's secrets. Her real name has been forgotten. As far as the Outside knows, she was never here. But she *was* here. And she's still here.'

'Still here?'

'She never left.' He turned to look out of the window, pointing at the headland. 'You know that cross on the highest point, above the rocks? That's my mum. She's buried there.'

Cairo knelt on the seat beside him, staring out at the promontory. She'd climbed it hundreds of times. She and Justin once stood right beside that cross, admiring the view. They must have been standing on Tripoli's grave.

'She isn't the only one buried there,' said Rome.

'No more secrets,' begged Cairo, but he was a runaway train.

'There's a stillborn baby. Gaza's baby.'

'*Gaza's* baby?'

'Gaza and Justin's. C'mon, Cairo—you must have noticed how often she goes to the island with him? Apparently she was so happy to be having a baby. But something went wrong during the birth, and he died. He was never even given a name, just quietly buried and forgotten. In return for her loyalty, Gaza was made a Companion.'

Cairo had nothing to say. She sat stunned, with her arm around Rome's shoulder, trying to process what she'd learned.

Footsteps galloped across the porch, and the door banged open. Damascus and Quito were home from tea at their Nana Kazan's.

'Rome's here!' screeched Damascus, and both boys piled on top of their favourite uncle.

Cairo's mind was cartwheeling. She had a duty to report Rome to the Companions. He'd brought Kerala's secrets—*or lies?*—into Gethsemane, and they could be lethally toxic. But she knew she wasn't going to betray him. She'd never forgotten what had happened to Sydney.

She needed a sanctuary. She needed time to think.

Leaving Rome with the boys, she fled to the laundry. She liked this building. It smelled of the coconut oil, lemon and lavender that were used to make soap, and was always warm because the water was heated in a wood-burning stove. She shut the door, dumped her basket and let out her breath in a long exhalation.

'Just the person I wanted to see,' said a voice.

Gaza was standing three feet away, watching Cairo with her taut smile. The white falcon, wondering which bit to eat first.

'Oh my God, Gaza!' Cairo felt a stomach-clenching rush of adrenaline. 'Gave me a fright.'

'Did Rome have something to tell you, after his trip to town?'

'Nothing important. He popped in to see the boys.'

'You're a bad liar.' Gaza stepped closer. Much closer. 'Secrets are always discovered. *Always*. I will do whatever it takes to protect the purity of Gethsemane.'

The woman's stare was like a searchlight. Even when your conscience was clear, she made you feel guilty. Cairo heard herself gabbling. 'Honestly, Gaza, there's no secret, I don't know what you—'

She didn't see the slap coming, didn't have time to flinch before her cheekbone exploded. The movement was lightning-fast, and its force sent Cairo reeling. Stars whirled in the gloom of the laundry.

'Watch your step.' Gaza's tone was casual. Chatty, even. 'You've got three children. That's a lot to lose, isn't it?'

'It is.'

'They'd miss you.'

'I know.'

'Well.' Another smile. 'Your choice.'

As soon as the door had shut behind Gaza, Cairo's knees gave way. She collapsed into a corner, nursing her aching cheek, refusing to cry.

It was dark by the time she walked back down the hill, carrying a basket of wet washing to be hung up on the line behind the cabin. She swung along as though everything was good in her world. She was smiling again. Smiling and smiling.

She'd slipped on some soap and banged her cheek on a porcelain basin. Yes, that was what had happened. She wouldn't tell anyone the truth. Not Rome, not even Aden. After all, she'd brought Gaza's anger on herself. It was her own fault; she wasn't worthy to be a Watchman. From now on she would strive to do better.

Thirty-seven

Diana

She cried when she saw Hamish on her doorstep.

She'd intended to be doughty and cheerful; made an effort to look like the woman he used to know. She'd even put on mascara and a bit of lipstick. Her hair was a disaster, more pewter than mouse, so she'd bundled it into a clip.

'Come in, come in,' she said, accepting his kiss on the cheek. 'Sorry to turn on the waterworks. It's just—seeing you large as life and twice as handsome . . .'

'I'm so sorry, Mrs Howells.'

'Diana. And don't be sorry,' she said, as he followed her into the kitchen. 'Who knows what your futures would have been?'

He'd filled out in the past five years and shaved off the designer stubble. Gold wedding ring; posh watch. He'd become exactly what she'd expected of him: successful, confident and ever so slightly smug.

'I think the rain's going to hold off,' she said, as she made coffee. 'Shall we brave the garden? It's rather a mess, I'm afraid. Gardening was Mike's thing. I've got a quiche in the oven but it needs a bit longer.'

There were still remnants of former glory: rosebushes and leggy lavender battled with bindweed and goosegrass. The potting shed was rotting under a feral buddleia while brambles crawled victoriously over the rusted swing. A couple of tea towels drooped on the washing line. Back in the day, that line had been a string of bunting: Mike's shirts flapping, the girls' colourful undies, and all the cheerful messiness of family life.

They sat at the picnic table. Pesky appeared from under the shed and settled on Diana's lap.

Small talk, at first. Hamish and his wife had a baby. He produced the inevitable photos on his phone. Diana expected Charlotte to be a toned goddess with Gucci accessories and matching offspring; she was pleasantly surprised to see a buxom girl with a lopsided smile, spoonfeeding a child whose face was covered in mush.

'Charlotte looks nice,' she said.

'She *is* nice.'

'I'm so pleased, Hamish. Well done.'

It was only a matter of time before he asked after Mike. When she told him about their split, his eyebrows lifted in polite astonishment.

'I never saw that coming. Not you two.'

'You never know what's around the corner.'

He nodded, looking wise; but he and—what was her name?—Charlotte clearly hadn't met any corners on their road. Not yet.

'Mike couldn't cope,' Diana said, stroking Pesky's ears. 'Not after Cassy made those horrible allegations. He blamed himself. He thought I blamed him too.'

'I'm sure you didn't.'

'Yes,' she said, after a moment's hesitation. 'If I'm honest, I think I did. It probably wasn't fair but you want to blame somebody. I never said it, but of course he sensed it. It came between us—that, and the unremitting sadness and worry. It was pretty awful in this house. He came home less and less. One day he didn't come home at all. I felt sorry for him, sorry for myself, but—I'll admit this—I gave up on our marriage. We never even argued, really. We're each still the best friend either of us has. We haven't had the energy to divorce.'

'He's still working?'

'Nonstop. Work, work, work. Hurt, hurt, hurt.'

'And Tara?'

'Dropped out of school.' Diana dabbed at her eyes with her sleeve. The mascara had been a mistake. 'She's had a string of boyfriends, all as dull as ditchwater. I think she's sticking herself to the ground with both feet in case she gets ripped away in a tornado.'

'Like Cassy?'

'Perhaps. The thing is . . . if Cassy had been killed in a road accident instead of getting into that bloody van, we'd still have happy memories. Instead she's alive and well, so far as we know, but she doesn't want anything to do with us. And we love her, Hamish. We do.' Diana was searching her pocket for a tissue, her voice dissolving. 'So that hurts quite a lot.'

He made embarrassed, sympathetic noises while she blew her nose.

'Cassy used to say she had a wonderful childhood,' he said stoutly.

'That's nice of you. Thank you.' She took a grip on herself. It wasn't fair on him.

'So now it's just you here,' he said.

She gestured at the cracked tiles on the patio, the wilderness in the garden. 'We should sell up, but how can we? This is Cassy's home. She'll be back one day.'

'You think so?'

'I *know* so. Every time the phone rings, I cross my fingers.'

'Hang on.' Hamish was holding up a hand, his head cocked to one side. 'Isn't that your phone right now?'

She listened. *Yes.* She could just hear it.

'Probably telesales,' she muttered, as she hurried inside. 'I'll answer it anyway—that quiche must be ready to come out of the oven. Excuse me . . .'

The kitchen was filled with the smell of warm pastry. Diana grabbed the phone in one hand, oven gloves in the other.

'Hello?' she said, fumbling with the oven door. *Please be Cassy.*

Not Cassy. Mike. He sounded as though he were losing his voice.

'Hi, Diana. Got a minute? Some news I'd like to discuss.'

Funny thing. He still relied on her. She relied on him too, in a way.

'I've got Hamish here for lunch,' she said. 'Remember I said he was coming?'

'Of course. Hello from me.'

'Could we talk this evening? Come for dinner.'

She heard heaviness in his breathing and wondered what had rattled him. Suddenly, she was afraid.

'Mike? What's this about?'

Several more breaths. When he finally managed to speak, his voice was calm.

'Bad news, I'm afraid.'

•

The quiche was burned. She steadied herself with one hand on the kitchen table, feeling her life shift and slide, yet again. The ground was never still. It hadn't been still for five years. This time, she felt as though she might end up on her knees.

The man who might have been her son-in-law was waiting. He leaned under the frame of the swing, one hand gripping the chain, pushing it back and forth. Vividly—oh, how vividly—she remembered standing in a kitchen very like this (which house was it? Colchester?), looking out on a pocket handkerchief of a garden, filled with lilac and sweet william and brilliant purple daisies. She saw Mike and Cassy playing with that same swing, while baby Tara snoozed in her buggy. Cassy was wearing a white sundress with yellow lemons all over it—*my lemon dress*, she called it. A bird's nest of brown hair, sparking with auburn lights; legs straight out in front, singing at the top of her voice—'*See saw, Margery Daw, John*ny shall have a new *mas*ter!' Mike was joining in the song as he pushed her. Hard to say whose singing was more tuneless.

They were ghosts, now. A ghost father and daughter, playing in a ghost garden among ghost flowers. Ghost happiness. Ghost love. All gone.

She walked back out to Hamish, almost tripping over a cracked tile.

'I'm afraid I've cremated the lunch.'

He was staring at her. 'You all right, Diana?'

So kind. And he's young enough to be my son.

'I don't know what to do,' she said. 'Mike is dying.'

•

Bless him, Hamish rose to the occasion. He opened every cupboard in the kitchen until he found the tea.

'Would you like me to contact somebody for you?' he asked, carrying a mug. It slopped as he lowered it to the table. 'Maybe Tara?'

'Thanks, no. Mike wants to tell her himself.'

'I'd better leave you in peace. I'm so sorry for your . . . all this.'

'Three months,' she said. 'Best guess. Maybe more, maybe less. He didn't even tell me he was having tests. Then his leg broke, and it turns out to be pancreatic cancer that's spread to his bones. So he *had* to tell me. Why didn't he want me to know? I'm still his wife.'

'Perhaps he didn't like to worry you.'

Diana chewed her knuckle. 'He wants her to come home. He wants to make peace with his girl. Not a lot to ask. Surely she'll come home to make peace with her dying father?'

Hamish murmured 'of course' and 'for sure'. But she could guess what he was thinking. She was thinking it too.

I wouldn't bet on it.

•

She found Mike in a hospital bed. He was hiding under a cloak of cheerful practicality, as though he'd broken his leg by falling off a ladder and would be right as rain in no time. She knew him too well to be fooled. He was already weakening, already diminished.

'I'm well insured,' he said. 'And there's the army widows' pension. You'll be better off.'

'Don't joke about it.'

They talked in a matter-of-fact way about timescales and treatments, and when he'd be coming home to her. There was never any question that he'd be going back to his flat.

'There's only one thing on my bucket list,' he kept saying. 'And that's to see Cassy again.'

They composed another desperate email to Gethsemane, though neither believed it would be answered. Then Diana kissed him on the forehead and left him alone in his condemned man's cell.

She was halfway home when the grief hit her. It was a physical blow, smashing the breath from her lungs. She had to pull over and stop on the verge as traffic rushed past, unknowing and uncaring. She had never, in her whole life, sat in a car and sobbed before.

•

From: Mike and Diana Howells
To: CallsopDCIT@universityofsussex.org
Re: Mike and Cassy

Cameron,
Mike has metastatic pancreatic cancer. He wants to see Cassy, so I'm going out there to try to tell her. We've nothing left to lose. Any advice?

Cameron rang an hour later.

'They must let me see her,' she said. 'Now her father's dying. Even the police will back me up on that. And if I can talk to her, I *know* I can get through to her.'

'Diana, you have to let go of the image you've got of that happy-go-lucky student you last saw at Heathrow Airport. After five years in a closed religious community, she will have changed beyond all imagining. You'll be meeting a stranger.'

'I know.'

'Do you really? *People are chameleons*. She's lived exclusively in that mindset. She's had experiences you can never understand. She's loved people, really loved them. She's danced to their tune, she's changed her moral code to synch with theirs. She's had to learn how to survive and succeed in that very odd, very rarefied environment.'

Diana sat down, daunted. 'What do you suggest?'

'Well.' A pause. A sigh. 'First. Remember they're *her* people now. If you walk in all guns blazing, telling her they're a crazy cult, you'll make things even worse.'

'I know that.'

'Second. If you do get her out, remember that lots of people go straight back. The hard part isn't getting out. The hard part is staying out.'

'Once she's with me—'

'She'll be a mess. D'you have a phobia? Spiders? Snakes?'

'Um . . . very deep water. That film *Titanic* gives me the heebie-jeebies.'

'Right. Imagine you've fallen off a boat. It's gone. You're alone, treading water. You know there are miles of water below your feet—*miles*—pitch-black depths, God knows what monsters. Nasty, isn't it? Believe it or not, Cassy may feel that same terror of the outside world. A real phobia.'

Diana shut out his image of the dark depths. 'So . . . how do I tackle that?'

'Let's take this a step at a time,' he said. 'First you have to see her. Then we'll know what we're up against.'

They talked a little longer before he wished her good luck and rang off.

Then she spoke to Fiona, who was horrified by Mike's illness and said of course, of *course*, she'd manage alone at the arts centre for as long as it took.

At midnight—eleven hours after first hearing Mike's news—Diana booked a flight.

•

The night before she left, she cleaned every corner of Cassy's room with superstitious fervour. Tara had come to house-sit. She stood in the doorway with her arms folded, wearing the cynical smile that seemed to have become her resting face.

'You can't turn back the clock,' she said, watching her mother plumping pillows.

'I can try.' Diana had been daydreaming. Cassy could still finish her degree, still live the life she'd planned. Perhaps, magically, the family could go back to being the way they'd been.

'Mum, don't get your hopes up. Even if she comes home, she won't be our Cassy any more. We've all moved on. We are what we are.'

'Such a facile expression.' Diana smoothed the duvet, removing imaginary wrinkles. She must get everything right. She must. '*We are what we are.* It's a tautology.'

'Doesn't make it any less true. How are you paying for this trip?'

'God made credit cards.'

•

She flew through two nights, listening to the hum of the engines.

Every hour brought her closer to Cassy; every hour brought Mike closer to death. When the plane touched down at Auckland Airport, she felt a thrill of fear and excitement. She was in the same hemisphere as Cassy. The same country. She was looking at the same sky.

So close. *So* close.

Thirty-eight

Cairo

It was an ordinary day, if any day could now be called ordinary.

Justin came to Early Call, but he was changing before their very eyes. His clothes flapped loosely, as though they were meant for someone else, and heavy lines had been etched down each cheek. He seemed to be sliding out of his body.

He sat down on the edge of the dais, drew one leg up and clasped his hand around his knee. He might have been chatting to an old friend over coffee.

'It's my turn to confess,' he said. 'Last night I had an unwelcome visitor. The Devil came and sat by my fire. She sucked the heat from the flames. She was laughing herself silly at mankind, because one single madman is about to destroy them. And she dangled temptation in front of me.' He imitated a husky female voice, seductively crooning. *'D'you want to save them all, Justin? Do you? Do you? I can fix it for you.'*

Damascus was sitting on the cushion next to Cairo, listening with his thumb in his mouth and very round eyes. He missed nothing. Before she could stop him, he'd put up his hand.

'Damascus!' cried Justin. 'Our wise counsellor. The first time you've spoken at Call. I'm listening, little mate.'

'Um,' said Damascus, 'is the lady going to fix it for you?'

Laughter rippled in the room, but Justin's expression was grave.

'Good question, Counsellor. I was so very tempted. She knows I long to save them all. But no. I told her no. I have my orders, and I will follow them.'

Damascus seemed satisfied with the answer. He leaned against Cairo, and his thumb went back in.

'I'm here to answer your questions,' said Justin, looking around. 'I know these are strange times for you. It's always strange to be packing up one life and moving on to the next, no matter how exciting and beautiful that next life will be.'

Jaipur's hand was up. He was squeezed onto a cushion between Malindi and Suva. 'Justin, who is the madman?'

'I can't answer that,' said Justin. 'There are plenty of candidates. But I'll tell you this: I've seen a mushroom cloud. A blinding flash, a giant shock wave spreading right around the planet. There may be days left, or there may only be hours. Be ready.'

•

Justin rowed back to his island after Call, taking Gaza with him. Cairo saw them go, and remembered the graves on the headland. She'd avoided Gaza in the weeks since that awful episode in the laundry. The bruise on her face had faded, but she still froze every time the woman came near her. She'd avoided Rome too. She couldn't afford to hear any more secrets. She was trying to be a perfect Watchman.

Her class spent the morning in the carpentry workshop, where Kyoto was teaching them how to make boxes. The carpenter was in his element, rushing around, pencil stub stuck into his wire-brush hair. 'A little bit of sanding here,' he said cheerfully, 'and a little bit of gluing there.'

One of the boys ran up to Cairo, holding out a cut finger.

'Let me see,' she said, squatting beside him. 'Ouch! Poor Moscow. What happened?'

'The hammer hit my finger, not the nail.'

'They do that,' said Cairo. 'Hammers. They don't always wallop the right place. Let's put on a plaster, shall we?'

The plaster—and the finger—took all her attention for a few minutes. She was putting away the first-aid kit when she felt a hand on her shoulder.

'Cairo.'

It was Liam's voice. He took her arm, drawing her away from the children.

'You've got a visitor,' he said.

Diana

The water-taxi man was waiting for her by the Landing Café, defying the cold in shorts and a blue-checked jacket, ready to cast off as soon as she'd put on her life vest.

He proved to be quite chatty, in a laconic kind of way. He was a retired farmer, apparently, and his name was Howard. 'Holiday-makers come in summer,' he said. 'People bring their boats. They fish. Their children water-ski. Pretty quiet at this time of year though.'

For twenty minutes or so Diana hunched into her winter coat, watching the scenery. She had to admit—grudgingly—that it was staggeringly spectacular. It reminded her of the Scottish Highlands, but the foliage was more exotic and there was a crystal-bright clarity to the air. Once they left the holiday houses behind she could see no sign of a road, or even a telegraph pole. Nothing. Just endless forest, and the desolate slopes of Mount Tarawera.

'Lonely spot!' she shouted over the roar of the motor.

'Bugger all out there. If you walked a hundred kilometres that way—' Howard pointed '—you'd see nothing but bush until you got to Lake Waikaremoana. Only you'd never get there. People get lost in that country. Never find a trace of 'em.'

'Do you know anything about Gethsemane?' she yelled. 'My daughter's with them.'

'You'd hardly know it's there. Seem like happy people.'

'Happy?'

He examined the word. 'Always smiling.'

She was tempted to tell him exactly what she thought of those smiling people, but the boat was slowing down. The water had stopped being a blur. She watched a bobbing family of coots slide by, as Howard steered into a bay.

And there it was. Gethsemane. A wooded valley, sheltered from the wind, drowsing in winter sunshine. She recognised the tumbling hillsides and low buildings from the website.

As soon as they were alongside the jetty she scrambled onto it and gave Howard a thumbs-up. He nodded, and motored away. They'd agreed on this beforehand—he was to leave immediately and pick her up at twelve. That way she couldn't be manhandled back into the boat, as Mike had been.

Two little boys were already racing to meet her. Both were barefoot, wearing pale brown shorts and blue jerseys. Both had pudding-basin haircuts.

'Looking for Gethsemane?' asked one. He might have been seven or so, with wide-awake eyes and a plaster on one knee. His sidekick was younger—four or five, she'd guess.

'Yes. Have I come to the right place?'

'Definitely the right place,' said the older boy.

'Def-nitly the right place!' echoed his friend.

Polite, she thought unwillingly. *And they look me in the eye. What nice little chaps.*

'May I take your bag for you?' asked the older one.

'Thank you, no. It's just a handbag.'

'I'm Monty,' he said. 'And this is Damascus. You have a kind smile.'

'I doubt it.'

'Would you like a cup of tea and some *very* yummy muffins?'

'No, thank you.'

'They're boysenberry muffins.'

Diana wasn't quite sure what to do next. She'd been geared up and adrenaline-fuelled for a shouting match. The last thing she'd expected was a welcoming committee of small boys, beaming up at her as though she were Father Christmas. Cameron Allsop hadn't written a manual for this.

Step 1: Locate your cult. Step 2: March in. Step 3: Fight off a pack of kids offering muffins.

More children pelted down the slope. A couple of teenaged girls brought up the rear. They had very short hair and were decked out in blue clothes. One might have been a young Marilyn Monroe: china-blue eyes, a wide, generous mouth and the sort of blonde hair most people got out of a bottle. The other was taller, thinner and more wary; freckled and sandy-haired.

'Hello and welcome,' said the freckled one, with an earnest smile. 'Have you come to stay with us? Are you enrolled in a course?'

'No. I've come to see Cassy.'

'Who?'

Diana sighed. 'I think you call her Cairo.'

It was as though she'd uttered a magic word. The smaller of the two boys danced a happy little jig on the spot. 'Cairo, Cairo! That's my—'

'Shush, Damascus.' The freckled girl took his hand. 'I'm not too sure where she is today.'

'Um . . .' Marilyn Monroe bit her lip thoughtfully. 'A group went to Rotorua, but I don't know if she was with them.'

'If you'll follow us,' said the first girl, gesturing towards the buildings, 'we'll try to find her. While you're waiting, can we get you some tea? I'm Suva, by the way. This is Malindi.'

Diana didn't want their bloody tea, but she could hardly tell them where to shove it. They were just children.

They formed a procession around their visitor, prancing up the grass. The two older girls were chatty. *Have you come far today? Oh—from Rotorua? Well, you're very welcome. You've got a lovely accent. Where are you from?*

When she mentioned England, they looked pitying.

'We hear a lot about the terrorists,' said Suva. 'And all those poor refugees, drowning and suffocating in lorries, but your government won't let them in.'

'It's a bit more complicated than that.'

They were walking among the buildings. Diana kept looking around, searching for Cassy.

'Is it true,' asked one of the younger children, 'that someone put a bomb on a train and a bus, and lots of people got killed?'

'Well, yes. A long time ago.'

'Is it true that there were riots and they broke shop windows and stole things and set fire to people's houses?'

Diana wished they'd shut up. Two women strolled past, carrying babies on their backs and washing in baskets (*not Cassy*); others seemed to be shepherding a gaggle of toddlers (*not Cassy*); distant figures were working in some kind of garden (*still not Cassy*).

'Are you a gardener?' asked Suva. 'At the moment it's early spring vegetables.'

Their smiling obstruction was maddening. She wanted to shake them. 'Look . . . just take me to Cassy. Cairo.'

'We'll find out where she is, I promise.'

Such wide-eyed honesty. Neither girl looked as though she'd ever told a lie in her whole life. *Guard against them*, Diana warned herself. *Even the children. They're cunning.* They were showing her up some steps and into a wooden building.

It might have been a campsite kitchen. Refectory tables filled the middle of the space, but there were armchairs around one window.

'Do sit down,' invited Suva, indicating an armchair. 'Tea, coffee, kiwifruit smoothie? Or a vegetable drink? It's nicer than it sounds.'

Diana could have cried with frustration. 'Please will you get Cassy? It's very, very urgent. Tell her it's her mother. There's bad news from home.'

'Okay. Malindi will take care of you. Monty and Damascus, please organise tea and muffins. Prague, run and find Liam and tell him this lady is here.'

Having issued her orders, Suva hurried out. It was an impressive piece of leadership. Diana noticed that all the children did exactly as they were asked.

She didn't touch the tea they brought her, nor the yummy muffins. The children seemed desperate to keep her entertained. The smallest boy—Damascus—stood in front of her chair, staring up at her with dark blue eyes, twisting a lock of his hair around his finger.

'Would you like to read my library book?'

'No!'

He winced at her vehemence, and Diana was ashamed. The poor little chap was only trying to be polite. Whatever lunacy was going on in this place, it wasn't his fault.

'All right,' she relented, through gritted teeth. 'Let's see it.'

He scurried off and was back in two minutes, clutching a picture book. It was a traditional take on the Christmas story, complete with angels and shepherds. The other youngsters gathered around.

How has this happened? she wondered in bewilderment. *I've come twelve thousand miles to see my daughter. Why am I reading to a pack of children?*

'See their wings?' asked Damascus, pointing at a picture of three angels. 'They don't really have those.'

'They don't?'

'No!' He was scornful. 'Angels don't *weigh* anything. They're not like bees! They don't need wings to fly.'

'Oh. I see. Actually . . .' All this relentless happiness was beginning to irritate Diana. She felt the need to strike a blow for rationality. 'Actually, angels don't exist at all. There aren't any angels in real life. None of this happened in real life.'

Her outburst was met by silence. It was a small victory, and it didn't feel as satisfying as she'd expected. She turned the pages of the book, reading fast. *Fairy stories. Why must the world raise its young on fairy stories?*

'"No room," said the innkeeper. "No room at the inn." "But my wife is going to have a baby," said Joseph. "Please help us."'

She galloped through page after page of soppiness to the inevitable end . . . *yep, yep, no surprises there: shepherds, angels, a star. And then the empty promises.*

'Peace on earth,' she read. 'Good will towards men. The end.'

'Thank you very much,' said Damascus, carefully closing the book. 'You're a really good reader.'

'You're welcome,' Diana lied. 'But you don't have to wait with me. Such a lovely day—I'm sure you'd like to be outside.'

No, they said, they wouldn't. The smaller ones began to play hide-and-seek among the tables. Diana felt as though she were in a horror film. Perhaps they'd killed Cassy in some satanic ritual before dumping her body in those vast forests or in the lake. That was why they were stalling.

She could see the lake through the windows, framed by the delicate fronds and peaty undersides of tree ferns. The pastureland and native bush looked improbably green, and the water improbably blue, reflecting hills and sky. It was all too perfect to be real. *It's a chocolate box view*, she thought. *And these are chocolate box children.*

As she watched the photogenic little band, something dawned on her. They weren't just being polite. They'd met her as soon as she set foot in the place. They'd escorted her here. Now they were keeping her in this room, and they wouldn't leave.

They're not hosts. They're guards.

Instantly, she was out of her chair and heading for the door.

'Are you looking for the toilet?' asked Malindi, moving to block her exit.

Diana looked at a blue-eyed teenager and saw a fiend.

'Get out of my bloody way! Where is she?'

They all stared at her, open-mouthed, holding one another's hands.

'Okay,' said Diana. 'I'm going straight back to Rotorua to fetch the police. I'll have this place taken apart piece by piece until I find out what's happened to her.'

The door had opened while she was speaking, and someone

came in: a smiling doughnut of a man, too round and sugar-sweetened to be dangerous. One eye didn't seem to be quite in step with the other.

'Hello there,' he said, twinkling benevolently as he shook her hand. 'I'm Liam. So sorry you've been kept waiting. Cairo's mum?' He answered his own question with a nod. 'Yes! I can see the family likeness. Welcome to Gethsemane!'

'Where's Cassy?'

'Cairo is a very special woman. You must be proud.'

'Where is she?'

'She's in retreat at the moment.'

'Don't play games with me.'

He didn't stop smiling. She had an almost irresistible urge to slap him. 'Another few minutes, Mrs . . .'

'Howells.'

'Mrs Howells. While we wait, why don't I show you around? See some of the things Cairo sees every day. It might help you to understand her world.'

'No, thanks.'

'Oh?' He looked confused. 'Don't you want to understand her?'

She wasn't sure how he got around her defences, but the next moment they were in bright sunshine, wandering about like a couple of octogenarians in a National Trust garden. She wanted to explode, to scream for Cassy, to curse them all, but Liam's affable manner made it impossible. He pointed out colourful beehives among the bushes, patting his own girth and ruefully admitting that he couldn't resist the honey cake. That was when she reached the end of her tether.

'Where is she?' she cried in desperation. 'Just tell me. Is she dead?'

Liam smiled over her shoulder. 'Not unless I'm seeing a ghost.'

Diana swung around. Two women were making their way through the trees. Both had cropped hair, blue clothes and scrubbed, shining faces. One was elderly and diminutive, the other younger, straighter and taller. Her complexion was clear, her eyes bright. She was smiling, but there was a waxwork quality to her expression.

For an awful moment, Diana was uncertain. *Is that Cassy? No. Yes. No, it isn't her. They're trying to trick me.*

This woman was much older than Cassy. Her face and body were far more angular. Her shorn scalp looked nothing like Cassy's dramatic mane of hair. She even held herself differently. And if it was really Cassy, why didn't she speak? Why the empty, Russian-doll smile?

But her eyes were dark blue, her nose slightly misshapen as though it had once been broken.

'Hi, Diana,' she said. It was Cassy's voice.

With a wordless yell Diana ran down the slope, throwing her arms around her daughter's neck, babbling *thank God, thank God*. She'd been pummelled over the past few days: the shock of Mike's diagnosis, the long journey, and now meeting this poised stranger. It was too much. She was overwhelmed.

Cassy embraced her mother, but it was a perfunctory gesture. She'd turned off the smile. 'They tell me you've brought bad news. I hope it isn't Tara?'

Diana forced herself to breathe. 'No, not Tara. It's . . . um . . .' *Wretched tears.* She appealed to Liam. 'Could you please leave us alone?'

'Better if we don't.'

'Why? Are you coercing her?'

'We don't coerce people, but you might. Ah, Aden! Glad you've come along.'

A man was striding up. He'd be somewhere in his thirties, with Viking size and colouring.

'Hello,' he said, holding out his hand to Diana. She shook it, because she couldn't bring herself to be openly rude.

'Aden is my husband,' explained Cassy, taking his arm. 'The father of my three children.'

'The father of . . . ?' Diana stared at her. 'We have three grandchildren? Cassy! Where are they? Can I meet them?'

There was a general shaking of heads.

'Please let me meet them,' pleaded Diana. 'Look, I promise I haven't come to make trouble. I've only come to tell you some news about Dad.'

'What about him?'

'Can't we sit down somewhere and talk properly?'

More shaking of heads. Apparently not.

'Okay.' *Breathe in, breathe out. Say the words.* 'He's got cancer. It's already spread to his bones. He might only have a few weeks. He—'

Her voice gave out. She pressed her knuckle to her mouth, willing herself not to dissolve.

Cassy had turned pale, but her waxwork expression didn't change. The Viking murmured something and drew her closer to him.

'We sent emails about this,' said Diana. 'Didn't you get them? There's only one thing he wants before he dies, one thing he *desperately* wants, and that's to see you again.'

'How can we believe you?' said the older woman. There was an accent. German perhaps, or Dutch.

'Here.' Diana reached into her handbag, dragging out a wad of folded sheets. 'His hospital notes. D'you really think I'd invent a story like this?'

The woman took the notes and glanced through each one.

'I'm sorry,' she said. 'I truly am.'

Diana sensed genuine compassion. Perhaps they weren't monsters after all; perhaps they'd let Cassy go.

'Please come and see him, Cassy,' she begged. 'He's never, ever stopped grieving for you. He's thought about you every day since you left. Not knowing if you're happy, not knowing if you're even alive . . . it's broken him. I've watched him fall apart.'

'I'd like you to stop the guilt trip, please,' said Liam. 'This is why we wouldn't allow you to speak to her alone. This is *exactly* why. Your emotional manipulation.'

Diana ignored him. She was looking at Cassy.

'I'll buy your return flight. You could be there and back in a fortnight. I'm asking you, in the name of all that's . . . Please don't let Dad die without making peace between you. *Please.*'

'I'll have to talk to the Companions,' said Cassy.

'*Who?*'

'The Companions. The elders. We make decisions together here. We don't act selfishly.'

'Can I talk to them too? I can't go home empty-handed. I can't let your father down. Poor Granny never stopped asking about you, right up until she died. It broke her heart.'

Cassy blinked. 'Granny's died?'

'Yes! Over a year ago.'

The waxwork began to melt, and Diana caught a glimpse of the real Cassy.

'I wrote to tell you,' she said, pressing her advantage. 'Haven't you been getting my letters? I've sent so many! Letters, emails, presents. So have Dad, and Tara, and Granny, and your friends.'

Cassy looked enquiringly at Liam, but he held up his hands.

'Not guilty! Maybe you used the wrong address.'

'We used the address on your website.'

'I think you'd better go now. I can see your boat coming in.'

You bastards, thought Diana furiously. *You lying, thieving, evil bastards.* All those carefully chosen presents. The hours spent writing, trying not to say the wrong thing. Not one word had reached Cassy.

But Allsop's advice had been very clear. Her only hope lay in being patient. She couldn't afford to insult these people.

'I'm at the Four Seasons Motel in Rotorua,' she said to Cassy. 'Room four, okay? I'll wait for you there.'

Cassy nodded. Then, at some unspoken signal, she and the Viking turned and walked quickly away. Liam and the older woman moved to stand side by side, forming a wall so that Diana couldn't follow.

'You do have to go now,' said Liam, taking her arm. 'We'll talk about your request, and get a message to you.'

They marched her back to the jetty. They were bouncers, seeing her off the premises.

'Stop,' said Diana, when they were almost at the boat. She wrenched her arm free from Liam's grasp. 'Let me say something else.'

She looked desperately from one face to the other, searching for some flicker of caring. Liam's smile was still firmly fixed, but the woman looked unhappy.

'Please!' Diana didn't care about dignity any more. If she thought it would make any difference, she'd hurl herself at their feet. 'I'm begging you as a mother, as a wife, as a fellow human being. Let her dad see her. Let her come home, even just for a week—even just for a day. We love her so much. She's our girl, can't you see that? Please, let her go.'

Thirty-nine

Cairo

'Out of the question,' said Gaza.

She and Justin had appeared within minutes of Diana's departure and called Cairo into the meditation room. All the Companions were there. Aden had insisted on coming in too, despite Gaza trying to block the door.

'I'm her Partner,' he'd said quietly. 'This affects me. It affects my children.'

Gaza had looked enraged, but she'd stood back from the door. 'Don't interfere, Aden.'

Seeing Diana's face had somehow telescoped time. It seemed to Cairo as though the years hadn't passed. It was only yesterday that she was packing, with her mother and sister sitting on the bed.

'Justin?' she asked, appealing to him. 'Isn't there a chance of redemption? Mike might turn to you, since he's facing death. Do you think I should go?'

Justin was standing with his back to the room, staring out of the window. He didn't answer.

'I promise to be back within a fortnight,' she said. 'I have children here. You know I'll come back.'

There was a long silence before he turned around. 'I'm sorry,

Cairo. You can't go. Here's the reason . . . are you listening? The Last Day is imminent. If you leave Gethsemane now, you won't be back in time. Believe me, you will not. They won't let you. They'll cancel your ticket, or steal your passport, or have you locked up in a psychiatric unit. They'll use every trick—lies, blackmail, bribery. They'll employ experts to mess with your mind. We've seen people driven mad by the mind games their families play. If you leave now, you won't come back.'

'You mean you won't *let* me come back?'

Suddenly, he was angry. He crossed the room in two strides, gripped her chin between his fingers and tilted her face to look up at him. She stood very still. For the first time ever, she felt afraid of Justin.

'I mean you *will* not come back,' he said, with quiet precision. 'Do you understand?'

She hardly recognised this man. There was no love in his gaze, no compassion or laughter. His mouth was a thin, contemptuous line. His fingers were bruising her face.

'I do,' she said. 'I understand.'

'So the subject is closed?'

She nodded.

His grip tightened. 'Don't question me again, Cairo. There isn't time.'

The next moment he'd walked out of the room.

There was a short, tense pause before Liam let out his breath. 'Okay. *Whew.* So that's decided. Gaza, you'll help Cairo write a letter to Mrs Howells?'

'Certainly,' said Gaza.

'I'll get someone to take it across as soon as it's written. Cairo, I know it seems hard, but this is a classic way for negativity to come in. We can't afford to lose you. The sooner we get shot of your mother, the better for everyone.'

Cairo knew what came next. She'd been through this before. They would go to the office, Gaza would dictate a letter, and Cairo would write it. All done and dusted. That was the Way.

Gaza was alight with energy and certainty. 'Right!' she said, opening the door. 'Let's get on with it.'

But Cairo hesitated. She stood as Justin had, gazing out at the scene she knew and loved more than any in the world. Dull thuds of pain throbbed on either side of her jaw where Justin had gripped her.

The face of the lake had darkened. Changes in the weather happened fast here. They caught people out. Boaters and trampers got into trouble and had to be rescued. She watched as rain made zigzag swathes across the water. A rainbow arched above the mountain, ghostly brightness projected over a granite sky, as though the air itself was stained with colour.

Mum will have got caught in the squall, she thought. *I hope she got back okay. She looked older than I remember.*

'He's dying though,' she whispered. 'He's really dying.'

'The world's dying, my love,' said Monika, laying a hand on her arm. 'He's just leaving a little early.'

They were all watching her.

They were waiting for her decision.

Diana

Hours had passed. Every time a vehicle pulled into the motel's car park she rushed across to the glass doors, hoping for a miracle.

A blue sedan with a family crammed into it.

A man in a yellow truck, delivering a parcel.

A motorbike carrying teenagers.

A rusting white van.

She watched as it circled around the car park before coming to a stop near the door of her unit. A young man swung out of the driver's side. Tall. Long nose, tidy hair. Canvas trousers and a jersey. Rather good-looking, in an old-fashioned way.

And then he was making a beeline for her door. She dropped the net curtain and stood with her back to it. Cassy wasn't coming. They'd sent a messenger.

His knock was rapid, rattling the glass.

'Mrs Howells?' He had an open, friendly smile. 'Hi, I'm Rome Calvin. I'm delivering a letter.'

She took the envelope and read Cassy's handwriting: *Diana. Mike.*

'Could you wait?' she asked. 'Come in, sit down for a minute. Perhaps I'll need to send another message back with you.'

'Sure,' he said, and perched on an armchair while she opened the envelope.

There were two sheets of paper. She stood beside the window while she read them. One hand held the letters up to the light; the other pinched the loose skin at the front of her neck.

> *Dear Diana,*
> *Thank you for coming all this way. I was very happy to see you.*
> *But I'm sorry, I can't come with you to England. It can't happen. It will not happen. This is my home now. Please go back to Mike and take care of him. I'm also writing a letter for him.*
> *I pray for both of you, and for Tara.*
> *Love,*
> *Cairo (Cassy)*

Diana let out a shuddering breath, shutting her eyes for a moment before turning to the second letter.

> *Dear Mike,*
> *I'm very sorry to hear you're ill. You must be frightened. I wish I could see you again, but it isn't possible.*
> *This does not have to be the end. You can live forever! Are you well enough to travel here? If so, please come. Give yourself to Justin and let him be your king. Even though you've never met him, even though you've left it so late, I know that if you come to him he'll open the gates and let you in.*

Don't worry about me. I want you to know that I am very, very happy. You have three grandchildren. Their names are Damascus, Quito and Havana. They are four, three and ten months old.

Damascus? Diana lowered the letter, narrowing her eyes. *Damascus. Damascus . . .* Wasn't that the name of the little chap who met her at the jetty? The smaller one? *I read my grandson a story today.* She was thinking back, frantically trying to remember what he looked like. If only she'd known! She would have read him ten stories. She would have taken a photo, for Mike.

Damascus looks a lot like me. Havana and Quito are fair-haired and blue-eyed and even-tempered, just like their father. Aden is a really wonderful man. He's a farmer, and very practical. I'm sorry you never got to meet him.

Mike, I forgive you for what happened in my childhood.

I pray that you will not die in ignorance, but will open your mind before it's too late.

With love,

Cairo (Cassy)

'Did Cassy write these?' Diana asked.

Rome blinked. 'Who? Oh—sorry. Yes, Cassy. Cairo.'

'I don't believe she wrote them herself,' said Diana. 'I don't believe it for one second. *Sorry to hear you're ill . . .* that's not Cassy's voice. And Mike's not just *ill*. He's dying!'

'Oh no.' The young man looked shaken. 'I didn't know that. I'm so, so sorry.'

Diana shoved the letters into her handbag. Her movements were quick and clumsy.

'I'm not leaving without her,' she said. 'I came to get her for her father, and that's what I'm bloody well going to do. If they think I've travelled twelve thousand miles just to go home alone, they've got another thing coming.'

'Have you talked to Cairo?'

'Five minutes! After five years! That's what they generously allowed. And they didn't give us a single second alone. There were bodyguards. A guy called Liam. Some woman—little, old . . .'

'Monika?'

'I've no idea. And a man who claims to be Cassy's husband.'

Rome was pacing around the room, tapping the van's keys against his teeth. He seemed so young. She'd assumed he was just a messenger.

'How long can you stay in Rotorua?' he asked.

'A few days. My husband needs me.'

'Okay. I'll see what I can do.'

'I'm desperate. If there's anything you can do, anything at all . . .'

'I'll try.' He drew an imaginary zip across his lips as he opened the door. 'Don't mention me to anyone. I'll be in touch as soon as I can.'

'Is this the van?' she asked, nodding at it. 'The one she got into?'

'Yep. I was there. We all knew, straight away, that she was special.'

Diana walked right around the vehicle, looking in with horrified fascination. For five years this thing had loomed in her imagination as somehow demonic. It was an evil trap. It was the Child Catcher's carriage; the Pied Piper's cavern.

It was just a battered old van, with a box of apples in the back.

Forty

Cairo

Gaza was edgy.

'Your mother's highly manipulative,' she said. 'I don't trust her. You're not to leave the valley until we're sure she's gone.'

'Of course not.'

'I wouldn't have let Rome deliver those letters. That was Liam's doing. I wasn't consulted.'

The Companions made sure Cairo was kept busy all day: laundering the bed linen of elderly Watchmen, chopping fire-wood, helping Monika with a stocktake in her surgery. She knew they were trying to distract her. The tactic didn't work.

Diana came all this way. And Mike's dying. And Granny's gone.

In the hour before Dusk Call she escaped to her own cabin on the pretext of changing Havana's cloth nappy. Rain was pattering on the roof, and the baby was babbling, but Cairo kept her ears open for another sound.

And there it was. The mosquito drone of a motor. She picked up Havana and rushed out to the porch to see Rome driving *Ikaroa*—head up, despite the rain in his face. She wanted to hear how her mother had taken her rejection; wanted to know if there was any message from her. But instead of pulling in to the bay, the red boat disappeared behind Justin's island.

Seconds later, Damascus came pelting around the corner.

'Mum!' he cried, sliding to a halt on the soaking grass. 'Otto says where are you? You're meant to be on the kitchen team and we've got a communal supper.'

Cairo hurried down the steps, holding out her free hand. 'Let's run together. You, me and Havana. One, two, three . . . go!'

They sprinted through the wet. She felt his small hand in hers and watched him trying to catch raindrops on his tongue. A thought came to her. It was unbidden, and unwanted, and unbearable.

Dad will never meet his grandchildren now.

•

It wasn't until they'd gathered for Dusk Call that she saw Rome. She leaned across to speak to him, but he shook his head and began an animated conversation with Jaipur.

Halfway through the song, Justin caused a stir by walking into the *wharenui* and stepping onto the dais. His movements were fast and jerky, his mouth compressed. He signalled to the musicians to stop playing, which they immediately did. Cairo had never seen this happen before.

'Rome has something to confess,' he said.

Stunned, anxious silence.

Rome stood like marble, arms folded. For an agonising stretch of time, he didn't move. Cairo felt her pulse throbbing. *What happens if he refuses? What happens then?*

At last, he stepped up onto the dais. Father and son stood shoulder to shoulder, facing the Watchmen. But this time they were like wrestlers in the ring, not comrades in arms.

'I argued with Justin,' confessed Rome, in his clear voice. 'I told him he was wrong. I lost my temper. I forgot to humble myself and be nothing.'

'And what else?' asked Justin.

'I swore. I shouted.'

'And what else?'

Rome's eyes flickered to his father's face. 'I said I was ashamed of Gethsemane. Ashamed of you.'

There was a collective gasp from the Watchmen, but Justin smiled.

'You're my beloved son,' he said, laying a hand on Rome's shoulder. 'My rock. My joy. And you disappointed me today.'

'I know.'

'Sometimes things are more complicated than they seem.'

'I'm sorry.'

Justin pressed his fingers to Rome's forehead. 'The touch of forgiveness. Love yourself again. And give me a hug.'

Father and son embraced, both smiling. The song started from the beginning, while Rome returned to his place among the Watchmen. All seemed well.

But Cairo was watching Rome's face. A muscle was working in his jaw. For the briefest of moments he met her eye. Then they both looked away.

●

After the communal supper, Cairo stood at the sink with Havana swaddled on her back, scrubbing pots and chanting under her breath: *No negativity. No negativity. Love, love, love.*

People were chatting as they wielded tea towels or ferried crockery to the sinks. Some were playing charades; others had got out the board games. Helike and Quito—born on the same day, and a bit like twins—had made a playhouse under one of the tables. Normally this would be a lovely time of the evening, when they'd all shared a meal and could hang out together. Not tonight. Cairo kept thinking about her mother, alone in a motel.

Rome hurried up, grabbed a tea towel and began to dry some knives. 'I've got to make this quick,' he muttered.

'How was she?'

'Upset. I didn't realise your dad's . . . anyway, she says she'll stay in Rotorua a bit longer.'

'What for?'

'Shh.' He ducked his head, talking out of the corner of his mouth. 'I think Justin's making a horrible mistake. He should trust you. I don't want us to be the kind of people who keep a father and daughter apart at the time of his death. Where's the compassion in that? Diana seems like a good woman. She's promised to get you back within two weeks.'

Cairo glanced around. There were no Companions in sight, but they weren't the only ones who might be watching.

'This is why you argued with Justin?'

'I thought he was going to kill me! He's changing, Cairo. There's something wrong. He's lost his peace.'

Aden strolled up, bearing a stack of plates.

'I'll take that tea towel,' he said. 'Thanks, Rome. You're a free man.'

Rome thanked him innocently and went off to play charades.

'Is he all right?' asked Aden, with a glance at his departing back.

'Who . . . Rome?' Cairo slid another plate into the water. 'Yes. He was on about Malindi. He's desperate for her to become his Partner.'

Another lie. Deceit and doubt were creeping in through every crevice.

Aden dried while she washed. He was talking about Damascus, who had a visit to the dentist in the morning. From time to time she felt his hand on her back or a kiss on her cheek. He was doing his best, and she loved him for it. When she pulled out the plug, he stood with his arms around her waist and his mouth nuzzling her hair.

'Going, going . . . gone,' she said, as the water spiralled down the plughole.

He dropped his mouth until it touched her ear. 'Don't go,' he whispered. 'Please, don't go.'

Forty-one

Cairo

In the morning, cloud slid like a blindfold over the eyes of the mountain.

Bali shivered when she saw the mist. 'You can feel the ghosts on days like this,' she said. 'You can imagine that phantom *waka*. It's eerie.'

A group was setting out on *Matariki*. Three of the flax weavers were delivering an order of exquisitely crafted *kete* and mats to a craft shop. Monika needed to stock up the pharmacy and Seoul the pantry. Five children, including Damascus, were booked in for check-ups with the dentist. He clung to Cairo's hand.

'The dentist doesn't hurt,' he said, as they walked down the jetty together. 'No, it doesn't. It doesn't, does it, Mummy? They just look in your mouth and they say *what lovely teeth* and then you go home.'

'The dentist will never have seen such beautiful pearly-whites as yours,' she promised. 'You'll go *aaaaah* for her.'

'Aaaah?'

'That's right, and you'll open your mouth.'

'Aaaaah.'

'Yes. And she'll give you a sticker for being so good.'

Cairo heard footsteps and looked around to see Rome trotting after them. 'Hi! Going to the dentist?'

'*Tag!*' The young man slapped her on the back. 'No, I've got a
foreign cheque to bank. Remember that Texan couple who came
on a course a couple of years ago? They just sent us a thousand
dollars, in return for our prayers. Damascus, d'you want to ride
on my shoulders?'

Damascus put up his arms, and a moment later he was aloft.

'Ask to come with us,' Rome whispered to Cairo. 'I'll take you
to see your mother.' Then he leaped aboard, making Damascus
laugh by pretending to be a pirate with a cutlass.

Cairo made a snap decision and followed him.

'I'd like to come with you,' she said to Monika. 'Suva can take
my class at the school. Damascus is a bit scared of the dentist,
he'd like me to be there.'

'I'll be there to hold his hand,' said Monika.

'Can't I come?'

'No.'

Cairo made a sound of frustration. 'I don't see why not. My
mother will have left Rotorua by now.'

'It isn't worth the risk.'

'There *is* no risk!'

'Ooh.' Monika winced, pressing her hands to her ears. 'Do
you know that you're shouting at me? Such negativity!'

'I'm sorry.'

'I know this has been horrible. But Justin's word is the last
word. You've valuable work to do in the school. Throw yourself
into that.' Monika shook her head, with a frown of warning.
'Your little ones need you. We *all* need you.'

It was a threat. It was primped and powdered and dressed up
as loving concern, but really it was a threat. And it hurt, because
Cairo thought of Monika as a friend.

She held up both hands, admitting defeat. 'Okay! Obviously,
if you think there's still a risk . . . Please will you look after
Damascus, then?'

'Ooh, yes! It will be my grandmotherly pleasure. And as a reward for being brave at the dentist, there will be ice-cream.'

Matariki was moving away. The water was dead calm, like a silk shroud. Soon the white boat was no more than a ghost in the mist.

•

Rome seemed to disappear into thin air. He didn't turn up for Call that night, nor the following morning, nor at Meridian Call.

'He's gone hunting,' said Suva, when Cairo asked if she knew where he was. 'A few of the guys went out last night. They were going to stay in one of the huts.'

Cloud hung in sullen layers, pressing down on the hills. Cairo struggled to keep her mind on teaching, and the children seemed unsettled too. From time to time they heard the sound of shots from the hills.

'Shall we go to Kereru Cove?' suggested Cairo, when she'd had enough of trying to be a real teacher. 'The hot-water beach, or the pools? Prague and Xian, zip along to the laundry and grab five swimming towels. We can share.'

It felt better to be galloping up the bush path, away from watching eyes. The children chose the beach and were soon playing in the water. Cairo hitched up her dress and waded in to her thighs, comforted by the warmth.

She was haunted by an image. Her father, in a hospital bed. He was looking towards the door.

He's waiting for me, she thought. *He's waiting right now.* Tears kept coming, no matter how much she brushed them away.

She looked around at the sound of running footsteps on the path. The next moment Rome had pelted onto the sand, carrying a rifle.

'Cairo.' He bent over his knees, breathing hard. 'Thank God I've found you.'

'Weren't you with—'

'Liam, Kyoto and Berlin.' He nodded, wiping his mouth with one hand. 'Yep. My guards—I've managed to lose them. They took me out hunting to stop me talking to you.'

'You'd better disappear, then.'

He shrugged. 'No point. They'll know I've been here. The kids will tell them.'

'They're children, not spies.'

'Cairo.' He was shaking his head, still trying to catch his breath. 'This is Gethsemane. Everyone's a spy.'

She waded back to the beach. The young man had aged in the past twenty-four hours. He looked unkempt.

'I didn't get a chance to see Diana yesterday,' he said. 'Otto never left me on my own, so I couldn't go to the motel. I couldn't even go into the library to charge my phone, so I can't call her. I don't know how much longer she'll wait if she hears nothing.'

'Rome—'

'Shh!' He spun around, scanning the trees. No footsteps. No rustle of leaves.

'There's nobody there,' whispered Cairo.

'I hate this. I hate having to slink around. Look, I've got something for you.' He'd pulled a small book out of his pocket. 'It hasn't expired,' he said, holding it out. 'I checked.'

She recoiled. She hadn't seen her passport since Monika took it for safekeeping five years earlier.

'Take it,' he urged, forcing it into her hands. 'You've got to leave today. Now.'

'Why?'

'Because Diana's waiting. And because they're going to take you to the island straight after school.'

She stared at him. 'You mean . . . like Bali?'

He laughed. 'No, not like Bali! This isn't an honour, it's a disgrace. They'll keep you there until they're sure your mother's left the country.'

'Does Aden know?'

'Not yet. But he won't be able to stop them.'

Justin is perfect, she chanted to herself. *Justin is divine. Justin is eternal life.*

'You need to move fast,' urged Rome. 'That's why I've been chasing up and down, looking for you. Don't worry about Justin, I'll talk to him, I'll make him understand. He loves you very much. He'll forgive you.'

'Oh God, oh God, oh God.' She stood irresolute, her hands pressed to her head. 'What about my children?'

'They've got Aden to look after them, and a hundred adoring relatives. You'll be back in a couple of weeks.'

She was terrified, searching for reasons not to go.

'Justin will stop me. He reads minds.'

'Mm . . . yes. And no.' Once again, Rome scanned the silent bush. 'The Companions speak to him through two-way radios.'

'No.'

'That's how he always appears at the right moment. And he's got satellite internet on the island. He uses it all the time, for all kinds of things.'

'I don't believe it.'

'And spies. That's how he knew you were pregnant when you first arrived. Remember how he seemed to know even before you did? It was a lucky guess, based on information received. Suva was told to watch for anything unusual, and she saw you throwing up every morning. She told Aden, who told Liam, who got on the radio and told Justin. And Justin is a master at looking for people's weak points.'

Ice was forming in Cairo's stomach. She needed Justin to be real. She *needed* him to be divine. The Last Day was coming! The world was on the verge of collapse! Without Justin's divine power, there was no hope.

'It's a shock, isn't it?' Rome looked haggard. He rubbed his forehead with his thumb. 'Turns everything upside down. Perth told me months ago. I didn't want to believe it, but then I watched, and it's true. It doesn't mean we don't love Justin. It *does* mean that he can't read our minds.'

Her God had lied. His omniscience was a trick. She was sitting on the sand—didn't remember when her legs gave way. There was no horizon, nothing steady.

Rome dropped to one knee beside her. 'Cairo, listen. If you want to see your father, you have to leave now. Your mother's waiting. You've got your passport. If you don't go now, it'll be too late.'

'How?' she whispered. 'I'll never get onto a boat without someone stopping me.'

He nodded. He had it all worked out. 'You know the paddocks at the top, where the hay barn is? There's a forestry track there that runs all the way to the public road. Aden knows it. We use it for bringing in stock and hay and stuff.'

'Are you sure?'

'I've driven along it! I'm the trusted son, remember?' Rome began to draw a map in the sand. 'The barn's here . . . follow this fence line. You'll see where the track comes out. Go along it . . . okay?'

'Okay.'

'It meets another track. Turn right . . . maybe ten kilometres . . . you'll get to another gate. It's probably locked. I'll find an excuse to take *Ikaroa*, collect the van and drive around to meet you at that gate. If I'm not there, it means they've stopped me. Keep walking. You'll eventually get to the public road.'

'And then?'

'You'll have to hitch a lift to Rotorua. I know you can hitch lifts—I've seen you do it! She's at the Four Seasons Motel, near the Redwood Forest.'

Cairo knew the hay barn; she should be able to find the track. But then what? Her Gethsemane mind was aghast. *Are you mad? People die out there!*

'I'll have to tell Aden,' she said.

'No.'

'I can't *not* tell him.'

'You'd be putting him in an impossible position. He'd have to blow the whistle on you, or be disgraced. The less he knows, the better it will be for everyone. I'll tell him after you've left.'

Damascus had spotted Rome. He skipped out of the water, holding up a small, wet hand to high-five. 'Coming in?' he asked hopefully.

Rome leaned down to stow his rifle behind a rock.

'You get going,' he muttered, as he pulled his shirt over his head. 'I'll keep the kids here. Buy you some time.'

'Quito and Havana are in the crèche.'

'You'll have to leave them. You'll be lucky to get out yourself. Don't risk anything unusual. Nothing at all.' He was wading into the water. 'Good luck.'

Cairo stood, still undecided, running the practicalities through her mind. *Get to the top paddocks, negotiate the track, somehow get to Rotorua* . . .

She opened the passport, flicking through its pages until she found the photo. *Is that really me?* The girl was about eighteen, long hair in a high ponytail, desperately *not* smiling because the authorities didn't allow it. This document had nothing to do with Cairo. It belonged to someone she'd thought was long dead. Someone who, according to her passport, was called *Cassandra Alexandra Howells.*

•

She hadn't seen her backpack since she'd arrived, but there was no packing to be done. She couldn't take anything with her. She tied an extra jersey around her waist; it would be freezing by nightfall.

She took a minute to scribble a note for Aden, and left it on the bed.

I've gone to see my father. I promise I'll only be gone two weeks. I WILL come back.

Please forgive me. I thought it was easiest and best to leave quietly and come back soon. I love you.

Please forgive me!

Cairo

The bed was spread with the ultra-soft blanket the community had given them as a wedding present. She wanted to lie down and go to sleep. She wanted things to be normal and good.

'Forgive me,' she whispered, straightening it.

Out on the porch, she stooped to lace her boots. Five years ago, she'd walked up those steps for the first time. She still remembered the magic of that day. Gethsemane had bewitched her from the moment she arrived, and she was still bewitched. As she looked across at the island, a skein of smoke spiralled from behind the trees and into a heavy sky. It smelled of happiness, of fish cooked on the beach, of sitting at the feet of her saviour. She stood transfixed. Her resolve was sliding away.

What do you think you're doing? It would be lovely to go to the island! Imagine being with Justin all day. Just being in his presence makes you happy, doesn't it? Yes! You'll get the full blast of his love. Heaven on earth.

'I'm coming back,' she said aloud. 'I'm coming back soon.'

Her boots sounded hard-hearted on the wooden steps. *Clunk. Clunk, clunk.*

The Gethsemane mind changed into top gear. *Where are you going? What are you doing? People die out there!*

She had no choice but to cross the pasture that ran through the settlement. From the corner of her eye, she spotted Monika emerging onto the surgery porch.

'Cairo?' called the doctor. 'Have you got a minute?'

Cairo turned around, walking backwards, grinning like an idiot. 'Can't stop,' she said, gesturing vaguely towards the school. 'Just nipped home to use the bathroom—better get back before there's a riot!'

Without waiting for an answer she carried on across the grass, trying to look as though she hadn't a care in the world. She expected to hear Monika shouting, demanding that she turn back—and then what? Justin would be called, and she'd have to face him and the Companions. They'd use power and love and threats and shame and guilt to bring her into line. They'd tell her children that their mummy wanted to leave them. Cairo knew she couldn't stand up to that. Gethsemane wasn't just about love; it was also about fear.

The hill path was close now. It led steeply away from behind the school building, marked on each side by rocks. Her instinct was to break into a run, but a glance over her shoulder proved that Monika was still watching. On a sudden wave of inspiration, she marched up to the school and into her own classroom, smartly shutting the door behind her.

From next door, she heard the murmur of Hana's class of older children. She stood in the gloom, surrounded by paintings, projects and child-sized things. She knew every inch of her dominion: the little chairs grouped around square tables, the whiteboard, that floorboard that creaked. She knew the smell and feel of the books, every splash of paint on the art cabinet. She imagined her class here—tomorrow, in this very room—being told that their teacher had left Gethsemane. They'd be horrified. The Outside was the hellish place of their nightmares. The monster under their bed was the human race.

Forgive me, she whispered to imaginary children, touching each empty chair. *Forgive me, Xian. Forgive me, Prague, Benghazi, Kat, Zanzibar, Moscow. Forgive me, Monty. Please forgive me, Damascus. I'm coming back*.

Moments later she'd crept out by the back door. She headed for the path, hiding behind the school building. Then she was running, while the Gethsemane mind sobbed and begged her to turn back. She forced herself up and up, leaping across streams and tree roots, edging around cliffs where the path had crumbled away. As she ran she chanted two words, again and again, though her lungs felt ready to burst. She *had* to say the words. They were for Aden, for the children, for her friends and for Justin, who was her God.

Forgive me. Forgive me. Forgive me.

When she looked back, Gethsemane was out of sight.

Forty-two

Diana

She hadn't dared to leave the motel room for more than five minutes at a time. The only foray she'd made was to a corner shop for bread and tinned soup, but even that wasn't without its hazards. The woman behind the counter liked to think of herself as a people person.

'You from Britain?'

'Mm.' Diana handed over a ten-dollar note, keeping an anxious eye on the motel's front entrance. 'Just a flying visit.'

'Long way to come for a flying visit.'

'Mm.'

'Visiting family?'

'My daughter.'

The shopkeeper pressed buttons on her till. 'Married a Kiwi, did she?'

'Yes. Yes, she did.'

'Three—fifty—and that's your ten.' The drawer slammed shut. 'Our Kiwi lads scrub up well. Grandkids?'

'Three.'

'Aw! You'll miss them. Mine's in Australia at the moment— Brisbane—lovely climate. She's got a boyfriend. Fingers crossed they don't get too serious.'

'Fingers crossed,' murmured Diana, though she'd lost the thread of the conversation some time ago. Fortunately another customer arrived, and she was able to make her escape.

Back in her room, she lay down on the bed while grey twilight gathered in the corners of the world. The fridge was humming. *This is limbo*, she thought. *A suburban motel room.* Beyond its net curtains, people were living their lives. She heard traffic on the road, a radio playing music, and Barry—*Your host! Welcome to the Four Seasons Motel*—whistling as he messed about with his recycling bins.

Rome Calvin hadn't come back. He hadn't phoned, either. He'd promised to do one or the other. Diana was losing hope.

Her eyes ached, so she closed them. She allowed herself the luxury of imagining the most magical thing: someone was knocking on the door. It was a glass sliding door, and it gasped every time it was pulled open or shut. Diana pictured herself hauling it open and seeing Cassy.

A shout jerked her out of her daydream. It was dark outside, though security lighting glowed behind the curtains. Just kids yelling, from the sound of it. Some giggling.

Footsteps. Diana held her breath as two shadows passed. Then they'd gone, leaving nothing but cigarette smoke. A little of it crept in, smelling of disappointment.

And so the evening went on: coming and going, talking and laughing and arguing. Human life.

Then she heard it: the low, steady rattle of an engine outside her door. It idled for a few seconds. Stopped. Silence. Diana lay rigid and alert, her eyes fixed on the net curtains. She didn't breathe at all.

A vehicle door opened—*creak*—and shut. A woman's voice seemed to ask a question. A male voice answered. They moved quietly, whoever they were. Just one or two words, mumbled and inaudible. Shadows loomed at the door.

Five years she'd been waiting for this. The shadows swelled and distorted until they became the distinct shapes of two people.

Then came the sound of knuckles, rapping on glass.

Diana was already sprinting across the room. The door gasped as she threw it open.

A woman stood under the security light. She was dressed in shapeless blue and carried nothing except a passport. Her eyes were like pools of oil, staring and empty.

'Hello, Mum,' she said.

Cairo

They left Rotorua within minutes. Diana had suggested spending the night in the motel, since it was already late. Rome and Cairo wouldn't hear of it. Cairo was sure they needed to get as far away as possible, and as fast.

'I don't know how they'll react,' said Rome. His eyes kept straying towards the road.

Diana didn't seem to understand their tension. 'They can't take Cassy away by force. I'd just call the police.'

Rome and Cairo looked at each other. It felt strange, after so long, to hear an Outsider's view of Gethsemane. Diana's sheer naivety was startling. Cairo didn't know how to explain that this wasn't about brute force; it was about a far more powerful kind of control.

'You ought to go immediately,' Rome insisted. 'Just believe me.'

They remained in the motel room while Diana packed and checked out. The tide of courage that had carried Cairo along the forestry track was ebbing away. Her Gethsemane mind was back in control and in a screaming panic. She paced up and down, wringing her hands. If she could have clicked her fingers and landed safely back in her cabin, she would have done it; if Aden had turned up at the motel she would have gone home with him.

Suddenly she froze, her heart thumping in her ribcage. There was another woman in the room, silently watching her. It took horrified seconds for her to understand that she was looking at herself in a full-length mirror.

'Is this who I am?' she asked Rome. 'Is this how I look?'

She stepped closer, fascinated by the thin figure with its blue clothes and short hair. Frightened eyes stared at her. Then she turned her back, vowing not to look at herself again. She wasn't going to add vanity to the list of shameful things she'd done.

'Right,' said Diana, at the door. 'I've paid. We can go.'

It felt odd to be sitting in a car. Everything felt so odd. Through the open window, Cairo saw Diana hugging Rome. That seemed odd too.

'I don't know if I'm allowed to do this,' Diana said fervently, as she kissed his cheek, 'but I'm going to anyway! Rome Calvin, you are my hero. I can't thank you enough. Thank you. *Thank you*.' She kissed him again. 'What you've done for this family can never be repaid. We're in your debt. If you need anything—if we can help you in any way—please, *please* ask.'

Rome was blushing. 'I hope it's all . . . your husband . . .'

'I hope so too.'

As Diana started the engine, Rome leaned down to Cairo's window.

'I'm worried for you, little brother,' she said. 'They'll know you helped me.'

'I went on a fishing trip and came back after dark. I do it all the time.'

'But you were meant to be hunting! And my passport? It didn't just jump out of the safe.'

Rome laughed, giving the car's roof a jaunty pat. She admired his courage.

'Relax. I've got friends in high places. I'm the son of God incarnate, remember?'

Forty-three

From: Mike and Diana Howells
To: CallsopDCIT@universityofsussex.org
Re: Cassy

Hi Cameron,
First the good news. I got her out, though it's only meant to be
for two weeks. That's the deal. But the nightmare continues!
This girl isn't like Cassy in any way. She doesn't think like
Cassy, doesn't talk like her. I hope she snaps out of it soon.
One minute she's in a state of gibbering terror. Then she with-
draws into her own head, can't do anything without specific
instructions, like a robot whose programming is buggered up.

   She walked out with just the clothes on her back, so I
took her to a shop. You'd think it was a snake pit, from her
reaction! I wanted colourful things to cheer her up, but she
insisted on blue and baggy, as similar to the Gethsemane
uniform as possible.

   She keeps asking if I think she's going mad. And I say
don't be silly, you'll be fine. But I'm starting to wonder.

   We fly tomorrow. Any thoughts are welcome.
   Diana

From: CallsopDCIT@universityofsussex.org
To: Mike and Diana Howells
Re: Cassy

Diana,
Well done. This is a massive step.

It sounds as though her body is out, but her mind is not. The hard part now will be keeping her out. They have long arms, these people. Expect intense pressure to return, especially as her husband and children are still there.

You're being patient. Keep it up! She's unlikely to 'snap out of it' any time soon, I'm afraid. Remember the phobia we talked about, the monsters of the deep? To her, the world is lethally dangerous. Look out for patterns of magical thinking, which you might call superstition. She may honestly believe that she is now cursed. She may believe that they can see where she is.

It's common for people to worry that they're losing their minds. Reassure her that she isn't. What she's going through has been experienced by thousands of others. But if she's still in this state when you get home, I'd suggest you get professional help ASAP.

GOOD LUCK!

Cairo

People everywhere. Pushing and shoving, jostling for space in the overhead lockers. Her heart was racing. If she stayed on this plane, she'd die. It would crash. You can't run away from God! She fumbled desperately at the buckle of her seatbelt, but her shaking fingers didn't seem to work properly.

Then she felt hands gripping hers, and Diana's voice.

'Cassy, stop. Stop. What are you doing?'

'I have to get out,' she said. 'Please let me get out.'

'You can't. They've shut the doors. We're moving, see?'

She tried to stand up, but the seatbelt held her. 'I'm going to die!'

'Look at me, Cassy. *Look at me*.' Her mother was leaning over her, holding her arms. 'Just two weeks. You'll be back in Gethsemane in two weeks. Okay? But first you're going to see Dad.'

'I don't like flying, either,' said the elderly woman sitting on Diana's other side. 'I've got some Bach Rescue Remedy. Like some?'

Unexpectedly, this unquestioning kindness helped. Here, at least, was a stranger who seemed to care. Cairo accepted a drop of the homeopathic remedy while Diana persuaded her to take deep breaths.

A flight attendant stopped beside their row. 'Did someone call out?' he asked.

'It's okay,' Diana assured him. 'Sorry. We're fine now.'

He nodded, and headed off to more demanding passengers.

'She's not afraid of flying,' Cairo heard her mother say to the kind neighbour. 'It's a bit more complicated than that.'

The Outside had proved to be everything Cairo dreaded. She was appalled by the traffic, the crowds, the frenetic emptiness. There was no bell, no singing, no loving community. No purpose. No hope. No joy. People looked frayed, with their downturned mouths and heads bent over phones. They never spoke to one another—they never even spoke to their children. And why was nobody smiling?

Airport buildings flashed past. Then they were in the air, turning and banking.

'It's okay, darling,' whispered her mother. 'It's okay.'

But it wasn't okay. It was terrible. She should be on Justin's island. She imagined the warmth of the fire on her face, the calls of birds, the lake stroking the shore. And Justin, her Messiah. His smile was deepening the crows' feet around his sea-green eyes. She reached out to him.

'I love you,' she said aloud.

'I love you too,' said Diana.

There was an electronic map on the screen in front of Cairo. A stylised plane inched across it, showing their position. There was Rotorua, with its scattered lakes. She worked out which was Lake Tarawera; and Gethsemane must be about *here*. It gave her comfort for a while, but every few seconds the little white plane moved further away from home. Soon it had left the coast of New Zealand and was heading across a lonely ocean.

Forty-four

Diana

Tara met them at Heathrow, looking ready to detonate. It wasn't a Kodak moment.

'Welcome home, Cass.'

'Thank you,' said Cassy. She was twitching, glancing over her shoulder. 'But I've left my home behind.'

Boom!

'You've blown our family into smithereens,' snarled Tara. 'Do you even fucking care? You don't want to be here? Fine! Why don't you just turn around and sod right off again?'

'Okay, okay,' said Diana, laying a hand on her younger daughter's arm. 'We're both dead on our feet. Cassy, we're going to drive you home. It's safe there.'

'It's *not* safe,' said Cassy.

'It's safe. You're going to have a long, long sleep.'

As they walked to the car park Diana gave Tara a warning shake of the head, mouthing *shush*. Tara scowled.

The car seemed to have a calming effect on Cassy. She and Diana both dozed. All seemed well until they were almost home, when Cassy suddenly sat up with a series of piercing shrieks. Tara swerved halfway across the road, and a bus flashed its lights.

'Bloody hell!' she shouted. 'Cassy, what the fuck? D'you want to kill us all?'

Cassy was gasping for breath, her eyes rolling in her head. 'Where am I?'

'Banshee impersonation,' said Tara. 'Right in my sodding ear!'

'My children were drowning. It was real. I saw them drowning. I heard them. Am I going crazy, Mum?'

'No,' said Diana, who'd been dragged out of sleep. 'Not crazy. But maybe you should talk to Dr Jacobs. You remember him? My GP.'

'So you *do* think I'm going mad.'

'No! But maybe you need something for your anxiety, just so you feel up to seeing Dad. You can't go to the hospital in this state.'

'This is what Justin predicted,' said Cassy. Her voice was flat again. 'This is *exactly* what he predicted. He said you'd mess with my mind. He said you'd have me locked up. If you try to make me see a doctor, I'll leave.'

Diana was floored. Cameron Allsop had advised her to get help, but if Cassy refused, what could she do?

'Here we are.' Tara was pulling into their drive. 'Home.'

Diana tried to be all energy and bustle—unlocking the door, ushering Cassy inside, turning on the lights—but she was in despair. This wasn't how she'd imagined Cassy's homecoming. Not at all.

'She's a basket case,' whispered Tara.

'She'll come right.'

'You think?' Tara blew out her cheeks. 'I dunno, Mum. I'm not sure she's even in there any more.'

Cassy seemed not to notice or care that she was back in her old home. She refused food, but accepted a cup of hot milk and one of Diana's sleeping pills. When she sipped the milk, she looked puzzled. 'This isn't . . . oh. I'd forgotten about cow's milk.'

'Bedtime,' said Diana firmly. 'Tara's staying the night.'

'Wouldn't miss this much fun for all the world,' muttered Tara.

Cassy followed her mother and sister upstairs like a sleep-walker; but when she arrived at her bedroom door, she came to a sudden halt.

'It's exactly the same,' she said, looking around in vague surprise. 'Nothing's changed. Hello, Pesky.'

The cat remembered his rescuer. When she bent to kiss him, he purred and fussed and rubbed his forehead against her face, which seemed to comfort her. Meanwhile Diana was patting the pillows, trying to be jolly.

'You said you'd be home in September,' she chirped. 'And it's September!'

'Yes.' Cassy's voice was a croak. 'I'm . . .' She sat down on the bed, still stroking the cat. 'Sorry. I'm just . . . sorry. I don't know who I am.' She picked up Babar, touching the toy to her nose.

'Don't worry,' said Diana. 'Just sleep. Everything will look better in the morning.'

'When I was in Gethsemane, I felt as though this world didn't really exist. But now I'm here, and this world *does* exist. It's just the same as I left it. I've been gone a lifetime, but time hasn't passed. I feel . . . I'm sorry, I can't explain.'

'You've been to Narnia and back?' suggested Tara, who was leaning in the doorway.

'Narnia and back.' Cassy almost managed a smile. 'Maybe.'

'Well, you've come out of the wardrobe,' said Tara. 'You're back in dear old Croydon. If you want, I'll grab my duvet and the spare mattress and kip down on your floor.'

'Would you do that for me?'

''Course, sis. We used to do it all the time, remember? But for Christ's sake, no more banshee wails. Okay?'

'For Christ's sake.'

'That's right.'

The sleeping pill was doing its job, and extreme exhaustion was taking over. Cassy lay down, stretching out her legs. She was wearing her blue Gethsemane dress.

You've brought Cassy home, Diana told herself, as she covered her daughter with the duvet. *She's safe in her own bed*. It was a wonderful feeling, despite everything. It was a dream come true.

'Justin is Jesus Christ,' mumbled Cassy.

'Sorry?' Diana hoped she'd misheard.

'He remembers being crucified. I wish you guys knew him.'

Tara shook her head pityingly, mouthing, *What . . . the . . . fuck?*

After that bombshell, the sleeping pill knocked Cassy out with almost comical speed. One moment she was talking about Jesus; the next, she was dead to the world.

'Did she say what I *think* she said?' hissed Diana.

Tara made her eyes cross. ''Fraid so. Fucking hell, it's like *The Exorcist* around here.'

Diana knelt to kiss Cassy's forehead. 'Goodnight, darling. Welcome home.'

The girl in the bed wasn't recognisable as their Cassy. She'd refused to eat since leaving Gethsemane; she'd hardly slept. Her face looked skeletal, more so because of the cropped hair. There were bruised half-moons under her eyes.

'She's lost the plot,' whispered Tara. 'Those bastards have totally screwed her up.'

'The journey's been a nightmare.' Diana reached to switch off the bedside lamp. 'She's been in a state ever since she turned up at my motel—I thought I'd never get her on the plane! I hate to admit it, but she looked fine when I saw her in Gethsemane. She looked well. She's got children. I told you that, didn't I? Three children.'

'Mm. And a hunky blond husband with massive biceps.'

'Who seems to care about her,' said Diana. She laid a hand on Cassy's shorn head. 'She was happy. Maybe I should have left her in peace.'

'With that bunch of moon-howling crazies? A guy who thinks he's Jesus Christ? *Seriously?*'

'But they were happy moon-howling crazies.'

'Go to bed,' ordered Tara, pushing her mother out of the room. 'You look about five thousand years old, and I'm not bloody surprised. You can rest now, Mum. You've done it. You've brought her home.'

Forty-five

Cairo

The night was almost over. Soon the valley would echo with birdsong and the steady tolling of the bell. The boys would sit up in their bunks and make faces at Havana in her cot, and she'd screech with laughter because she found her brothers hilarious. The family would walk across the grass to join their friends at Early Call.

But the bell didn't toll. Instead a car's horn blasted, then someone shouted an obscenity. The Gethsemane mist was thickening around her, bringing the chill of fear and shame and loneliness. She was in a frightening, familiar house, and a stranger was sprawled under a duvet on the floor.

Sliding out of bed, she crept to the bathroom. Perhaps, if she washed enough, she could rid herself of the shame. She stripped off her dress and stepped into the shower, sitting on the floor with her legs drawn up and her face pressed into her knees. Water cascaded over her bent head.

Rain was thundering onto the roof of the *wharenui*. She could smell the sweet wax of the candles. Justin was nearby. She couldn't see him, but she felt the glorious comfort of his presence.

He spoke into her ear. *Cairo?*

She lifted her face, letting the water flow over her eyelids. 'Justin! I'm here.'

I think you have something to confess.

He sounded desperately sad. She heard her own sobs as she stepped up onto the dais. People were staring at her. All the people she loved, their faces distorted in the candlelight. Shame weighed on her chest.

'I'm sorry,' she said. 'I'm so sorry.'

You've betrayed our trust. You've hurt us. You've hurt me.

Cairo held out her hands, trying to find him. 'I'll be back soon, I promise.'

You can never come home. You're lost.

She heard thumping and banging. A voice shouted through the dark reaches of the universe. *Cassy? What's happening in there? Let me in, you daft tart!*

She felt herself falling and knew that this was hell.

Diana

'We found her in the shower,' she told Cameron Allsop. 'Curled up in the flood she'd caused by lying on the drain. We had to break a panel in the bathroom door.'

'How is she now?'

'She's asleep, thank God.'

'Floating,' he said. 'It's horrible for relatives to see. The pull of the place is extremely powerful, so sometimes a person dissociates from real life and slips back to them.'

'What on earth do I do? She will come back to us, won't she?'

'It's early days. Wait and see how she gets on. You've had a long journey, she'll be sleep-deprived. Don't try and get her to see Mike just yet. She might need some kind of medication, or she might need a lot more help. What she needs most of all is for you to stay calm and listen without judging.'

'I feel sorry for her.'

'Mm? I can hear a "but" in that statement.'

Diana laughed tiredly. 'Good hearing! Okay. *But* . . . I sometimes want to slap her. She's safe. We're doing our best. What
more does she want?'

There was silence for a moment. She imagined him marshal-
ling his thoughts. Then he said, 'Cassy's been through things you
can't imagine. Bad things, and good things. Her sense of self has
been broken down. Give her time.'

'How much time?'

'Piece of string, I'm afraid.'

Once the call was over, Diana sat and fretted. *Give her time.*

Mike knew Cassy was home. He'd already rung, asking when
she'd be visiting. Time was the one thing he didn't have.

Cairo

Justin stalked her dreams. He took her fishing, or walked with
her among the crosses on the promontory. *How could you betray
me?* he asked, and she woke up in tears. Sometimes he stood
on his island beach and shouted across the water. His voice was
vivid, ricocheting in her mind: *Cairo, come back!*

By day she hid indoors, gazing out at grey concrete and
endless traffic, trying to find the courage to visit her father. On
the second afternoon she spotted a family out on the street. The
mother pushed a toddler in a buggy. The eldest child whizzed
merrily along on his scooter, and a white-hatted baby peered out
from a carrier on her father's back.

'They look like my family,' said Cairo wistfully.

'Who?' Tara put down her tablet. Her hair was dyed jet black,
bundled into a knot. She wore jeans and a sweatshirt, and for the
first time Cairo noticed that one eyebrow was pierced. 'Those
guys? Wow. It's really weird to imagine you with three rugrats.'

'And Suva. Don't forget Suva.'

'What's your man like?'

'Aden's a great father. Never flustered. Sexy smile.'

'Got any photos?'

'Sorry.' Cairo *was* sorry. She'd love to show Tara some pictures of her family. 'We don't use cameras.'

'That's ridiculous.'

Cairo didn't argue. 'And how about you?' she asked. 'Have you got anyone?'

'I'm off men at the moment. They're all so frickin' needy.'

For a few wonderful minutes, the veil of Gethsemane seemed to lift. Cairo felt her anxiety lessen. Her mind cleared a little.

'Tell me what you've been doing,' she asked, turning away from the window. 'I've missed so much! When I left, you'd just taken your GCSEs.'

Tara seemed pleased that she'd remembered. 'I did all right in those. After that, it was downhill all the way.'

They began to talk—and even if it was stilted, it was better than nothing. So much had happened, so much had been lost, so much was carefully left unsaid. Cairo listened while her sister described the trouble she'd got into at school, and the apprenticeship she was doing, and the young men whose hearts she'd broken.

Then Tara mentioned the elephant in the room.

'I dropped out of school because this family fell apart,' she said.

'I'm sorry.'

'Bloody hell, Cass. Didn't you get *any* of my messages? Why did you shut down your Facebook page?'

'We don't use the internet at Gethsemane.'

'Not at all?'

'Only certain people, for specific purposes. I'm not one of them. The internet is a door by which negativity can come into a person's mind. We're all much happier without it.'

'So how d'you manage?' Tara seemed genuinely perplexed. 'How do you keep in touch with what's going on? How do you *live*?'

Cairo smiled. 'We just live.'

'Yeah, in the Dark Ages!'

'The children play real games. The adults have real friendships.'

Tara rolled her eyes and left the room, muttering about making tea.

Describing Gethsemane had brought the veil down again. Cairo wasn't seeing the street any more. She was rounding the headland. Wood smoke. Sunshine. Diamond flashes on water. There was the jetty, and her children scampering to meet her. *Home. I'm home.*

Tara was tapping her on the arm. 'Hey. Hey! You there?'

Cairo shook herself. 'I'm here.'

'Tea, just the way you like it,' said Tara, holding out a mug. 'I remembered, sis! Ridiculously strong. Milk and no sugar.'

Cairo thanked her, and sipped dutifully at the alien taste.

'So . . . I'm assuming there's no Netflix in that place?' asked Tara, as she sat down again.

'What's Netflix?'

'Never mind. Telly? Radio?'

'Nope.'

'No Olympics, no Royal Wedding, no *Downton Abbey*. Sounds like some kind of weird social experiment. How d'you know what's going on in the world?'

Cairo thought about this. 'The Companions monitor the news,' she said. 'It's their job. They always tell us when there's been a disaster.'

'Who the hell are the Companions? Don't worry, I can guess . . . so they only tell you about disasters? Don't they pass on any good news?'

'What good news?'

'Are you serious?' Tara laughed. 'You know what I think? I think they treat you like mushrooms. They keep you in the dark and feed you shit.'

Cairo put down her mug, stood up and walked out of the room. She knew exactly what the Companions would say about Tara: *Your sister is pure negativity. Cut yourself off from her. Leave that house today.*

There was nowhere to hide. Her bedroom was festooned with pre-Gethsemane life: books, photos, jewellery, makeup, toys.

Even the clock was alien. These things belonged to Cassy, not Cairo. They were soaked in Cassy's emotions and memories. They disturbed her.

She tore everything off the noticeboard and hurled it into the cupboard—followed by Babar, the books, the dreamcatcher, the wooden dolls and everything from the dressing table. She locked the cupboard door. Then she lay down and pulled the duvet over her head.

She could hear Justin. He was calling to her from across the lake. He sounded heartbroken. *Cairo! Cairo!*

But his voice was growing fainter.

Forty-six

On the third night there were no dreams.

She woke before dawn, but she didn't listen for the tolling of the bell. Streetlights shone through a gap in the curtain, forming three intersecting ovals. Those lights had made the same pattern ever since her family first lived here. It always made her think of a Venn diagram.

Tugging her duvet off the bed, she slipped downstairs. Another memory: on Sunday mornings in the school holidays, when her parents were sleeping in, she'd creep down to watch telly, snuggled on the sofa under this duvet. Bliss.

They'd lived in a lot of different houses, but this sofa had always moved with them: old, now, and ragged. She wrapped the duvet around herself and dropped into her comfy spot. Pesky arrived from nowhere and smooched happily. Apart from the two of them, nothing stirred in the house. There was nothing to interrupt her thoughts. No bell. No Call. No work. No rules. No tiredness. No hunger.

As daylight gleamed over the rooftops of South London, she began to feel something shift in her mind. The veil was thinning; ideas took shape in the mist.

She thought about two-way radios, and clouds of sadness hanging over people's cabins. She thought about the internet on Justin's island, and all the things he could do with it. Watch the news. Contact people. Book hotels, taxis and flights. Move money around.

No negativity, screamed the Gethsemane mind. *Negativity is poison!*

She thought about being coached to bring back recruits: to smile, and gush with love, and keep Gethsemane's secrets. She thought about Skye and Tripoli: lost girls—so young—with nowhere else to go. Tripoli was dead and buried on the headland, her real name forgotten as if she'd never existed.

She remembered Sydney, who'd been exiled so brutally. *Ask how Justin gets about when he goes on his mysterious jaunts*, he said, the last time she saw him. *He doesn't use the van.*

The back door rattled when she opened it. *Always did, just like that.* The daylight seemed diffused, as though there were gauze over the sun. She caught an evocative breath from some neighbour's smouldering bonfire. The effect was instantaneous. It was a wisp of smoke, curling up from the island. Justin would be waiting.

'No,' she said aloud, snatching at her mind before it could float back to Gethsemane.

Ah, there was her swing! She touched the seat—not too wet—before sitting on it and surveying the garden. The weeds were completely out of hand, and leaves lay in rotting drifts against the fence. Her dad loved gardening. When they'd bought this house, the only thing he insisted on was having a decent-sized garden. He used to rush about the place, digging, mowing, composting, planting. *Come and help me, girls! I'm having a bonfire!* But now it lay in ruins. So did he. She was looking at the destruction of her family, and she'd caused it.

She pushed off with her feet, setting the swing in motion. Forwards, back. Forwards, back.

Dad gave me this swing. He'd brought it home in a giant box—grinning as he carried it into the house—and he and she bolted it all together. It was *their* thing. Whenever they moved, they took it with them. She sang their song quietly, as she jack-knifed backwards and forwards, and the rusted chains groaned.

'See saw, Margery Daw . . .' Forwards, back. 'Johnny shall have a new master.'

But he's a violent man, moaned the Gethsemane mind. *A monster. He smashed you with a wooden spoon.*

'He shall have but a penny a day, because he can't work any faster.'

Remember? REMEMBER?

She swooped higher and higher, singing louder and louder. Blackbirds took flight from the lawn, darting over the hedge.

'See saw, Margery Daw, Johnny—'

She dug her heels into the ground. Her swinging stopped with a jolt. She sat with her elbows around the chains, peering through the cobwebbed window of the past, screwing up her eyes to see what the truth looked like.

Yes. She remembered him losing his cool when she ran in front of that car. *Yes.* She bit her nails before school reports arrived. And yes, there was a time—when she was small, and he'd just come home from some war zone—when his shouting used to make her mum cry. But Count One on the Indictment: The Wooden Spoon? When she faced the memory square on, without Justin's voice in her ear, it seemed to slide away. It didn't feel like a memory; more of a dream. She wasn't sure it was real at all.

The model she had—of the world, of her place in it—was changing shape again. Memories were treacherous. They could lie. When she thought about her father now, she didn't see a monster. She just saw her dad. Sometimes obsessive, for sure. Sometimes controlling. A terrible fusspot when it came to her education. But he'd brought home a swing in a giant box, and sung as he pushed her. He'd waved goodbye at Heathrow. He'd come all the way to Gethsemane. And now he needed her.

●

Her mother was on the phone. Cairo noticed that she started
guiltily at the rattle of the garden door.

'Cassy!' she cried. 'Um, tea?'

While Cairo was filling the kettle, she caught murmured
snatches of conversation.

That's right . . . yes, please . . . definitely urgent.

'You're up to something, Mum,' she said, when the call was
over.

Diana looked as though she were tiptoeing over a landmine.
'I've got a confession to make.'

Humble yourself, and be nothing.

'I've asked Dr Jacobs to come and see you,' said Diana.

'Why?'

'Just routine.'

'It's not routine at all! You want him to pack me off to a
shrink.'

Cairo felt herself begin to laugh. The sensation startled her;
it was as if her facial muscles had been frozen since she'd left
Gethsemane.

'Never mind Dr Jacobs,' she said. 'I think it's time I saw my
dad.'

●

Travelling through the streets of South London was an unsettling
experience, and the weather wasn't helping. The morning had
rapidly deteriorated. By noon the sky was a lowering mass, lit by
camera flashes of lightning.

Cairo's sense of doom was back, pinning her to the ground
like a giant hand. As they crawled around the car park, she gazed
out at the hospital's massive sprawl. Her dad was there, behind
one of those hundreds of electric-lit windows. She was going to
have to face him.

At last, Diana parked and turned off the engine. Kettledrum
thunder. A drop of rain splattered on the windscreen.

'Marvellous,' said Diana. 'All we need.'

More drops. Then a deluge. People scurried for their cars.

Cairo was balancing—teetering, whimpering—on the tipping point of a seesaw, balanced above an abyss. She was a circus performer with no safety net. For a few hold-your-breath moments one end of the seesaw seemed heavier, and she slid in that direction . . . sliding, sliding . . . and saw clearly that Gethsemane was a beautiful lie, and Justin was a beautiful liar, and the universe was empty.

It was impossible. It was unbearable. It meant death for the human race, with no protector.

So she forced the seesaw to tip the other way, and let herself slide. She relived the ecstasy of meditation; the absolute, euphoric certainty that she was in the presence of the Infinite Power. *Justin is love. Justin is divine. Justin is eternal life.*

She wobbled—slipped—and found herself paralysed with fear, suspended between two equally terrifying truths.

A man strode past: tall and thin, with an umbrella. He glanced into the car as he passed, and for a moment he was Justin. She was sure of it. *You can't run away from God. He sees everything. He reads your thoughts.*

'You all right?' asked Diana. 'Penny for them.'

'I think Justin's watching me.'

'No.'

'You don't know him. He's everywhere.'

'Calvin doesn't have magic powers.' Diana unclipped her seat-belt. 'Look, I'm not meant to say this kind of thing, I'm meant to keep my trap shut, but I can't do it any longer. Justin Calvin is not—repeat *not*—Jesus Christ.'

'How can you be sure?'

'Well . . . because he just isn't!' cried Diana, with an incredulous burst of laughter. 'It just seems improbable to me. Isn't the Messiah meant to be descending in clouds of glory, with angels and trumpets and lots of pizzazz?'

'He never said so.'

'Oh come *on*, Cassy.'

'They didn't expect him to arrive in a stable either.'

Now that Justin was under attack—and, by implication, the Watchmen were being called deluded fools—Cairo felt she must defend him.

'Well,' Diana snorted. 'I certainly wouldn't expect the Messiah to pop up in rural New Zealand.'

'Why not?'

'Because it's so . . . ooh, how do I put this?' Diana twisted her mouth. 'So terribly *nice*! People go on adventure holidays and send back annoying selfies. Gethsemane looks like the photo on a chocolate box. I don't think Jesus would come all this way to live in a chocolate box. Do you?'

Cassy was thinking about the man who'd walked past. *Was that Justin?* An ambulance crawled along the service road, leaving a wake on the flooded tarmac.

'I've just spent a week in New Zealand,' said Diana, 'and I can tell you that the greatest crisis they reported on the radio was the earth-shattering news that users of the Park 'n' Ride service in Auckland may have to start paying. Seriously, that was headline news. Meanwhile we've got ISIS rampaging across the Middle East, murdering and raping and threatening to sack the city of Rome. We've got Syria. We've got the worst humanitarian crisis in history. If Jesus Christ turned up today, he'd have his work cut out.'

'Exactly! Armageddon, as prophesied.'

'It's not Armageddon.' Diana sounded weary. 'It's human beings being utter jerks, as per usual. I'm sure the world felt apocalyptic in 1914 too. Or in the thirties, watching the rise of fascism. My mother's generation saw the Holocaust, Hiroshima, Nagasaki, the Cold War. Go back further: the Black Death killed half the population of Europe. Was it the end of the world? No!'

The rain seemed to be moving on. Lightning flickered, but the answering rumble of thunder sounded distant. Cassy was transfixed by a raindrop on the windscreen. It inched across the glass: right, left, down, gathering others on the way.

'You're telling me,' said Diana, 'that the Second Coming—the

event Christians have eagerly awaited for over two millennia—
you're telling me it consists of a jailbird lounging around by a lake
all day? Second Coming, my arse. Calvin's just a clever conman,
exploiting a lot of good people.'

'You don't know him.'

'I know enough.'

Cairo felt a rush of panic. The seesaw was slipping, tipping,
sliding towards an agonising emptiness. She scrabbled and tried
to hold on, but there was no handhold. She threw her door open
and retched, bringing up the morning's cup of tea.

'Darling?' asked Diana. 'You all right?'

They sat for a long time—Cairo half out of the car, while
Diana apologised anxiously.

'Stupid of me,' she said, handing over a box of wet wipes.
'That was my fault.'

'It wasn't.' Cairo wiped her mouth. 'I just have some things to
face, and it's pretty terrifying. Okay. I think I'm ready to go in.'

Across the flooded car park. Into the entrance hall. Disinfect-
ant, and oxtail soup. Bewildering, crowded corridors. The squeak
of a wheelchair, the wailing of a child. Up the concrete stairs and
onto a ward.

'You go on,' suggested Diana, stopping at the nurse's station.
'Fourth door along. Bed on the left, by the window.'

'You're not coming?'

Diana blew her a kiss. 'It isn't me he's waiting for.'

This is it, thought Cairo, as she walked down the hallway.
This is why I'm here. This is why I'm risking everything.

People about to visit dying relatives are like actors, preparing to
burst out of the wings and onto the stage. They summon cheerful
energy and optimistic smiles. Cairo's Gethsemane training stood
her in good stead. *Smile! Be happy!* She walked past each open
door, glancing in at the patients in their beds, at the families
making awkward conversation. Each room held a story. Her own
story was waiting for her, through the fourth door. Her footsteps
slowed. Time slowed. *One . . . two . . . three . . .*

Four.

She'd known it was going to be bad. She'd known he was doped up to his eyeballs. She'd known he was dying.

She had steeled herself; but it wasn't enough.

The man in the bed was broken. Fading hair failed to cover his scalp; sagging pouches dragged at his eyes. He lay propped up, with a drip attached to one arm and a leg in plaster. His head was turned on the pillows, his gaze fixed on the open doorway. He was waiting for someone.

It isn't my dad, she thought. *It can't be my dad.*

His eyes widened at the sight of her. His mouth dropped open into something that was both a smile and a gape of astonishment. It took a long moment for him to find his voice.

'Is it September already?' he asked.

•

Half an hour can change everything.

At first they talked about safe things—not about death, or betrayal, or wasted years. There were other people in the room, but nobody paid any attention to Cairo and Mike. She sat on his bed, and they behaved as though she'd just come back from a week in Ibiza. Just a father and daughter, discussing the weather and the standard of hospital catering.

But all the time, her heart was aching.

Did I do this to you? Is this my fault?

'So you've got kids,' he said, reaching for her hand. 'Tell me about them.'

She described her family. He smiled as she talked, sometimes chuckling and shaking his head. She told him about Damascus, the thoughtful boy with dark blue eyes who loved stories, could swim like a fish even though he was only four, and followed his best friend Monty around like a puppy. She described Quito, the clown of the family, who'd finally mastered somersaults. Mike's eyes watered when she described Havana's big cheeks and predilection for getting every pot out of the kitchen cupboard.

'They're very happy children,' she said. 'The boys adore their sister; they're always making her laugh. She's got this gorgeous giggle, like she's burbling.'

'Oh!' Mike looked entranced. 'I wish I could see them.'

'*I* wish you could.'

She imagined what they'd make of their English grandfather. She saw them in his garden, helping him make a bonfire. Normal kids, living a normal life.

'I have a stepdaughter too,' she said. 'Suva. She's just turned sixteen.'

'Photos?'

When Cairo shook her head, his face fell. 'None at all? Of any of 'em?'

She shrugged miserably. 'Sorry, Dad.'

'But they have photos on their website.'

'They're out of date. The children in those pictures are adults now.'

'Not to worry!' he cried, rallying. 'I can imagine them. Now, what about this son-in-law of mine?'

'Mum met him, did she tell you?'

Mike smiled, but his speech had begun to slur. 'She calls him the Viking.'

'Does she? That's funny. He's a farmer, but he'll turn his hand to anything.'

Mike closed his eyes. 'Never got to see you married.'

'Sorry, Dad.'

'No, no. Don't waste time regretting things.'

A nurse brought in the blood-pressure kit. She was about forty, short and brisk.

'Hazel!' exclaimed Mike, opening his eyes. 'Just come on duty?'

Thinking of his dignity, Cairo moved away to look out of the window. She heard the word *catheter*, and the nurse drew the curtain along its tracks. The room didn't have much of a view. Clouds. Roofs. A plastic bag caught on an aerial, streaming out like a white flag.

Then again, it was real. Not a chocolate box.

The nurse emerged, pulling the curtain open.

'Isn't he great?' she said to Cairo.

'He is.'

'This is Cassy, my daughter,' said Mike. He sounded proud. 'She's just walked in! All the way from New Zealand.'

Hazel looked suitably impressed. 'How long can you stay?'

'Only a week, I'm afraid.'

The nurse's eyebrows went up. 'That's a short visit.'

'She's left three small children behind,' explained Mike.

'And a poorly dad here.' Hazel glanced meaningfully towards Mike. 'Maybe you could stretch it a bit? Stay longer? It wouldn't be the end of the world.'

I hope not, thought Cairo.

Forty-seven

Those few days with her father had a special quality. It seemed as though they were woven out of threads of gold: intensely fragile and immeasurably precious. She and Mike learned more about each other in those hours than they had in the twenty-one years before she left.

She discovered a man she never knew existed. She was fascinated to hear him reminiscing about his own childhood in Northampton, and how he refused to go into his father's shoe-making business.

'The truth is, I didn't really join the army for the career,' he said. 'Certainly not for the pension! I joined up to get as far away from Northampton as I could. I wanted to see the world, be my own person.'

'What did Grandpa say?'

Mike shook his head. 'I was a disappointment.'

He talked about his brother Robert, who'd done the right thing and was still making shoes. They'd never got on very well. There were swathes of army life that he still glossed over, especially the years of the Bosnian war. It struck Cairo that there were things he'd done—things he'd seen, and feared, and loved, and been a part of—that changed him forever. He had his own version of Gethsemane.

Sometimes she had to share him with others, but there were hours alone together. She brought in books to read, and sat beside him while he dozed. Often they played cards, desperately pretending that he wasn't very ill at all, and that she wasn't leaving again. In a week. In six days. In five. In four.

It was too soon. The gold-thread days were passing too quickly.

'Looks like I might get home before you leave Blighty,' said Mike on Tuesday. 'That's Friday, right? Well, I'm hoping to escape before then. We'll make some new memories. Be a family again, for a night or so.'

'Fingers crossed,' said Cairo. 'I bet these poor nurses are desperate to get rid of you.'

That evening, the girls turned the conservatory into a bedroom. They were carrying a chest of drawers down the stairs when Diana came into the hall.

'Cassy?' she said. 'There's an email from Rome. I think you'd better read it.'

Hi Mrs Howells,
I hope you are well. I was given your email address by Barry at the Four Seasons Motel. Please could you pass on this message (below) to Cairo (Cassy)?
    Yours truly,
    Rome Calvin

'Good old Rome!' cried Cairo. 'He's found a way to get in touch!'

'Not stupid, your boy,' said Tara approvingly.

Cairo leaned closer to the screen.

Hi Cairo,
I hope you got home in time to see your father.
    I'm in Rotorua. Don't worry, I'm not on the streets, but I

have been expelled. When Justin heard that you'd left and I'd helped you, he went mad. That's the only way I can describe it. He called me Judas. He said he knows I've been telling people he's paranoid and sick, he knows I'm trying to turn the Watchmen against him. He punched me in the face. He's a fighter, and I'm not. He knocked me over, and he shouted that he never wants to see me again, that I'm not his son. He used words I've never heard him use before. He was like a different man.

I was on Ikaroa five minutes later, and I couldn't take anything with me except what I could fit into a pillowcase. I couldn't find your mother's phone number and assume they'd already found and destroyed it. Otto and Kyoto drove me to Rotorua, gave me a hundred dollars and left me by the side of the road in the rain. Those men are like uncles. I've known them all my life. I sat in a bus shelter for a while because I didn't dare move. I have never felt fear like it! And I never want to again!

But in the end I got too cold. I knew about the dormitories in the hostels being the cheapest place to stay, so I walked into town and found one.

Cairo read this with guilty horror, knowing that Rome had lost everything because he'd helped her. She imagined him by the side of the road, clutching a pillowcase. He was born in Gethsemane. He'd worked for years, seven days a week, for no pay. He'd put one foot wrong, and he was out.

'How could they?' she said. 'How *could* they?'

I'm okay compared to others who've been expelled. I know my way around, can drive and use technology. When I told the girl on the desk at the hostel what had happened she fetched the manager, Phil. They helped me claim some emergency cash from the benefits office. Phil's letting me stay here in return for work.

I've begun to look for jobs. Life out here is complicated though! I don't have any references and I've had to sort out things like a tax number. Phil's friend works at the hospital, and he got me an interview for a job as a porter. They've offered me a week's trial, starting tomorrow.

I must face the fact that Justin is just a man. A man I love, but just a man. He's not even a very good man. And if that's true, then what hope is there for the world? What meaning is there for me? Who AM I?

Your children were okay last time I saw them. I'm afraid Suva is VERY angry with you. The Companions have separated them from Aden at night, to make sure Aden can't leave. They're all staying with different families.

Aden understands why you left. He believes Justin will let you come back, for his sake if nothing else. He said if I managed to contact you I was to tell you that he and the children are counting the days until you come home.

That's all for now. I'm staying at a hostel called Kit and Meg's. I'm feeling quite lonely. Please write back soon.

Rome

•

Such a lovely afternoon for fishing. Aden was showing Suva how to cast while Damascus and Quito waited their turn. From time to time the two little boys shared some hilarious joke, understood only by three- and four-year-olds. Havana sat in a wicker basket, wearing nothing but a nappy and chewing on a nectarine. There were wispy curls at the nape of her neck.

A family day out. Sunlight flashing on mercury, under a burning sky.

Then the boat tipped, flinging Cairo overboard. The mercury was cold and heavy, dragging her down. The children were screaming for her. She saw their wide-open mouths.

Aden leaned over the side of the boat—*Grab my hand, Cairo*—but she couldn't touch him. The waves were smooth and silver and poisonous. She was going under.

Then the children were pointing, they were smiling—Justin was coming! He was walking across the water, straight towards her. A ray of brilliance moved with him because the sun was his own personal spotlight. His feet made little dents in the surface of the mercury, as though he was walking on a silver cushion.

She held up her hands, gasping, 'Save me, Justin!'

But he didn't reach out his hand to her. He watched her struggles, smiling beatifically.

'I've been keeping an eye on you,' he said. 'Oh dear. You can never run away from God.'

'I'm dying! Please, Justin, help me.'

'I know you're dying. But hey—good news!' He opened his arms. 'It's your turn. I died for you once. Now *you* get to die for *me*!'

The last sounds she heard were the wails of her children. Then the mercury closed over her head.

Blinding light. Electric light.

'What the fuck?' snapped Tara. She was standing in the doorway in her nightie, one finger on the switch. 'Someone being murdered in here?'

Cairo was staring around the room, heart pounding. The dream was still with her. She could still hear the screams.

'He can see me,' she gasped. 'He can hear me. He knows everything.'

'Well, if he can hear you, I feel sorry for the bugger because you've got one hell of a set of lungs.'

'He smiled. He watched me drown.'

'Seriously, sis,' said Tara, throwing herself onto the bed, 'you should train as an opera singer.'

They both lay on their backs, sharing one pillow, staring up at the ceiling. Gradually, Cairo's heart rate slowed.

'I can't believe they've separated my family,' she said. 'All sleeping in different cabins, so Aden can't leave.'

'Isn't that a breach of his human rights?'

'They're a little unit, the children. Every morning, the boys go and get Havana out of her cot. They'll be bewildered now, they won't understand.'

'Mean bastards,' said Tara. 'Poor little kids.'

Cairo didn't even try to defend Gethsemane. The Companions had gone too far.

I'll be with them soon, she thought, as she listened to a police siren wailing in the night. *Just another few days. We'll all be together again.*

Forty-eight

'Don't you want to drive?' asked Diana, as she backed out of the driveway.

Cairo shook her head. She hadn't seen her licence for five years. She supposed it was in the safe at Gethsemane.

Diana glanced at her. 'D'you really have to leave the day after tomorrow?'

'The children are counting the days, Mum. But I'll try to come back soon.'

'I don't think that's very likely, do you?'

The radio was on. The presenter was talking to a scientist who thought the human race was headed for extinction within a hundred years. *Take Easter Island!* he exclaimed exuberantly. *Excellent example. The human population outstripped the environment. The result? Extinction.*

'Charming,' muttered Diana, retuning to a music channel. 'Remind me not to invite *him* to dinner.'

'A hundred years is a lot longer than Justin predicts.'

'You don't still believe that stuff, do you? About the end of the world being nigh?'

Cairo looked out at the traffic, at people walking along with

phones clapped to their ears and cheerful advertising hoard-
ings. She saw a party of children with their teachers; a man in
an anorak, stooping to pat a dog. It all seemed very humdrum.
Not remotely apocalyptic. But the darkness of the mercury dream
clung to her.

'There's not believing,' she said, 'and then there's *really* not
believing. It's hard to unbelieve things you've built your life
around.'

'It must be bloody depressing. I mean, why would you bother
to do anything? I think I'd just give up and eat a lot of chocolate.'

•

Cairo arrived on the ward in time to see a gaggle of medical
types filing out from behind Mike's curtain. She pressed herself
against the basin as they swept by. It was hard to believe that so
many people had somehow jammed themselves around his bed; it
reminded her of jokes about elephants and fridges.

Mike's mood was upbeat.

'Tomorrow morning! The consultant and his sidekicks just
had a pow-wow. They're sick of me.'

'Great, Dad!'

'I'll feel more human once I'm out.' He pointed at his bedside
cabinet. 'Grab my phone for me? Better let your mum know.'

He called Diana while Cairo rearranged the Get Well cards.
He looked *so* much better today. Perhaps the prognosis was
wrong? Her children might meet their grandfather after all.

'Think we could go outside?' he asked. 'I've got cabin fever.'

Cairo asked Hazel, who produced a wheelchair. The nurse
dosed her patient up with pain relief and, with the help of Cairo,
manoeuvred him into the chair.

'What a palaver,' said Mike. 'I could get used to being treated
like royalty.'

It *was* a palaver, but it was worth it. As soon as he was in the
open air, Mike seemed ecstatic.

'I haven't been outside since this whole thing began,' he said.

'Funny, the things that don't matter. I was on my way to work, on my phone, bitching about someone's mismanagement. Stumbled over a kerb, and—*snap!*—leg's broken, and I'm sitting on the pavement.'

'Just like that?'

'Yep. Ambulance. Faces getting more and more solemn. It dawns on me that we're not talking about a broken leg any more, we're talking about what's caused it to break. A load of tests. Then the news nobody wants to hear. Not a great moment.' One hand strayed to his ear, and he tugged at the lobe. 'Anyhoo. Onwards and upwards. I might be one of those miracles who baffle their doctors. And right now I'm out here in the sunshine.' He tipped his head back, basking. 'And I'm with Cassy. That makes me glad I've got the Big C.'

'No, Dad. No.'

'Yes, yes, yes. I'd rather die at the age of fifty-five, knowing you and I are friends, than live to a hundred and think you hate me.'

They'd arrived at a lily pond. It was really just a trough full of water, raised to a wheelchair user's level. Tiny fish flitted under the algae, like shining copper coins. Cairo parked Mike's chair and sat on the brick surround of the trough. She and her father didn't have much time left, and there were things that must be put right.

'I want you to know I'm sorry,' she said. 'I just . . . want to say that.'

'For leaving us?'

'For everything. For accusing you.'

'Ah. Yes, that did hurt a bit.'

'I honestly believed what I was saying. I thought I was remembering real events. It all seemed so vivid.'

He flicked his fingers, shooing her words away. 'No more apologies. Life's too short—literally too short. I've been an idiot of a father. I made a God-awful fuss about things that didn't matter at all.' He pretended to slap his own face. 'Stupid.'

A fish came up, its copper snout breaking the surface.

'Justin says the only measure of success is whether we love one another,' said Cairo.

'Does he?' Mike raised a cynical eyebrow. 'And how does JC score on that criteria?'

'I used to think he scored top marks. One hundred percent. But now I wonder whether the only person he really loves is himself. And I'm not even sure of that.'

'Can I ask . . . is it true that he thinks he's Jesus Christ?'

'An embodiment of the divine spirit of Jesus. Yes.'

'Ah.' Mike wasn't quite suppressing a smirk. 'What's the difference?'

'Well, he teaches that the mysteries of the universe are far beyond human understanding.'

'How convenient.'

'Dad!' She splashed a little pond water over him, and he looked contrite.

'Sorry. Please tell me, I won't interrupt again.'

She had to think. The Watchmen didn't ask these questions. 'He teaches that when he—the risen Jesus—was taken up to heaven two thousand years ago, he was rejoined, or reabsorbed, into a kind of cloud of power . . . that's the Infinite Power, which we also call God. His true state of being is a part of the Infinite Power. See? Then he became human for a second time. And that's Justin.'

'Really? Wow.'

'*Wow*, Dad?' Cairo mimed astonishment. 'Is that all you've got to say?'

'It's all I'm allowed to say. Your mother's forbidden me—on pain of death, though that's not much of a threat—to use expressions like *whack job* or *psycho* or *string the bastard up*. She's afraid I'll drive you back into that whack job's arms.'

Cairo could see that he was tiring, but she didn't want this time with him to end. This might be their last chance to sit and talk, alone in a sunny garden. Every second was priceless.

'Tell me more about Gethsemane,' he begged. 'I won't scoff

any more. I'd like to understand where you've been. Those lost years! I want to live them with you.'

Cairo held back at least half of the story. There were things she never wanted her family to know. Her life in Gethsemane was deeply personal. She couldn't explain the euphoria of meditation, or her sense of soaring into the presence of God, or the fear of being expelled, or the way Justin seemed to bend the very air around him. She was ashamed to admit that she'd been out recruiting; that she'd helped to play people like fish. She was embarrassed to have welcomed hunger and sleep deprivation, and public confession, and being told when to have children and how many she was allowed, or what she should think and feel, or how she should spend every second of every day.

Instead she talked about picnics, rope swings and hot springs; gardens, goats and swimming in the lake on summer nights. She talked about community and friendship. Mike was especially interested in her teaching.

'I bet you're good at it,' he said.

'Well, I do get a buzz. I'd like to be properly trained.'

He'd been smiling as he listened to her.

'I'm starting to understand why you stayed,' he said. 'I think I'm finally getting it.'

She dipped her hand into the pond, and a water boatman skittered away. That little creature really *could* walk on water. Simple, when you knew how.

'I was looking for answers,' she said. 'I thought I'd found them.'

'We're all looking for answers.'

'You too, huh?'

He was watching the fish as they darted around their microworld. 'I lie at night in my bed by the window, and I look out at this fascinating, mysterious, mind-blowingly vast universe—or at where it would be, if it wasn't for the light pollution—and I wonder if there's any chance of finding an omnipotent being out there, who created the whole shebang. And I wonder what kind of omnipotent being would just lounge about, watching the mess we're making down here, and let it happen anyway. I mean, what a bastard. It all seems pretty unlikely to me.'

'Are you scared?'

'Of dying? Yes. But not so much of death. I've seen a fair bit of it, one way and another. It's just the last stop on the line. My brain will shut down, and my atoms will break down, and go off and re-form themselves into new structures, and that will be that for me. *Finito*.'

His view seemed impossibly bleak. She wanted to save him from it. 'Millions of people think you're wrong, Dad.'

'I do hope not! Oblivion's a *much* better option than eternity.'

'You don't believe that.'

'Bloody well do. The very idea of eternity gives me vertigo. I'd rather be non-existent than sitting on a cloud making eternal small talk with a whole load of Christians. Or Buddhists, or Jews, or Muslims, or Hindus, or Jehovah's Witnesses, or Zoroastrians . . . or whichever bunch turns out to have backed the right horse. Think how smug they'll be!'

Cairo laughed, despite everything. She took her hand from the water and shook it dry. An elderly couple were approaching the pond; he was leaning on a Zimmer frame while she guided him.

'Might be time to move along,' said Mike. 'We mustn't hog the ornamental lake.'

Cairo struggled to turn his chair around and ended up driving over the edge of a flowerbed.

'Women drivers,' jeered Mike.

'You haven't changed, Dad. You're still a wanker.'

She pushed him slowly, sensing that neither of them was quite ready for this time to end. She'd never felt so close to her father. She'd never quite seen him as human.

'I suppose your man Calvin thinks I'm going directly to hell, not passing Go, not collecting two hundred pounds?' he asked.

'Ah! That's where you're wrong! Justin says hell is a figment of mankind's imagination.'

'*Does* he?'

'Mm. He says most doctrines, from all the world's religions, are a figment of mankind's imagination. He says science is much closer to understanding God than religion. He insists on Gethsemane children learning about evolution, lots of history, and proper science.'

'I'm starting to like this guy!'

They were back on smooth tarmac, and soon she was pushing the wheelchair up a ramp towards a set of doors. Mike had closed his eyes.

'Is the pain relief working, Dad?'

'Well enough. But they'll be doing the tea round soon, and we don't want to miss that.'

'No, we mustn't miss that.'

'I think I've become institutionalised. Good thing I'm getting out tomorrow. You know you're in trouble when you look forward to a witch's brew with cardboard biscuits.'

For the rest of the slow and clumsy journey—corridor, lift, corridor—they earnestly debated the dunking of biscuits. It was a much more cheerful subject than oblivion. Or, for that matter, eternity.

•

The internet was pretty miraculous. Cairo had forgotten what could be done with it. Tara needed less than a minute to find the phone number for Kit and Meg's hostel in Rotorua. Three minutes after that, Cairo was talking to Rome.

'Cairo!' He sounded overwhelmed. 'This is . . . it's great to hear your voice. Oh wow, I'm happy to hear your voice.'

They talked about life Outside, swapping notes and agreeing that it was lonely and frightening and confusing and—above all—noisy. But Rome was doing well. His first day as a hospital porter had been a success.

'It's just so exhausting, being out here,' he said. 'I've never had to meet so many new people before. I sometimes find myself . . .'

'Sliding back?'

'Sliding back. Yes.' There was hesitation before he asked, 'Is the Last Day coming, do you think?'

'No,' she said firmly. 'I really don't.'

'I'm worried about what's happening at Gethsemane. People have started leaving.'

'People have left? Who?'

'Kiev and Tunis, for a start.'

Cairo was surprised. Kiev and Tunis were the couple she'd helped to recruit in Hamilton, years ago. They'd seemed like perfect Watchmen.

'They've ended up in this hostel,' said Rome. 'Kiev is so scared, she won't leave her room. Her brother's flying up from Christchurch to collect them.'

'What made them leave?'

'Well, this is the thing . . . according to them, the atmosphere's got much worse since I was expelled. All five flax weavers have gone! They walked out along the top path, same as you. Justin keeps having those thunderclap headaches. He keeps shouting at Messenger, all night long. He says the Last Day is imminent. Like . . . *imminent*. He's doubled the numbers at every Vigil. Nobody's allowed to leave the valley, for any reason. *Matariki* and *Ikaroa* can't be used any more. Tunis and Kiev only just managed to get out on a kayak.'

'Justin's closing the gates.'

'That's right. He's got everyone sleeping with their shoes on, ready for a journey. Tunis said the valley feels dark. *Dark*. I don't like the sound of it, do you?'

No, Cairo didn't like the sound of it. Her mind began to work fast: weighing choices, making decisions. She had woken up at last.

Take the flight on Friday, as planned. I wouldn't be able to get one before then . . . save a lot of time if I take a domestic flight down to Rotorua. I'll have to borrow the money from Mum for that. Find Rome. Get myself back into Gethsemane. Quickly.

She had to hurry. The gates were closing, and her family was inside.

Forty-nine

Mike was coming home today.

They'd worked hard to make the conservatory look like something other than a sick room. They'd carried in the most comfortable armchair, swapping it for two of the wicker ones. They'd arranged a pile of his travel books, and his chess set, and the leather-cased telescope that had been his father's. Diana had fetched clothes and a flat-screen television from his flat.

Tara was edgy. By twelve o'clock she was pacing around the house, hair in a ponytail, car keys in one hand.

'Ready to go?' she asked Cairo. 'Well, you don't look it! Where's Mum? It's not fair to keep poor Dad waiting.'

Cairo found Diana in the conservatory. She was sitting on the bed, clutching a cloth and a bottle of window-cleaning fluid. Cairo had the feeling she'd been sitting there for a long time.

'Tara thinks we should get going,' said Cairo.

'I heard her bossing you around.' Diana stood up and sprayed too much liquid onto the glass. The cloth squeaked as she wiped.

'How're you doing, Mum?'

'A bit nervous.' Diana was rubbing as though her life depended upon it. 'I signed up to seeing him die, didn't I? I knew it was on the cards when I married him. Just didn't expect it yet.'

'I'm sorry.'

Diana shrugged. 'I'll have to learn to be a nurse. Hope I'm up to it. There's so much to remember in the way of drugs and appointments. I've got the GP visiting, and the hospice, and an OT and the district nurse. It'll be like Paddington Station around here. To tell you the truth, I don't want a visit from the hospice. He's not *that* ill.'

'They're the experts on pain relief, I think.'

'They should be concentrating on a cure! This defeatist attitude.' Diana stopped trying to clean the window and leaned her forehead against it. 'The thing is, I love him. I know we don't normally use the "L" word, he and I. But I do, in fact, love that man.'

They heard Tara's voice in the hall, yelling for them to get a move on. What the bloody hell were they *doing*?

Diana put down her cloth and straightened her back.

'Let's go,' she said.

●

Mike was waiting for them, sitting on a chair with the broken leg stuck out. The hospital had issued crutches; the physio had made sure he could use them. He'd brushed his hair and put on a collared shirt. He looked boyishly eager, as though they were all going on holiday.

'Ah!' he cried, when Diana and the girls appeared in the ward. 'The old gang, come to spring me from the clink!'

All the nurses came to say goodbye. They genuinely seemed to like him. Hazel had arranged a wheelchair to get him as far as the car, but he wouldn't use it.

'Makes you feel decrepit,' he said. 'Sitting in a bloody bathchair. Once I get rid of this pot on my leg, I'll be mobile again.'

Hazel smiled indulgently. 'Skateboarding and hang-gliding, Mike?'

'I might try a marathon.'

He thanked them all and swung himself out of the ward. Diana walked close by his side as though he were made of china and might smash at any moment. His daughters followed behind, carrying medical paraphernalia and his overnight bag.

'Quite fun,' Mike was saying. 'Crutches.'

His desperate courage made Cairo want to cry. His trousers hung from his hips, and he hunched slightly, perhaps because of the pain. Diana slid into the back of the car next to him and sat holding his hand in both of hers. Tara drove without a word. Twenty minutes later they were welcoming him home.

'Here's your bedroom,' said Diana, showing him the conservatory. 'Got the view across your beloved garden. Sorry about the weeds.'

'Wow! How did you move the furniture?' asked Mike, looking around.

'Cassy's turned into superwoman since she got matey with Jesus,' said Tara. 'Just picked up the chest of drawers in one hand and—*whoof!*—flew down the stairs.'

'Don't be bitchy,' said Diana.

Cairo wasn't sure how to respond; she felt disorientated by Tara's change of mood. She knew her sister was grieving, but struggled to understand why she was so brittle. There was a moment's awkwardness before Mike dropped into the armchair.

'I'm home,' he declared, with a sigh of contentment. 'Hurray! I'm home! Why did I ever leave?'

'Because you were an idiot,' said Diana.

'I don't deserve you.' He began to say something else, but words failed him. His eyes reddened; his mouth folded in on itself. Diana dropped to her knees on the floor beside him, and they clung together. Cairo glimpsed her father's fist, gripping the softness of her mother's sleeve. Until today she hadn't thought of them as people who loved each other.

Tara spun around. 'Coffee!'

Cairo said she'd help, and followed her into the kitchen. 'Good to see them together,' she said.

'Yeah? I think it's shitty. He's on death row, after all they've been through.' Tara's voice was wobbling. She used her teeth to tear at a bag of ground coffee. It split open, its dark richness spilling across the bench. 'Fuck.'

'I'll get that,' said Cairo, and grabbed a cloth from the sink. 'Um . . . have I upset you?'

'Ha! Why would you think that?' Tara was banging about, making far more noise than was necessary. 'You weren't around when they split up. You *caused* the whole thing, but you weren't here to see the results of your handiwork. You didn't have to visit Dad in that sodding awful flat, trying to hang on to his dignity for dear life. And guess what? Surprise, surprise! You're making a break for it tomorrow! You won't be around when he gets worse and worse and ends up wearing nappies and being in agony.'

'I'm sorry.'

'You ought to be sorry. You've swanned in, done your prodigal daughter act, and now you're swanning out again. Nice one, sis.' *Clatter, crash* went the mugs, out of the dishwasher and onto the table. 'And we all have to pretend that's fine and dandy. We're not allowed to say what we're all thinking—that you're the dizzy bitch who destroyed this family.' The dishwasher door got in her way and was smashed shut. 'Bye-bye, Cassy, off on a nice plane to a cute place where they sing hymns and prance about by a lake. Naked, I expect. Wearing daisy chains. Lovely husband and kids.'

'My children—'

'Oh, shut up. Shut up about your kids needing you. That's such bullshit—do they have cancer? Are they dying? They're just an excuse for you to run away again, like a bloody coward. But Mum and I can't run away. No. We have to see this through. Right to the end. Right to the miserable, horrible end.'

Tara seemed to have ranted herself to a standstill, and went about her coffee-making task with jerky movements. Cairo dried everything on the draining board, wondering what she could possibly say or do that would make things better. She wasn't used to open conflict. She'd forgotten that people sometimes expressed themselves as Tara had, with bitterness and anger and honesty. It went against the Gethsemane grain.

'It's true,' she said in the end. 'I *did* destroy the family. I *was* a dizzy bitch. I'm sorry.'

'Takes one to know one.' Tara's fury had dampened as quickly as it flared. She stood with her hands flat on the bench, her head hanging. 'I kind of hoped if you came home, you'd wave a magic wand and save him. We'd all be back the way we were. But it hasn't worked. He's still got cancer, he's still dying.'

'I wish I had a magic wand.'

'Does he have one? Your Jesus man? Can he heal the sick?'

'No,' said Cairo. 'No, the magic isn't real. I've finally seen the smoke and mirrors. Once you get that, everything else looks different. He's an amazing man—I still believe he's amazing—but he's deluded, and so is everyone around him.'

'Like the emperor in his new clothes.'

'Ha! Yes, that's right.'

'You're the little boy who sees he isn't wearing a stitch.'

Music came floating out of the conservatory. The first bars of Dire Straits' 'Telegraph Road'. The sisters heard Mike say something, and Diana's quiet laughter.

'And what did the emperor do,' asked Tara, 'when the boy pointed and laughed and yelled, *You're butt-naked, you silly sod*?'

'I don't know,' said Cairo. 'But I think I'm about to find out.'

•

Such a bittersweet evening. To an outsider it might even have looked ordinary. Supper at the kitchen table, a game of Scrabble.

But to the four people who shared them, those hours would never be forgotten. It was a first and a last. None of them wanted it to end. None of them wanted tomorrow to come.

They agreed that Tara would drive her sister to the airport. Mike tried to insist on going too, but Diana put her foot down.

'All that hassle, the escalators, and you're on crutches. No, Mike. You and I will see her off from here. I don't want to watch Cassy leave from Heathrow again. Not after last time.'

He stuck out his lower lip, pretending to sulk.

'Bossy baggage,' he said and winked at Cairo.

'You look just like Quito when you do that,' she said. 'And he's three years old.'

'Really? Good old Quito! Pleased to think I've left a legacy. My grandson has inherited my pout.'

Mike was doing a brave job of pretending to be well, but pain and exhaustion broke through in the end. After he fell asleep in his chair for the third time, they persuaded him to go to bed.

'This has been wonderful,' he said, when his daughters came into the conservatory to say goodnight. 'Thank you. We've been a family again. Nothing can take that away.'

Cairo was packing her very few belongings—all blue, still—when there was a tap on the bedroom door, and Diana's face appeared, wearing a too-bright smile.

'Can I come in for a minute?'

'Sure, Mum.'

'I know you need to get some sleep. But you're going to be gone in a few hours, and I'm bloody well going to miss you.'

'And I'm bloody well going to miss you too,' said Cairo, patting the bed.

Diana sat next to the duffle bag she'd bought Cairo for the journey, glancing into it. 'Gosh, you're travelling light! You could take just one or two nicer clothes, couldn't you? There are such lovely things in your cupboard.'

'I won't wear them, Mum. I still feel guilty if I wear anything, do anything, even *think* anything that isn't allowed by Gethsemane. And anyway, we can't keep our own things. There isn't room in the cabins for personal possessions. They'd just be taken off me.'

Diana nodded. She seemed determined not to make a scene.

'I just caught the end of the news,' she said. 'A volcano's

erupted in Japan. Amazing footage, really dramatic! Clouds of ash and smoke.'

'Anyone hurt?'

'I don't think so.'

'All the same, that'll go on the board in the *wharenui*. They'll make it sound terrifying. More evidence of the Last Day.' Cairo zipped her bag and sighed. 'Well. I'm ready.'

'It's been lovely having you back in this room. Your room.'

Cairo sat heavily on the bed, swallowing, not quite trusting herself to speak. Pesky had come in while they were talking, and he leaped onto her lap.

'The vet's right,' Cairo whispered, stroking him. 'You're getting a little porky, my man.'

'Cassy,' said Diana, 'please don't be cross, because I have to say this. I'm so afraid we're going to lose you again. I really, really don't want you to go back.'

'I have to go.'

Diana had jammed her hands under her thighs as she sat. She was rocking—backwards, forwards—as though she were in pain.

'Let me ask, just one more time: are you *sure* you have to go? We can raise the money for a lawyer. We'll make an application to get the children out. Surely the courts will be on your side. They could come and live here.'

'Thank you, Mum. But even if the courts agreed, it wouldn't be fair to them. They've never even seen a road.'

'Children are adaptable.'

Cairo smiled, despite her distress. 'And poor Aden! My marriage was arranged, in a way, but I do love my husband and I won't hurt him any more than I already have.'

Diana nodded. She was still rocking. Backwards, forwards.

She's being so brave, thought Cairo. *She's facing so much hurt.*

'So what *is* your plan?' asked Diana.

'I'm going to try to persuade Aden to leave.'

'And will he?'

'Maybe. I hope so. But it's an awful lot to ask. He'd have to give up everyone and everything, and accept that his faith is a delusion. Whatever happens, I'll stay in touch with you. I promise.'

Diana nodded, whispering, 'Okay.'

She sat for a while, fidgeting with her wedding ring.

'I'm being silly, I know,' she said. 'Very silly. But is it safe there? Waco, Jonestown, Heaven's Gate. We're not going to be seeing Gethsemane on the news, are we?'

•

The night was peopled with dreams of Mike and Justin—though in the dream, she wasn't sure which of them was her father. Aden and the children were there, and Diana and Tara, as though her two worlds had merged into one. They were all huddled together in a dark *whare*, watching the roof bending under a deluge of ash. Havana was a wide-eyed bush baby in Aden's arms. The boys clung to Cairo. Only Justin seemed happy.

'The Last Day,' he said exultantly. 'Told you so!'

The collapse came suddenly, with a dull crash. Then they were choking. Blackness and chaos. She tried to shield her sons with her own body, but as the ash buried her she realised she was crushing them to death. *I can't breathe, Mummy*, whimpered Damascus. Then he was silent.

She woke at five, with a sinking heart.

Breakfast was awful, though Mike gamely tried to make conversation. When the time came for her to leave, Cairo was afraid she might actually throw up. It was like going back to boarding school, multiplied by a thousand. She kept finding excuses to walk around the house one last time. She touched everything. She cuddled Pesky, burying her face in his fur. She went outside to sit on the swing.

'Come on, Cass.' Tara was tapping her watch. 'You never know what the traffic's going to do.'

'Shush!' said Diana, putting a finger to her lips. 'We *want* her to miss her plane. There's plenty of time, darling. Have another cup of tea.'

'No,' said Mike. 'There are three little children waiting for their mum. Right, Cassy. I'll walk you outside. At least, you walk—I'll hop.'

Even when she was on the point of getting into the car, he refused to say a real goodbye.

'I'll see you again,' he insisted doggedly. 'And if I don't, so be it. Let's not say goodbye. You know I love you, eh?'

She hung around his neck, feeling his frailty. She didn't want to let go of her dad. In the end, it was he who firmly pushed her away.

'You've got a plane to catch. If you don't come back soon, I think I'll pay a visit to New Zealand and see those grandchildren of mine.'

Don't cry. Don't cry. She hugged him again, thinking, *Just one more time.* She did the same with Diana before forcing herself into the passenger seat, winding down her window so that she could still talk to them. Precious, precious last moments.

Tara started the engine.

As the car began to back down the narrow drive, Cairo looked out at her parents. Mike had his crutches under one arm; the other arm was around Diana. He was smiling.

'Can't wave,' he said ruefully. 'I'll fall over.'

'Bye, Dad,' she said.

'Bye, darling.'

Fifty

Cairo stepped off the domestic flight and onto the tarmac, shielding her eyes. It was a balmy spring morning with the sharp intensity of light she'd never seen anywhere else but here. The pungent, geothermal smell struck her at once. She'd forgotten that. She felt disorientated, as though she were in two hemispheres at once.

Rome was waiting for her in the little terminal building. The gangly figure looked barely recognisable in jeans, a hoodie and trainers. One eye was distorted by bruising, deep mauve fading to a pale brown. He sported a black baseball cap, which turned out to be a present from the hostel's manager.

'So good to see you,' he cried fervently, draping himself over her. 'So, *so* good. Oh, you don't know how great this is.'

He'd lost weight in the past fortnight. He was too thin, and nobody his age should have lines of anxiety drawn across their forehead.

She touched his eye. 'Ouch! Was this Justin?'

'Never mind. Fading now. Look, something's happened. Something you probably ought to know about.'

He'd come in the hostel's van—black, with *Kit and Meg's Backpackers* written in jaunty lettering—and was meeting four

Korean tourists. They asked a hundred questions on the way to the hostel: did Rome recommend the Zorb? Which geothermal area was best? Where were the liveliest bars? He reeled off answers with complete confidence, as though he was an old hand at the Zorb—whatever that might be—and was familiar with the vibe of every bar in town.

'You haven't changed,' muttered Cairo, as he handed them their room keys. 'You still lure people into your van and tell them what they want to hear.'

'I resent that remark.'

'I admire you. I can't believe how well you're doing. I was a quivering mess for days. I'm still having nightmares, *still* can't bring myself to wear anything but blue.'

'There's a lot of paddling under the water.'

He made Cairo a cup of tea and showed her into the lounge, where they sat on a sofa with broken springs. Some English guys were playing table tennis. They seemed to be stoned, laughing wildly at non-events. Cairo felt a little stoned herself. She'd managed a few hours' sleep in a hotel near Auckland Airport, but it wasn't enough.

'Tell me,' she said. 'What's up?'

'You know I'm doing a trial at the hospital? Well. I was there last night.' He ran his hand through his hair, screwing up his face. 'Um, this is breaking the rules. We're not meant to repeat anything we see or hear.'

'I'm sure you aren't,' she said. 'But you're going to, aren't you?'

'I really need this job. I don't want to lose it.'

'Rome, this isn't Gethsemane. There are no Companions, the walls don't have ears.' She patted his arm. 'Tell me.'

'Justin's in hospital.'

'*Justin?* How come? What's wrong with him?'

'I don't know. I stayed well away. Last time he saw me, I got this.' Rome touched his swollen eye. 'He was brought into the ED by ambulance, and later I saw him being taken up to a ward.'

'Anyone with him?'

'Nope. He was alone.'

She thought about this news. Perhaps Justin was dying, like her father; perhaps he needed help. 'Are you working there today?'

'Not till tomorrow.'

The stoned boys were in hysterics. One of them was trying to balance a ping-pong ball on his nose.

'I think Justin needs a visitor,' said Cairo.

•

She was heartily sick of hospitals. She'd hoped not to see the inside of another one for many years to come.

Rome drove her in Kit and Meg's van, dropping her at the main entrance. As they pulled up, he reached across her and opened the glove box.

'Here,' he said, pulling out a mobile phone. 'A guest left this behind. It's just a cheap one, got a few dollars of credit on it. I'll put my number in . . . there we go. Under *Rome*, see? Text me once you've seen Justin. I'll give you a lift to the forestry track. You can walk back in the same way you came out.'

She thanked him, sliding the phone into the pocket of her Gethsemane dress.

'Are you nervous?' he asked.

'Terrified. I'm about to meet my God. I'll be lucky if I get away with a black eye.'

•

The hospital receptionist was very obliging. 'Calvin,' she said, after checking on the computer system. 'Medical assessment. I'll ask if he's still there.'

She lifted the phone and had a conversation with somebody.

'He's gone for an MRI,' she said to Cairo. 'Pop along to radiology. You might catch him.'

Cairo followed the signs to radiology's waiting area. A handful of patients sat around in plastic chairs. One was leafing through torn magazines; another was staring at his phone. A couple of women had their heads together, discussing some disgraceful thing a mutual friend had done. The walls were painted the colour of bile.

High in one corner, a television wearily churned out infomercials. A model draped herself over an exercise machine. She was wearing a crop top and shorts, pushing a bar up and down with improbably lean legs. She looked enraptured. *The Multi-ciser all-in-one home gym is so easy to use!* she crooned. *In just ten minutes a day, these exercises can give you the tight buns you've always wanted!* A message looped along the bottom of the screen: *Thirty-day free trial! One hundred percent refund with no questions asked if you're not TOTALLY IN LOVE WITH THE MULTI-CISER™ ALL-IN-ONE HOME GYM!*

Justin was there. The lonely figure was folded into a chair, bent forwards over his knees, fingers curled around his head. He was in his own clothes, not a hospital gown. Cairo felt a jolt of love and indignation. The Messiah shouldn't have to sit in a bile-coloured waiting room, surrounded by sticky magazines.

'Justin,' she whispered.

His fingers slid away from his hair. She was looking into the vivid eyes she knew so well, with their smile lines and depths of sadness. There were tears on his face, though he wiped them in the crook of his arm. The gesture reminded her of Damascus, when he was crying and wanted to hide it.

'You're back,' he said.

'Two weeks. I promised.'

He coughed carefully. 'I knew you'd come. You heard me calling for you?'

'Oh yes,' she said, thinking of her dreams. 'I heard you.'

He was coughing again. She spotted a water cooler in the corner, and filled a plastic cup.

'What's happened?' she asked, as she handed it to him. 'Why are you here?'

'I collapsed on a street in Rotorua. My head exploded, and then . . . I don't know. They're looking for a bleed, or a clot, or a tumour.'

'What do they think?'

'They haven't got a clue.' He gestured gracefully with both hands, encompassing the whole hospital. 'All this marvellous technology! They want me to go through another machine, but no. I was only waiting for you. And now you're here. So I'm leaving.'

'Why don't you let them help? It could be something quite simple. Maybe a trapped nerve, or a migraine, or—'

He was shaking his head. 'The breakdown of this body is inevitable. Built-in obsolescence. Mix divinity and humanity in one body, and you're going to get a conflagration in the end. I had a moment of weakness last night, when I was half crazy with the pain. They gave me drugs, and I accepted them, and I slept. Haven't slept for a long time.'

'That's good.'

'I don't have time for sleeping.' He looked at the palms of his hands, as though he might find comfort there. 'I'm God incarnate, God made human. Sometimes I've prayed to lose the God part, and just be the human. Sometimes I've wished I was just plain Justin Calvin. Perhaps he'd have spent most of his life in and out of prison, but at least—' He broke off with a whimper of agony, wrapping his arms over his head.

He was clearly in appalling pain. Cairo looked around for help. The other patients in the waiting area were ostentatiously taking no notice.

'Shall I get someone?' she asked, but he held up a hand. Gradually, she sensed the tension leave him.

On the television the crop-topped model was on all fours. *No more hiding behind bulky clothing*, she purred into the lens. *No more saying 'no' to pool parties. In just ten minutes a day, the Multi-Ciser can transform your life forever!*

Justin pushed himself to his feet. 'Let's go.'

'Listen, Justin,' she said. 'Listen. You don't have to *be* the Messiah.'

'Not the Messiah?'

'Not the Messiah. You can be just an ordinary guy. Think about it! I bet the pain would go away. I bet you'd live to be a hundred. You've got friends who love you, and they'll still love you! You can shack up with some jolly woman like Bali—be a real dad to Helike—and have takeaway lamb madras in front of the Saturday-night movie. You can watch your children and grandchildren grow up.'

Justin had sunk back into the chair. He was motionless, staring at the pile of magazines on the table. He seemed to see something truly wonderful laid out there. 'Could I really do that?'

'Yes!' She crouched on the floor beside him, whispering urgently. 'You can sleep. You can eat. Stop waiting for the Last Day and start working for a better world. It isn't about to end, it really isn't. If and when it does, somebody else can be the Messiah. Put this burden down, Justin! Why does it have to be you?'

'I could be free.'

'Yes! You can be free.'

He gazed at the beautiful vision. Slowly, he stretched his fingers towards whatever was laid out on the table. Then he jerked his hand away, as though he'd touched an electric fence.

'If I'm not the Messiah,' he said, 'what's the point of me?'

'What's the point of any of us? To do our best. To make other people's lives a little bit better.'

He looked puzzled. 'But if I'm not divine, I'm mad.'

'You're a man with a vision.'

He was wary now, glaring at her with a frown of deep suspicion. 'I'd just be a fool who fooled others. Is that what you believe?'

'No.'

'If I thought that was true, I'd put an end to myself.'

'Justin—'

'I know you!' Suddenly, he seemed to overflow. His eyes were wide, showing white all around the green. He lunged to his feet, towering over Cairo. 'I know you!' he bellowed. 'I know your evil whispers.'

The gossiping women stopped to gape.

'You're right,' said Cairo. She forced herself to speak calmly, but she was shaking from the swift eruption of his rage, his mistaking her for the Devil. 'Of course you're right.'

He grabbed her arm, dragging her along with him. 'Let's go home.'

The television news had begun. The Multi-Ciser girl was gone, replaced by footage of people screaming and running from shops while buildings shook. Justin stopped in his tracks and turned back to look. A powerful earthquake had rocked Chile. A million people were being evacuated as giant waves raced towards the coastline. A tsunami warning was in force across the Pacific, all the way to New Zealand.

'No time to waste,' said Justin.

•

They took a taxi out to Tarawera, and Justin—who had a lot of cash in his wallet—bribed the driver to go through the gate and try to negotiate the track. Understandably, the poor man wasn't happy. He fussed about his car's suspension. There had been rain, and the track was in a worse state than ever. Eventually he stopped. 'I'll get bogged,' he said. 'I'm turning around here. Sorry, mate.'

So they got out and continued on foot. Cairo had to walk fast to keep up with Justin's long stride. He seemed euphoric now.

'I've passed the last test,' he said.

'Test?'

'Look at me!' He pumped a fist into the air, a victory salute. 'I've come out of the wilderness.'

The van was parked in its usual place. When she saw it, she remembered Sydney. *Ask how Justin gets about when he goes on his mysterious jaunts.*

'How did you get to town yesterday?' she asked.

If he heard the question, he ignored it; he marched straight down the jetty to where *Ikaroa* was waiting.

'Quick sticks, Cairo!' he yelled, leaping into the boat. 'So much to do. So little time.'

Seconds later, *Ikaroa* was skimming over the lake, and Cairo was sharing in Justin's euphoria. In a few minutes, she'd be home, hugging Aden and the children.

When the boat was a long way from shore—too far to swim—Justin leaned close to her. 'Now,' he said, 'we won't talk about my trip to hospital, will we, Cairo? No need to frighten the Watchmen.'

'Okay.'

'Not one word. Not to anyone.'

'I promise.'

'I know I can trust you.' He touched her cheek with his knuckle before sliding his hand around her neck. It could almost have been a caress, until his thumb pressed hard into her windpipe. She felt the pain on her throat; felt the constriction in her airway; felt the rising of her own fear. He left his hand there until she tried to pull away from him. Then he let her go, laughing as *Ikaroa* danced across the ripples.

Fifty-one

Her homecoming was just like one of her dreams. They were rounding the headland, and there was Gethsemane. Half the children in the community swarmed to meet her. Damascus and Monty were at the head of the posse.

'See how they love you?' said Justin.

Damascus reached them first, despite being one of the smallest. He cannoned head first into Cairo's stomach, tight-lipped and determined, as though his life depended on getting to his mother. She kissed him five—ten—twenty times.

'I had to sleep in Monika's cabin,' he whispered, clinging like a monkey. 'Havana was in Nana Kazan's. Quito got to stay with Monty and Helike and Bali.'

'I'm so sorry. I'm home now, we'll be together again.'

'We're all going on a journey soon,' Monty told her. He looked awed by this information.

'A journey! Where are we going?'

'To the Kingdom of Peace.' He pointed solemnly at his feet. 'We have to sleep with our shoes on and keep food ready, like the people of Israel in Egypt, because we could be leaving any time.'

The troupe headed towards the buildings. They were halfway

up the hill when Liam emerged from the office. Nothing smiley or twinkling about him today. He barrelled up to Cairo, fists clenched.

'You've got a bloody nerve, showing your face here.'

'It's all right,' said Justin calmly. 'Cairo heard me calling, and came back to me from the other side of the world.'

Liam was spluttering. 'Right. I see . . . right.'

'This is the prodigal daughter.' Justin laid his hand on Cairo's arm. 'I've forgiven her. We're going to celebrate.'

'We are?'

'Do we have a fatted calf to kill?'

Liam looked sulky. 'I'm sure something could be arranged.'

'A feast it is, then!' There was a jubilant music to Justin's voice. 'This isn't the season for anger, Liam. It's the season for love and forgiveness. Tonight we'll celebrate Cairo's return; tomorrow we must get ready for our last Vigil.'

'But the damage she did—Cairo, do you realise what you did? We've lost about ten people because of you!'

'They weren't true Watchmen,' said Justin. 'Liam, come and see me on the island, will you? Come for lunch. You and I have things to arrange.' He put an arm around Liam's shoulders, drawing him close. 'My wingman,' he whispered. 'We're coming to the end of our journey together. I need your help.'

Then Liam did something inexplicable. He began to cry. He grabbed both of Justin's hands and kissed them.

Cairo was watching in astonishment when she heard running footsteps and looked around to see Aden sprinting across the grass towards her, startling the tethered goats. Her heart lightened at the sight of him.

'Go and be with your family,' said Justin. 'They've missed you.'

•

You don't know what it is you love about a place, she thought, *until you've been away.* Breezes ruffled the lake, and daffodils nodded among the cabins. Kazan and Berlin brought a tin of muffins to welcome their daughter-in-law home. Monika bustled down the steps of the surgery to show her how much baby Fez had grown. Even Gaza managed a frosty smile.

It was as though Cairo were reliving the mystery of the day she arrived here; she was falling in love all over again. She thrilled at familiar, everyday things: the plaintive piping of fantails, the echoing call of a coot. Children climbing in the trees, and a *thud-thud-thud* as someone chopped wood. The smells of pasture, wood smoke and fresh water.

When she went to collect her younger two, the women working in the crèche greeted her with real warmth. They even asked after her father. This was Gethsemane, after all. There was no negativity. Quito tottered merrily into her arms; Havana burst into guilt-inducing tears and had to be cuddled.

'Now the harder part,' Aden said with a sigh.

'Suva?'

'Mm. Sixteen-year-olds are less forgiving than babies.'

Suva must have seen Cairo's arrival, but she hadn't come out of the cabin. She was sweeping the place with angry jabs of her broom.

'I've missed you,' said Cairo. 'How've you been?'

Suva kept sweeping, her face set and pinched. The kitchen floor had never looked so clean.

'Enough.' Aden took the broom from her hand. 'Love, not negativity.'

'That doesn't apply to traitors.'

'Cairo kept her promise. She said she'd be back in a fortnight, and here she is. Justin's forgiven her. Remember the prodigal son, and the father who ran out to welcome him? Well, that father is Justin.'

Suva wouldn't look at either adult. 'My mother didn't do half what you did. How come you get off so lightly?'

And she stormed out, slamming the flyscreen behind her. Quito and Damascus peeped through it, watching their sister's departing back.

'She's been frightened,' said Aden. 'But oh, it's great to have you home!' He sank into the window seat, pulling Cairo with him. The children climbed all over their parents. Havana fell asleep. Damascus was sucking his thumb, leaning his head against Cairo's chest. Quito doggy-piled on top of everyone.

For an hour the family made the most of being together again. They talked about Mike, and about Tara, and Diana. Cairo described the panic she'd felt when she first left Gethsemane, and how the memory of her childhood abuse seemed to melt away like a mist in the sun. Aden seemed disturbed by this, but he didn't argue.

From time to time Damascus and Quito joined in with random stories about their lives. Nana Kazan had made them a tamarillo cake, and that was yummy. Damascus claimed to have seen a kiwi in the bush, and did a fair imitation of its shrill cry.

'And Justin shouted in Call,' he said.

'Yeah!' Quito held up miniature hands in a pantomime of dismay. 'Really loud!'

'Why did he shout?' asked Cairo.

'Because of Rome. He said Rome let the Devil into his heart.'

'Things have changed here,' murmured Aden. 'It hasn't been peaceful. Justin—oh, here we go. Another tremor.'

The ground shuddered and shook beneath them. Cups swung on their hooks.

'Last Day coming,' said Damascus. 'Lots of earthquakes.'

Cairo wanted to get out of the cabin, to somewhere they couldn't be overheard. She stretched her arms, trying to hug the whole family at once.

'I need fresh air after being cooped up in aeroplanes. Shall we go for a walk?'

They took one of the bush trails, heading inland from the lake. Sunlight trickled through the canopy, forming brilliant pools on the peaty earth. A twittering pair of fantails flickered on and off the path. Aden carried Havana on his back. Damascus and Quito ran ahead. Every few minutes they stopped to hide behind rotting logs and jump out at their parents, screaming *boo!*

'I'm worried,' said Cairo, once they were safely away from the settlement. 'I don't like all this talk of the Last Day.'

'It's what we're here for, isn't it? We're the Watchmen.'

'Yes, but—'

Boo! roared the boys, and Aden pretended to leap in fright.

Cairo waited until they'd scurried off again. 'What d'you think the Last Day will be like?' she asked. 'In practice?'

'We don't know the details. It's one of the mysteries. We trust Justin to lead us.'

'Yes.' She looked sideways at him, weighing her next words. 'But *should* we trust him?'

It was heresy, and it was a gamble. Aden carried on walking. So far, so good.

'I can see more clearly now I've been away,' she said. 'Everything looks different. There are things I've discovered, things I've worked out. We've got to make decisions about our future.'

'Our future's here,' said Aden. He sounded bemused. 'Where else could it be?'

She played her trump card. 'They claim Justin's omniscient. He always appears when something's happening. Right? Well no, because he's got internet on the island! Internet! And—you won't believe this, but it's true—he and the Companions communicate through two-way radios. They tell him everything he needs to know.'

Not a trump card, after all. To her amazement, Aden nodded calmly. 'Yes, I know about that. I've used those radios myself.'

'But it's a trick!'

'It's practical.' He had the grace to look embarrassed, rubbing his nose with the back of his hand. 'Justin gave up most of his divine power when he became human, so he needs a bit of help. But he *does* sense things, he does prophesy accurately. I've seen him do it. It's amazing what he knows.'

'Every tarot card reader knows how to convince people they can read minds or see the future. Every fortune teller—every teenager with a ouija board, for God's sake.'

'I wouldn't know about that.'

She took his arm in both of hers. 'Justin's just a magician. A brilliant magician. He's a genius! And for his next trick, he's somehow got to make the Last Day happen. And that scares me.'

The boys were lying under the roots of a fallen tree, giggling helplessly. *Booo!* they howled, and Havana gurgled with laughter, in her papoose.

Cairo racked her brains for some way to open Aden's eyes. It seemed blindingly obvious to her now that the emperor had no clothes. She reminded Aden about Tripoli, and about Skye, and asked whether he didn't think it un-Christ-like that Justin had a habit of bringing very young, vulnerable girls back to his island. She pointed out that he controlled all the investments, all the pensions, all the income Gethsemane generated.

'What's he doing with that money?' she demanded. 'I'm pretty sure he's got a car parked somewhere. He might own a penthouse, he might take luxury holidays.'

'I'll tell you one thing he *does* do,' said Aden. 'He pays the care home fees for more than one faithful friend of Gethsemane.'

She was beginning to despair. She'd arrived here as an adult, brought up by cynical parents, yet even when she was twelve thousand miles away she'd struggled to escape her own magical thinking. It wasn't a logical thing, she knew. It was like having a different model of the world in your head. She was asking Aden to abandon everything he'd ever believed.

'Imagine something for me,' she said. 'Just imagine it, okay?'

He didn't refuse point blank, and that gave her hope. He could have denounced her negativity and gone straight to the Companions. But he was listening.

'What if . . .' She squeezed his arm. 'Please don't be shocked, just try to imagine it. What if Justin's just an ordinary human being? What if his divinity exists only in his mind? *Think* about it, Aden.'

'Do I have to?'

'Yes. Imagine it. Think about what it would actually mean.'

He'd stopped, and was looking down at his feet. He stood there for a long time.

'Then we're all fools,' he said quietly. 'All of us. And our lives have been wasted.'

'No, not wasted! Gethsemane's achieved wonderful things.' She followed up her advantage. 'Justin spent last night in hospital.'

'How d'you know?'

'Because I saw him there. He may have a brain tumour, or a blood clot, or it may be nothing to worry about, but he spent the night being pumped full of morphine.'

'So he's sick?'

'I think so. We've all seen the changes in him. Did you know he punched Rome, gave him a black eye?'

'He hit *Rome*?' Aden looked appalled.

She told him about Rome meeting her at the airport; that he was doing well, coping in the outside world. She described his half-closed eye, and his place at Kit and Meg's. Aden seemed relieved to have news of him.

'I'm glad he's okay,' he said. 'But I wish that whole thing hadn't happened. After he was expelled, it felt as though Gethsemane would never be the same again.'

'What is it that's so different?'

'The atmosphere. Everyone's on edge. We've never had so many people leave before. I can hear Justin shouting at night— keeps me awake! He seems to think we're disloyal, that we're plotting against him. But nobody is.'

'What's he going to do next?' asked Cairo. 'What's going to happen if the Last Day comes, and there *is* no host of angels or cloud of glory?'

The small boys were running out of steam. Their joyous enthusiasm for nonsense was wearing off, and Quito had banged his knee. Cairo kissed it better before the family turned around and began to wander home.

'We can leave,' whispered Cairo. 'We can leave whenever we want. We can walk along the track at the top—hey, we could even use the tractor! We'll take the children, and anyone else who'll come with us. Maybe your parents. There must be others who're worried.'

There was no response from Aden. She could imagine the chaos in his mind. She was asking for the impossible.

'Think about it,' she begged. 'Please.'

•

By the time they returned to the settlement, Seoul had a wild pig roasting on a spit. News was out that Cairo was back, and people rushed to welcome her with varying degrees of sincerity. The well-oiled machinery of Gethsemane had swung into action. Justin had called for a feast to celebrate the return of the prodigal daughter, and all stops were being pulled out.

Cairo and Aden lingered on the beach, watching the last light bleed from Mount Tarawera while the boys threw handfuls of sand into the water. They saw Justin row Liam back from lunch on the island. Justin seemed spry, but Liam's shoulders were slumped. The two men stood on the jetty for a long time, with Peter sitting patiently at his master's feet. Justin was doing most of the talking. Eventually Liam climbed into *Ikaroa* and set off towards the van.

'Where's he going?' wondered Cairo.

Aden shrugged. 'Some errand.'

Justin waved at Cairo and Aden, and was walking along the jetty when the ground trembled again. Ripples spread across the water as though some monster were stirring in its depths. Peter howled, but Justin smiled.

'The earth knows,' he said.

•

Gethsemane celebrated Cairo's return to the fold with wine, song and love. Later, as she and Aden fell asleep, she promised never to leave him again.

'If and when I go,' she said, 'you'll be coming with me.'

The next day, everything changed.

Fifty-two

It was a cold night, and sunrise was lost in icy drizzle. All day long the mountain hid itself. London seemed like a dream.

Cairo's class were tired from the feast the night before, and her long journey had left her poleaxed, so she spent the afternoon reading them stories as they lay on cushions in the library. When the school day ended she stayed in the classroom to talk to Bali's parents, Hana and Dean—who were touchingly pleased to have her home—and get ready for the next day's lessons. The light was fading by the time she and Damascus hurried up to the crèche, sharing a cloak. He was telling her a complicated story about something he and Monty were planning to do in their tree den. She said *gosh* and *wow* in the right places, but she was peering out at the lake.

Liam was rowing away from *Matariki*; the grand old lady was moored in her usual place in the bay, behind a lace curtain of mist and drizzle. It would be miserable out there on the water, and Liam looked bedraggled. Still, there wasn't time to worry about him. The children would be hungry, and she'd have to hurry if she was going to give them a drink and some of Kazan's muffins before Dusk Call.

As it turned out, tea wasn't such a rushed affair. Call was at least an hour overdue when the bell began a fast, frantic peal. Watchmen came pelting from all over the community, crowding into the *wharenui*. There were anxious faces. They feared horrible news from Outside.

The Companions were already standing on the dais. Liam was among them, but he wasn't bustling or jolly. He looked pale, and he kept blinking compulsively. By contrast, Gaza seemed incandescent.

'Listen up!' she cried, when everyone was gathered. 'All nature has fallen silent. All the world is waiting.' She cupped her hand to her ear. 'Don't you feel it?'

There was a murmur. Cairo listened. *Yes!* She did sense expectancy in the air.

Gaza's eyes were glittering. 'News from Justin. It's over. Tonight will be our last Vigil. Tomorrow is the Last Dawn.'

Pandemonium erupted in the hall. Cairo heard someone— Paris, she thought—screaming, *At last! At last!* People cheered and high-fived, though Cairo noticed some frightened faces.

Gaza held up her hands. 'This is the countdown to the last hour, the last minute, the last second! Justin has had his final orders from Messenger.'

She made way for Liam, who stepped to the edge of the dais, donned a pair of reading glasses and began to read from a piece of paper. His voice, by contrast with Gaza's, sounded flat.

'Here are Justin's orders . . . These are the last hours of this world. By the time we return to this place, Justin will have been transformed into the divine King of Peace, and Gethsemane will be his heavenly court. But we'll need to stay away while the radiation and death are purified. So every workshop, every cabin, every building must be left tidy. All tools are to be put away. All food is to be stored so that it won't spoil. The stock must have enough food, water and other essentials for at least three days. We put our affairs in order. We tie every loose end.' Liam swallowed painfully, looking around at their faces. 'Every Watchman and every child is to come to the *whare kai* tonight, when the bell calls us. There will be a midnight supper before we begin our last Vigil. Nobody is to return to their cabin after that Call, so make sure you bring everything you need for a Vigil. Bring warm clothes for a journey. Wear shoes. Be watchful. Be ready.'

While he folded up his list, Gaza took centre stage again. Her icy serenity had melted.

'This is it!' she cried. 'Soon Justin will be bathed in the Infinite Power!'

Kyoto yelled, *Yes!* and punched the air with both fists. The grizzled carpenter was laughing as though he was drunk, and others followed his lead. The hall exploded with sound for a second time.

'Hurry!' shouted Gaza, above the noise. 'Come back when the bell tolls tonight. Be watchful. Be ready—and stay awake!'

They streamed out of the big double doors of the *wharenui*. Damascus and Quito both stood clinging to Cairo's waist.

'I forgive you, Cairo,' said Suva, laughing. She took both of Cairo's hands. 'I love you! Nothing matters now because it's happening! Can you believe it's finally happening? I feel as though it's my birthday times a million!'

She and Malindi scurried away together, to work for Gaza in the greenhouse.

'I've got ewes due to lamb,' said Aden, swinging Quito onto his back. The little boy clung there, arms and legs around his father. 'I'll go and see what I can do for them. It'll take me a while to organise three days' feed for the stock. Could you let the goats off their tethers? They can fend for themselves. Except Marigold—I think she might be going into labour. I'll put her in the barn.'

'Aden.' Cairo grabbed his arm. 'Wait. Can we talk?'

'There's no more time for talking.'

He began to jog away through the deepening twilight. She could see Quito's blond head bobbing. He laughed when his father jumped clean over a fallen log, pretending to be a horse.

'Where will we be going?' asked Damascus, burying his face in her skirt. 'Gaza said we need our shoes. Will we be walking?'

'It'll be all right.'

'Will you be coming too?'

'I'll be coming too,' she said, stooping to cuddle him. 'I promise.'

She kept him close beside her. He helped her tidy the schoolroom, mop the floors and even clean the composting toilets—though why they were doing it, and for whom, Cairo had no idea. When Havana grumbled, Damascus lay on the floor and entertained his sister with a wooden abacus.

Otto turned up with one of his lists, handing out tasks. He sent Cairo to help in the kitchen, preparing for the night's communal meal.

'The world's ending,' protested Cairo. 'Why does it matter how we leave this place?'

His eyebrows beetled. 'And a new world is beginning. We don't understand the mysteries. We just carry out our orders.'

There were seven kitchen helpers, including Aden's parents. Otto and Monika's daughter Breda and her husband Chernobyl were there, as excited as children on Christmas Eve. Havana crawled around, unpacking all the saucepans from the cupboards. Aden's father, Berlin, sat in an armchair with Damascus on his knee, reading their way through a pile of picture books.

When her mother-in-law went into the huge pantry, Cairo followed her.

'I'm so glad you came home in time, Cairo,' said Kazan.

'I'm happy to be back.' Cairo pretended to be collecting kumara from a basket. 'Um . . . you're not at all worried?'

'Worried?'

'About the Last Day. About what it might mean.'

'No!' Kazan seemed amused by the question. 'This is what we've been waiting for. This is our purpose.'

It felt very late by the time they were back in their own cabin. There was no sign of Aden, Quito or Suva. Poor Damascus was flagging. His thumb was firmly in his mouth, and he stretched his eyes to keep them open. Cairo wished he were safe, snuggled down in an ordinary bed, in an ordinary house, far from whatever was happening in the valley.

'Shh,' she whispered. 'Lie down on the window seat and have a little snooze.'

'Gaza said we have to stay awake.'

'Never mind what Gaza said. *I'm* saying you can lie down. Havana's sleeping too, see? I'll cover you up with my cloak.'

The place was already clean after Suva's angry ministrations. Cairo remade the beds and put away every garment. Weariness swirled around her brain, displacing logical thought. She rubbed her forehead with her fist. Think. *Think*.

What's Justin planning? Where's he taking us? A walk into the bush? A pilgrimage?

At last she heard Aden's footsteps on the porch, and Quito's high voice. Then they were in the cabin, bringing the smell of sheep with them. Quito had the sagging look of a very tired child but he refused to lie down. Instead he dragged out Justin's box of blocks and began to build a tower.

Aden took Cairo's arm. 'Come outside,' he said.

She followed him onto the dark porch. Cloud covered the stars. They stood together, their eyes drawn to a flicker of firelight on Justin's island.

'I've done a lot of thinking,' Aden said. 'I know you're worried about all this. So am I.'

'You are?'

'Of course I am. But look at it this way. If Justin *is* who he says he is, the world's in its final hours. And if that's the case, then the only place we're safe is right here.'

'True. I can accept that. But if he's not?'

'Well, nothing will have happened, will it? Tomorrow won't be the Last Day; tomorrow will just be another day. You and I will be back here again, on this porch. We'll know for sure that Justin's not divine. And then we'll make decisions.'

The words weren't quite out of his mouth when the bell began to toll, calling the people of Gethsemane to their last supper.

Fifty-three

The atmosphere in the *whare kai* hit Cairo before she was through the door. It was like being drawn into a vortex of joy. She'd never known anything quite like it; the only event that came close was a U2 concert at Wembley Stadium, when she was one of a crowd of ninety thousand. She'd been caught up in the hysterical sense of anticipation that night, but this was on another scale. Everyone was smiling—not just with their faces, but with their whole bodies too.

Ah well, thought Cairo. *Aden has a point. When all of this turns out to be a hoax, Gethsemane will cope. They're eternal optimists. They'll invent some reason why they haven't been taken up in a fiery cloud, and then they'll go on exactly the same as before.*

Or perhaps it isn't a hoax? Perhaps this really is the end of the world.

'Justin's preparing for his transformation,' said Liam, as he stood on his chair. 'He'll join us in the *wharenui* later. So let's thank the Infinite one last time, as we have thousands of times before.' He lifted his hands. 'For this food, we thank you!'

We thank you!

'For your love, we thank you!'

We thank you!

'For this new journey, we thank you!'

The chorus was a roar of sound. Liam jumped down from his chair, spoke briefly to Monika, and left the hall.

Seoul and his team did themselves proud yet again, producing cold meat, sauerkraut and roast vegetables. Bali was playing the piano, and wine was flowing. Cairo felt herself being swept along on the high. She let her eyes rove around the room, taking in the rock-concert atmosphere, the feverish joy and chatter.

Then she spotted a false note. Monika. She and Otto were at a table among their own large family. Breda was sitting beside her mother, talking animatedly to Palmyra, but the old doctor looked to be in another world. Her hands clutched at the collar of her jersey. Cairo noticed Washington say something in her ear, but Monika ignored him.

After the meal Aden hurried off to check on Marigold, who was struggling to deliver a large kid. Cairo helped to clean the kitchen, scrubbing pots and taking leftover food out to the hens. She was wiping the long tables when she stole another glance at Monika. The doctor had moved to an armchair, where she sat cradling Fez. Her eyes were closed. She held the baby fiercely, as though someone was trying to take him from her.

When the bell tolled for the last time, the Watchmen filed into the *wharenui*. The kitchen was left in darkness, the stoves damped down, the doors shut. Last Call.

•

The *wharenui* looked festive, with every candle blazing in the honey-scented air, but the night was half gone and energy levels were falling. Children's eyes drooped. Havana spotted her beloved Nana Kazan, crawled across to her welcoming lap and fell asleep. Cairo and the boys sat on a nearby cushion. She'd brought cloaks for everyone, because the night was very cold. She guessed there were still several hours before the first hint of dawn.

At first the Companions led Vigil. Gaza and Kyoto walked up and down, getting everyone to chant rhythmically while Dublin drummed: *Justin is per-fect! Justin is divine! Justin is e-ter-nal life!*

Aden reappeared—muttered that Marigold had one kid, but there was another on the way—and sat with Cairo and the boys. After hundreds of repetitions of the chant, the Watchmen were punch-drunk.

Must be about three or four in the morning, thought Cairo. *A good time for manipulation.*

And then, at last, Justin was among them. There was an electric intensity and vitality about him tonight; a presence so palpable that people cried out and rushed to touch him as he stepped into the circle of candles.

'God so loved the world,' he began quietly—then had to wait, because those five words were met by ecstatic applause, as though he'd played the first bars of an iconic song. He waited for calm before speaking again. 'God so loved the world, that he gave his only begotten son; that whoever believes in him shall not perish, but have everlasting life.' He turned slowly in a full circle, holding his palms upwards. '*Do* you believe in me?'

People were screaming. They'd screamed in Wembley Stadium too.

He really is a terrific showman, thought Cairo. *I can see it now.*

'I know you believe in me,' he said. 'And because you believe in me, you *will* have everlasting life. Hush, now! Hush! Monty's going to sing.'

The room shivered at the sound of Monty's silver voice, especially when the flute joined and interwove with him. Dazed people murmured and swayed.

'The time is coming,' said Justin, as the music charmed them. 'Be silent. Be open. Empty your minds.'

The Watchmen were good at this; they'd been doing it for years. In the early hours of the morning, dulled by emotion and exhaustion, it was easy for them to slide into a state of enchantment. By the time the music fell silent, they were well on their way to the Infinite.

The process of meditation took an hour, perhaps two, but nobody noticed the passage of time. Cairo had to use all her self-control to avoid being carried on the wind. *It's all just smoke and mirrors*, she told herself. *It's hysteria.* She was an observer. She watched Skye and Bali clutching at Justin's feet; she saw Kyoto on his knees. Almost all the Watchmen were laughing and sobbing— every generation, even children like Zanzibar and Xian. Some rolled on the floor, twitching, with wails that sounded like pain. It was like being in a room full of people who'd taken a hallucinogenic drug. *Was that me?* she wondered in horror. *Did I behave like this, in front of my children?*

Some stayed sober: Justin, the ringmaster. The youngest children, many of whom were asleep. Havana had curled up like a snoozing puppy between her grandparents, and was oblivious to the ectasy all around her. Monika and Aden quietly patrolled the hall, making sure nobody got hurt.

Justin was bringing the Watchmen back to consciousness when another earthquake shook the building. Candles toppled over.

'Just the poor old beleaguered earth,' he said, once the ground was still again. 'Falling apart. Like me. This planet and I are both longing to be renewed.' He looked out of the window. 'Ah! It's time to begin our journey. Are you ready to greet the Last Dawn?'

People were scrambling to their feet, shouting, *Yes! Yes!*

Justin laughed. 'Come on then, and follow me. Bring candles, bring lanterns. We have a rendezvous with a divine army!'

He ran down the hall, threw the double doors open with one push and led his people into the frozen night. They followed in delirious excitement, many of them still in the trance of meditation. Kazan was carrying Havana, who was just waking up. Peter appeared from the shadows and padded beside his master. On the far horizon, along the ridge of the volcano, a luminous band of orange broke the darkness.

'Thank God,' Cairo muttered to Aden. 'Light. We need light.'

'Where are we going, Justin?' asked Monty, taking Justin's hand. 'I brought my shoes.'

'On a boat trip.'

'Ooh! On *Matariki*?'

'Yes. *Matariki* is going to take us to the meeting place, where we'll greet the Host. Oh, hello, Damascus! You going to hold my other hand? Great. Let's sing as we greet the Last Dawn!'

Every voice was raised in a chant while they marched down the grass towards the jetty. *Jus-tin! Jus-tin! Justin is eternal life!* Washington played a voluntary on his trumpet, Dublin crashed the cymbals, Beersheba and Malindi and Suva clapped their hands and skipped along. The Watchmen followed Justin without question. They always had. Candles and lanterns floated in the dark.

'I'd better take another look at Marigold,' muttered Aden, peeling off.

'Don't go.'

'Won't be long.'

Cairo had begun to follow the procession when she felt someone tugging on her arm. Monika was stumbling, clinging to Cairo as though she might be about to faint.

'The children,' she quavered. 'Cairo, help them. The children.'

Cairo stopped dead. 'What about the children?'

'Oh dear God, forgive me. I've delivered every one of them. My little Fez is only nine weeks old. I can't let—' She broke off as Kyoto passed by. When she spoke again, she was whispering. '*Matariki* isn't coming back.'

'What? Monika, what do you mean?'

The doctor's mouth was open, her cheeks tear-stained. 'Liam couldn't carry the guilt of it by himself. He told us. Nobody's coming back. Whether or not the angels come to meet us, nobody is ever coming back.'

'You mean Justin's going to sink her?'

'I don't know.'

'But how—'

'Otto's watching me.' Monika let go of Cairo's arm and was swept away in the procession.

Cairo stood on the slope. Her heart was punching from inside her ribcage. *They'll die in the lake.*

She began to scream at the Watchmen, waving her arms— *stop, stop!* The cymbals crashed. The trumpet sounded. Over a hundred voices belted out songs, drunk on hysteria, euphoria, fatigue and wine.

She shrieked again, running up and down the line, and this time one or two of her friends faltered. Paris stepped out of the procession and pushed her in the chest.

'Not now,' she snarled. 'Keep your negativity to yourself.'

'Help me, Paris. Justin's going to sink *Matariki*.'

'I don't care.'

'But people will die!'

'Cairo, you're a fool. We trust him. *I* trust him. We'll follow him anywhere. So either leave or shut up.'

Cairo ran around the crowd, frenziedly searching for allies. It was as she was passing the laundry that she remembered she had a phone. *Two bars*, Rome had said. *Behind the laundry.* She brought it out of her pocket, trying to see in the dark. Her fingers were fumbling in panic.

Calm down. Breathe. She found the right switch to press, and the screen lit up as she felt her way around the back of the building.

Something tangled on her ankle, making her sprawl full-length. The phone bounced out of her hand. She was winded, sobbing for breath, hunting blindly until she felt smooth plastic under her hand. Still in one piece, thank God, and it came to life when she touched it. And—miraculously—there were two bars of signal.

Contacts. Rome. Call.

Silence. Then ringing.

Rome's voice was befuddled with sleep, but it was the most welcome sound in the world. 'Hi?'

'Help,' she gasped.

'Cairo?'

'He's getting everyone into *Matariki*. All the children, everyone. It'll be overloaded. I think he's going to sink her.'

'Sink *Matariki*? Why would he do that?'

'It's the Last Day.'

'Try and hold him up—' The line crackled, and for several seconds Cairo thought it was dead. Then Rome's voice was back: '—him talking. I'll call the police. But it would be really hard to sink *Matariki*. He could open the stopcocks, I guess, but it would take ages. Everyone on board would have to just sit there and let it happen and—'

His voice cut out.

She turned around, trying to get a better signal. 'Rome? You there?'

But he wasn't there. The signal was gone, and she was alone.

The sky was paler now, the stars beginning to melt. A thin mist lay right across the lake. Justin had reached the beach. Watchmen were milling around him—still chanting, still playing the trumpet and cymbals, still swinging their lanterns and clapping the rhythm. It was a party.

Matariki had been moved during the night. She was moored at the end of the jetty with her gangplank down. Liam and Otto were aboard, bustling around in the cockpit before disappearing into the cabin below.

As she peered at the boat, Cairo's stomach lurched. Three excited little figures were running down the jetty and across the gangplank. They climbed up on the cabin roof and began to prance about: one small, one even smaller and one who was little more than a toddler. Monty, Damascus and Quito. Three boys who loved boat trips.

She pelted down the slope, past the singing crowd. Nobody in the procession paid any attention as she headed straight for *Matariki*. By the time she got there, Zanzibar had joined the boys and was cavorting too.

'Guys,' hissed Cairo, crouching on the gangplank. '*Guys.*'

They saw her. Reluctantly, they slid off the roof and came to see what she wanted. She led the four of them well away from the boat before pulling them into a huddle.

'Will you do something for me? It's very, *very* important. And it's secret. Monty and Zanzibar will be your leaders.'

The small ones nodded. Monty was always their leader.

'You're going to play a game, okay?'

'Okay.'

'I want you to sneak up to the school. It's like playing Kick the Shoe. You have to get there without anyone seeing you. Zanzi, hold Quito's hand and make sure he can keep up with you. You *all* have to get there. Creep along the beach on this side—away from all the people, see?—then run through the trees and in through the back door, very, *very* quietly.'

'Shall we shout to you when we get there?' asked Zanzibar.

'No! No, don't make any noise. You have to be ever so quiet—' Cairo held her finger to her lips '—like little hiding creatures in the bush.'

Monty glanced longingly at the boat. 'Aren't we going on a very special trip?'

'*Matariki*'s broken down. They're trying to fix her, and in the meantime we're playing hide-and-seek. So hide in the library and read stories. Don't come out until I fetch you. Otherwise you'll have lost the game. Promise?'

They promised. Quito was pleased at the prospect of a game, hopping from foot to foot.

'Don't come out,' warned Cairo. '*Don't* come out. Okay? Good luck. *Shh.* Ready, set, go.'

The four children jumped down to the sand. Within seconds they were a blur in the half-dark. At the same moment Otto and Liam reappeared in *Matariki*'s cockpit. Cairo heard Liam say something about a signal, and Otto grunted.

It took a long time for the whole community to gather on the beach. Some people seemed almost to be dreaming and moved slowly; some were carrying children. Quite a few had gone to the ablutions block behind the *wharenui* and were only now reappearing. Cairo spotted Suva arm in arm with Malindi and Jaipur, all three of them alight with the spirit of adventure. She saw Havana riding on Kazan's shoulders. The baby was beaming now that she'd had a nap. She loved her nana, and she loved a party.

Justin waited patiently for the last stragglers to join him. Once they were all there, he gave another rallying cry and began to lead them towards the jetty, flanked by Kyoto and Gaza. The Watchmen followed, still chanting, beatific joy glowing on their faces.

Cairo dropped down from the jetty and planted herself directly in front of Justin. He couldn't pass without pushing her aside, so he stopped. Gradually people noticed that something was happening. The chanting petered out.

Justin seemed completely calm. He stood with the dawn breeze lifting his hair, staring into Cairo's eyes. It took all her courage not to give way to him. He still had power over her. She still felt as though the air was bending around him.

'What are you doing, Cairo?' he asked quietly.

'Don't take them. Don't, Justin. What about the children?'

'You want them to die in a nuclear holocaust?'

'Listen, everyone!' she shouted, with all the power of her lungs. 'Listen! He's going to sink *Matariki*.'

Justin looked astonished. 'How on earth would I sink a boat as big as that? It isn't as easy as it sounds. And all the Watchmen are strong swimmers, so it wouldn't be a very efficient way to carry out mass murder.'

There was laughter. People surged forwards, and the chanting began again.

'Monika!' called Cairo, desperately scanning the crowd for the doctor's face. 'Where are you? Help me! Monika knows this boat isn't coming back.'

Justin wasn't smiling now.

'Enough. Get behind me, Cairo.'

'No.'

'Shut up, you snake,' said Kyoto. He moved closer to Cairo, standing over her with his fists clenched.

'I've called the police.' Cairo held up her phone. 'I don't want to see you in prison, Justin. Let them find everyone safely asleep in their cabins.'

Kyoto was laughing at her. 'You think our Lord is scared of a couple of coppers from Rotorua? Have you forgotten who he is? He wasn't afraid of the Roman army!'

'He's not Jesus Christ. He's not. I know about your two-way radios, and your satellite internet, and—'

The carpenter bellowed as he drove his forehead into her nose. Cairo's knees buckled. Flecks of white spun in her vision; she tasted blood on her tongue. Then Havana was wailing from her perch on Kazan's shoulders, and Peter was barking, and Aden had run up and was shouting, 'What the hell are you doing?' as he shoved Kyoto away.

Justin remained supremely calm. He stepped around the scuffle, climbed onto the jetty and faced the Watchmen.

'Do you trust me?' he asked, pacing the wooden boards. 'It's a very simple question. Do—you—trust—me?'

He was answered by applause and shouts. He smiled, nodded, held up his hands for quiet.

'Good. Then follow me now. And yes—*yes*—that will mean leaving your human bodies behind.'

As his meaning sank in, the exultant cheers faltered. People drew back, glancing across at *Matariki*. Aden helped Cairo to her feet. She still felt dizzy, her eyes watering from the pain in her nose, but her vision had cleared.

'You mean we'll die?' someone asked.

'No. I mean you'll live! What do you need your bodies for?' Justin pointed towards the blushing horizon. 'See that? You're witnessing the Last Dawn. At this very moment—*this very moment*—nuclear weapons are being unleashed. There are people out there whose dream is to destroy the earth for their religion, and that's exactly what they're about to do. This planet has just become a giant suicide bomb. Mankind is finished! Follow me now, or you *will* die today.'

He turned around and strode aboard *Matariki,* with Peter at his heels.

'Which of you wants to live forever?' he shouted, swinging easily onto the roof of the cabin. 'Who will follow me?'

'Aye!' whooped Kyoto, as he ran aboard.

There was silence. Stillness. At last, the Watchmen understood. Justin was asking them to give up their lives. Families clung to one another, utterly at a loss. This wasn't the golden dawn they'd been expecting. Cairo darted across to Kazan and grabbed Havana from her, cuddling the little girl tightly to her own chest.

'Who will follow me?' Justin cried again. He was a tall silhouette on the cabin roof, with radiance at his back. 'Who will pass the final test?'

'I will.' Monika appeared from the back of the crowd. 'Who needs this old body, anyway? But please, Justin, don't take the children. They can join us later, can't they? In the Kingdom of Peace?'

She kissed baby Fez, who was smiling at her from his papoose on Palmyra's back, and nodded her thanks to Cairo. Then she hurried up the jetty—duck-footed and determined—and into Otto's waiting arms.

Monika was the torchbearer. She'd delivered their children; she'd sewn up their wounds and soothed their aches. Others followed her lead. Her daughter Breda, with Chernobyl. Hana and Dean. Skye, Gaza and Malindi danced across the gangplank like a jubilant troupe of cheerleaders, clapping and chanting, *Jus-tin! Jus-tin! Justin is eternal life!* Malindi looked radiant, a young bride on her wedding day. *Jus-tin! Jus-tin!*

'I can't find Zanzibar,' said Skye, when Cairo tried to stop the three of them. 'But tell her not to worry. Justin will send for her.'

'Who else?' Justin shouted. 'Which of you is worthy of eternal life?'

Turmoil on the beach. People were sobbing, fighting, panicking. Some were desperate to board the boat; others were trying to hold them back. Seoul was on his knees, begging Paris not to go. Aden rugby-tackled Suva when she tried to follow Malindi. Meanwhile the people on the boat were smiling and chanting and hand-clapping. *Jus-tin! Jus-tin! Justin is eternal life!*

'What do we do?' cried Washington, distraught in the chaos. His trumpet had dropped onto the sand, and he huddled with Palmyra and their baby. 'My parents have gone. My grandparents have gone. What do we do?'

Dublin and Beersheba made a last-minute decision to follow.

'No,' said Cairo, grabbing Beersheba's arm. 'Not you two.'

'Justin set me free from a demon called meth,' said Dublin. 'I owe him. We don't have children, and we're both pretty good swimmers.' He winked at Beersheba. 'It's a win-win for us, isn't it, Sheba? If he scuttles the boat, we'll be swimming back in time for breakfast. If he's Jesus Christ incarnate, we'll have breakfast in paradise.'

Cairo was still trying to dissuade them when she heard something far out on the lake—the high whine of an engine, still distant. A moment later she glimpsed a dark insect crawling across the expanse, heading towards Gethsemane.

The police, she thought. *Thank God. They'll stop this madness.*

Liam had seen it too, and shouted to Justin. That was the turning point. Suddenly, everything was hurried. *Matariki*'s propeller began to churn the water while Otto swiftly untied the mooring ropes. Paris tore herself from Seoul's grasp and dashed aboard.

'Anyone else?' yelled Justin. 'You have twenty seconds!'

All this time, Bali had been running up and down the beach, calling hysterically for Monty. Three-year-old Helike stood on the sand, bewildered, rubbing her eyes.

'Wait, Justin!' shrieked Bali. 'Monty? Has anyone seen Monty? Cairo, have you seen Monty?'

'Yes,' said Cairo. 'You won't find him. I've hidden him.'

At that moment *Matariki*'s motor roared. Bali spun around in time to see Otto pulling up the gangplank. She screamed—'Wait, Justin! Wait!'—then picked up Helike and sprinted with her along the jetty. Liam was driving *Matariki* away at top speed, but Bali didn't stop. She kept on running, hurled herself off the end of the jetty and hit the water with a dull splash. She didn't even try to swim; just let herself and Helike sink.

The next moment, Seoul had leaped in after them and was lifting them up. Hands reached down to help. All three were hauled out, shivering while their friends draped cloaks over them. Helike's eyes and mouth were wide open, shocked by the intense cold.

'Why did he leave me?' Bali was wailing. 'Why? Why?'

Aden let Suva go, now that the boat was out of her reach. She stumbled into the water, up to her knees, crying for Justin to come back and get her.

With Havana balanced on her hip, Cairo took Aden's hand. They stood side by side on the beach, watching the lake. The Watchmen were spread out along the shore and on the jetty. Every face was turned towards *Matariki*. Some people were sobbing, saying they wished they'd gone too.

They could see Justin standing on the roof of the white boat as it slid across the water, with his people at his feet. *Just-in! Just-in! Justin is eternal life!* Cairo thought of a Maori war canoe, racing through the morning mist, ferrying the souls of the dead to the mountain.

'I hope he *doesn't* sink her,' said Aden. 'My dad's not such a good swimmer since he damaged his knee.'

'Berlin isn't on there, is he? I didn't see him.'

'Yes.' Aden was deathly pale. 'And Mum. I couldn't stop them.'

'The police will pick them up, if anything happens.'

Cairo was trying to reassure them both; but the crawling insect was still a long way off. Its progress seemed painfully slow across the great openness.

Once *Matariki* was far out on the lake, her engine was cut. She was drifting. Cairo could make out Malindi's very blonde head, and Monika's grey one. The chanting ended. The people on board turned—all at once—to face the mountain. A glittering aura blazed along its summit, heralding sunrise. It was a mystical moment. Cairo half expected to see an army of angels come swooping down, flying without wings, singing with a million voices.

The watchers on the shore fell silent. Nobody spoke. Nobody breathed. They watched as the sun made its grand entrance, filling the valley with golden light. They all heard Justin shout—though later, they couldn't agree about what he'd said. It wasn't an angry yell, more a cry of victory or greeting. He sounded gloriously happy. They saw him lift his arms, stretching them towards the mountain.

Time seemed to slow. A breeze rippled the water. The watchers stood very still, waiting for the fiery cloud of glory.

Nothing happened.

Nothing.

'You were right,' whispered Aden. 'No angels.'

Nothing.

And then the lake exploded.

Matariki disappeared in a mushroom cloud of flame, followed a second later by a blast of sound and energy that sent both Cairo and Aden staggering backwards, stunned by the sheer force of it. Debris flew upwards and outwards; the cabin roof was catapulted high into the air, rising and falling in surreal slow motion.

Cairo's first thought was that she was witnessing the fiery glory, or perhaps the nuclear holocaust. She saw Aden shouting as he ran into the water, but she could hear nothing because the blast had deafened her. The watchers were throwing themselves into the lake, screaming for their friends and families, for the people they loved. But nobody could have survived the power of that blast. They were all gone. People's children, people's parents, people's partners. Old people, young people. All gone.

Fifty-four

Diana

She'd brought Mike a cup of tea along with his pills, as was their morning ritual. The doctors hadn't been wrong. He was courteous and patient and brave, but he was fading.

'Glad Cassy came home,' he said, when she sat down in the armchair by his bed. 'Made all the difference.'

'I wonder how she's doing? I wish she'd phone.'

'So do I, but she'll be all right. I'll get up in a minute—feeling good today.' But he didn't get up; he dozed off.

Diana sat beside him, listening to his breathing and longing for a miracle.

Later, he opened his eyes. 'You'll go and see her, won't you? You'll be a rich widow. Not in bad shape, either.'

'Mike!'

He smiled. 'Go and meet our grandchildren.'

He'd drifted away again when she heard the phone. She hurried to answer before it woke him up.

'Mum.' Tara's voice sounded strained. 'Have you seen the news?'

•

TRAGEDY IN NEW ZEALAND, the headlines shrieked. MASS SUICIDE IN APOCALYPTIC CULT. HELL IN PARADISE.

Over the weeks that followed, the media reported on the Gethsemane disaster from every possible angle. They rootled around in Justin's life and dug up all sorts of salacious details. There was his criminal past, and the tantalising possibility of a tumour in his final weeks. One newspaper interviewed a psychologist who'd never met him but was happy to hold forth about psychosis, religious mania and narcissism. Secrets came to light: an opulent flat in Wellington, a four-wheel drive kept hidden on one of the forest tracks. Apparently Justin had been fond of taking holidays around the world, accompanied by various young women—all of whom now claimed to have been his long-term mistress.

Cassy was being hailed as the heroine of the hour whether she liked it or not. A Sunday magazine ran an in-depth article on Gethsemane. They interviewed Kiev and Tunis, who made the community sound sinister and abusive. They also sent a journalist to meet Cassy. She cooperated, because she wanted to set the record straight.

The article was spread over six glossy pages, complete with an arty photograph of a whaleboat on the lake. There was also a picture of the blackened shell of *Matariki*, half submerged in picture-postcard water; another of police divers on a rubber boat; and a rather flattering shot of Cassy holding a brown hen. Tara shared the piece all over Facebook and Twitter. Mike cut it out and made all his visitors and medical helpers read the section about Cassy. It was quite short, because she hadn't dished any newsworthy dirt.

'They wanted me to say Justin held wild orgies,' she said to Diana. 'And that Gaza was . . . I dunno, a pimp, grooming children for satanic ritual abuse. But it wasn't like that. So they didn't print most of what I said.'

THE GARDENER OF GETHSEMANE
At dawn on 19 September 2015, the 34' launch Matariki *exploded, killing all seventeen people on board. Eight men*

and nine women died, their ages ranging between sixteen and seventy-five. Had it not been for Cairo Howells, the toll might have been far higher. But Ms Howells is a reluctant heroine.

I first met her as she greeted me at the jetty of Gethsemane, the isolated Tarawera settlement where she's spent the past five years, and which she had offered to show me around.

There's no denying the physical beauty of the place, set in its own lush valley on the shores of Lake Tarawera. But this community was more than a pretty face. In its heyday it seems to have been a sophisticated, carefully constructed machine, with ingenious methods of electricity generation and food production. Looking over the vegetable gardens, the beehives, fishing boats and the great kitchen, I was reminded of pre-Reformation monasteries.

Ms Howells insists that Gethsemane was about more than religious fervour. In its original inception it was focused on sustainable living, its members passionate about their duty as stewards of the land. Her attitude to the structure of Gethsemane is one of pride. She is almost—dare I say it—evangelistic.

'The media have painted us as brainwashed morons, and Justin as a diabolical Mad Hatter. But he had a vision and we shared it. We weren't just hippies. We had a wide skill base: a doctor, a teacher, a mechanic, a farmer, an accountant, a manager, a joiner who built cabins from scratch. Artisans and cooks. Experts in permaculture. These people lived in harmony for a quarter of a century and achieved incredible things. We were self-sufficient and we were sustainable. There was manipulation—yes, okay, hands up to that—but there was also real community. Nobody was ever lonely. Children and the elderly were safe and loved. The world has a lot to learn from Gethsemane.'

As we stroll, I note that many of the cabins are empty. Ms Howells explains that about half of the survivors have left since the tragedy. Professional counselling and support have been provided for those who remain, and the community is grateful for that, she says.

'Some people have lived here all their lives. Readjustment will be very difficult.' She sees the future as 'perhaps a different kind of set-up. Somewhere less isolated, where the children can go to school and people can work and be part of the real world.'

When pressed about Justin Calvin, the man who caused the deaths of himself and sixteen others in a mass suicide, Ms Howells admits to a personal conflict.

'People died. People I loved. But it wasn't like Jonestown, where they were forced to drink poison at gunpoint. Justin told them they'd be leaving their human bodies behind yet they still chose to follow him. I've heard him called a monster and a murderer but that isn't the whole picture. He was fatally misguided in the end, but he understood the power of love, of real listening, of a simple life. How many people understand those things?' Cairo thinks for a moment before adding, 'To be honest, the world seems colourless without him.'

Quietly spoken yet confident, the mother-of-three is modest when she talks about the day she saved a hundred lives.

'I had a lot of help, and a lot of luck,' she says. 'And anyway, who's to say I was right? For all I know, Justin and the others are laughing at me right now.'

'That's my Cassy,' said Mike, kissing the photo. 'She saved a hundred people! So it's all been worth it. This whole bloody thing.'

•

In retrospect, Diana was pleased the article came out when it did. It seemed to give Mike a last surge of energy. He was able to stay at home, with wonderful help from the hospice. His legs were swollen and it was difficult to manage the pain, but he kept smiling for a stream of visitors. His brother Robert came to visit in early November and stayed for several days. The pair of them covered a lot of ground.

Then the bulb dimmed. It happened quickly in the end. His hands lost their strength; his eyes lost their focus. Diana saw that he was packing to leave, and grieved, and let him go. He slept more and more, spoke less and less. Finally, he slipped into unconsciousness.

He died early one morning, before the sun was up.

Fifty-five

'Fireball,' said Howard. 'Absolute fireball. Never seen anything like it.'

Diana huddled into the plastic poncho he'd given her to wear. The lake was a sulky, white-capped green today.

'You actually saw it?' she asked, as they set off.

'Saw it—heard it—even bloody felt the bastard. Never witnessed anything like that in my life before, hope I never do again. They heard it as far away as the Buried Village—thought the bloody mountain was erupting again!'

'But wasn't it very early in the morning?'

'Bit after six. I was taking some trampers up to the trailhead. Coastguard and police screamed down here with their sirens and their disco lights, threw a boat into the water and set off like a rocket. Broke all the speed restrictions, I can tell you. Apparently they were hailing the vessel when it blew up. They were lucky not to get bowled by the blast.'

'I didn't know that.'

'We've had a lot of relatives visiting,' he said. 'I took a Swiss guy out last week, throwing flowers on the spot. He lost his brother. A guy from Scotland the week before that—his daughter died. Sad, eh? To be honest, with all the investigation people, the families, social workers, journalists and hundreds of rubber-necking tourists, business is booming. Nothing like a mass suicide to stimulate the local economy.'

It was black humour, but she didn't blame him. She could imagine the local community's reaction, the shocked excitement in pubs and offices and schools. There must have been endless speculation about what had happened, and how, and why.

'Police divers had their work cut out,' said Howard. 'Deep part of the lake, freezing cold, body parts everywhere. Not a job you'd catch me doing. But they got there, more or less. What those nutters did was pretty simple when you know how.'

'Some kind of gas, wasn't it?'

'Mm. Well, for a start, that boat was running on ethanol. Now, you don't want to mess with ethanol—it's volatile.'

'More than diesel?'

'Oh yeah.' Howard was warming to his theme. 'And what they did is, they put a load of propane tanks in the cabin. Ordinary propane tanks, we've all got them on our boats and barbecues. They put about ten of them in the cabin and then they just opened them up. So while they were going along—doing all their singing and chanting—propane gas was filling the cabin. Made the bloody thing into a floating bomb.'

'I see.'

'So then all you need is a stick of gelignite and a detonator—that's not hard, plenty of farmers have a stick in their shed, for blasting tree stumps.'

'Really?'

'Yep. Used to use it myself. Or, simplest of all, you just soak a rag in ethanol, light it, chuck it in. Either way the whole lot goes up. Which it did. *Kaboom*. They won't have known what hit 'em. That's one comfort.'

Diana didn't feel very comforted. A wave breasted the bow, and the boat lurched. Her poncho was streaming.

'The oldest pair was seventy-five!' yelled Howard. 'The

CHARITY NORMAN

youngest was a kid, only sixteen. Sixteen, for Pete's sake. Younger
than my granddaughter. That's murder, if you ask me. No way
that's suicide. Hang on, might get a bit lumpy here . . .' He throttled back, turning the boat to hit a wave side on. 'So you're going
to catch up with your daughter?'

'Yes! And my grandchildren, and my son-in-law.'

'Glad she's okay.'

Cassy hadn't come home for Mike's funeral. She and Aden
were working hard to support those survivors who hadn't left
Gethsemane. The police and other authorities had wanted
answers, and Cassy had become a spokesperson.

'The social services came swooping in,' she'd said, during
one of her frequent phone calls home. 'Big boots they've got.
They threatened to remove all our children—*all* the children in
Gethsemane! Apparently we're an abusive cult.'

'No! Can you stop them?'

'It's okay—don't panic, Mum. We've managed to hold them
off, as long as we jump through their hoops. We've enrolled the
kids into Correspondence School. The one they really fussed
about was Bali.'

'The woman who almost drowned herself, along with her
toddler?'

'That's right. Her brother pulled her out. Seoul. He's looking
after poor Monty and Helike now, in a hovel in Rotorua. They're
homesick and lonely but he's not allowed to bring them back. The
authorities think Bali's a danger to them.'

'*Is* she a danger to them?'

'Um . . . possibly.'

'Well then.'

'Yes—but Mum, it feels like an invasion. Some of these social
workers are as authoritarian as Gaza ever was. Seems to me this
democratic society of ours is just another controlling cult.'

There was a small silence before Diana asked, 'You *are* joking,
aren't you?'

'Yes and no.' A sigh. 'Maybe. We had our own kind of freedom.'

The boat had slowed. They were approaching the headland.

'Seventeen more crosses than there used to be,' grunted Howard, looking up at the white markers. 'They thought they were going to kingdom come.' He smiled grimly. 'Blast like that, they probably made it.'

'Where did it happen?' asked Diana. 'Where on the lake?'

'Way over there—see the buoy? That's the marker.' Howard chuckled. ''Course, there was one survivor.'

'No! Surely it wasn't survivable?'

'One.' Howard looked pleased. 'The dog. He was the only one with any sense. Leaped off the boat a couple of seconds before the blast. Police hauled him out of the water.'

Diana pulled off her poncho, scanning the idyllic scene. Ducks snoozed on the beach, and children kicked a football around the grass with whoops and laughter. They were all in rag-bag clothes, perhaps from a charity shop: colourful scarves were draped over skirts, t-shirts were worn on top of sweatshirts; ribbons were tied around heads, and even—on one little chap—red tinsel.

A woman was waiting on the jetty. Chestnut hair curled over her collar, and there were gold hoops in her ears. A smiling toddler clung to her hip, while two small boys jumped up and down by her side.

'There she is!' cried Diana, standing up to wave. 'There's Cassy!'

Howard grinned. 'You've come a long way,' he said. 'But at least she was here to meet you.'

•

Strange, disturbing, wonderful days. Over the past months Diana had played several unexpected roles: rescuer, nurse, widow. Now she was grandmother to three children with whom she immediately fell in love. The trickier job was to be mother-in-law to a thoughtful, burly Viking who'd lost both his parents.

She and Cassy took the grandchildren for outings to Rotorua—even the luge, which involved go-karting down a hill while Damascus shrieked, *Faster, Granny!* They visited the Buried Village, and learned all about the 1886 eruption. They lazed in hot pools and hiked through native bush. To her surprise, Diana was a rather popular grandmother. She could play football, at a pinch, and tell stories that made small boys—and one-year-old girls—laugh uproariously. She was soon falling under the spell of the dazed, half-empty community, living in limbo in the shadow of a volcano.

The survivors of Gethsemane clung together in their shared grief, and meals were often communal. Diana got to know many of them. She quickly befriended Athens, perhaps because both women had just lost their husbands. The bell still tolled five times a day, but most people ignored it. The days of euphoric singing were over. There were too many faces missing; too much sadness. Only the hard-core Justin followers kept the Calls any more.

'Who are those followers?' Diana asked Cassy, as they listened to the bell.

Cassy blew out her cheeks. 'Suva's one of them, I'm afraid. I'm their arch-enemy. I ruined the Last Day.'

'And saved their lives.'

'They don't see it that way! There are about seven of them, led by Bali.'

Diana hadn't yet clapped eyes on this woman, Bali. She seemed a mythical figure. Apparently she'd moved to the island and was living in Justin's cabin with his dog. Her children were still in Rotorua.

'They call themselves Justinites,' said Cassy. 'They keep the Vigil and the Calls. They're waiting for Justin's Second Coming.' She considered this statement. 'Third Coming, I suppose. Technically.'

'Oh dear,' said Diana. 'That sounds awfully familiar. I'm afraid they may have a long wait.'

Most evenings ended on the front porch of Cassy's cabin, sitting on the step, sipping Gethsemane wine out of clay cups. Sometimes Aden joined them; more often he had things to do.

'Is he coping?' whispered Diana.

Cassy held up crossed fingers. 'I think so. He's been in touch with his sons and his sister, so that's one happy thing to come out of all this. Our biggest worry at the moment is Suva.'

Diana thought of the thin, silent teenager. 'She seems angry.'

'She *is* angry. Aden stopped her following Justin. She was screaming at him to let her go.'

'And she's not grateful?'

'No! She says she'll never forgive him. She lost Malindi. She lost her grandparents. And worst of all, she lost her God. She was brought up with one plan, one goal, one promise—everlasting life. She's having to face the horrible fact of her mortality.' Cassy was pouring more wine into their cups. 'That's why she's determined to believe that Justin is alive.'

Diana rested her head against a post, listening to an owl calling in the hills. It was a lonely cry.

'I can understand why you love this place,' she said.

'But it's time to move on. Rome wants to sell up and relocate everyone to somewhere less isolated, with no ghosts. He's hoping people will drift away in the end. Live their own lives.'

'Why is it up to Rome to make these decisions?'

'You don't know? Didn't the papers get hold of this story? Justin left a will.' Cassy gave a bark of cynical laughter. 'Why would you leave a will, when the world is going to end and you're going to rise again? Anyway, he did. It was very organised. Lists of his assets and his lawyer's phone number. Turns out he was rolling in it—and I do mean *rolling* in it, partly because of mugs like me who gave him all their savings. Rome gets the lot. Which is quite funny, since he's working as a hospital porter. He says the work's keeping him sane.'

The rangy young man had come to the luge with them and blasted down the track with a squealing Quito on his lap. He hadn't thought to mention that he was a multimillionaire.

'He wants to repay me, once the probate's all finished,' said Cassy. 'But most of the assets came from people who're long gone.'

Diana tilted back her head, tracing the shape of Orion. She

still hadn't got used to the dizzying immensity of the night sky
here. She imagined Mike sitting on the porch beside her, pointing
out the constellations.

'Who were they?' she asked.

'Who were who?'

'The people who died. Your friends.'

'Oh, Mum.' Cassy took a mouthful of wine. 'Where do I start?'

'Start with Malindi. I met her. She seemed a gentle soul.
Blonde hair and china-blue eyes?'

'That's Malindi. She'd been waiting for the Last Day all her
life, wouldn't have missed it for the world. She and her mother
danced on board together—danced and clapped and chanted!
They were ecstatic.'

'Her mother was . . . ?'

'Gaza. The gardener. Scary as hell, but loyal to the end. I think
she knew what Justin was planning.'

'Wow. And she still danced to her death?'

'Oh yes. Like millions of martyrs over the centuries. It's called
faith, Mum. *Faith*. Gaza was prepared to die, and let her daughter
die too, because she had unshakeable faith in Justin's divinity. So
did Skye. She would have taken poor little Zanzibar if she hadn't
been hiding in the library.'

Diana had tried to befriend the orphan, but without much
success. She spent most of her time clinging to Athens—who was
now her long-term foster mother—or standing on the edge of
other children's games.

'The media talked about a young couple,' Diana said.

'Dublin and Beersheba. He was our drummer—and a hell of
a good one! Justin saved him from meth. Beersheba was twenty-
two, she was born here. She made my wedding dress, but she
still seemed like a child. She had a laugh like Betty Rubble—you
know, from *The Flintstones*?'

'I do know.'

'Her parents were watching from the shore when *Matariki*
exploded. You can't even imagine . . . I don't think they'll ever

get over the guilt of still being alive. They're Justinites. They're waiting for him to come back, and bring Beersheba with him.'

Diana was shaken. 'Poor people. I think I can understand that.'

'Paris.' Cassy sighed. 'A bit like a sister to me. She and Seoul had only been married a few weeks. She loved him, but she loved Justin more. Her father came over from Edinburgh. He spent two nights in their empty cabin. Paris always said he didn't care about her, but she was so wrong. He was broken.'

That could have been me, thought Diana. *Mourning in an empty cabin, throwing flowers on the lake.*

'And dear old Otto,' said Cassy. 'All jowls and beetle brows and lists. It was him who first suggested I could be a teacher. His wife was Monika.'

'I met her.'

'You didn't see her at her best! Dr Monika. She broke ranks by warning me about *Matariki*. Seventy-five years old, though you wouldn't know it. She could be strict but we got on pretty well—we were friends. She was a kind of grumpy grandmother.' Cassy chuckled. 'We used to drink a lot of tea together—gawd, she made some weird brews. Her daughter Breda died, along with Chernobyl. So Washington and Riyadh lost their whole family.'

Diana listened to the tremble in Cassy's voice and understood that she loved these people. She knew their faults, and their weaknesses, and all the messiness of their lives. They were *her* people. They were her family.

Cassy started talking about two men. Kyoto and Liam.

'They could be absolute bastards, but they honestly thought they were doing the right thing. Faithful to Justin—unfailingly, unquestioningly faithful. Except that Liam told Monika about Justin's plan, and he saved Bali and Helike—and probably some others too—by speeding away from the jetty when he did, while Otto was still pulling up the gangplank. I'm sure he did that on purpose. It was all he could do.'

Cassy was silent for a few seconds, perhaps in homage to Liam, who had done his best.

The owl hooted again, lamenting in the darkness.

'Aden's parents,' prompted Diana.

'Aden's parents. Kazan and Berlin. I didn't even see them going aboard. Lovely people, lovely grandparents. *So* kind. We all miss them very, very much.' Cassy dropped her chin onto her folded arms. The bleak rollcall was obviously draining her. 'Hana. Another friend. She gave me the gift of teaching, trained and supported me, and worked alongside me for five years. Dean, her husband. He wore thick glasses and always had a peaceful smile. They were Bali's parents.' She paused, repeating all the names under her breath, counting on her fingers. 'And Justin. And that's all.'

'Too many.'

'*Too* many. I wish I could have saved them.'

'You did all you could.'

'Did I? I don't know.'

The bell began to toll. It sounded profoundly calm.

'I think about them all the time,' said Cassy. 'I wonder why I got to live, when they died. I wonder whether they were scared in those last seconds. I wonder whether there was more I could have done. But I've run out of tears, Mum. How do you keep crying for so many people?'

•

Someone is playing a piano. Rippling triplets, with a wistful melody woven through them. In this strange and beautiful place, after so much loss, the music seems to drag with the weight of sadness. It makes her want to cry.

Diana has taken an hour off from grandmotherly duties. She's just returned from a morning stroll through the bush, delighting in the discovery of a secret little stream and the glimpse of a kereru. She's wandering back into the settlement when she hears the piano.

For a time she simply listens, entranced. Then she turns in a full circle, looking for the source of the sound. Jaipur is huddled on the back step of the laundry. He's often there, using the two bars of phone coverage to talk to Rome. *Nice boy*. He grins and gives her a thumbs-up as she passes by.

The music seems to be coming from the *wharenui*, and Diana remembers noticing a piano in there. The big double doors stand open. Crossing the porch, she steps out of the morning light and into gloom.

A woman sits at the keys, playing with her eyes almost closed. She's wearing a blue dress, exactly like the one Cassy used to wear. Youngish. Dark hair, cut very short. As soon as she sees her listener, she stops.

'Don't mind me,' begs Diana.

But the pianist has already jumped up.

'Hello!' she cries, with a charming smile. 'Welcome! I'm Bali.'

Diana blinks. Bali, who lives on the island and tried to drown herself and her little girl. This smiling woman has seen both her parents die, and her children have been taken away from her, and yet she seems perfectly sanguine.

'Have you come to join us?' Bali asks.

'No. No, I'm just visiting.'

'You should stay! We've got lots of empty cabins.'

While they've been talking, the two women have moved outside. A dog comes trotting onto the porch to greet them: a magnificent creature with a shaggy coat. Diana stoops to stroke his head.

'This is Peter,' says Bali. 'He's lost his master.'

'I'm so sorry.'

'You don't need to be sorry. It's okay—didn't they tell you? Justin's alive.'

'Is he?'

'I've seen him.' Bali's eyes are gleaming. 'The very first time, he was on his island. Sitting by his fire. I saw him from the jetty.'

'Are you sure it was him?'

Bali bursts out laughing. 'There's no mistaking Justin! That's why I moved to the island, to be near him. He comes to me in dreams. He bargained with the Infinite Power to give mankind another chance. He's postponed the Last Day. He's going to return and build a new Gethsemane.'

'You mean right here?'

'Right here. Until then we'll keep the Vigil, and the Calls, and the Way. We'll be ready when he comes back.'

What do I do? Humour her?

'You think I'm delusional,' says Bali. 'But I'm not the only one. Suva sees his shadow every time she keeps Vigil. She feels his presence. This is exactly what he did the first time, isn't it? In Palestine. He first showed himself to a woman who loved him! Then he appeared on the shores of Lake Tiberias, and on the road to Emmaus, and even in a locked room.'

'True!' Diana begins to back away. 'Well, it was nice to—'

'We saw *Matariki* yesterday.'

'Couldn't it have been some other boat? This is a very big lake. Lots of boats. And yesterday was misty, visibility was—'

Bali laughs again. 'There *was* mist, and we saw Justin standing on top of the cabin as it passed us by. You didn't know him, did you?'

'I didn't.'

'You can't kill God incarnate. They found that out the hard way, last time.'

A door slams, followed by children's voices. 'Sounds as though school's out!' breathes Diana in relief. 'I'd better go and meet my grandson.'

'My children were taken away from me.'

'That must be terrible for you.'

Bali's smile doesn't slip. 'Ah, well. Persecution is on the cards. I can only expect it to get worse. Won't stop me spreading the good news.'

Diana mutters again about meeting her grandson, and says goodbye. She's on her way down the steps when the other woman calls after her.

'He's coming back!' she shouts. 'You'd better be ready. Justin Calvin is alive!'

Fifty-six

Cairo

Three weeks haven't been long enough. She doesn't want her mother to go.

The family drives Diana to Auckland Airport: Cairo, Aden, the three small children. And—wonderfully—even Suva has agreed to come.

'Can't believe I've been running around the countryside in this bloody thing,' says Diana, when they set off. 'The white van of my nightmares! I used to think of it as the Child Catcher's carriage.'

'The Child Catcher's carriage won't last much longer,' grumbles Aden, as he steers around potholes on the track. 'Not without Dad to keep it going. It's done about a million kilometres. I don't know why Justin didn't replace it for us, since he was running around in that swanky jeep.'

'Dad,' warns Suva. 'Don't.'

Aden makes an apologetic face at her in the rear-view mirror. 'Sorry.'

Cairo thinks rapidly for some way to change the subject. She doesn't want anything to upset Suva. Her coming on this outing is a breakthrough.

'Promise you'll be back next year, Mum?' she asks.

'Definitely,' says Diana.

'And Tara?'

'She's already making plans! Says she's going to marry Rome because he's rich as Croesus. Her words. She's been stalking him on Facebook.'

'That's creepy.'

'That's the twenty-first century.'

Cairo is remembering the day she first got into the van. She was scared and lonely and cold, and Gethsemane welcomed her. Maybe they had an agenda, but they welcomed her. If she hadn't got in, she might never have heard of Gethsemane. She might be a corporate lawyer like Hamish, or divorced and battling like Imogen. *No*, she thinks, *I don't regret accepting that lift.*

She leans forwards in her seat to kiss Aden on the ear.

'What was that for?' he asks, laughing.

'For being my getaway driver.'

•

It's a long day. Damascus cries when they say goodbye to his granny, and Quito joins in the general lamentation. Havana continues to grin, because that's what she does best.

'We can Skype!' Diana promises, kissing them all. 'Ooh, I love you, gorgeous grandchildren! I'll see you very soon.'

They make their way home, stopping to visit Rome at Kit and Meg's. Suva says she doesn't understand why he'd want to live in such a horrible place, but Cairo thinks she can hear wistfulness in her tone.

The small children are asleep by the time they moor *Ikaroa* at the jetty. The sun has already sunk behind the western hills, and a blanket of mist is settling on the lake. Aden carries the boys, one in each arm, sleepy heads resting against his shoulders. Suva follows with Havana.

Cairo lingers for a while. She sits on the jetty, dangling her feet over the edge. The water rises and falls and whispers, calmly slap-slap-slapping against the piles. A black swan coasts by, dipping his beak to drink.

The peace of Gethsemane. The peace.

If she half closes her eyes, she can conjure a white boat gliding among the skeins of mist. Yes, there it is. A familiar figure stands on the cabin roof. She can almost hear his voice. She can sense his divine presence. If she tries hard enough, she can resurrect him.

'Justin,' she whispers. 'Justin? Are you there?'

Then she hears Aden calling. She stands up, and turns her back on the Risen Lord. It's time to dance to a different tune.

Fifty-seven

Justin
19 September 2015

Soon. Very soon. He saw the volcano's glowing halo, and knew that his power was growing. Soon he'd be brighter than a thousand suns.

The faithful few were chanting. Their faces shone, reflecting his radiant divinity. They were beyond happiness. They chanted and clapped and laughed as Liam steered the boat into the deepest part of the lake and stopped the engine.

In the last seconds of the world, *Matariki* waltzed in a gentle swell. The chant had ended. Poor old Liam was wiping away a stream of tears as he peered out of the cockpit. His squinting eye had turned inwards, as though it wanted to hide. He was frightened, but he would carry out his final duty. It was Liam who would ignite the fiery cloud of glory. He was watching for the signal they'd arranged: the moment when Justin closed his eyes and stretched his arms towards the sun.

'You've passed the test,' Justin told the faithful few. 'Today the earth will know the hell of Armageddon, but you and I will feast in paradise.'

A buzzing little boat. A buzzing little voice, trying to get his attention. Some of his disciples glanced towards the sound. There had been police on the quay in Wellington when all of this began, and they were here at the end. Irrelevant, both times.

'Ignore them,' cried Justin. 'Face the mountain. Look into the sunrise—here come the Host!'

With a roar, heaven came billowing over the lip of the world. Dazzling fire hurtled across the water, like an arrow from a bow, straight into his eyes. It was a pointer. It was marking him out.

And then Messenger was back, yelling a joyous greeting as he led his army to earth. They flew in shining squadrons, filling the valley with the power and glory of their singing. They were made of white light, blindingly bright, pieces of the sun. Justin felt love like a swollen river, lifting him up and carrying him in a tide of shining gold. His life had come full circle.

His shout of triumph was carried on the wind. It marked the end of this world, and the beginning of life everlasting.

'It has begun!' he cried.

He closed his eyes. He stretched his arms towards the rising sun.

Acknowledgements

This book wouldn't exist without the help of many, many people. I'm grateful to all of them.

In particular I thank Jane Gregory, my agent, for whose wisdom and support I owe so much. Thanks to all her team— especially Stephanie Glencross, whose editorial instincts helped to salvage that dodgy first draft.

At Allen & Unwin: heartfelt thanks to my publisher, Annette Barlow, for all she does for me; to Ali Lavau for her brilliant editorial input; Kate Goldsworthy, whose eye for detail avoided some real howlers; and Sarah Baker for her efficiency and calm in managing the process. Also thanks to Sam Brown and Clare Drysdale in London for their unfailing friendship and advice.

To my friends, Mary-Clare and David Reynolds: thank you for lending your cliff-top hermitage. It saved the book as well as its author's sanity. I can still hear the waves rolling in. I'm also indebted to Napier Library, my day-to-day office and refuge.

Above all I thank my husband, Tim Meredith, and children George, Sam and Cora. I'm sorry I threw away a perfectly good career, and life changed, and you had to starve in a garret.

Thanks for being so nice about it. Thanks for all the cups of tea and late-night chats. Thanks for everything.

Finally, I'd like to reassure any undercover agency who may be monitoring my internet use: yes, I know I've been Googling things like *how to brainwash people* and *how to blow up a boat*, but it was all entirely innocent. I was writing a book, see? Please take me off your watch list. Thank you.